ROBERT WILSON

Robert Wilson was born in 1957. A graduate of Oxford University, he has worked in shipping, advertising and trading in Africa. He has travelled in Asia and Africa and has lived in Greece and West Africa. He is married and writes from an isolated farmhouse in Portugal.

He was awarded the CWA Gold Dagger Award for Fiction for his fifth novel, *A Small Death in Lisbon*.

Praise for Robert Wilson

A DARKENING STAIN

'Unmissable . . . Unflinchingly imagined and executed. No hint of competition. First in a field of one' *Literary Review*

BLOOD IS DIRT

'For once a novelist influenced by Raymond Chandler is not shown up by the comparison, matching his mentor's descriptive flourishes and screwball dialogue . . . A class act'
Sunday Times

THE BIG KILLING

'Something special in the line of original crime fiction . . . If I come across as original and blackly funny a thriller again this year, I'll feel myself doubly blest' *Irish Times*

INSTRUMENTS OF DARKNESS

'An atmospheric and absorbing debut, *Instruments of Darkness* vividly paints a credible picture of a world I know almost nothing about. Now I feel I've been ther~~~ ~~~ert Wilson writes like a m~~~ ~~~ife'
~~~cDermid

ROBERT WILSON

Blood is Dirt

HarperCollins*Publishers*

HarperCollins*Publishers*
77–85 Fulham Palace Road,
Hammersmith, London W6 8JB

www.**fire**and**water**.com

This paperback edition 2002

1 3 5 7 9 8 6 4 2

First published in Great Britain
in 1997 by HarperCollins

A catalogue record for this book is
available from the British Library

ISBN 0 00 713041 4

Set in Meridien by
Rowland Phototypesetting Ltd,
Bury St Edmunds, Suffolk

Printed in Great Britain by
Clays Ltd, St Ives plc

For Jane
and
my mother
and
in memory of João

'Blood's dirt,' he laughed, looking away
Far off to where his wound had bled
And almost merged for ever into clay.
'The world is washing out its stains,' he said.

From 'Inspection' by Wilfred Owen

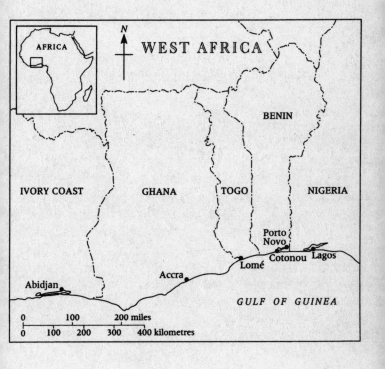

Chapter 1

The sheep stood in the car park looking at its African owner with interest but no concern, which was a mistake. The animal had arrived from the market on a moped lying across the lap of its executioner whose sackful of knives was resting on the sheep's back. He'd lifted the sheep off with a gentleness normally reserved for sick children. The sheep was no more than dazed at seeing life passing it by a little quicker than usual. The butcher tethered it to the bumper of a Land Rover and arranged his knives on the sack.

A boy arrived in a sweat on a bicycle which he leaned against the wall. He ran into the building. His feet slapped on the tiles in the stairwell. A while later the feet came back down again. And a while after that someone wearing steel tips on their shoes followed. They appeared in the car park.

The sheep looked from the owner to the boy and then to the very tall, athletic Lebanese with the steel tips who was about to be the new owner but with one drastic difference that the sheep had not, as yet, rumbled. The Lebanese inspected the sheep, drumming the fingers of one hand on his washboard stomach and using the other hand to spin his gold chain around his neck. He nodded.

1

The African took hold of a horn on the sheep's head and wiped a blade across its neck opening up a red, woolly grimace. The animal was puzzled by the movement and its consequences. It fell on its side. Blood trickled down the concrete ramp of the car park, skirted a large patch of black oil and pooled in the dirt of the road where a dog licked it quickly before it soaked into the sand. The Lebanese clipped away.

I'd come out of the office to catch what could hardly be called a breeze that was playing around on the balcony, but it was better than sitting in the rise of one's own fetor. I had nothing on my plate which was why I was taking an interest in *al fresco* butchery and it was lucky I did. Glancing up from the twitching life struggling to get away from the future mutton roast, my eyes connected with the only white man in the street. He was looking at the sign hanging on my first floor balcony which said 'M & B' and below that *'Enquêtes et Recouvrements'*, 'Investigations and Debt Collection'.

The white man was wearing a cream linen suit which must have seemed like a great idea in the shop window in London but out here quite quickly achieved the crumpled, downtrodden look of a copywriter or a graphic artist. He slipped a card into his pocket and was about to walk across the car park when he noticed the dead sheep with accusatory eyes and lolling head. The sight of it jerked something between his shoulder blades. His head flicked up, he looked left and right and went on to his back foot, preparing for a cartoon scram. The butcher, who was kneeling down by now, took out a wooden tube and with a small knife made a nick in the back leg above the sheep's elbow. He inserted the tube and blew down it. The boy stood adjacent with a machete in his hand almost trailing on the ground. At a nod from the butcher he raised the machete. I pushed myself off the balcony rail and shouted, 'Yes!' at the white man and pointed at the entrance to the building below me. It gave him just enough courage to skitter past the sheep and gave me half a chance at our first client in more than a week. The boy beat on the belly of the sheep with the flat of the machete blade. Whump, whump, whump.

I stepped back from the balcony into the office. Bagado, my partner, who had been a detective on the Cotonou force up until a few years back, looked up from behind the single bare desk in the room. The door opened without being knocked.

'What the hell is going on out there?' asked the white man.

'They're butchering a sheep.'

Whump, whump, whump.

'A sheep?'

'What did you think it was? A white man?'

'No, I . . . Jesus. What's he blowing down its leg for?'

'Get some air under the hide. Makes it easier to skin.'

'Don't they have a shop or anything?'

'No,' I said, 'I don't think they have, Mr . . . ?'

'Briggs. Napier Briggs.'

'Bruce Medway,' I said, without holding out my hand.

'I know,' he said. 'Why the hell do you think I'm here?'

'I've never been a great guesser.'

'No, what I meant was . . .'

3

'I know what you meant.'

He ran his hand through some hair on his head in a way that made me think it had been a lot thicker until recently.

'I've lost some money,' he said, looking shambolic enough so that we'd believe him. 'A great deal of money. I want you to get it back.'

We didn't say anything. I looked him up and down and thought about two things. The first, his name. How to make 'Briggs' more interesting – stick 'Napier' in front of it, get yourself an eyepatch and a black silver skull-topped cane. The man was missing some props. The second thing was whether he had enough money left to pay us to find what he'd lost.

Bagado's head came out of the wreckage of his blue mac like a tortoise that's caught a whiff of spring. He had his hands steepled and the spired fingers were itching up and down a scar he had in the cleft of his chin.

'How much is a great deal?' he asked, and Napier jumped as high as he had when he'd seen the dead sheep. He rushed at me and drove me out on to the balcony.

'Who the fuck is he?'

'My partner, Bagado. M & B. Medway and Bagado.'

'He's not . . . ?' he asked with ferocious intensity.

'What?'

Briggs wiped the sweat off his face with his hand and flicked it on the ground. He dropped on to the balcony rail with his elbows and looked over. He reared back.

'Oh, my God.'

The sheep's intestines were out of the belly now. They slipped and jostled against each other, still warm. The sheep was on its back, skinned, the hide underneath it to keep the meat clean.

'Take a seat, Mr Briggs,' I said. 'Take a seat in here.'

I got him on to a chair. Bagado raised his eyebrows. 'Coffee?' I asked.

'Black,' he said. 'I mean black-black.'

'White,' said Bagado, *au lait.*

I roared down the stairwell to the *gardien* who came up to take 2000 CFA off me and I added three croissants to the order. Briggs moved his chair back from the desk. He took out a packet of Camels from his linen jacket which had now become a relief map of a mountainous desert in the thick unsliced heat. He took three matches to light up and flicked each dud through the hole in the wall where the air conditioner should have been.

At least he wasn't overwhelmed by our new office. The single plant on the floor in its concrete pot, the view of the neighbouring block out of one window, a mango tree and a tailor's shack out of the other, a local stationer's calendar on the wall, and the two of us evidently with only one desk to sit behind, didn't even have any schoolboy chic let alone adult consequence.

'Ours is a new business,' said Bagado, trying to pull some cheer into his voice.

'Delicately balanced between start-up and instant bankruptcy,' I added.

'A great deal of money could be as much as . . .'

'. . . five hundred dollars,' I said. 'We need perspective, Mr Briggs.'

He sucked on the Camel, pulling an inch of it into his lungs without even glazing over. His yellow cigarette fingers were shaking and his thumb flickered against the filter. He was tall and thin. The sort who could eat like a pig and never get themselves over 150 pounds, the sort who kickstarted the day with four espressos and five Camels, the sort who could live off whatever their latest stomach ulcer was secreting. His eyes were sunken and dark, his face lined deeply with creases that dropped from the outsides of his eyes to the corners of his mouth. He tugged at his tie, which was down by his sternum, as if it was crimping his windpipe.

'You do do this kind of thing?' he asked. 'Getting my money back. I mean, that is your . . . bag?'

'We run a debt-collection service. We call it debt to be polite. People feel better about returning money which has been "extensively borrowed" rather than "stolen".'

He nodded and threaded an arm through the back of the chair, trying to break it off.

'Has your money been "extensively borrowed"?' asked Bagado.

'No. It's been stolen. I've been ripped off like you wouldn't believe.'

'Oh, we would, Mr Briggs,' said Bagado. 'Have no fear of that, we would.'

Napier Briggs screwed the cigarette into the corner of his mouth and struggled out of his jacket as if he'd been strapped in there and we were a paying audience. He sat back exhausted with one wrist still stuck in a sleeve's gullet. Bagado opened a drawer and produced an empty sardine tin, which was the office ashtray. He nudged it towards him. Briggs tore his fist out of the sleeve and whipped the cigarette out of his mouth, taking a lungful of quality filter. He lit another from the butt and crushed

6

it out in the tin and licked and blew on a finger. He looked blasted by sun, booze and nerves. His skin was stretched tight over his skull, and the remains of his blond hair looked as if it had been stitched in. His lower teeth were stained brown from nicotine and bitumen coffee.

'How much money, Mr Briggs? You didn't say.'

'One million eight hundred and fifty-seven thousand and small . . . dollars.'

'Gold bars in a trunk? Cash in a suitcase? Diamonds in a condom?'

Napier Briggs bent over and gripped his forehead. The pain and suffering of money loss getting the better of him for a moment. A man bereaved. You'd have seen more control at an English graveside.

'Take your time, Mr Briggs. Ours has been passing slowly enough without you,' said Bagado. 'Begin at the beginning; now that we know the end we just need to fill in the middle. Colouring by numbers. It couldn't be easier. What do you do for a living? That's a start.'

He took a card from his wallet and flipped it across the desk at us.

'Napier Briggs Associates Ltd. Shipbrokers,' read Bagado. 'How many associates?'

'One.'

'Who's that?'

'A sleeping one. Nonexecutive. Nothing to do with the business. Just an arrangement.'

'So a one-man band,' I said, 'with nearly two million dollars in liftable cash.'

'A specialist in chemical, and clean and dirty fuel transportation,' read Bagado. 'You didn't get muddled up in a Bonny Light Crude scam, did you, Mr Briggs?'

'What's a Bonny Light Crude scam?'

'It's not as cheerful as it sounds.'

'Businessmen come here,' I said, 'they get introduced to people who are close personal friends of the president of the Nigerian National Oil Corporation. They visit offices with an NNOC brass plate on the wall. They part with money to register their company as a buyer of unbelievably cheap Nigerian crude oil. They part with money for advance expenses and ship's bunkers. They part with money for a bill of lading for a few hundred thousand barrels of Nigerian crude that doesn't exist. That's a Bonny Light Crude scam.'

'I take it you haven't done business in West Africa before, Mr Briggs?' asked Bagado. Napier looked up, confused, too many things bowling around in his head. 'You specialize in dirty fuel transportation but you don't know what a Bonny Light Crude scam is.'

'No. Yes. I see what you're getting at.'

'The truth, Mr Briggs, that's what we *want* to get at. That way we can help you. Many of these scams sound incredible in the telling and absurd on paper, but if you're involved in them they become a part of your life, a part of your business hopes and aspirations. You've no need to be coy about . . .'

'. . . my greed?' asked Napier, his head tilted to one side like an intelligent dog.

'Be brutal with yourself, by all means,' said Bagado. 'But tell us what happened too.'

'I received a letter from a man who described himself as a senior accountant at the Ministry of Finance of the Benin Republic living and working in Porto Novo.'

8

'Do you have this letter?'

'The letter,' said Napier, surfing over Bagado's question, 'offered me a percentage of something over thirty million dollars. The money came from overinvoicing on a contract awarded to a foreign company.'

'All you had to do,' Bagado cut in, 'was supply them with signed letterheads, signed invoices and the name of your bank along with the account number and telephone/fax number.'

Napier Briggs sat rigid, Bagado's words as good as a glance across a crowded room of Gorgons.

'Hundreds of these letters are coming out of Nigeria every week. What's happened to you Mr Briggs is that you've been four-one-nined.'

'Four-one-nined?'

'Obtaining Goods by False Pretences, section four-one-nine of the Nigerian Criminal Code. You really haven't done much business in West Africa, Mr Briggs.'

'I've done some deals,' said Napier, finding a carat of professional pride from somewhere, and then giving himself away by scratching the crown of his head and picking at imaginary specks on his face.

'The senior accountant at the Ministry of Finance in Benin, did he come to you via one of your successful deals . . . as a reward for something, perhaps?'

If we'd been impressed by the range of Napier's nervous tics before, now we were spellbound by the sheer speed with which his hands shifted over his face and head. He tugged his ears, scratched his head, picked at the side of his nose, smoothed his eyebrows, pulled at the point of his chin, pinched his eyelids, the cigarette changing hands all the time, not having enough to do,

9

he could have used six or seven smokes to keep himself occupied.

'Why don't you just show us the letter, Mr Briggs?' I asked.

'Napier. For Christ's sake, it's Napier.'

'Napier?'

He lit another cigarette from the butt, and dragged on the stub, hauling the most acrid smoke deep down into his lungs. Bagado nudged the tin again, wincing at what the X-rays must look like. Napier brutalized the tin with the butt and walked to the window holding his forehead with his free hand as if the nicotine rush might drop him.

'Mr Briggs,' said Bagado, still not comfortable with Napier, 'I'm not one for turning down custom. As you can see, we need the money. But, in this case, I think you would be better served, and I will write a letter of introduction, by going back to Nigeria to see a man called Colonel Adjeokuta. He has set up an investigation bureau within the Lagos police force specializing in 419 cases. He knows how these gangs operate, he has case histories, he knows some of the gang members, he has some of them available for comment in the Kirikiri Maximum Security Prison in Lagos, some of them are on death row and are interested . . .'

'I want a private investigation,' said Napier Briggs, in a quiet intense voice that seemed to have stopped the traffic for a moment. 'Anyway, this is a Benin thing.'

'It's a Lagos gang using a Benin scenario. Porto Novo is on the border. There are many crime links between Benin and Nigeria. Stolen cars, hi-fi, petrol, drugs . . .'

'I don't want the Nigerians involved.'

'I'm half Nigerian myself, Mr Briggs.'

'Then perhaps you'll know why.'

'Do you mean the Nigerian *authorities*?'

'No,' he said, his head seeming to operate independently of his neck, the puppeteer getting his fingers crossed. The three of us exchanged code through the volumes of smoke leaking out of Napier.

'They used the letterheads to clear out your account?' I asked, trying a new line.

'They said the invoices would show goods and services I'd supplied,' said Napier, 'the letterheads would be used to give covering information. They'd put the whole lot through the system and effect a transfer. They needed a foreign company account to pull it off.'

'What were you doing with nearly two million dollars in your account?'

'They were freight payments from contracts and time charters and I'd had some good months on the spot market. It was all money due to go out to the shipowners in the New Year . . . apart from my two per cent.'

'Timely,' I said. 'All that money being there, Napier?'

'Not for me. Not for my owners.'

'Who would have known about that kind of money being in there?'

'The charterers, the owners, the bank . . . myself.'

'You have someone else in your office?'

'Karen. Out of the question, she's been with me for years.'

'She'd have known, though?'

'Yes.'

'Your associate?'

'I told you. Nonexec. Remember?'

'Do you have a wife, an ex, a girlfriend, a partner in life?'

'Divorced. Three years ago.'

'Bitter?'

'This isn't relevant.'

'You're not giving us much to go on this end, Napier. I'm just coming at it from a different angle. Did your wife know about your business?'

'She used to.'

'You talked about it with her?'

'She was a broker. She covered the Mediterranean small ships market.'

'Was there anyone else involved at that time?'

'Back off,' Napier snarled. 'This is none of . . .'

'It's only a question. Has your company always been called Napier Briggs Associates?'

'No. It used to be Atkin Briggs Shipbrokers Ltd.'

'What happened to Atkin?'

'Blair Atkin.' He said it as if he'd just got a mouthful of coffee grounds.

'Your wife ran off with Blair?'

Napier had his back to us now, his hands above his head, leaning against the window, two fingers trailing smoke.

'Yes,' he said, taut as a drum skin.

'You're sure this isn't relevant?'

'They split up a year later. I haven't seen or heard from her since. Nor has . . . anyway, she was a bitch.'

'Was?' asked Bagado.

'Still is. I doubt it was the kind of expertise she could drop.'

'*You* broke with *her*?'

'*She* broke with *me*. I was very bitter about it. It bust

12

up the marriage, tore the company in half, screwed up lives, all because she couldn't keep her knickers on. Now let's forget my wife, my ex-wife. She's not involved. She's out of the picture.'

'How do you suggest we get ourselves into the picture, Napier? No letter. No proof. Scant information which we have to wring out of you *and* you turn down the offer of the Lagos fraud squad. What do you want us to do? Hang around on street corners in downtown Lagos looking at people's back pockets? Time-consuming. Expensive. How much money have you got on you? Maybe not much beyond your own expenses. You're not *giving* us anything, Napier. Chuck us a bone, for God's sake. Spill your guts or bow out. We've got some paperclip chains to make.'

'Perhaps Mr Briggs is concerned that he's done something illegal,' said Bagado. Napier kicked himself back off the window and turned on him. 'Transferring funds from overinvoicing on a government contract. Whose money is it?'

'Ah, yes,' said Napier, backing down, leaning against the window, easing another smoke out, keeping the chain going. 'Embarrassing.'

'What percentage did they offer you?'

'Forty. Thirty-five for . . .'

'Who was the other five for?'

'Someone called Dan Emanalo. He doesn't exist, nor does the company he works for.'

'Which was?'

'Chemiclean Limited. I supplied them with chemicals in drums. They had a government contract to supply sewage treatment systems.'

'But they didn't exist?'

'No.'

'But they miraculously paid you for supplying the chemicals?'

Napier Briggs fell silent. He wasn't a topnotch liar. He was pretty good at shutting up or spinning out half truths and he was an outstanding smoker, but lying . . . he just didn't have it.

'You're binding up on us again, Napier.'

'I have to think about this.'

'Nothing's going out of this room, Napier. Strictly P and C and all that.'

'Where's that coffee?' he asked.

'Coming.'

Napier clasped the back of his neck and tried to squeeze the anguish out.

'Why can't I think?'

'Maybe you're scared, Napier?'

'Did you have particular need of this ten million?' asked Bagado.

'Ten million?'

'Thirty-five per cent of thirty million dollars.'

'Yes. No,' said Napier, and his face crumpled. He was losing it. We sat in the silence left over by the traffic. The coffee and croissants arrived. Two *cafés au lait* for Bagado and I, and a double tarantula juice for Napier. He sipped it, rattling the cup back into the saucer each time. Thinking. Thinking. The brain turning and turning like a hamster's wheel.

'What did you make supplying the sewage treatment chemicals?'

'Two per cent of the shipping, about three thousand

dollars, but I did the product as well. Took five per cent of that. I don't usually do product.'

'Who did you get the product off?'

'Dupont,' he said, too quickly.

'French Dupont?'

'Yes, it was,' he said, wanting to fill that out a bit more but having nothing else to say.

'Sweet deal?'

'Very.'

'What are we talking about? Two hundred, three hundred grand.'

'Something like that.'

'Takes care of your running costs for a bit.'

'Sure.'

'Now, the ten million dollars, that's different. That's retirement money. Don't have to push the pen any more, hump the phone to your ear. It can solve big problems, too, that kind of money.'

'Like?'

'Debts. Payoffs. Muscle.'

Napier slugged back the last dram of tar and refitted the cup. He lit another cigarette and threw the old butt out on to the balcony. He folded his jacket over his arm and shook his legs in his trousers, which were clinging to those parts where dogs like to stick their noses. He picked up his zip-top briefcase by the ear.

'It's like going to a shrink, Napier,' I said. 'You have to relive the trauma to get over the neurosis. Have a think about things. Straighten them out in your head. Come back and talk to us again.'

'Do you have a home number?'

'I do, but I don't give it out. This kind of business and

a happy home life don't go together. You've got a card, I take it?'

'Yeah. The guy in the British High Commission gave it to me.'

'We have an answering machine here. Office hours are eight a.m. to one p.m. and five p.m. to eight p.m. Where are you staying, Napier?'

'The Hotel du Lac, just across the lagoon there.'

Bagado and I listened to the man who'd nearly been our tenth client scuffing down the untiled concrete stairs.

'That was close,' said Bagado.

'We can still nail him.'

'You better be quick.'

'With all the competition out there, you mean?'

'I think he's a dead man, or heading that way.'

'Really? He just looked a little scared to me.'

'Victim,' said Bagado, shaking his head.

'Hotel du Lac,' I said, thinking about that for a moment. 'That's middling, but they're doing it up. It's still cheapish. He must be a bit short. If he'd been in the Aledjo or the Sheraton, even the Golfe, I'd have felt better about him.'

'Is that why you asked him?'

'No. I thought I might go and hustle him some more this evening.'

'Even if he's a dead man and he hasn't got any money?'

'Nobody's got less money than us, Bagado.'

'Do you want his croissant?'

'See what I mean?'

Chapter 2

Bagado didn't show for the evening sitting-around session. He had a sick daughter and a wife who'd had to take to the streets selling live chickens from a calabash. Life was getting hard for him. All the money he earned went straight out into the extended family, and worse than that – there just wasn't enough for his brain to chew on.

If I hadn't heard from Napier Briggs by the close of business I was going to go round to the Hotel du Lac and try and necklock him into being a client, even a nonpaying client. Maybe we could do something on a commission basis for him like those ambulance-chasing lawyers do. Us, desperate? Forget it.

I turned the light out to save on electricity and hobbled out on to the balcony to see if I could hook any other passing suckers who'd want help from a couple of strapped PIs working from a stripped-down cell in a dog-poo coloured apartment block at the epicentre of Cotonou's pollution.

I hobbled because I'd had gout. A bad bout of it, but I was coming out the other end. Sympathy had been low on the ground – with lepers on the street it tended to be. I tried telling people it was the purine in anchovies and sardines rather than a weekly intake of a bottle of . . . what's the point, you wouldn't believe me anyway.

I sniffed the air over Cotonou and caught the usual gagging mix of sea breath, rubbish, drains, grilled kebabs all wrapped in a heady concoction of diesel and two-stroke fumes. Yeah, the bicycles have gone and we've been overrun by a million mopeds. Marxism is finished.

We had the Francophonie conference here at the end of last year and they stripped the place down, repainted it, repaired the roads and introduced mobile phones. In three months the Beninois became capitalists.

The transition wasn't completed without pain. The economy, in the jaws of the free market, was given a kick in the pants by the French who devalued the CFA franc by a hundred per cent to one hundred CFA to one French franc. The whimpering is still going on. Imports are hellishly expensive, trips to France are out, supporting kids in school in Europe is painful; on the other hand, exports are cheap. But who gives a damn about that if the wife can't afford twelve metres of Dutch Wax African print to adorn her body? No one.

I dragged myself back inside and called Heike – my English/German girlfriend, the one who towed me out of the desert all those years ago, the one who works as a latterday saint for a German NGO* aid agency – to see if my priapic driver Moses's blood-test results had come through. He'd been sick for a month and a half and my toe had been through hell on the brake pedal. Heike had persuaded him to go and see a doctor last week and it had been like a child's first day at school.

The receptionist told me that Heike had left the office, and the blood tests hadn't come through.

* Nongovernmental Organization

I sat in the dark and listened to the radio playing Africando from the tailor's shack across the street until it seemed like the time to close up for the night and get down to the Hotel du Lac to see if Napier was in pieces yet and needed gluing.

It was a thick, hot night and the stench in the stairwell from the overflowing septic tank added a ripeness that had the mosquitoes dancing for blood. I hacked through it and folded myself into my battered Peugeot estate which was so old and decrepit that I'd quite often been mistaken for a bush taxi on the open road.

The mopeds were out in force and their blue exhaust had been changed into a sickly orange by the streetlighting. People were sitting on the first-floor verandah of the redecorated La Caravelle café. They were drinking and trying to stay alive in the small pockets of air still available. Some Lebanese lads with baseball caps on back to front hung over the balcony rail looking at a couple of policemen wrestling with a Nigerian street hawker. A huge diesel locomotive, pushing a line of open wagons, honked and grumbled between the stationary cars and trucks on its way across the lagoon. I turned left, overtook it without disappearing into the usual two-foot-deep Peugeot trap, and crossed the lagoon. The day-glo sign of the Hotel du Lac was easily visible from the bridge, as was the scaffolding on its side. I turned right past the Hotel Pacific, which seemed a long way from home, and parked up behind the hotel. The mosquitoes were screaming out here and I was all over myself like a flea-ridden dog.

I walked by the pool and down the steps to the well-lit bar in the front. There were hunched people in there and a po-faced barman scraping foam off the *pressions* with a throat spatula.

'Looking for me?' asked Napier, jiggling something amber in my face from his side-saddle position on his bar stool. He nearly launched himself on to the floor and was only saved by the boniness of his elbow on the lip of the bar.

'This isn't one of my usual haunts.'

'You're a drinking man then?'

'It has been known.'

'What'll it be?'

'A beer.'

'One of these to chase?'

'I've never said no.'

The barman settled the drinks and I backed up on to a stool. A woman eyed us coolly from the other side of the bar.

'I told her to fuck off before she even got her bum up on the stool,' said Napier.

'You're learning, but it pays to be polite here. It's the French in them.'

'Couldn't get any life into the old boy even if I wanted to.'

'Anxious,' I said, and we drank.

'No,' said Napier, squeezing his lips with his fist. 'Fucking petrified.'

'Petrified?'

''Swat I said.'

'Have you heard something?'

'What's it to you?'

'I'm sitting next to you in a bar. That's what people do. Tell each other what's on their minds.'

'What's on your mind?'

'Money. I want to make some.'

'Out of me?'

'If there's any to be made.'

'Do you mind getting killed?'

'It's not high on my list of goals.'

'You have goals?'

'No, it was just something to say.'

'I had goals,' he said, sniffing at his Scotch and then taking a pull of beer.

'What happened?'

'I scored too many in my own net.'

'Don't get maudlin on me, Napier.'

'I thought we could say what was on our minds.'

'You cheated. You were going to tell me why you were petrified. You lost some money. That's worrying but it doesn't make you scared. You asked me if I minded getting killed. Who's going to kill me if I stick my nose in?'

Napier waggled his finger at the barman. Two more *grandes pressions* arrived and two more Red Labels. He lit a Camel. The phone rang in the hotel.

'*Gardez l'écoute*,' said the receptionist.

A short fat fellow came into the bar from the hotel and held up a finger. '*M. Napier. Téléphone.*'

Napier squirmed off his stool and leaned back for his cigarettes in case it was a long one.

'Keep my beer warm,' he said, and let me know how drunk he was by pinballing his way out of our tight corner before getting on the straight and narrow.

He was back in ten minutes, looking frisky and not half as drunk as he had been. He hopped up on to the

21

bar stool and clapped me on the back. I didn't like the turnaround in mood, especially as it looked as if it was going to involve me.

'Still wanna make some money, Bruce?'

'Not if I've got to lay down my life for it,' I said. 'You can't take it with you, Napier, remember that.'

'Sure I do,' he said and socked back the chaser. 'That was them on the phone.'

'Who's *them*?'

'They said there's been a mistake.'

'That's big of them. Who's *they*?'

'They said they want to give me my money back.'

'Why should *they* suddenly want to do a thing like that?'

'I don't know . . .' he said, without letting his confidence falter, before he remembered not to lie. 'Pressure.'

'Tell me about the kind of person who can exert that kind of pressure.'

'Well, you know, like you say, you meet people. You tell them what's on your mind. Sometimes they help you. Sometimes they don't even have to be asked. You coming?'

'Napier, you're going to have to tell me what you're talking about.'

'I want you to hold my hand.'

'That's not . . .'

'I'll give you five. No. I'll give you ten thousand . . . dollars.'

'What's wrong with your hand?'

'Nothing you're going to catch.'

'I don't know about that,' I said, and drained the first

· 22

grande pression and started in on the second. 'Let's get this straight. The gang that stole your money from your UK bank account have called you here in your luxurious Beninois hotel and have volunteered to give you your money back. In cash. In dollars.'

He nodded.

'Ten hours ago you came into my office so frazzled you wouldn't even tell me their shoe size. Half an hour ago you tell me you're petrified . . . seem to think your death is required in all this. Ten minutes ago you get a phone call and you've kissed and made up. Now you want me to hold your hand out there in the dark. What annoys me, Napier, what you have to tell me right now is – do I look that much of a sucker?'

He nodded.

'You're on your own,' I said, and stood up to finish the beer.

'No, no, Bruce. Sorry. I didn't mean that. What I meant was that if I start telling you what it's all about we're going to be here until six in the morning and the meeting is at nine tonight. There just isn't the time to fill you in. You've got twenty minutes to say "yes" and get me there. But look, what I can tell you is that the person gave me a name. The name of a very powerful man who has guaranteed the handover and my personal safety.'

'What about mine?'

'Yours too.'

'What the hell do you need me for?'

'How do you get a moped taxi to stop in this town?'

'You shout *kekeno*. It's Fon for "stop".'

'Now you don't want me to get on the back of a

moped with two million dollars in a suitcase, do you?'

'I'm your chauffeur,' I said, getting it. Napier laughed.

'If you like.'

'Since when have you paid your chauffeur ten thousand bucks for a night's work?'

'As a matter of fact this is the first time,' he said, and socked back the chaser.

'What's the name of your guarantor?'

'You don't need to know and you don't want to know.'

'Maybe I'd like to know. See if he's on my party list. Get an invitation to him for my next one. If he's this powerful I could use him in my business.'

Napier got another Camel under way and used his thumb to get an imaginary plank out of his own eye.

'The less you know about this the better. You help me. You take your money. We never see each other again.'

'Just as we were getting beyond the small-talk stage, getting to know each other a bit . . .'

'Nobody knows me, Bruce, least of all myself. Time's short. Are you in or out?'

'Where's the meet?'

'Are you *in* or *out*?'

'Why do you think I'm asking?'

'That's not a yes and it's not a no.'

'It means if we're meeting in a private room in the Sheraton it's a "yes". If we're meeting in an empty warehouse in the industrial zone it's a big "no". There are places to do these kind of things. I did one of these out in the bush in the Côte d'Ivoire and nearly found myself as dead as the guy I was supposed to be meeting.'

'In a coconut grove opposite the Hotel Croix du Sud. They tell me there's a bit of beach there where people go for picnics at the weekend.'

'Harmless enough during the day.'

'But you need your hand held at night.'

'This is not a good idea, Napier,' I said. 'What if I say no.'

'Nothing's going to stop me going out there to take a look.'

'You're a bastard.'

'Am I?' he asked, innocent as cherry blossom. 'You're the one who said you wanted to make some money out of my . . . out of me, if it could be made.'

'That's right. I'm upfront about what I want. You, on the other hand, won't tell me a damn thing and then you corner me into feeling responsible for you . . . a white man in West Africa with . . .'

'You're not doing it for free,' he said, and smiled. Now that his face wasn't a chiselled mess of fear and worry I could see what got him into a lot of trouble and what probably got him a lot of women too – a little-boy look. I dropped the chaser down the hatch and we went out to the car. I fitted the keys into the ignition and thought ten thousand dollars could solve a lot of problems and then stopped myself in case the next time I looked in the mirror I'd find Napier staring back at me.

'I don't suppose you've got a gun, have you?' he asked.

'Firing a piece of lead into human flesh, watching a man drop with a gut shot, seeing his life crawling away from him, takes something that I haven't got. And you – if I remember rightly, Napier Briggs – got spooked from seeing a dead sheep in the car park, got the vom from seeing a little offal on the pavement. I don't think you're in any frame of mind to be going around pointing guns at people.'

We drove back across the lagoon, up the main drag past the remains of the evening fish market and past the port which was lit up with ships being worked and loaded trucks queuing to get out on the road. The ship's agents offices were dark and quiet on either side of the Boulevard de la Marina. We continued up past the Hotel du Port, the Présidence, the Hotel Croix du Sud and the huge expanse of *cocotiers* between the road and the sea. Napier watched it all go.

'Where are we going?' he asked.

I took a left before the conference centre on to a short causeway out to the new Novotel and parked up in its floodlit car park. The flags of all nations snapped in the sea breeze, their ropes pinged against the metal poles.

'The Croix du Sud was back . . .'

'Your two million dollars is out there,' I said, pointing across him back towards the port. 'About three hundred metres.'

'You're still going with me . . . aren't you?'

'Now that we're away from the bar, the beers and the chasers, now that you can see how black it is out there in the *cocotiers*, now that you can hear the sea and the wind, I thought I'd give you a chance to think about whether you reckon there's somebody standing out in the middle of that lot with two million in a suitcase.'

Napier looked to where I'd been pointing. In the bright lights of the Novotel car park I saw the sweat start out on his forehead. He wiped a finger across his brow and dabbed the palms of his hands on his trousers. His tongue came out to try and put some lick on his lips.

'Where's this guarantor you've just spoken to on the phone?'

'Lagos,' he said, turning back, his mind drifting off to a time when this was all over and he was on a flight back to Paris with his cash in the overhead.

'Why don't we *drive* in there?' he asked, the light bulb coming on in his head.

'We could, but there's only one way in and one way out and once we're in there we're stuck in the car, an easy sedentary target. If we're on the hoof we can leg it through those palm trees and there's nobody who'd be able to get a clear shot at you through that lot.'

They were good words to use, 'target', 'leg it', 'shot', but they didn't infect his judgement with a germ of terror. He sat in silence, staring into the dash, mouth open, jaw tense, gunning himself up.

'You don't think this is a funny place to hand over two million dollars?'

'No,' he said, pinching the septum of his nose, thinking about something else now, and then making up his mind about it. 'If anything goes wrong out there, Bruce, you should . . . you will get a visit from my associate.'

'The nonexec one you didn't tell us anything about?'

'That one,' he said. 'She's my daughter. The company put her through an MBA, that's all. She runs her own business, nothing to do with me.'

'She have a name?'

'Selina,' he said.

'Well, I hope I never get to meet her.'

'No,' he said, turning to the window where he set about filtering all the doubt out of his mind while his eyes drank in the blackness of the wind-rattled coconut palms.

He started out of the car. I grabbed his arm.

'No talking. Quiet as possible. If they're out there they'll know we've arrived. The first person to talk is me and' – I whipped the Camel out of his mouth and tossed it out of the window – 'no smoking.'

We walked to the edge of the tarmac. The security guards at the gate had their backs to us. We dropped off the raised car park and trotted into the coconut palms. We waited a few minutes until our eyes were used to the dark and walked on. The ground was firm between the palms. It wasn't long before we found the patch of beaten earth and a rough table where the city people came to drink beer and breathe air with a dash of the sea in it.

I sat on the ground with my back to a coconut palm and watched Napier in almost no light at all sitting on his hands on the table under a palm-leaf lean-to trying to forget about smoking Camels. We sat there for more than half an hour. The wind whistled up quite a few false alarms for us but in the end nobody showed. A little before a quarter to ten I stood up and whacked the back of my jeans.

'I've got to take a piss,' I said. All the beer I'd drunk sat like a medicine ball in my lap. Napier hissed.

A car, with its headlights on full beam, rippled across the coconut palms and silhouetted two figures on the pavement. The car slowed and stopped. The lights died. One of the figures bent to window height. There was a discussion. The door opened and the figure who'd done the talking got in.

'It's a pick-up, Napier. This is a smart part of town. Girls come here to get taken for a ride by men in Mercedes. That could have been you if they'd showed.'

I walked off to the edge of the palms about thirty or forty metres and kicked a hole in the sand.

'Maybe they didn't show because of you,' he said to the back of my head.

'I didn't crash, I was invited, remember. You cleared me with your big man. And anyway, I'm going now. I've got dinner. You want to stay, you can find your own way back.'

I urinated for at least two minutes. I closed my eyes to the relief spreading through me. The wind got up and blew with some force through the palms and their leaves clacked together like empty scabbards. I walked back to the table shivering, suddenly cold and clammy in the salty breeze.

'Napier,' I called, seeing he'd moved from the table. I looked around for the red glow of a cigarette butt, knowing he wouldn't have been able to hang on. I made a 180-degree sweep of the coconut grove. The Hotel Croix du Sud's gate lights winked on the other side of the boulevard, the aura of the new conference centre lit the night sky, the Novotel and its car park looked as if they were out in a sea of black, but there was no Napier. I shouted his name. The breeze took it off me and shuttled it through the trunks of the palms, but nothing came back.

Just like that – he'd gone.

29

Chapter 3

I ran like a wild man through the trees looking up and down and all around until I was dizzy and freaked at finding myself in the imagery sequence of a sixties TV drama. I walked back to the car and drove home, trawling the streets like an idiot, hoping for a sight of Napier. Everybody was African apart from four huge sailor types who'd washed their hair in beer and, now that they were fragrant, had their rods out casting for some dangerous sex.

The lights were on at my house, our house. I parked up behind Heike's year-old Nissan Pathfinder, a car that came with her job, that came with a housing allowance to pay the rent. I sat with my forehead on the steering wheel and worried at the Napier Briggs fiasco like a cat with a dead mouse trying to pretend there's still some life in it.

I went upstairs to our part of the house and found a single place setting on the dining-room table with an empty bottle of Bourgogne Aligoté beside it, which was better than our usual Entre-Deux-Mers. With Heike's smarter salary we'd moved off the paint-stripper gut rot from tetrapaks and we didn't drink whisky called Big V any more. It was minimum Red Label now.

Heike was asleep on some cushions on the floor, a half-full ashtray next to her head and a tumbler with melted ice in the bottom with nearly a full bottle of nothing less than Black Label by the chair leg. Were we celebrating? I took a right turn into the kitchen and found the lamb tagine on the stove and lit the gas underneath it. I went back into the living room and snitched the Black Label and poured myself a good two fingers. I stirred the tagine and found some cold cooked rice in the pot next to it.

'I waited and I waited for the birthday boy,' said a tired voice from the door.

My birthday! Goddamn. Hit forty and go senile. What year is it?

'How old am I?' I asked her reflection in the window.

'Come on, Bruce, it's not all that bad.'

'Forty-one?'

'There you are – mind like a steel trap. What happened to you this evening?'

'I got held up.'

'What's new?'

'I lost someone.'

'Someone you'd already found?' asked Heike.

'Worse. Someone who was right bang next to me.'

'Jesus,' she said, as sympathetically as possible. 'They beamed him up?'

'As if, Heike, as if. And who's "they", anyway?'

She shrugged and concentrated on fitting a cigarette into her holder.

'I drank your share of the wine,' she said, lighting up.

'I saw.'

'I started on your birthday present too.'

'The Black Label? Yeah, thanks. I mean for the present.'

'Don't mention it. How's the foot?'

'It's OK. I haven't thought about it.'

'In the heat of the moment?'

'Right.'

'Too scared?'

'Maybe.'

She sighed. A birthday treat. Most other times she'd have hardened up, cool as marble, no give at all until the whisky loosened off her throwing arm. Heike didn't like my job, but it *had* nearly got her killed one time which was why she'd put me out to that kennel down the road. She kneaded my shoulder and turned me round. We kissed. My hand went up her bare back. She didn't bother with a bra after her evening shower. I cupped a breast and ran a thumb over the nipple. She tensed and backed off.

'Eat first. Shower. Then I've got another present for you. Two, in fact.'

I finished off the tagine. Heike and I shared the second bottle of Bourgogne Aligoté. I was about to join my Black Label but Heike pushed me off to the shower. I cleaned up and sat on the sofa in a towel. Heike dropped some ice into my glass and splashed another finger over the top.

'Birthday treats,' I said.

She shrugged her eyebrows and sat behind her knees in a corner of the sofa. She sipped her Scotch and smoked at me.

'What about these presents then?'

'Gerhard wants to meet you,' she said.

'Who's Gerhard?'

'Bruce,' she said, her voice taking on a serrated edge.

I raised an eyebrow. She reined back. 'Gerhard Lehrner. He's my boss. The new one.'

'*That* Gerhard. Right. The new one. I'm not used to hearing his name.'

'How many Gerhards . . . ?' She stopped herself. 'Forget it.'

'Come here,' I said, lunging at her.

'Not yet,' she said, inching her feet back. 'Gerhard's going to stay in the office tomorrow afternoon. He wants to talk to you about a job when there's nobody else around,' she said. The glass of Black Label stuck to my lips. I sat up straighter and looked her in the eye. No kidding.

'You've been telling him about my charitable soul,' I said. 'How long did it take?' She smiled. I stroked her big toenail. She twitched it away.

'I didn't tell him about your charitable soul, in fact. I told him what a complete bastard you are. And you know, he's interested.'

'He's got some poor people need kicking.'

She laughed this time. Appealed to her, that, a man with gout kicking a poor person. The suffering.

'He's got a job for Medway and Bagado Investigations. He's looking for someone who can't be fobbed off, who doesn't have the word "no" in their language, who will run something to ground and go down the hole after it and . . .'

'Above all, someone who's . . .'

'Cheap.'

'Thanks for the write-up,' I said, and took a measure off the Scotch.

'He tells me it could be dangerous. So you better listen to what he has to say before you say yes.'

'Well, there's never been any harm in listening.'

'Then why don't you do it to me?'

Our eyes connected. Our whisky glasses hit the table together. She stretched a foot out and undid my towel with her toes. She kicked it away and toyed with what she found underneath until I was gritting my teeth. She sat astride me, yanking her skirt up around her waist and took hold of me with a surprisingly cool palm. Watching herself as she did it she lowered herself with infinitesimal slowness until our lips drew level.

'Better?'

The tension went out of me and I sat back and let Heike do all the work.

I woke up at 6.30 a.m. with too much light in the room because, in the urgency of the moment, closing curtains had been the last thing on our minds. Heike's arm was across my chest and the phone was ringing. I was too content to answer it. It stopped.

Heike's hand slipped down below the sheet line and came across some eagerness she hadn't expected which made her start and look me in the corner of the eye.

'Is that for me?'

'More presents.'

She bit me hard on the shoulder so that I yelped. I rolled over her and she gripped my hips with her hands to steady me on. The phone started ringing again.

'Shit,' she said.

I thrust, but she held me back. The phone banged on.

'Come on,' I said. 'It'll stop, for Christ's sake.'

'No. I can't stand it.'

I dropped on to my knees and waited. And waited. And waited.

'Answer the damn thing and get back in here.'

I stormed into the living room and yanked the phone to my ear.

'Bagado here. Sorry to disturb you. He's been found.'

'Who?'

'Who do you think?'

'I don't know. Who are we looking for?'

'Napier Briggs.'

'Where is he, the bloody idiot?'

'Down on the railway tracks. He's dead, Bruce. Dead as the sleeper he's lying on.'

Chapter 4

Cotonou. Saturday 17th February.

There'd been no *harmattan* this year. That cooling, drying wind, which made all the Africans miserable and
me feel human for once in the year, never arrived. It
stopped about 100 kilometres north of Cotonou and
wouldn't come any further. Some said it was the pollution, others that it was just a weak *harmattan* this year
but most put it down to the devaluation – anything out
of the ordinary just had to be.

Now it should have settled down into the dry season
before the April rains, but the weather, like the currency
markets, the world economy and my left foot was a
mess this year. Cotonou, and other cities along this
stretch of coast, had been thumped about by short, savage night-time storms which had left it flat on its back,
with no power and secreting fluids from orifices which
should have been free and dry. The town got up groggy
in the mornings, the people pasty-mouthed and irri-
table. The buildings shed their conference paint jobs
and looked bruised and broken, with mud spattered up
the sides from the rain's kickback. The mud roads were
steaming lakes and the first post-conference potholes
opened up in the new tarmac like a teenager's night-
mare acne.

There was nothing refreshing about these storms. The sun eased itself into position in no time at all and hammered down so that at eight in the morning, out on the railway tracks, it was already close to eighty degrees, and a thin mist like kettle steam hung in the air. The place stank of putrid salami. My head was coming apart like a coconut after the first machete blow and there was the same flesh-tearing, sucking noise in my ears.

Bagado was walking ahead of me, pacing the sleepers between the tracks, towards a group of people who were standing around Napier's body. Bagado was looking over the toes of his shoes for clues, small change, anything that might get him through his current lean patch. I limped behind. Yes, it was back.

I wasn't really thinking about the *harmattan*. I wasn't that upset by the night-time storms, which I slept through anyway. The heat and the humidity were hell but you either got used to that or you got out. I wasn't even torturing myself over Napier Briggs. Bagado had talked me out of that kind of thinking some time ago. Not even the gout was penetrating. It was rolling over a short few minutes with Heike that had left me feeling uneasy.

After Bagado's news about Napier the flag was well down by the time I'd come back to the bedroom. Heike was lying there with her arms folded across her bosom with no expression in her face.

'I suppose you don't like me now that I'm not the birthday boy?' I'd said. It was a joke but I could see from her look that there was some truth in it.

'Bagado with some bad news?'

'Don't ask.'

'I won't.'

I'd pulled on my clothes with her not saying anything and the room full of it. How had it happened? How had the dynamics changed? It hadn't been Bagado's call. She was resigned to that kind of intrusion once in a while.

'Don't be late for the meeting this afternoon,' she'd said.

'I wouldn't dare.'

I'd pulled her to me and kissed her goodbye. She was stiff, wooden, unyielding as if a stagehand was standing in for the leading lady.

The policemen standing around the body parted as we arrived. Some of them knew Bagado and there was an exchange of pleasantries, the asking after immediate relatives which can take some time in Africa. Then Bagado tried to get down to business with them and they froze. He was speaking to them in their own language, Fon, and they were looking sheepish in more ways than one.

'They've been told not to talk to me,' said Bagado. 'They won't touch the body until the senior officer on duty comes. Commandant Bondougou.'

'Your favourite. Is he out of bed yet?' I asked, and he shrugged.

'Let us, you and I, Bruce, go and sit for a while and . . . mull.'

'Mull? You've got some vocabulary on you, Bagado.'

'Education – the only thing they can't take away from me.'

We crouched down and sat on another rail in the

siding. Some crows had collected on the corrugated-iron roof of a warehouse opposite. Their toenails clinked on the hot roof, their wings clasped behind them, polite, waiting for the police to have their fill before they moved in. Bagado and I mulled.

'I made some expensive calls after you left for lunch yesterday,' he said.

'What'd you want to do a thing like that for? He wasn't even a client.'

'Professional reaction.'

'Who'd you call?'

'Dupont in France.'

'I hope it didn't take too long to find out they'd never heard of Napier Briggs?'

'It did and they hadn't and they said they certainly wouldn't use a shipbroker to sell their product for them.'

'He might have used another company name.'

'And an alias to buy the product? I don't think so.'

'OK, I'll buy it. Anything else?'

'Napier Briggs was a very nervous man. He didn't want to tell us anything about what he'd been doing and he didn't want the Nigerian authorities involved. He only wanted a private investigation from here, so we can assume his business wasn't legal. I mean the original business, supplying what he said were sewage treatment chemicals to Chemiclean . . .'

'Who he told us didn't exist.'

'But who paid him for supplying the chemicals, so they did exist. They just weren't legal, they weren't registered as a company.'

'Was that another one of your calls?'

'Yes.'

'How does an unregistered company import goods from overseas?'

'We're talking about Nigeria, my friend, not Benin. You couldn't do it here, but over there . . .'

'You pay your money,' I said. 'So your next expensive call was to . . . ?'

'Colonel Adjeokuta, the head of the four-one-nine squad, the man I offered to put Mr Briggs in touch with. He hadn't heard of Chemiclean, but he was going to make it his business to find out if there was anybody in his department who had. He wasn't surprised about the Benin connection on the second scam. There's been a number of those recently.'

'They never stop, these guys.'

'It costs a stamp and an envelope and there's a sucker born every day,' said Bagado. 'So what happened to you last night?'

'Do I look that bad?'

'No worse than usual, but you said you were going to see Napier at the Hotel du Lac. Did you?'

'I did. He got a call from the boys while I was there saying they wanted to give him his money back.'

Bagado chuckled to himself.

'So we went and had a look.'

'You did what?' he said, setting solid on the rail as if he'd seen a train coming. 'What did you want to go and do a thing like that for, he wasn't even a . . .'

'Yeah, yeah, Bagado. I know. He offered me ten grand to hold his hand. Dollars. He said there was a big man who'd guaranteed his personal safety. I went because if I hadn't he'd have gone by himself and . . .'

40

'Got himself killed.'

'Point taken.'

I told him how it had happened.

'Now that's a problem,' he said, and we did a quick stick-and-paste job on what we were going to tell Bondougou if he was predictable enough to ask what the hell we were doing out on the railway tracks at that hour of the morning.

Commandant Bondougou arrived a little after 8.30 a.m. and stood over the dead body with his hat in his armpit. His head was fat and broad with the eyes widely spaced, as sinister as a halloween pumpkin. He passed a hand over his shaved head and plugged a finger and thumb in each of his nostrils to keep his brain in neutral. A junior policeman muttered something. He glanced Bagado's way and looked as if he'd spit if he could be bothered to drag up the phlegm. I wouldn't have liked to rely on him for an introduction to Cotonou society, we were lower than bilharzia on his dance card. We kept our distance.

An ambulance arrived. The policemen rolled the body over and stepped back in formation horror. All we could see between their legs was the mass of blood which had poured down Napier's chest and was now clogged with dust and insects. Bondougou checked Napier's wrists for a watch and his pockets for money. Nothing. He found a passport in the jacket and opened it. A card fluttered out which a junior pounced on. Bondougou beckoned us over. It was one of our cards. We looked down at Napier. It was a shock.

Around his neck was a length of rope and two knots evenly spaced along it. It must have been used to squeeze the eyeballs out of their sockets because two black holes stared out of Napier's face. From his ears, protruding about two inches, were the ends of what must have been two six-inch nails. Most horrific of all was his mouth. It gave him the appearance of an African mask because it was set in a terrible grimace – all teeth and gums. Too many teeth, too much gum and too black inside. Whoever had picked him up in the *cocotiers* last night had hacked out his tongue and then used the knife to cut off Napier Briggs's mouth.

Commandant Bondougou released us at lunchtime. I'd been lucky not to get too much of his ugly attention. Bagado had caught most of that. I'd been lying on a bench outside his office and the few occasions the door had opened I'd seen a surprisingly tranquil scene. Bondougou slouched with his tunic open, his gut humped up under a string vest, a toothpick jammed between his teeth which he was sucking on when he wasn't talking. Bagado upright in a chair, his mac rucked up on his shoulders, his head still, listening.

We'd both written up short and inconclusive statements about our meeting with Napier Briggs which, after our mulling, fortunately matched. We left the station and picked up some sandwiches at La Gerbe d'Or patisserie and drove thirty kilometres east, nose to tail with a thirty-five-ton *Titan*, to the Benin capital Porto Novo, for our meeting with Heike's boss.

We parked in the agency's compound, empty except for Heike's Pathfinder and a Land Cruiser, just before 2 p.m. I broke the silence by asking Bagado if he'd mind me doing the talking during the meeting.

'White man to white man, you mean?'

'No, it's just that we have a habit of shouting each other down. I think it'd look better if one of us took control to start with until the meeting turns into a free-for-all. I'm volunteering.'

'Or insisting?'

'No. I like to talk. You're a good listener.'

'This isn't what you British would call excluding me in? I've been in those meetings before. Token nigger in the corner whose word and opinion doesn't count.'

We stopped in the car park and faced off.

'What's brought this on?' I asked. 'Since when have you been or felt excluded?'

'I didn't like the way you assumed to be boss.'

'I have *not* assumed that. You want to control the meeting, that's fine.'

Bagado shook his head. He put his hands in his mac pockets and slumped. He didn't like himself for some reason.

'What's going on, Bagado?' I asked, putting a hand on his shoulder. 'Bondougou said something to you?'

'Let's do this meeting,' he said, morose, looking at the dust on his shoes. 'You do the talking. You're right. I'm a listener. I listen too much.'

Gerhard's office was as large and cool as Gerhard Lehrner himself. The man had all his blond hair on his head and all of his stomach behind his belt, even though Heike had told me he was on the nearside of fifty and had lost one wife to Africa – not killed, just couldn't take it. He disposed of most preconceptions Englishmen drag up when they hear they're about to meet a German. He had blue eyes in an uncreased face and a soft, full-lipped mouth which made him look kind to strangers, especially if they were women. He was courteous. He called me by my Christian name. He sat on the front edge of his desk so there were no barriers between us and revealed that he wasn't wearing any socks under his brown loafers. He spoke perfect English and didn't sound as if he was keen on extracting something without anaesthetic.

Heike wasn't in on the meeting, otherwise I might have had to disguise the fact that Gerhard didn't strike me as a bad guy at all. This, despite the fact that his first question was not one you'd come across in Trivial Pursuit.

'What can you tell me about the Yoruba god, Orishala?'

Bagado smiled benignly and looked at me as if I'd recently vacated the Yoruba mythology chair at Lagos University. I waved him through.

'Orishala,' said Bagado, slitting his eyes, looking through the thin Venetian blinds of the window for inspiration and starting to sound like a lecturer with a roomful of captured arseholes to talk to, 'is the creator god of the Yoruba. He's not the supreme god. That is Olorun, "owner of the sky" and creator and judge of man. But the two are connected. In the beginning Olorun gave Orishala the task of creating firm ground out of the water and marsh that existed all around. To do this Orishala was given a pigeon, a hen and a snail shell full of earth. Orishala emptied the snail shell and the two birds scratched around and spread the earth over the marsh so that it became dry land.

'Later on, Orishala made plants and people but, this

is the important bit, he could only *shape* people. Olorun being the supreme god was the only one who could invest them with life. Orishala wanted to know how Olorun did this, but whenever he spied on him, Olorun would make him fall asleep. This made Orishala unpredictable so that when he saw human beings they would sometimes remind him of his frustration and the powerlessness he felt in his work. It could make him angry, incensed that he didn't hold the ultimate power of life and because he could shape people he would take revenge by deforming them. This is the Yoruba people's explanation for occasional aberrations.'

'I've always liked that part about the pigeon, the hen and the snail shell,' said Gerhard, letting us know he was on top of it all along and getting within a hair of thanking Bagado for handing in a good piece of prep. It was a line that wiped out previous goodwill and made me feel more expensive than I had done yesterday.

'We have a small project in a town called Kétou just over a hundred kilometres north of Porto Novo. We're very close to the Nigerian border. The project is agricultural but we have a medical service there too. Pregnant women have been coming from a small village called Akata across the border. They're very frightened pregnant women. They've been talking about the anger of the god Orishala. Five women from the village have already given birth to deformed babies. They've been telling my staff about how their livestock are sick and their crops are dying.'

There was a knock on the door. Heike came in. Gerhard didn't need to stand up, suck in his gut and swell his pecs but he did it anyway. His blue eyes flashed across the room like police lights at night. Now I knew at least one of the reasons why we'd got the job and that made me feel even less cheap. Bagado was leaning forward with his thumb on his chin and two fingers astride the ridge he had coming down his forehead to the bridge of his nose, squeezing.

Nobody misses love walking into a room.

Heike was self-conscious. She knew the attention she was getting and she knew I was there watching her get it. I now realized that she hadn't let me into the sanctity of her workplace for the simple reason of a cheap job. There were messages. How to read them, that was the thing. There was no doubt that Gerhard had got himself all atremble with Heike in the room, but what was I there for? Was this Heike telling Gerhard, 'This is my man, back off'? Was Heike telling me, 'I'm still attractive, watch your step'? This could be Heike giving Bagado and I a break, knowing we needed the money, or it could be a little punishment, a helping of self-knowledge.

I didn't think Heike was going to try anything on with Gerhard. He seemed too reasonable and she'd already run that one past me with another guy she'd worked with – Wolfgang. They'd gone back to Berlin together after some ugly business of mine had spilled over into our private life. Wolfgang had been no match for her. When she'd disappointed him he'd cried in the street, sat on the edge of the pavement with his elbows on his knees and his fists banged into the side of his head and added to the rains in the gutter – inconsolable.

I'd spent some time thinking about Wolfgang's scene while Heike slept beside me with the sweat of sex still on us. She'd always accused me of holding things back from her, not letting her in, building up walls around myself. Maybe she was right and I was just doing some self-protection, making sure I didn't end up crouched in a street somewhere making mud out of dust.

'Bruce?'

I looked up to find three pairs of eyes on me. Bagado's were the friendliest.

'What was the question?' I asked. 'I was thinking of the good god Orishala.'

'There was no question,' said Gerhard, sounding German for the first time, and looking more triumphant than he should have been.

'You were looking strange,' said Heike.

'You're sending me up country to find out why Orishala is angry and you think *I* look strange?'

'Yes,' said Gerhard, smiling and walking behind his desk to sit in his leather swivel chair, 'I see your point.'

Heike's eyes remained wide open, two divots of concern on her forehead, looking good with no make-up, no perfume, just with an African pin I'd bought for her up in Abomey in her hair and a light tan. She softened her mouth into a smile and her teeth showed white against her dark lips with the defined cupid's bow. Heike wasn't a model beauty. She had too much intelligence and resilience in her features for that – you'd take your eye off the clothes – but I hadn't met the guy who wouldn't sit up straight for her.

Bagado had released his face from his grasp now that the sex had subsided in the room and was staring at a wooden African head on Gerhard's desk, being patient, which was one of his great strengths. Bagado and Heike had become good friends over the last few years. She'd conveniently forgotten how he'd led me off the winding path of my bread-and-butter business work and into the jungle of more sinister crimes. He wasn't just my partner. He had a much higher status than that. He was a husband, a father and a totally honourable man. I was the lover, the bastard and as dependable as an island of weed in a mangrove swamp.

Heike crossed her legs and cued Bagado.

'What do you want us to do, M Gerhard?'

'We respect Orishala,' said Gerhard, 'but we are not convinced. I want you to find out what is happening across the border. I can't, and I don't want to involve my own people. They have enough trouble in Benin. You will have to be discreet. You'll have to come up with your own reasons for being over there. Anything that doesn't bear the agency's name. Talk to our people in Kétou if you like, they may have something to add. *Sie haben den Akten, bitte, Heike.*'

Heike gave him some files and he stood them on end and tapped the desk.

'Perhaps, first, we should talk about money,' he said. 'Unless, of course, you don't want the job.'

'We're interested,' I said. 'The money, well, the money's got a little complicated since devaluation. We used to charge a hundred thousand CFA a day for the two of us.' A wince shot across Gerhard's brow like a snake across tarmac. 'We've been finding it difficult to double our rate since devaluation. But that's what we'd like to do. Two hundred thousand a day plus expenses.'

'Impossible,' said Gerhard. 'I can't justify that. I have no budget for private investigations, you understand.'

'You have contingency, don't you, Gerhard?'

'Yes, but you are asking me to pay more than three hundred dollars a day which is my budget for the Kétou station, *and* this is not our business. Our mandate is for Benin.'

'But it affects you.'

'Yes, but when the accountants ask, "What is this thousand dollars?" I have to give an answer within the mandate or I have to ask *my* boss in Berlin to . . . to . . . pacify the money men. I can't do that very often in a year. I need to keep favours in reserve.'

'Don't want to use them up early on?'

'Precisely.'

'What sort of money did you have in mind?'

'*That* for the whole job . . . including expenses.'

'Two hundred thousand? You've got to be kidding. Three hundred and seventy-five dollars for the lot? It'll cost seventy-five dollars to get up there and back. Three-day job. A hundred dollars a day. Fifty dollars each if we don't eat, sleep or bribe anyone. That's very little, Gerhard. That's so little . . .'

'You might as well do it for free?' he said, finding some cheek to slap me with.

'Not *that* little.'

'Two hundred and fifty thousand is my limit.'

I looked long and hard into his unflinching, blue, Aryan eyes. The sort that had spent their youth looking out over cornfields and thinking of Valhalla. There wasn't even a hairline crack of pity in their blue glassiness. I felt Heike's tension. She was sitting three feet from me and looked ready to snap up like a roller blind any second. She hated talking about money. I did it so rarely I loved it.

'Gerhard, I don't know what Heike's told you about me. I can be difficult. Unconventional. In this case, I believe your intentions are good. I know Heike's are. If it wasn't for her we wouldn't be here so, for that, and because of the charitable nature of the work, we'll do it. But you mentioned favours earlier, favours from your boss. Favours are something I'm big on. Favours are my kind of barter system. I'll do this job for two hundred and fifty thousand and one favour.'

'What is this favour?'

I thought I might get it over with now and tell him to keep his Teuton muscle out of Heike's fishing limits and go and be handsome, stable and bossy elsewhere. But that would not be cool.

'I don't know, Gerhard. It'll come to me. It won't be anything dangerous or unpleasant. It won't involve money out of your precious budget. You might have to put yourself out a little, that's all. Are we on?'

Gerhard liked it. He leaned across his desk like a winner and shook hands as if he was crushing beer tins. He handed me the file. We all stood and Heike shook herself out. Gerhard's jaw muscles were as bunched as a chipmunk's cheeks.

Chapter 5

We read the file in Heike's office. It was a longer version of what Gerhard had covered in the meeting. Heike walked us to the car. When I kissed her goodbye our noses somehow got in the way, which they hadn't done before. She touched me on the shoulder as I got in the car. I looked back and her face crumpled a little with pity or worry, I couldn't decide. Things had been smooth for just over a year, and now, since this morning, I could sense the levels changing, could feel myself being brought to the edge of something.

I checked the camera for film, there was still some in. We bought some whisky and mineral water and drove north in the late afternoon.

It was hot enough for the sweat to curl round the back of my ears like a little girl's silky hair. Bagado opened up his mac a little and let the hair-dryer-air warm his flat belly. I hadn't found the day that could make Bagado sweat. His mother called him her little lizard because he always had to be out in the sun. He'd been with the police in both Paris and London. The cold and a desire to find a wife had driven him back, and in that order. He still had nightmares about London – being down on the Thames on a January afternoon with an east wind direct from Siberia blowing up the estuary. I just had to say 'chill factor' to him and he'd go into the foetal position.

This was Bagado's season. The dry season, when the heat squirmed up off the tarmac and the beaten earth so that after two minutes out in it a white man would feel sure he'd eaten a bad prawn somewhere. The abnormal rains had unsettled him. He didn't like rains. They brought malaria with them and he always caught it – hit *him* like a flu bug, nearly killed me, gave me a headache like the earth must have had when the Grand Canyon opened up.

'What did you think of our German friend?' asked Bagado.

'Looked more of a director for Mercedes or Siemens than an aid agency.'

'He wasn't wearing any socks.'

'Well, yeah, apart from that.'

'Heike looked . . . very pretty,' he said. Bagado had a liking for non sequiturs. He looked out of the window, as if there was anything out there that could interest him. Trees, earth, more trees.

'Yes,' I agreed.

We carried on in a silence that not even a town called Pobé could break.

'She seems to like him,' said Bagado, and then, 'Gerhard,' as an afterthought.

'That's a shame,' I said.

'Oh, why's that?'

'Because he's a vain, arrogant, opinionated, self-centred fake-liberal with the sensitivity of an Alabaman cockfighter,' I said, as calm as a triangle of cucumber sandwich.

'I thought he handled *us* very well.'

'Did you?'

'Two hundred and fifty thousand for all this talent.'

'Plus the favour. You've no idea how expensive that favour's going to be.'

'You said no money.'

'Services, Bagado, services.'

'I see.'

Another half hour went past, the car packed tight with the unsaid thing.

'So what did Bondougou say?' I asked. Bagado looked blank. 'You tore my ears off before that meeting and now you don't remember?'

'I remember,' he said, quietly so that my nerve quivered. 'Bondougou offered me my job back.'

'He wants you on the inside pissing out and you told him where to go . . .' Bagado didn't respond. 'You did tell him where to go, Bagado?'

'The way he put it was that since the trouble in Togo and with the regime in Nigeria, Cotonou has become the new business centre. More business, more money, more crime.'

'And if there's anybody who should know about crime, Bondougou should. He's a one-man gangland.'

'The job offer is political. The politicians want a safe place. They don't, for instance, want dead British ship-brokers with their mouths cut off lying face down across the railway tracks. Bondougou has to make a show of getting things done. The Cotonou force is short of the right kind of manpower and, for a change, they have money to spend. I am one of the most experienced people in Benin.'

Bondougou was right. The Togolese capital, Lomé, had been an important centre of the business community in West Africa. It was a free port with hard currency, good restaurants, smart hotels and a congenial atmosphere. It had also been the largest exporter of gold along this coast and it didn't even have a goldmine. There'd been political problems, multiparty democracy riots and one day the army had opened fire indiscriminately on a crowd of civilians and hundreds had been killed or injured. In the three days after the incident three hundred and fifty thousand people left Togo for Benin. Lomé was a ghost town now, the people who remained imposed their own curfew. All the business was in Cotonou, which was itself a free port and had hard currency, too, but more important, the army didn't feel the need to impose its authority on the civilian government, something that had happened in Nigeria. There, the elections had been annulled, pressure applied on the press, and key figures put under house arrest. On top of that there were strikes, petrol shortages, piles of stinking refuse in the streets and the odd corpse. The locals were getting very restless.

Bondougou needed policemen in Benin, good ones, who could handle big numbers and get the politicians off his back. The only thing he'd never liked about Bagado was that the man didn't have a corrupt cell in his body. That made Bondougou nervous. He didn't know where Bagado was coming from and he could never rely on him to keep his mouth shut at the right time.

'Has Bondougou told you your duties?'

'In outline. Nothing specific.'

'But we know there's no such thing as a gift from Bondougou. Did you talk about Napier Briggs?'

'No. He started off playing the patriotic card. He teased me about working for the white man. He told me I had more important things to do for my country. He called me *un caniche Parisien*. A Parisian poodle. He made it sound as if I'd thrown it all in for the money. I felt like showing him our accounts. I felt like reminding him why I lost my job in the first place. It made me very, what's that word Brian used, you know, my detective friend in London . . . narked. That was it. He go' me bloody narked.' Bagado finished with a perfect glottal stop in his imitation South London accent.

'Bondougou is a . . .'

'We know what Bondougou is.'

'Bondougou is the biggest bastard in the Gulf of Guinea. You go work for him again and you know where you'll end up . . .'

'The same place as last time.'

'Uh-uh, Bagado, no way, not the shitheap this time. You won't just get fired *this time* . . .'

Bagado nodded. The tyres roared on the hot tarmac, which glistened in the sun as if glass had been shattered across it. He passed a hand over the dusting of white in his hair – tired of all this.

'He's giving me no choice,' he said.

'You're going back to him?'

'If I don't, we're finished. That was his last card, Bruce – he'll close us down, strip you of your *carte de séjour* and have you deported.'

A dog slunk across the road and I braked. The tyres squealed in the heat and women walking with their heads loaded into the sky shot off the road into the bush followed by their children who maintained line like chicks after a hen. The car kicked up a jib of dust from the edge of the road. The women stopped and turned, their necks straining under their loads to see if anybody had been hit.

'Christ, Bagado, what did I ever do to him?'

'You know me, that's enough.'

'This is it then?'

'What?'

'The last job.'

'Until . . .'

'. . . until they find Bondougou down a storm drain. The pies he's got his fingers in are very hot.'

'Yes. It might not be so long.'

'Then it'll be Commandant Bagado, maybe, and we'll all have to bow and scrape.'

'Kiss the hem of my mac.'

'I'd rather worship the ground you walk on, if that's OK.'

'You don't sound very annoyed.'

'Oh, I am, Bagado. I am. But what can a poor boy do?'

We drove on in silence. The car fuller now with that and the unsaid thing still there. Another half hour passed.

'What did you make of the Napier Briggs thing?' I asked.

'It looked like a warning to me. Don't see, don't hear, don't speak.'

'To who?'

'Anybody that's got half a mind to be nosy.'

'From who?'

'A big man. Probably the guarantor you talked about

56

who said it would be fine to go out into the *cocotiers* and pick up two million dollars of an evening . . . What the hell were you thinking of, Bruce?' said Bagado, suddenly annoyed.

'I'll tell you exactly what I was thinking of, and I'm not proud of it.'

'Ten thousand dollars?'

'You got it in one, Bagado. You're wasted here, you should be a criminal psychologist.'

'Criminal?' he asked the inside of the car. 'I suppose it bloody nearly was, what you did.'

He looked off out the window and shook his head. We drove on in silence. The unsaid thing still inside me, bigger than a full set of luggage.

'Has Heike spoken to you?' I asked, unable to bear listening to the roar of the road any longer.

'Aha!' said Bagado. 'No.'

'What was the "Aha!" about?'

'Nearly an hour and a half for you to get it out.'

'What?'

'What's been on your mind since first thing this morning. You're improving.'

'I am?'

'A year ago you'd have waited until nightfall and the third whisky.'

'I've given up whisky.'

'During the week.'

'It hasn't helped.'

'Take it up again.'

'The gout's still niggling.'

'I don't suppose you know that there's almost no incidence of gout in Scotland.'

'You're kidding.'

'They don't think whisky brings it on. Beer, red wine, port's more the thing.'

'What about the purine?'

'The purine?'

'All the Arbroath smokies, the oak-smoked kippers, the tinned pilchards, the wild salmon leaping up the glens – all that purine.'

'What's that got to do with it?'

'Purine brings on gout.'

'And you think . . . ?' Bagado roared and then settled back. 'You better go back on the whisky before the rest of your brain packs in.'

I gave him a bit of slab-faced silence after that. He didn't notice. So I told him what had happened before I left home this morning.

'Maybe she doesn't like you,' he said.

'Give it to me straight, Bagado. I can't take all this faffing around the bush.'

'Well, I don't mean permanently. Just for the time being. She's gone off you. It happens. I asked a woman in Paris once how she came to kill her husband. She said it all started when she saw him cleaning his ears with his little finger and wiping it on her furniture.'

'I took your call in the living room, went back into the bedroom and she was off me. No reason. Just dead to me as if she was in a state of shock.'

'Maybe in your distracted state you scratched yourself, you know, unattractively.'

'That's interesting,' I said, dismissing it. 'So what d'you think that was all about back at the office? The Gerhard thing.'

'Maybe that an attractive woman like Heike could do better than the deadbeat she's decided to live with.'

'Deadbeat?'

'Your expression, I think.'

'Deadbeat?'

'I don't think that's it, by the way. She doesn't mind you being a deadbeat.'

'But I'm not a deadbeat. A deadbeat's someone . . .'

'It's part of it, but it's not it.'

'I'm not a deadbeat. I get up in the morning. I go to work . . .'

Bagado gave me the yackety-yack with his hand.

'What was your annual income last year?'

'Come on, she's got a job, Bagado. It's different, for God's sake. I'm a street hustler – different ball game altogether.'

'We're missing the point, but you understand me, I think.'

'I do?'

'Sex is not the only thing.'

'The Great Leap Forward, Bagado, I missed something. The link. Let's have it. And what do you know about my sex life?'

'That it's very good.'

'She told you that?'

'She didn't have to. Whenever I come to your house the two of you are in bed together.'

'What's wrong with that?'

'Nothing, but it's not the only thing.'

'Even a "*deadbeat*" like me knows that.'

'What do you think the difference is between you and Gerhard?'

'He's stable, got a good job, he's older, he's German, he's got a sense of humour like an elephant trap . . .'

'He's been married and he wants to get married again to someone who likes Africa.'

'Heike's not interested in Gerhard. We've been through all that crap with Wolfgang.'

'And look how far you've come in a year. She needs some reassurance that there's a point. A year's a long time for a woman creeping through her thirties.'

'She doesn't creep.'

'You're being weak, Bruce. You make out you look and don't see but you know better than I do. You just can't bring yourself to the marks. You're afraid that she'll leave you. You're afraid to move on. You're being a modern man.'

'That's enough of that kind of talk, Bagado. Enough. You're getting very close to using that word and I don't want to hear that word in this car . . .'

'Commitment? There, I've said it. Better in than out.'

'You can hear the ranks of bachelors' bowels weakening,' I said, cupping a hand to my ear.

'I don't know what you're afraid of,' he said, sawing the scar in the cleft of his chin. 'Compromise?'

'You've been pulling some vocab. out of the bag today, Bagado.'

'Is that it? You're afraid of compromise? You should see what I'm going to have to do when I go back to Bondougou.'

'I've already done some compromising. It wasn't half as painful as I thought it was going to be. What I'm afraid of is that if I cross the line it might not work and

60

I'll be in a deeper problem than if I don't cross the line in the first place.'

'She'll go,' said Bagado. 'That'll solve your problem.'

We arrived in Kétou at nightfall. The aid station was closed, with a *gardien* outside who showed us a restaurant where we had some *pâte* and bean sauce and a couple of bottles of La Beninoise beer. We drove out into the bush, set up a mosquito net against the car, rolled out some sleeping mats and had an early, very cheap night out under the stars. I lay on my back and felt like a deadbeat. The pattern had held for more than a year. Now things were falling to pieces and all out of my reach. Bagado going back to his job, Heike tapping her feet and behind it all the dark shadow of Bondougou, his eyes flickering in his head.

Chapter 6

Sunday 18th February.

Gerhard's people were dedicated and came in as early on Sunday mornings as they did during the week. They gave us coffee and directions. We crossed the border into Nigeria just after 8 a.m. and headed north from a town called Meko on a dirt road. After ten kilometres we hit a roadblock guarded by men wearing army fatigues and holding AK-47s loosely in capable hands.

'They look like the real thing,' I said, as we cruised up to the soldier standing with his hand raised.

'This is no place for armed robbery, unless they're very stupid.'

The soldier came to my window and looked in and over our shoulders.

'Where you going?' he asked.

'Akata village.'

'Closed.'

'For why?' asked Bagado.

'Big sickness. Nobody go in. Nobody come out.'

'What sort of sickness?'

'Typhoid. Cholera. We don't know. We just keeping people from going there 'til doctah come telling us.'

'Which doctor?'

'No, no, medical doctah.'

62

'I mean, what's his name, this doctor. Where's he come from?'

'Oh yes,' he said and looked back at the other soldiers who gave him about as much animation as a sloth gang on downers. He turned back to us and found a 1000-CFA note fluttering under his nose. His hand came up in a Pavlovian reflex and rested on the window ledge. He shook his head.

'This not that kind thing. You get sick, you die. A white man out here, what do I say to my superiah officah?'

'You give him this,' I said, and produced a bottle of Red Label from under the seat.

'No, sah. You go back to Meko. No entry through here, sah.'

'Who is your superior officer?'

'Major Okaka.'

'Where's he?'

The soldier shrugged.

We drove back to Meko and headed west for about fifteen kilometres before cutting north again, but not on a track this time, through the bush. Within twenty minutes we were stopped by a jeep and a Land Rover, one with a machine gun mounted on the cab. Four soldiers armed with machine pistols got out of the jeep and stood at the four points of the car. An officer type levered himself out of the Land Rover and removed a Browning pistol from a holster on his hip. The gun hung down his side in a slack hand. He approached the window and rested the gun on the ledge and looked at us from under his brow.

'We're looking for Major Okaka. This is Dr Bagado from Ibadan.'

Bagado leaned across me and said something in Yoruba to the officer. The officer's other hand came up on the window and he leaned on the car as if he was going to roll it over. He grinned and spoke with an English accent that he must have picked up from the World Service in the fifties.

'There is no Major Okaka on this exercise. We're not expecting a Dr Bagado. You have entered a restricted area. If you return to the main road nothing more will be said. If, however, you prove yourselves troublesome we shall have to escort you down to Lagos for interrogation. Your passports, please.'

He flicked though our passports, the Browning still in his hand, his finger on the trigger and a certain studied carelessness in where he was pointing it.

'Who is the officer in command of this army exercise?' asked Bagado.

'That is none of your business. You just go back to the main road. It's dangerous out here. If you wish, my men can escort you back to the frontier and ensure that you cross the border safely.'

'That won't be necessary . . . er, Major . . . ?'

'Captain Mundo.'

He returned our passports and took us back to the main road. We drove towards Meko. The two vehicles disappeared back into the bush. Four kilometres outside Meko we came across a man walking in the dust at the side of the road, his jacket thrown over his shoulder and his white shirt filthy and patched dark by the hot morning sun. His trousers were no better. He looked as if he'd been kicked around. We offered him a lift. He removed a pair of black-framed glasses held together above his nose by electrician's tape. He wiped the sweat out of his eyes and got in. His name was Sam Ifaki and he worked for a weekly news magazine called *Progress*.

'Are you making any?' I asked.

'Not here.'

'What've you been doing?'

'Looking around.'

'Akata village?'

'Not any more.'

'Those army people roll you around in the dirt and send you back?'

'Army people,' he said. 'They're all the same, army people.'

'So you're not interested in Akata any more?'

'It's not my job. I was looking at a farming project outside Ayeforo. Some people told me there's something happening near Meko. I come. These people are rough with me. Tell me this business is none of mine. They tell me to go. So I go. If I don't, they kill me. They say it's nothing to them.'

'What did you hear about Akata?'

'Some sickness. They talk about the gods and such. That's why I'm interested. *Progress* likes to report on witchcraft. You know, we like to show the people this pile of rubbish. When people get sick it's not because of the gods, unless they think it's god business putting faeces in the water supply. Nine times out of ten this is the problem. We've been having some rain. Strange for this time of year. Things are messed up, is all.'

'We've heard about deformed babies in Akata.'

'And sick cattle,' said Sam, squeezing the bridge of

his glasses, 'and crops dying. Orishala is angry. Always the same thing.'

We arrived in Meko at lunchtime. Sam took us to a chop bar where an old man wearing a shift patched together from polypropylene fertilizer sacks sat outside. He had cataracts over both eyes and tapped the ground in front of him with a heavy stick as if summoning an audience for a foreign potentate. Inside, a couple of petrol barons, who sold cheap Nigerian gasoline in Kétou for half the Benin price, sat in full robes and started making elaborate gestures at each other so that we could see their Rolexes. Sam let us buy him a beer and some chop. The food was *eba*, a ball of steamed gari, cassava flour, which you could build a brick wall with if the cement works went out of production. It came with a red-hot sauce and two pieces of meat which looked like knee cartilage but turned out to be school rubbers. I ate the *eba* and sauce and left the rubbers for Sam and Bagado. The petrol barons were drinking Nigerian Guinness, which, at eight per cent alcohol, can creep up on you. Their mouths widened and their tongues flopped out. Occasionally they sat back from each other, stunned, as if they'd inadvertently called each other sons of whores.

The chop-bar owner was playing draughts with himself using beer-bottle tops on a board scored into the counter. He was roughly half the size of his wife, who appeared from the kitchen behind him and looked over his shoulder to make sure he wasn't cheating. Bagado asked him about Akata village. He left the bar without a word and roared at the old man outside who stumbled in behind him, fresh from some pilgrimage of the mind.

The barman gave us a bottle of *ogogoro*, distilled palm wine, which could get you nowhere quicker than a sandbag across the back of the neck. That was how they got the name for it, it was the noise a man made as he went down.

The bar owner suggested that we get our questions in between the first and third shot of *ogogoro* which proved to be good advice. After the first shot the old man looked around him as if his cataracts had demisted. Bagado spoke to him in Yoruba, sounding solicitous, respecting his elders, and made notes in his little book. Once Bagado had it straight on paper he gave the old man his third shot. Something short-circuited and the wavering twelve-volt lamps behind the white discs of the old man's eyes went out.

Sam gave us a treasured business card and we left him in the chop bar with the sleeping petrol barons. The bar owner walked the old man outside, where he sat down and fell asleep with his head balanced on the end of his stick. He'd given Bagado directions on how to get into Akata from the north where there should be fewer patrols. It involved crossing a river twice. We hoped it would be dry. I bought some tinned corned beef and some old bread, which they'd coloured pink, and we set off into the bush in the mid-afternoon.

By 5.30 p.m. we'd crossed the river for the second time and abandoned the car, which we hid in the thick bush. I took the camera and a couple of empty water bottles for samples and we walked up to the top of a ridge and down a dry tributary to the river which the old man had said would take us close to Akata village.

A team of buzzards had found something and we watched them spiralling down in ones and twos into the trees. I was sweating cobs and not just from the heat – the gout didn't like the shabby treatment it was getting from walking over rough ground and it seemed to have set up some kind of carpentry class in the joint of my big toe. The insects remembered there was a feast to attend and started rubbing their hands at the prospect. A type of fly which had a proboscis geared for getting through cow hide had just found that human skin was as buttery as the finest beef fillet. Bagado strode ahead with his hands clasped behind his back.

The light was failing rapidly as we broke out of the trees and on to a rough but graded track. This didn't sound right from the instructions the old man had given us. Maybe that *ogogoro* had burnt more out of his brain than the bar owner thought. From the dusk came a deep, farting noise of a diesel engine – a tractor or an old truck. We walked towards it. As we drew closer the gearing of the engine changed, manoeuvring with more urgency. There were voices around it. We dropped off the graded road into a ditch and worked our way forward to what we could now see was a construction machine with a hydraulic shovel at the front end and an excavating arm crooked at the back.

Another engine started up and headlights flared across the road, lighting up the bush and attracting a whirl of insects. It blew out the last of the dusk and darkness floated down, black and velvety, with just a hole slashed by the truck's lights. A transmission growled. Air brakes hissed. Universal joints shrieked. The slash of light arced across the forest and pointed down the graded road. The driver stirred the pudding and found another gear with a gnashing of teeth and shredded metal. The truck pushed forward. We sank back into the trees. The huge exhaust baffled past, the lights blinding us, the cargo invisible.

Torches floated like fireflies in the night. A single voice shouted orders. Then silence and the insect metropolis moved in.

'Are they building?' asked Bagado. 'Out here?'

'If they're excavating why truck the stuff away?'

'At night?'

Bagado gripped my arm as if he'd had some premonition at what was about to come screeching out of the forest.

A terrible scream, a horrific mortal howl ripped open the night, the noise so loud and piercing that life paused for a moment before rumbling on. We stiffened as if shivved in the back. A cold steel bowl of fear grew in my stomach and pressed on my guts. Another scream. The trees crouched. Voices panicked in the dark. The start of the third scream shredded the man's voice box and the rest came out like fingernails tearing down a granite rock face.

Another engine started and simultaneously a blue flash of light exploded through the trees. The clearing had become a dome of light, a circle watched over by the ferocity of a dozen halogen lamps. We jogged, keeping low, and crashed into the trees just in front of the arena under whose brilliant whiteness all colour was drained from the scene.

The strangeness of it, like black-and-white, incomplete stop-frame animation of life. The sweat steeled cold on my face. A group of men were huddled, just away from a body lying on the ground, their hands on their knees as if completely out of breath. Squares of halogen light stared out unflinching all around. Two other men converged in such a way that I knew they didn't want to but they were drawn. The body, my Christ, the body was smoking. Smoking thin trails of God knows what into a light so brutal it prickled the vision to graininess. Ten feet beyond the men, stacked up into the darkness more than twelve foot high, higher than the light dome, were hundreds of drums, some dull and plastic, others with the sheen of metal, some whole, some split. A gap in the edifice showed where a single drum had fallen from. The drum, capless and split, lay some feet from the body. The cap, stuck upright in some sludge, was at the foot of the drums. A slicked track from the open drum showed where the man had tried to crawl out of himself.

Details crashed into my mind, some magnified by horror. The man's skull was visible, his ribcage too. Rubber gloves and boots on his hands and feet twitched. Two men stood up from the huddle and vomited black. Four armed men appeared from the circling darkness. Their rifles were pointed at the group. The two men converging finally arrived. One of them said the single word.

'Acid.'

The armed men put their hands up to cover their noses and mouths. One of them peeled off and went to talk to the man in the digger. The digger started up, moved to the edge of the lights and planted its feet. The driver manipulated the levers and the elbow straightened at the back. He scooped out a deep trench in the earth. The soldiers herded the group of men away from the body, their rifles pointing at the ground. The digger lifted its feet and reversed in a wide arc and dropped the hydraulic shovel. The shovel tilted. The machine moved forward and consumed the top six inches of earth and the dead man before throwing its neck back and swallowing. The digger manoeuvred to the side of the trench and tipped out the shovel and scraped the earth in over it.

'Toxic waste,' said Bagado.

The soldiers stood with their backs to the drums, the other workmen in front of them. The noise from the generator and digger overwhelmed the scene. I stepped out from the trees and shot off half a roll of film. Bagado and I moved back into the trees. We made a rough calculation of the size of the dump and put the figure at around a thousand two-hundred-litre containers; a lot of them were in poor condition and all the ones we could see had Italian language printed on them.

From where the soldiers had come into the light we guessed the direction of Akata village. At the back of the dump there was a track of dead vegetation leading from the drums down a slight incline. At the end of it we found a stream running towards the village. Bagado filled the water bottles.

We circled back round to the other side of the dump to get some shots of the machines and men with the dump in the background. The digger was scraping more earth away from in front of the drums and dumping it in the forest. There was a jeep parked up near the generator with its licence plate facing our position. The workmen were on their haunches, eating. The soldiers looked down on them, still with their rifles but at ease.

I was more nervous this time and didn't step close enough to the light. When I reeled off the shots the automatic flash operated. I might as well have used a heliograph to yoo-hoo them over here. One of the soldiers pointed at me. I stumbled back and fell hard on my shoulder tying to protect the camera. Bagado dropped a water bottle and hauled me up by the collar. We bolted into the trees. All I could see was the black-and-white scene burned on my retina – two soldiers running, the other two kneeling and loading. I blundered through the forest. Bagado was gone. The first bullets snapped through the foliage, hungry but wide, well wide.

I ran like all people in films should learn to run who've just seen the lunatic making his selection from the Sabatier block. I ran with no control over my tongue. I ran faster than my bowels. I found the quickest cure for gout – three pints of adrenaline injected directly into the heart.

Just when I'd begun to think I could see something beyond the X-ray of the halogen-lit scene in my eyes, the generator cut. The light imploded behind me and with a jack-hammer jolt a jagged crack of light opened up in front of me. I ran into it, but it was too small, too tight. Then I wasn't running any more and it was dark. So dark I thought I hadn't been born.

Chapter 7

Near Akata. Nigeria. Monday 18th February.

I surfaced from a liquid heavier than mercury into chaotic night where distant voices shouted incomprehensible things – *bola numasabba hanipitti tibiwanna subsub nabbitihib*. Why did I feel sandwiched in sponge cake? There was a popping sensation. No noise. A soap bubble bursting. A smell. I was never so glad to smell that smell. Earth. Rich, damp, black earth. The voices were speaking language this time. Yoruba. Not one of my strengths. Bad-egg saliva squirted into my mouth, my tongue was as huge as a zeppelin in a hangar.

A mechanism clattered. A man checking to see if there was a round up the sleeve. I lay flat on my back. A ridge of pain was scored down my forehead, over my right eye, my cheek and jaw. I wanted to put my hand to my face but my arm was as heavy as a truck axle. The voices, movement, came closer. Shafts of thin light swept above the undergrowth, boots shuffled by my head, a word repeated close enough to hear the plosive on a lip. Voices moved off. High-lifted boots crushed leaves and such. I wanted to move now. I wanted to take off through the trees. The darkness pinned me, pressed me into the moist ground.

The voices vanished. Only the faintest shuffling remained.

A frog offered a tentative croak. He got a couple of replies. Insects rubbed themselves up to full volume and somebody brought in a whole percussion section of football rattles, whistles, maracas and castanets.

A man, no more than two metres from my head, sighed and moved off.

The ground released me with the reluctance of setting concrete. A body check revealed that I hadn't been shot. I was lying at the bottom of a two-foot-thick tree which should have my face imprint on its bark even now.

The lights remained shut down in the clearing. There was a small fire going where some silhouettes passed the time with each other. A truck double-declutched in the distance. I moved towards the noise and found the track and the ditch at the side of it. I remembered the camera. I was in no mood or state for heroism. The camera would have to stay lost.

The break in the forest where Bagado and I had first hit the road appeared and I went back in there but it was too dark. I sat down to wait for first light and propped my head up on a bolster of terrifying dreams which left me raw and jangling and asking for my mother.

By 6.30 a.m. I'd found the car with Bagado screwed up and tossed in the back. I lifted the boot and poked him. He came to, speaking Yiddish, and crawled out of the car and sat on the tail.

'I was worried,' he said, with a yawn wide enough to show me he hadn't had any breakfast. 'I was very worried.'

'You should have seen it from my angle.'

'Judging by your face I imagine it was somewhat sharp.'

'Big and blunt. I ran into a tree.'

'Best thing you could have done. This terrain isn't built for men your size.'

'I lost the camera.'

'But you're here. That's the thing.'

'What happened to you?'

'I have a very strong sense of direction,' he said, 'and good eyes. I managed to hold on to one of the sample bottles.'

We ate the stale sweet pink bread and corned beef. I washed it down with a single slug whisky to two slugs water. The gout was subdued, not used to such contemptuous treatment. We drove back to Meko and straight out across the border to debrief Gerhard's people in Kétou. They repaired my face. We had lunch, slept and drove back to Porto Novo.

We gave our report to Gerhard, who arranged for the contaminated water to be packaged in sample bottles and addressed it to a laboratory in Berlin. He paid us. We took the parcel to the DHL office in Cotonou and went back to the office. There were two messages on the answering machine.

The first was Colonel Adjeokuta from the 419 squad in Lagos. Bagado called him back and caught him leaving the office. I listened in on a separate earpiece. All he could give us on Chemiclean was what he'd found in his file. A single copy of a letter sent through to him anonymously with the receiver's address blacked out. The postmark on the letter was the City of London.

From the opening paragraph it was clear that the company that Chemiclean had mailed were specialists in the transportation of hazardous cargoes and Chemiclean were touting for business. They said they had a large tract of land in the Western State of Nigeria, close to the Benin border, where they had built a concrete bunker. They were offering this as storage space for pretreated toxic waste and inquiring of the company if they knew anybody in need of that kind of service. The colonel's team were working on getting the name of the addressee of the letter and would be back in touch later.

'Why didn't you tell him what we'd just found in the Western State of Nigeria close to the Benin border?' I asked.

'My instinct told me to wait.'

'Your instinct told you that your friend the colonel is in the army and those boys sealing off Akata village were army too?'

'It could be very complicated for us to reveal our involvement at this early stage,' said Bagado. 'I'm also very tired.'

'How do you feel about Napier Briggs now?'

'I can understand why he was a very scared man.'

'Not so scared that he couldn't be tempted into the *cocotiers* for two million bucks.'

'They knew Napier Briggs well enough,' said Bagado, 'and it didn't take him too long to figure you out.'

'I didn't know what he was involved in at that point.'

Bagado gave me a look that let me know I was a pretty sorry specimen.

The second message was for me from David Bartholomew, the guy who worked in the British High

Commission in Lagos and pushed the occasional no-hoper our way. I called him, Bagado on the earpiece this time, and we talked about nothing until I asked him why he'd left the message.

'Just wanted a chat,' he said, and Bagado cocked his head to one side which meant that David had told his first lie.

'I thought you might be calling to ask after that guy you sent us.'

'Which one was that?'

'You mean you've sent us half a dozen in the last few weeks?' I said. 'Because they haven't turned up.'

'Did that Napier Briggs chap turn up?'

'David, you might have a brain the size of a small block of flats, which is why you're working for the Foreign Office in the British High Commission and I'm doing a poor job of kicking shit in the street, but for God's sake credit me with something.'

'I don't follow.'

'They haven't given you an interrogation-techniques course in your entire time at the FO? Or did the only one you get consist of standing around in a room with a bunch of other guys all with gin and tonics in your hands.'

'*Gins* and tonic, Bruce, and absolutely not, Scotch and soda in the evenings and pink gin at lunchtimes.'

'I suppose that's Scotches and soda . . .'

'Well, it certainly wouldn't be one. You've never been to an FO "do" if you think that.'

Bagado had his head on the table, a gentle snoring issuing from his nose.

'Napier Briggs is dead,' I said. Silence from the FO.

'He was found on the railway tracks in Cotonou with his eyes squeezed out, two six-inch nails in his ears, his tongue ripped out and his mouth cut off.'

'My God.'

'You didn't know he was running with such a fast crowd?'

'He was just pathetic, like all those other ones who come to see me. I told him to go home. He said he couldn't leave without the two million he'd lost. So I sent him to you.'

'Why didn't you send him to Colonel Adjeokuta?'

Bagado sat up and shook his head. I held up a hand.

'I thought you'd rather have had the business.'

'Thanks for thinking of my welfare, David. That must be a first for the FO thinking of a British citizen in distress.'

'There's no need to be like that,' said David, getting a little camp. He was a homosexual and could resort to that kind of thing with people he knew and if he needed to hide for a bit.

'I thought you'd have heard about Napier by now. Didn't the Honorary Consul call you, or was he doing a Graham Greene?'

'Are you coming to Lagos sometime, Bruce?' he asked, surfing my question.

'I've got no need to at the moment ... now that Napier Briggs is dead. If I do, I'll call you.'

'Or maybe I'll come to Cotonou.'

'You'll be welcome.'

Bagado was pacing the room, hands in pockets, his processor whirring – his hard disk snickering.

'We've got something here,' he said. 'It looks as if it's

flying higher than we thought. When you asked him about Adjeokuta why didn't he just say that Mr Briggs didn't want an investigation by the Nigerian authorities?'

'Because . . .'

'He obviously didn't offer Mr Briggs the four-one-nine squad option in the first place. Why not?'

'He wanted him out of there. He was a potential embarrassment?'

'Could they have known about the toxic waste?' asked Bagado. 'What could the British government's involvement be in a loser like Briggs?'

'All the writing on the drums at the dump was Italian, but maybe it's British waste, or there's a British connection in there somewhere?'

'It could, of course, just be something private between your friend at the High Commission and Briggs.'

'Anyway, we're finished with Napier Briggs now. He was never even a client.'

'*You* might be.'

'Ah, yes. I forgot. You're a policeman again.'

Chapter 8

By the time I'd dropped Bagado at home and climbed the steps up to my own house it was 8 p.m., but the lights were on, which promised cold beer.

I was about to open the door when I heard Heike and another woman, whose voice I didn't recognize, talking. The other woman sounded English from the expressions she used but I could tell she'd spent some time in a foreign country. She was used to speaking to foreigners, choosing her words, even though Heike was completely bilingual. The woman was talking about a lover, or a husband maybe.

'. . . there always had to be this ritual,' she said. 'We couldn't just go to bed together and get on with it. The bedroom door had to be locked, the lights positioned, the mirrors in place. He would say things, strange things like, "You and me," which made me look around the room, you know, relieved. I wasn't allowed to say anything. I had to be wearing the right things. Normally black, occasionally red, but always the whole bit, suspenders, stockings. He spent a fortune on my underwear and there was always the other things . . .'

'What other things?'

The woman paused.

'Oh Christ,' she said, not embarrassed, just remembering it all.

'That bad?'

'One word. I'll give you one word.'

'Go on then.'

'Cufflinks.'

'Cufflinks?'

'Right.'

'*Cufflinks*,' said Heike, completely stunned, 'are you sure you mean cufflinks?'

'Oh shit,' said the other woman, slapping the table, 'of course I bloody don't. Handcuffs. I mean handcuffs.' They roared.

I opened the door. Heike was sitting on the floor in a big white calico dress propped up on a cushion facing me. The other woman I couldn't see, apart from her size-nine bare feet hanging over the edge of the sofa. My bottle of Black Label was on the low table between them and it had taken quite a pounding. Heike was still laughing and blowing smoke into the ceiling. The other woman's hand appeared on the back of the sofa. It was huge, as big as a man's hand. I went to the sofa and looked down. A blonde-haired woman in her mid-twenties, who I'd never met before, looked back up at me, giggling.

'The man with the cuff . . .' she started, ready to hoot. 'What happened to your face?'

'You guys pissed or what?' I asked. They forgot about my face and roared at me, which was all the answer I needed.

Heike stood up and skipped around the room to me. She put an arm around my neck and kissed my ear with whisky breath.

'This,' she said, pointing down at the sofa with her

cigarette, 'is Selina Aguia. Selina Aguia, this is Bruce Medway.'

'He's very pretty, isn't he?' she said, with mock seriousness. 'Apart from the lump on his head.'

'Not when you get to know him,' said Heike, and they giggled some more.

'I've got some catching up to do,' I said. They weren't listening. I went into the bedroom thinking of Selina, the associate/daughter, paying her visit as Napier said she would.

'What happened to your face?' Heike shouted after me.

'I kissed a tree and the others got jealous.'

I had a shower and changed and drank half a litre of Eku straight from the bottle. In the living room they were back under control. Selina was sitting cross-legged on the sofa with her skirt up around her hips, cradling a glass of whisky in her lap where her knickers were in full view. A strap of the loose vest she was wearing had slipped off her shoulder and a torpedo breast was seeking the light. Heike was back on the cushion, fitting another cigarette into her holder. They were both still smouldering with laughter. I eased myself down on to a cushion at the head of the low table.

'How long were you listening in for, Big Ears?' asked Heike.

'Oooo, 'bout half an hour,' I said.

'In that case I was lying,' she said to Selina.

'About him?' she said. 'Shame.'

'All right, a couple of minutes,' I said. 'I heard the cufflinks line, that's all.'

'Then you'll never know,' said Selina, smiling up at me.

'Was the ice frozen in the fridge yet?' asked Heike.

'I didn't look.'

She went into the kitchen, trailing smoke. Selina went back to lying down on the sofa, her short skirt not doing the job it was supposed to. Heike came back in and dropped ice over Selina's shoulder into her glass and topped up her own with more Scotch.

'I'll buy you another bottle,' she said, running a still cold, wet hand through my hair.

'Are we eating?' I asked.

'There's nothing in,' she said, 'and Helen's gone for the evening.'

'I'll take you out, both of you. Gerhard paid up.'

'You finished the job?'

'Yes. There was a toxic-waste dump north of the village contaminating the water supply. I've just DHLed the samples to Berlin for analysis.'

The smoke rolling in the air and the ice chinking in the glasses stilled into a brittle silence. I took a long pull of cold beer and positioned the bottle on a curling coaster on the table. Selina broke open a new packet of Camels and lit one up. Her head sagged and she hid behind the curtain of her long blonde hair. More silence. Heike brought her knees up to her chest.

'If I've interrupted something,' I said, 'I'll leave. No problem.'

Heike shook her head and said, 'Selina is Napier Briggs's daughter, she flew into Lagos last night from London and took the hop to Cotonou this morning.'

I started to say something. Selina put her hand up to stop me. Grief cracked her mouth, which was huge, and split her face like the beak of a foetal bird. Tears spilled.

83

The saliva made her want to swallow but there was something big in the way. It looked like anger to me, in rarefied form, which seemed capable of burning with very little oxygen. She didn't speak, not with the fight going on in her throat. She crushed the cigarette into the ashtray and stood with a loud crack from the signet ring on her finger rapping the table. Heike stood with her.

'You didn't see him, Heike,' she said. 'You didn't see what they did to him.'

She took three strides into the bathroom, the door banged behind her. I took a long pull of beer. Heike drained the whisky in her glass and hissed at the alcohol racking down her throat. She sucked on her cigarette holder which bubbled with the tar collecting in its stem. She looked steely.

'I don't know how she found us,' I said, thinking this might be the problem.

'I don't mind that,' said Heike, sharply. 'I'm glad. I like her. She found your card in her father's passport. She's the persistent type.'

'And what does toxic waste have to do with anything?' I asked. Heike showed me her palms.

The bathroom door opened. Selina's face was raw but repaired, her hair tied back in a ponytail, both straps of her vest up on her shoulders now. She was a good-looking woman, even amongst the wreckage. She leaned across the sofa and pulled another cigarette from the pack and lit it. She sucked on it with a wide straight mouth which had no cupid's bow to the top lip and frowned with very dark, thick, straight eyebrows.

'I'm sorry,' she said. Heike and I drivelled nothing.

'I'm going to have to cut this all off.' She sat down, sheafing her ponytail. 'I'd forgotten how hot it gets.'

'You've been here before?' I asked.

'Not to Benin. Ivory Coast and Ghana.'

'Business or travel?'

'Buying palm oil and cocoa. I trade commodities.'

'They say that can be volatile.'

'If you're greedy you can lose your shirt.'

'I've heard it can get worse than that.'

'It can. But I don't put all my chips on one number and pray. I've been in a lot of casinos, the Golden Nugget *and* the London Stock Exchange to name two. I don't like them. I spread my risk. Lose some. Win more. Percentages and hedge. That should be the name of my company . . . but then I wouldn't have any clients.'

'What *is* the name of your company?'

'Selina Aguia Limited,' she said, smiling. 'Boring but true.'

She took a slug of her drink and stretched her long tanned legs out on the sofa and smoked. She was tall, taller than Heike, maybe over six foot and big boned, strong like an athlete. Her arms were muscular, not as defined as they would have been if she'd pounded yam all her life, but they'd seen some work. The corner where her shoulder joined the pectoral had been sculpted and the stomach under the vest looked flat and board hard. She had a narrow back and big unsupported breasts which stood firm. And those hands. The wrists. She was a powerful woman – put her in a charcoal suit and some sharp shoes that were big enough and watch the directors of the board collapse.

'There was something about the toxic waste . . .' I started.

She swung her legs off the sofa, found her briefcase and took out a file which she handed to me. Written on the cardboard flap was: 'Briggs/OTE/Chemiclean'.

'That was all I could find in my father's office. The short happy life of Napier Briggs. He thought he was on a roll.'

'Was he the one who took you to all those casinos?'

'Best thing he ever did,' she nodded.

'Another one of your father's gambles?' I asked, holding up the file.

'Not all of it. The toxic waste was good business. I mean, it was bad and illegal but he made money out of it. The scam was the gamble.'

'Is there a site for the dump mentioned in this file?' I asked.

'It says something about a traditional ruler who owns land in Western Nigeria. They've built a concrete bunker . . . something like that.'

'This toxic-waste dump I've just seen . . .' I held up a hand to stop her interrupting. 'This toxic-waste dump which my partner and I have just uncovered, *and* got shot at by the army doing it, is located in Western Nigeria, just across the Benin border.'

'You were shot at by the army?' asked Heike.

'I ran into a tree *while* I was being shot at which is why I'm not dead. Bagado came through too. The army were being oversensitive and a little renegade too.'

'You mean . . .'

'I mean there was an informal and impromptu burial of a man who died after a tub of acid fell on him.'

The silence was broken by Heike slapping her leg. The mosquito was full of blood – very full.

'Do you think,' I asked Selina again, calmly, 'that Napier arranged the shipping for the dump I've just seen?'

'I don't know,' Selina started, uncertain of her ground for a moment, unable to detect the tone. 'How many shipments are going to the site in Western Nigeria mentioned in that file. Heike just told me you've been investigating a village in the same area. You come back saying it's toxic waste. We can make an assumption but we can check it too. There are copies of the bills of lading in the file, there are the container numbers and the discharge port which, in this case, was Tin Can Island, Lagos.'

'How much of it was there?' I asked.

'Three hundred and eighty tons in drums, in forty-five containers.'

'There was over a thousand two-hundred-litre drums at the dump which, if they all had water in them, would be about two hundred tons. But toxic waste is heavy – acids, metallic sludges, chemical wastes, they all have specific gravities much higher than water . . . so the quantities could be about the same. If it's relevant, the language on the drums was Italian.'

'OTE were the shippers,' said Selina. 'They're Italian based out of Leghorn.'

'Aguia?' I asked. 'Is that Italian?'

'I was married to an Italian fashion designer for six long months. I was telling Heike about it before . . .'

'The cufflinks man?' I asked.

'Handcuffs,' she said, getting shrewd.

Something uncomfortable hung in the room and, after we'd sent out enough signals to agree on that, we all laughed.

'Let's go to La Verdure,' said Heike, 'before I kill him.'

We drove the short distance to the La Verdure restaurant. I offered Selina a bed at our place for the night. Heike had already moved her in. I told her she could stay as long as she liked, as long as she could stand the friction. She said she'd test the friction for at least tonight and she wanted to talk some business with me in the morning. She said she was glad of the company. So was Heike. She didn't have to say it. But she did.

We sat out in the garden under an awning where there was some crappy fishing montage consisting of a stuffed varnished fish, some rotting net and some spherical blue-glass floats. We ate steak and chips with salad and drank a lot of cold red. Selina had the sharpened senses of the recently bereaved. She savoured everything – the food, the wine, new people, the dippy waiter, the size of the three white guys in the bar, the beauty of the six hookers waiting for someone to buy them a drink, even the heat, which was monstrous because the fans were being ornamental rather than working. Death brings the living to life, has a way of showing you that at your worst moment it's still worth going on.

We went back home and took it in turns in the shower. Heike and I drank whisky. I was allowed to after I told her what Bagado had said about the Scots and gout. I said a couple of funny things about it but she didn't laugh. Maybe they weren't funny but it was that time of night after a good time when you're prepared to cough at anything. I had that uneasy feeling that she could only bear me in company, could only bear me as long as she didn't have to talk to me directly.

I was last in the shower and found Heike lying naked under a damp-patched sheet, staring at the ceiling, when I came into our room with a towel around my waist. Only a small lamp was on at the bedside, just enough to read by. A single rectangle of light shone in the top left corner of the window frame – a room lit in a higher floor of another house. A man stood with his hands on the windowsill looking down into his black garden. An aura of streetlighting hung over the roofs.

Heike propped herself up on an elbow and looked me up and down. The antagonism was still there, along with plenty of drink.

'What's going on, Heike?'

'Ach, nothing.'

'You haven't liked me much since Bagado called the other morning.'

She didn't say anything but fell back on to her pillow and looked at the ceiling again through half-closed eyes.

'Can't stand being in the same room as me?' I asked.

She shrugged, which meant she knew what was bothering her and I did too, but how to get it out. She stuck the heels of her palms into her eyes.

'I was glad you went away for a couple of days,' she said. 'Then I wasn't glad. Then I was again. It's been like that. Moody. It was good having Selina around. She pulled me out of myself.'

'How do you feel about me now?' I asked. 'Am I on the couch?'

89

'Not with her next door,' she said, taking her hands away from her face. She propped herself up on an elbow and smiled with some resignation in there. She looked me up and down with other things starting to work inside her head. It excited me. She saw it and sighed from down around the back of her knees at what she recognized in herself.

She threw back the sheet, sat on the edge of the bed, her legs apart, the dark triangle visible, and pulled the towel off my waist. She gripped my buttocks and pulled me to her and kissed my belly, her breasts nudging at the painful hardness of my erection, her nipples hard and cool around my loins. I stroked her head and bent down to kiss her. She turned her back on me, crawled to the wall and leaned a forearm up against it. She stretched the other hand behind her, took hold of me and guided me into her. I kissed her madly over her shoulder, our lips never quite touching, the column of tendon in her neck frequently between my teeth. I smoothed a hand down her belly to her thighs, to our moist, tense connection. We moved rhythmically, her face up against the cool wall, the sweat pouring down my chest, rivulets running down her arched spine. My hands were full of her breasts. I clamped my mouth on to the roll of muscle at her shoulder and desperately tried to thrust harder, and further in, so that I could become a part of her.

At the last moment, Heike already trembling in my hands like a frightened bird, a feeling shivered over me. We were being watched. It was so strong that I turned on shuddering thighs to see the door open, the light from the street painting the edges of things in the living room and something, someone. Then an ecstatic light burned fast and wide in my head with the brightness of magnesium and I collapsed against the wall which was slick with sweat gone cold and clammy.

We parted and slid down to the pillows, Heike feverish now with her hands up to her mouth. I pulled the sheet over her. Where our bodies touched were like spot welds. I could hear Heike's clotted breath from her overwrought throat. She turned into the wall. I stroked her back and she started as if my fingers were live. Her shoulders shook with each breath and then smoothed out. She slept.

I got up and glanced around the living room. I checked the front door. Selina's bedroom door was shut. I padded back to bed, lay down and watched the ceiling recede. Emptiness grew in my stomach as the moment of union seeped out of my mind. In the absence of something new we'd always fallen back on the old way of communicating.

The line had been crossed twice. Forwards but then, as usual, backwards. Now I was out in the cold again, which even the hot African night, jammed into the room, couldn't warm.

Chapter 9

I woke up as stiff and sore as a wind-dried duck. Heike's space was empty. I was lying diagonally across the bed. She was in a T-shirt and knickers looking out of the window, her hair wet, staring at the overcast day.

'It's six thirty,' she said. 'I'm late.'

'Did it rain?'

'No.'

'I didn't ask you last night . . . what was all that about with Gerhard?'

'All *what* about with Gerhard?' she said, some needle in her voice.

'There was something going on with Gerhard . . . In the meeting.'

'Why did you have to be so tough with him . . . about money?' she said.

Well, even I knew that wasn't the reason but we were started now.

'Why *I* had to be so tough?'

'We're an aid agency. Aid not ad. We don't have the money for it.'

'I'd like to be a charity too but I don't want to see Bagado's kids starve . . .'

'I still have to pay the rent whatever . . .'

92

'Stick it in, Heike.'

'Look, Bruce, I have to work with Gerhard. He assesses me and reports back to Berlin. He puts pressure on me.'

'So you wanted to say to him, "This is my man." You didn't have him in mind as a role model?'

'Gerhard. A role model for you? You've got to be committed, Bruce Medway. It's dangerous having you and your ideas out there.'

She stepped into a skirt and left the room. I pulled on a pair of jeans, went into the kitchen and squeezed the juice out of some oranges from the fridge. Why did my eye always land on the whisky bottle? The last thing I wanted was a drink, wasn't it? Heike poured herself a glass of juice. I wondered how these things happened to people. How did people bring themselves to the marks? What do people say these days, you know, to take things forward? Let's get married? Get off the grass. Nobody gets married these days. Let's have kids? Yikes. One minute I'm an arm's-length bachelor, the next I want little versions of ourselves running around. Who's going to believe that? Not me. There's got to be a half-way house, for Christ's sake. Then you find yourself saying words like 'sharing' and before you know it . . .

'What's going on in there?' asked Heike.

'Nothing.'

'The usual,' she said.

'You're a bit sharp this morning, aren't you?'

'I've a small hangover and I'm a little annoyed.'

'About the Gerhard thing?'

'No, about the you thing.'

'More juice?'

'Why should I introduce you to the role model? Why

not just run off with him? You know, cut out the duffer, go straight to the real thing.'

'Maybe you wanted me to learn something from Gerhard.'

'He's a divorced workaholic.'

'And talking about workaholics. Do you think I'm a deadbeat?' She snorted a laugh out at that.

'You don't want to ask that question looking like you do this morning.'

'Do you mind paying the rent?'

'I get a housing allowance. You're broke.'

'It's not drawing us together though, is it?'

She laughed at that, too.

'You're like a dog wandering around a park barking up trees.'

'I'm working my way round.'

'Good luck,' she said. 'I've got to go to work.'

Out of the kitchen window, I saw the same man I'd seen last night but on the balcony this time, staring down into the same garden, looking as if he'd got nowhere in a whole night-time.

Bagado arrived while I had my head over the sink contemplating a puke.

'I was just on my way down to my new office,' said Bagado.

'You're sounding cheerful. I suppose you've got your own desk and phone, your own office plant, don't have to share with whitey any more.'

'There's something about a fresh start I've always liked. Even this one, which will stay fresh for as long as a calabash of fish in the sun.'

I took another slug of the orange juice, which burned down my oesophagus. I tried to get some baguette down after it to stop it stripping off my stomach lining but it got stuck in my neck and I had to cough it back up.

'I've got to go,' said Bagado, slapping my back.

'Hang on. There's somebody for you to meet.'

I knocked on Selina's door. No answer. I pushed the door open. The room was empty. I told Bagado about Selina Aguia and we opened up the OTE/Chemiclean file which had been left on the table. The telexes and letters had been filed in chronological order. This whole big bad problem started with the simplest inquiry you could imagine:

> 380 mts Chemicals
> Ex Leghorn
> IMMY

'No destination but immediate shipment,' said Bagado. 'Is that usual?'

'Very unusual for this kind of business. They might fix crude oil from the Persian Gulf with no destination or just Med or Western Europe, but chemicals are products you don't ship without a buyer. They're too specific, especially only three hundred and eighty tons of the stuff. It's not as if it's three thousand tons of benzene or toluene. It also says "chemicals", which would normally mean a number of parcels. Even more specific.'

'So he should have known it was wrong from the start.'

Selina had photocopied notes from Napier's day book. There was an Italian phone number, then OTE and scribbled alongside 'ready-treated industrial waste' and the name Fabrizzio Franconelli. Underneath the name

Napier had written, '45 × 20 ft containers. Chemical products in drums'. There was a line and the workings of some cargoes for a North Sea contract for BP Chemicals. On the next sheet was a massive doodle of what could have been the left flank of an armadillo and underneath a circle with OTE and Chemiclean in it. Then there was a fax from Chemiclean.

CHEMICLEAN INTERNATIONAL LIMITED

Postal address:
PO Box 735 Lagos.

Office Address:
28, Campbell Street
Lagos Island
Lagos. Nigeria.

Napier Briggs
Napier Briggs Associates
204, Old Street
London ECI

CIL LAGOS W. AFRICA.
Dealer in Chemical
Materials
Disposition of Chemical
Waste
Oil Materials. Company
representation.
Import/Export services.
Phone (234) 01–441 441
Fax (234) 01–441 442

30th August
FAX MESSAGE

Dear Mr Briggs,
   We have been informed by the International Chamber of Commerce that your company specializes in the transportation of hazardous chemicals.
   I am writing to introduce our company to you with

the hope that you might be of our need or help in scouting out some industries in Europe in need of evacuating waste products emanating from their company's productive activities.

My name is Daniel Emanalo (Operations Manager). My father is a tradition ruler in the Western State of Nigeria. We own a vast tract of land close to the border with the Republic of Benin. On this land we have built a reinforced concrete bunker 60 ft below the surface for the storage of industrial waste.

Please note that we are only able to accept pre-treated industrial waste. We are not having the facilities or know-how to treat waste products. We cannot accept any radioactive material as this is a serious offence under our nation's penal code and punishable by death.

Our handling, transportation and storage charge is fixed at $30,000 per ton of chemical products as a one-off payment for life.

If you would in anyway assist in scouting out for some industries in Europe who need our services we would pay a commission on all trade of 5 per cent. Please don't hesitate to contact us immediately to enable us to furnish you with our operative modalities.

Looking forward to hearing from you and doing business with you.

Yours sincerely,

Daniel Emanalo (Operations Manager)

P.S. All communications will be in strictest confidence.

After this fax Selina had filed a permit from the Office of the Pharmacist's Board of Nigeria allowing Chemiclean to import pretreated industrial waste and a notice from the Federal Ministry of Health, Environmental Protection Agency confirming that the Chemiclean facilities had been inspected and pronounced A1.

All the negotiations had been typed up on to a single sheet of paper. Napier had fixed a vessel called the *Paphos Star*, some Cypriot rust bucket, for $2500 per container ex Leghorn/Tin Can Island Lagos on a laycan of 10/15 October subject to contract. Napier's opening offer to OTE had been for $30,500 per ton and they'd come back with $7000 per ton which looked like an unbridgeable gap and would have been between serious business people. As it turned out, Chemiclean would have agreed to store the waste at $12,000 per ton but not in the concrete bunker – OTE wanted to be in that concrete bunker and eventually agreed a price of $23,000 per ton.

'A lot of money,' I said.

'A lot of money,' agreed Bagado. 'Too much money. I looked over some files I kept at home on a toxic-waste-dumping scandal in Benin four years ago. The cost of disposing a two-hundred-and-five-litre drum of intractable hazardous waste in Europe is somewhere between four and seven thousand dollars, depending on what it is. OTE are supposed to be shipping pretreated waste so it should cost even less. Even if the waste has a specific gravity of water that's still more than four thousand dollars per drum. It's not what you'd call commercial business.'

'Money laundering?'

'Italian company. Mafia money?'

'Drug money.'

'Maybe the full circle. The drugs come into Nigeria from Columbia and the Far East. They courier them to Europe. The money goes through OTE, through Napier Briggs, back to Nigeria, by which time it's clean.'

'How much are we talking about?'

Bagado flipped over to the next sheet. An early December bank statement showed an underlined credit for $8,740,000 and another for $112,500 – the product and the freight. The mid-December section of the statement showed $8,303,000 going out, followed by another $110,250 – the product money less the 5 per cent commission and the freight less a 2 per cent commission. Napier Briggs had cleared nearly $440,000 with a few phone calls.

Then came the sting.

M. M. Aounou
Victor Ballot No 28
Porto Novo
Rep. Bénin
Postal Address
BP, 741
Porto Novo.
Rep. Bénin.

29th November

Dear Mr Briggs,

I am senior accountant with the Ministry of Finance in the Benin Republic. I have been given your name by Daniel Emanalo, the Operations Manager at Chemiclean. He has told me that you have recently

99

concluded a very successful business transaction with OTE in Leghorn. He has asked me to contact you with my proposal as a reward, I think you call it a 'success fee', for bringing Chemiclean and OTE together.

In my position at the Ministry of Finance I have many contacts in government and in the banking system. Some friends of mine at the Banque Beninoise de Dévélopment (BBD) discovered a government account containing $38,742,480. Through my files here in the Ministry of Finance I have traced this money to the overinvoicing of a contract awarded to a Danish company for clearing untreated toxic waste which had been illegally dumped in Benin during the previous administration. As you know from your dealings in West Africa, the powers of the old regime were dramatically reduced by the multipartite national conference in March 1990 and a new cabinet resulted with a new Prime Minister. This new administration know nothing about this account.

Through my offices at the Ministry I have been able to effect a payment authority but I require a foreign company account to make the transfer, it being in dollars and originally designed for a foreign firm. I hope you can see how your cooperation in this business might be of mutual benefit.

We have decided to offer you 40 per cent of the fund if you will allow us to make use of your bank account to make the transfer. Out of your 40 per cent you will have to pay 5 per cent to Daniel Emanalo for making the introduction but this would still leave you with a net gain in excess of $13,000,000.

All we would require from you is the following:

1) Three (3) blank copies of your company's letterhead, signed.
2) Three (3) blank copies of your company's invoices.
3) Name and address of your bank, account number and telephone/fax and/or telex numbers.

The invoices will be used to show goods and services which your company supplied and the letterheads will act as covering letters to back up the invoices. We will fill them in with all the necessary information that would have pertained to the original contract and can then push them through the BBD system and effect the transfer.

Please note that your letterhead and invoices should not only be signed but stamped as well as is the custom in West Africa. All communications should be sent by DHL as the local postal system is too unreliable.

We will update you with the progress of the transfer. On the day that the monies arrive in your account two officials will make contact with you in London – Mr B. Segun and Mr A. Idris – they will effect disbursement of the funds.

Please keep this business strictly private and confidential.

Awaiting your immediate response.

Yours sincerely,

M. Aounou.

A copy of a letter from Napier to M. Aounou showed that he sent the letterheads and invoices out on 6th

December. Selina had typed up his December/January diary making the note that the secretary, Karen, had left the office on 21st December and gone on holiday until 5th January. Napier had been all over the place – Genoa for the launch of a gas ship called the *Amedeo Avogadro*, Madrid for a meeting with a broker called Navichem, Hamburg for a meeting with a shipowner called Hamburger-Lloyd, Copenhagen for a Christmas party, Bergen to see an owner's broker called Steensland, Paris to discuss a Far East time charter with some brokers called Gazocean and Manchester to see a Shell refinery. He didn't go back into his office until after the Christmas break and he didn't see a bank statement until Karen tried to effect a freight payment to an owner on 10th January and was informed by the bank that there were insufficient funds.

The printout of the January statement which Karen had asked for immediately and had gone to the bank to pick up showed the accumulation of money in Napier's account while he was travelling. He hit a maximum of $1,932,724 before three debits on 5th January of $728,965, $514,496 and $613,768 which took $1,857,229 out of his account.

He applied for a Nigerian visa on 10th January afternoon but didn't receive it until 29th January. It took him six days to get a flight to Lagos, where he arrived early in the morning on Monday 5th February. He spent the first night in a hotel called the Ritalori but there was no record of subsequent nights. He moved to Cotonou on the 14th February and set himself up in the Hotel du Lac where he spent two nights, getting himself killed on his third night on Friday 16th February. The last three sheets in the file were copies of the signed letterheads received by Napier's bank instructing them to transfer three different amounts to three different banks in three cities in the UK.

'How did they know how much money he would have and when it would be in the account?' I asked.

'Somebody in the bank, somebody in Briggs's office or outside information.'

'They timed it well, didn't they? Over the Christmas break.'

'What did he do and who did he see for those ten days he spent in Lagos?'

'That's what I want you to find out,' said Selina, who'd come in silently and was standing by the door with all her hair cut off into a spiky bleached crew cut. She had a plastic bag in her hand.

'That's a bit radical, isn't it?' I said. 'The hair.'

'You don't like it?'

'It looks cool.'

'I'll take that both ways.'

I introduced Bagado. It was clear we'd looked through the file.

'What do *you* think, Mr Bagado?'

'Very nice,' he said, 'but I didn't see the "before".'

'It's in the bag. I thought I'd bury it with Napier,' she said, lightly. 'My father always loved my hair.'

Bagado was experienced in grief. He knew how to handle these blank spaces where weighty things said breezily send emotions into free fall and paralyse speech. He didn't suddenly start talking about the heat, which was folding itself into the room and expanding, or comment on the weather, which everybody knew was always hot. He radiated sympathy without tilting his head or drawbridging his eyebrows into a 'sincere' expression. He felt for the woman and she could sense it.

'Maybe this isn't a good time to be impulsive,' he said. 'You should think about your father now while everything is still fresh. You don't have to do anything. Just reflect. If you don't you'll miss out and you may regret that later.'

Nobody had ever spoken to Selina like that before in her life. She was astonished, as if Bagado had proposed some primitive rite that people like her just didn't do.

'It was hot,' she said. 'I didn't think.'

'What's there to think about?'

'My father and who killed him.'

'That might take some time to uncover. You've done all that's necessary by organizing the file for us. Now take care of yourself.'

'But you've found the toxic waste.'

'We've found *some* toxic waste.'

'The same quantity my father shipped, Bruce said . . .'

'We need more to go on than that. The toxic waste is out of our jurisdiction. I have to make contact with the Nigerians to see if they will cooperate. We have to tread carefully doing that. The army were present at the dump. That could mean government involvement or someone with a great deal of power. We don't know who we're up against and we are already in a political situation here in Benin starting with my appointment.'

'I have *some* idea of who we're up against,' she said.

'Somebody here?'

'The Franconellis,' she said, shaking her head.

'You've spoken to them?'

'I found out about them through my ex-husband's contacts in Milan. They're from a large Neapolitan mafia family. They have representation in government and powerful contacts in industry. They're in construction and shipping, and further down the line olive oil, wine, the rag trade, almost everything you can think of. They also run drugs – cocaine from Columbia and heroin from the Far East. The eldest son, Fabrizzio, is fifty-eight years old. He runs a shipping company out of Leghorn. Roberto is the youngest. He's just hit fifty. He runs a construction company and an import/export business out of Lagos. Between them and their sons and one of the daughters they run a drug-distribution network in Europe and CIS countries. There are two other brothers in the States with three sons between them. Two of those sons are in Russia. The father is eighty-two years old and never leaves Naples.'

'Well,' said Bagado, 'now you see that this is not such a simple investigation.'

'If you want to do something,' I said, 'perhaps we could have a quiet look around in Nigeria and find out who we're up against.'

'I *do* want to do something,' said Selina, 'and I have money to do something.'

'Bagado?' I asked. 'Where are you in this?'

'I didn't say? I've been put in charge of the Napier Briggs murder investigation, reporting directly to Bondougou.'

'What do you think that means?'

'I've been sent barefoot down a causeway of broken glass.'

'Bondougou wants you in his lap with his hand up your back.'

'As usual. But I don't intend to allow that to happen.'

'You reckon he has an interest beyond law enforcement?'

'You know as well as I do that the only law Bondougou enforces is his own.'

'You might be interested to know,' said Selina, 'that yesterday they said I could take my father's body. They're just doing the paperwork this morning and I can fly him back this afternoon.'

'That's quick,' said Bagado, 'and not strictly correct in a murder investigation. The defence can make a case for doing their own autopsy. But then, perhaps, they're not anticipating a trial.'

Selina paced the room like a caged panther needing bigger horizons. Bagado looked at his watch and said he had to be going now that he was a public servant. He didn't interrupt Selina who wasn't noticing anything outside the inside of her own head. More heat leaked into the room. Sweat started in my scalp, the orange juice staged a revolt and made me feel nauseous. I threw up in the bathroom.

'Where's Heike?' asked Selina, when I came out.

'Gone to work.'

'I didn't think you were supposed to drink during the week,' she said, looking at me carefully so that I knew that she knew – women talk to each other all the time, even strangers.

'I'm not, but I'm a shocking little rule-breaker when I want to be,' I said, swallowing something nasty. Selina looked as if she was about to step in with something, but she didn't feel sure of her ground yet and swerved away from it.

'How much do you want?' she asked instead.

'To find out what Napier was up to in Lagos? Five hundred thousand CFA to get started.'

'What's your fee?'

'Ten thousand a day.'

'That's more than a hundred quid,' she snapped. 'Are you worth it . . . without your detective friend?'

'I'm double with him. He'll help us out and draw official pay. You're getting two for one.'

'I thought you'd be cheaper. Heike . . .'

Women talk about even more than you'd imagine.

'Heike draws a salary. People who draw salaries don't understand. You run your own business. You know that much.'

'I thought you did a three-day job for two hundred and fifty thousand all in.'

'Charity work. I nearly got killed doing it too. Now I know we've got the mafia thrown in there, some heavy hitters in Nigeria and Bondougou on the edges, I'm going to make sure I get paid this time.'

'Maybe I'll wait and see what the official police investigation comes up with.'

'I'll be in my office.'

'Who pays the bills around here?'

Women talk about literally everything.

'None of your business, Selina.'

'Probably the one with the salary.'

'Still none of your business.'

They must have gone through the household accounts once they'd sorted me out and slammed down a half bottle of Scotch. It wasn't that surprising. Heike was low on sympathetic ears to gab to. The German girls in her agency were a little vegan for her taste. Well, she'd found a meat eater in Selina and the tough bitch was using everything she'd learned. I couldn't think why she needed that MBA her father had put her through, she had the head and muscle of a barrow boy. Maybe those boys from the Lagos school of business were going to learn a few things. All I had left on me was the stonewall.

'You know where the office is,' I said, and headed for the door.

'It's all right. I've found the right man for the job,' she said to the back of my head.

'But not the right money.'

'I opened an account in the Bank of Africa yesterday morning. They said I'll have to wait a week for a cheque book. You'll have to wait a few days before my transfer arrives from Paris. I'll give you the half million cash as soon as it's there. Is that going to delay you?'

'That's fine.'

'Napier was a weak man, Bruce. It was my mother who wore the pants. She had more men after she married my father than before. He didn't say a word or lift a finger. I think he was too scared of losing her. She took it as humiliation and she returned it in full by running off . . .'

'. . . with Blair.'

'The old man told you that?'

'It took some time to prise it out of him.'

'I don't like weak men,' she said, pinching her bottom lip. 'I tolerated it in my father because I loved him but I won't have it from others.'

For a moment I became aware of the plus and minus ions in the room. Selina Aguia ran a hand through her new crop and painted a layer of gloss on to her top lip with the tip of her tongue.

Chapter 10

You'd have thought there was a refugee situation at the Benin/Nigerian border that morning. The number of people and the quantity of gear they were carrying made me ask if there'd been some trouble, but no, it was just the regulars passing through and getting indignant with the customs officers who snitched something here and brutally shoved someone over there. I was through by 9.30 a.m. and started working through the police posts on the coastal road to Lagos.

Before Selina Briggs had left the house to go and pick up Napier's body and fly with it back to London, I'd agreed to do various things for the three days she would be away burying her father. I was now heading for Tin Can Island to find out what had happened to the containers Napier had shipped on the *Phaphos Star*. I wanted to get a handle on who was behind the toxic waste before I went to the Hotel Ritalori to find out what Napier had been doing in Lagos. I'd already called the foreign office man, David Bartholomew, and arranged to meet him for a drink in the evening. David and I had been drawn together by boredom and booze and he'd taken a stack of cards to hand out to the numerous unfortunates who broke down and wept in his office. Only the biggest losers made it to us because David Bartholomew's policy was to hand out the advice that now the lesson had been learned, now that the welts across the wallet were still fresh and painful, it was time to go home and forget about making it big or getting it back in Nigeria.

I joined the torrential traffic on the Apapa–Orowonsoki Expressway and let it channel me into Tin Can Island which lived up to its reputation, if for 'tin can' you read 'container'. The island was a town, a huge bewildering grid of twenty-foot and forty-foot boxes stacked on top of each other. Gantry cranes rumbled to and fro on rusted rails while giant mobiles, hugely weighted at the rear with extendable arms out front and wheels higher than my Peugeot Estate, stalked the lanes between the high rises and removed blocks and placed them else-where for someone else to move on later. Tin Can Island was a good place to lose something whilst knowing exactly where it was.

I found the offices of the agents Ogwashi & Ikare and parked up under the midday sun. The staircase up to their first-floor hole smelled of school right down to the stink of overboiled cabbage. I knocked on the frosted-glass door and entered a long, narrow office where four men sat at wooden tables piled with stacks of paper. What was going on inside was a microcosm of what was happening outside. One wall of the office was floor to ceiling with cardboard boxes of soap powder and bleach filled with paper. At the far end was a glass partition, an isolation tent for a larger man who sat at a desk of polished mahogany with a computer monitor on one corner and a telephone on another. Behind the man's head was an optimistic photograph of the current military leader which clashed with the sullen and brutal features on the live face below. He passed a finger across his forehead, wiping the sweat of accumulated bribes off his brow.

I told the nearest clerk my business and handed him the container numbers I wanted him to check. I'd selected just two from Napier Briggs's shipment and mixed them in with some of my own inventions. He nodded and looked at the numbers, hoping to divine the answer without having to hit the reference system. His concentration broke and he handed the paper on. All four men gave the numbers their very best but nobody could crack it. I sat down.

Number four clerk pushed himself up from his desk and headed for the boss sitting in his idling capsule. The boss slipped his phone off the hook and started talking. I hadn't heard it ring. The clerk stopped, switched his brain into 'loaf' mode and barely ticked over.

The clerk was called in and the paper torn from his pathetic fingers by the instant dynamism of the boss who dismissed him. He switched on the computer and tapped in the numbers. He picked up the phone again and dialled a number. He spoke for three minutes. The clerks looked up at the ceiling where three fans turned slowly enough not to ruffle any papers down below. A faint cry from the glass case invited me into the air-conditioned, carpeted, slightly more fragrant bubble.

'What do you want to know?' asked the boss.

'If any of those containers are here, where are they? If they're not, who took them away and where?'

'Same shipment?'

'No.'

He tapped in the numbers and picked his nose while he waited for each container to be 'searched'. He wrote 'NR' against my inventions. He reached behind him and, from a shelf, took a Motorola radio phone which he played with. Then he put that down and picked his nose some more. The first of Napier Briggs's containers arrested his finger mid-pick. He wrote a date and a truck's registration next to it which began with the letters LA for Lagos. He carried on until the next one and did the same. The registration began with OG which was Ogun state whose capital was Abeokuta about 100 kilometres north of Lagos.

'We were agents for only two of these.'

'The London office must have given me the wrong numbers . . .'

'Which London office?'

'. . . or the wrong agents, perhaps.'

He folded the sheet of paper and tapped the edge of his desk with the crease. I took a 5000-CFA note out of my pocket, smoothed it out and pushed it to the middle of the table. He must have been to the minimalist school of bargaining because he managed to convey his disappointment, his utter contempt, for this sum without moving a pore from the neck upwards or breaking the metronome tap of the paper on his desk. I laid another 5000 on top. Still not enough for him, but as far as I was concerned, with that tap, tap, tap chipping away at my head, I'd reached my ceiling.

'That's it, my friend,' I said. 'I live here.'

'Who do you represent?' he asked, looking up from the 10,000 CFA.

'Myself.'

'The clerk didn't give me your name.'

'I didn't give him one.'

'Do you have a card?'

'No.'

'Why do you want this information?'

'Because I've been asked to find it,' I said. 'And what do you care? You've got ten thousand for nothing.'

'It's not just a question of money,' he said, picking up the two notes and stuffing them in his pocket.

'What's it a question of?'

He found himself on the brink of an admission he didn't want to make. I held out my hand and he slid the paper between two fingers. We stood and shook hands. He held on.

'You didn't say your name.'

'Galen Persimmon.'

'What was that?' he asked, his eyes opening to full size.

'People call me G. P. Thanks and goodbye.'

I strode through the office, each clerk's head coming up with the rush as I passed. By the time I had the door open the boss man was standing at the window in his bubble looking out over the container city with the Motorola clamped to his ear. I dropped down the stairs two at a time and felt that gout twinging again which made me lope towards the car like a shinsplit giraffe.

I started the car; the steering wheel had been dipped in molten tar and the seat clung to me like the hottest whore in La Verdure. The four clerks' faces appeared at the window, the boss at the end with his gut flattened against the glass. I dumped the clutch and squealed six foot of rubber on to the hot tarmac.

I drove without thinking for a few minutes and got myself lost in the container maze, which had been my intention. The smell of diesel in the heat and the mixture of sea and lagoon air polluted by the industry and effluent of the city's ten million people was making me feel queasy. There was the sound of distant thunder but the sky was clear. Then a gantry crane rumbled and screeched across one of the container canyons.

I found myself in a large square in which a series of massive generators supplied electricity to banks of refrigerated containers. The noise was held down in the box city and crashed around the ribbed metal cliffs of blue, white and orange, reverberating, penetrating, shuddering my insides. Back in the Manhattan gorges the massive mobiles haunted the lanes, and smaller but still giant forklifts pirouetted expertly through carefully choreographed routines.

I turned into a broader lane with forty-foot containers on either side, some of them looking as if they were rusted there for life, not so easy to ship a forty-footer out of there as it was to put them in. A huge mobile appeared at the end of the lane with its arms raised and a forty-foot container above its head. There was a crossroads about fifty yards in front of it and I accelerated to turn into it and let the mobile past. Its exhaust blatted black smoke and the tyres which had momentarily quivered in the sickening heat rolled solidly forward to block the crossroads. The driver in his cab was on his feet talking into a Motorola. I reversed with a panicked howl from the engine when the reverse gear popped out of its socket. I held the shift in place and smelt the blue smoke whining out of the wheel arches.

There was three hundred yards to cover to the next turning. My head flicked back to see the mobile in front of me moving forward again, rollicking over the undulations in the tarmac, its glassless cab door swinging open and banging shut. I held the gear shift in place with my foot, gripped the back of the passenger seat and looked behind in time to see another mobile swing into the lane with a forty-footer held a few inches off the ground, bulldozing its way forward. I slammed on the brakes, the engine stalled and the car slewed across the lane. I tried to restart. The engine turned over without catching. I went to open the door but the sky darkened as the rusted cliff of the container closed in.

It hit the car broadside and shunted it sideways with such violence that I heard the whiplash crack of my neck vertebrae. My body was jolted over the handbrake. The colours, names and numbers of parked containers flashed in front of the frame of the windscreen like dull footage through an old Moviola. There was an explosion of compressed air and the passenger side dropped as the tyres were torn off their rims. The light dimmed on the passenger side. There was another crash and the Peugeot sandwich was complete. The clear glass of the windscreen crystallized, held for a second, and with a buckling of the frame and a popping of the rubber seal, diamonds of glass fell into my lap from all sides. The mobiles paused and strained as if constipated and then farted loudly and backed away.

116

I scrambled through the rhomboid frame of the windscreen out on to the bonnet. It flickered through my panic that there was no feeling in my left hand and a hot iron bar was being held to the side of my neck.

I slid off the bonnet. My knees dropped from underneath me. I fell on my side, a burnt oil smell from the tarmac in my nostrils. The sun was blocked again. The mobiles had raised the forty-footers above their cabs. I rolled over to the parked containers and found a crack in the wall and slipped in, one arm hanging limp and dead. The first mobile dropped its container on to the roof of the car. The shock absorbers did not absorb the shock. The chassis thumped on to the ground, a wheel was sheered from an axle, the front grille and headlights popped out. Steam hissed from the radiator like pained breath between teeth.

The mobile lifted off its container and backed away. The second mobile dropped its load. Between them they dropped their containers six times and flattened the car. The metal crumpled, folded, and compacted. The mobiles roared approval at each other like conquering leviathans. Gasoline and metallic steam patched the ground. When the car was no more than a six-inch block the mobiles took their containers and backed off down the lane.

The sunshine continued, the generators pounded in the distance, the heat boxed in, my mouth remained slack and open and my elbow felt as if it had a four-inch screw being drilled into it down the ulna.

I've always admired ambiguity as a subtle tool that can both interest and confuse, however I have a huge respect for the clear, bold statement, especially accompanied by violence.

I ran. My gouty foot bleated. My dead arm swung like an empty sleeve.

Chapter 11

The Port Authority were sceptical. What did you expect? I had to drop my trousers, pull up my shirt tails and deposit quarter of a windscreen in gem form on the brown lino floor before I could even get a nod of possibility from them.

The Port Authority police took me for a drive down the forty-foot container lanes. We found the spot, and that was all it was, a dark patch on the tarmac from the gasoline and a brown tinge from the evaporated water, but no crushed Peugeot Estate. The police exchanged puzzlement. Whatever book they were going by had no procedure for crushed cars making contact with another world. They asked me what I wanted from them. I lost my head and demanded a full investigation, as if I was fresh off the plane from London and had never been to Africa before. Their entire inner workings seized. The senior officer gave me a sinister look and started talking about the seriousness of cars coming into the port but not going out. I backed off.

'Hey, guys,' I said, digging out some light expressions I never used, 'it's only a car. What say you write out a crash report and give me a half chance of getting some insurance.'

They all laughed at that. They knew I had no chance. I put my hands in my pockets and came out with two handfuls of glass. I let them fall from my lifeless fingers and asked for a lift back to the port gates.

There's nowhere left for the traffic to go in Lagos. It has now filled every road and side street in the capital so that nothing moves except between two and four in the morning. A meeting downtown could take the whole day. If the appointment was for any earlier than four in the afternoon and you set out any later than six in the morning the meeting will take you two days and cost a night in a downtown hotel. Throw in the accumulation of carbon monoxide which goes nowhere in the high humidity. Add the dammed frustration of rivers of volatile drivers who could go up like sparked avgas. Tack on the neediness of impotent traffic cops, wedge in a dash of armed robbery, and lying under the bed in a darkened room seems a much better option than trying to earn a living. Unfortunately, not many people in Lagos thought like that and even in the tense days after the military annulled the free and fair elections for civilian rule the traffic barely faltered. Even when the oil workers went on strike and there was no petrol people still found time to get together and make a traffic jam.

This was why I took a taxi to 'Mile Two', which was well outside Lagos but had a ferry station which went down Porto Novo Creek to the Apapa Docks and then across Lagos Harbour to Marina which was on Lagos Island and downtown.

I called David Bartholomew at the British High Commission from a restaurant on Marina and arranged to meet him in the evening in the five-star luxury of the

Eko Meridien Hotel on Kyrano Waters. This hotel was on the other side of Victoria Island from the British HC. Lagos and Victoria Islands are joined by a bridge across Five Cowrie Creek which I crossed on foot at dusk. I found a taxi outside the British HC which took me to a guesthouse called Y-Kays on Adeola Hopewell Street which was close to the Eko Meridien geographically but a long way off in style.

I met David Bartholomew at 7.30 p.m. by the hotel pool. I'd showered but it hadn't made any difference. I hadn't changed my clothes. They were in a bag in a very small cavity in a crushed Peugeot. David had detected the element of stress in my voice over the phone and had decided I needed pampering. A whisky with a real live Löwenbrau chaser was parked on the table in front of my empty chair.

'I love you, David,' I said.

'There's no need to go that far,' he said, with a camp flick of the wrist which he occasionally pulled out of the bag but which, for most of his professional life, he kept tied down. 'There doesn't have to be any love, you know.'

David was tall, just an inch shorter than me. He had thick, dramatically moussed jet-black hair, a full and very red mouth, dark-brown lustrous eyes with long cow lashes and a kind of prewar elegance that I thought had been blown away by the sixties. He was forty-four years old and people were still saying, 'Funny how he never married.'

His slacks were so exquisitely tailored, as were each of his seventy-two suits. His shirt, which he was wearing outside his trousers, was of such fine cream silk. His intelligence and conversation, when he wasn't talking politics, was of such sophistication that it was impossible to believe that what he really wanted from life was to be taken by a six foot three, black stevedore from Apapa Docks and given a very rough seeing-to. This, and it was not for lack of wishful thinking, had never happened.

'Live in hope, Bruce,' he'd said to me, at the end of a long drunken night in Cotonou when that admission had eased its way through the glasses and bottles on the table. 'Live in hope, that's the thing.'

More astonishing than this, *even* more astonishing than the blue/white Omo pallor of his skin which could make the London tan look erotic, was that this revelation came on top of the gradual unveiling of David's extremely rightwing views.

What he required from the Apapan docker had slipped out after a mean and unpleasant row about UK immigration policy. David marshalled his views and put them across with a combination of irrefutable logic and devastating timing from a highly educated head, while I bellowed injustice from an inadequately prepared and inconsistently fed heart.

David had a first in PPE from Oxford University.

'They gave me the clap,' he'd said, feeling wicked that night – not professorial VD but a degree so brilliant that when he walked in for his *viva voce*, or as mortals call it, his 'interview', the panel of dons stood and applauded. The two A-levels I'd squeezed out of my London grammar were no match for the air-cooled recesses of David's massive brain.

When I'd digested that unlikely union of David with an Apapan docker I'd said: 'Don't you think your sexual needs and political beliefs are somewhat at odds, David?'

'How close you come to calling me a hypocrite, Bruce,' he'd said, tossing back another whisky. 'I'm not. The African in his own land is a noble man, a man who belongs, a man with history and culture behind him. They are a beautiful people in their own country. Compare them to the trash we have on our own streets, those gangs of dissolute youth with their . . . what did Tom Wolfe call it . . . their "pimp roll", their bristling, recidivistic aggression, their . . .'

'That's enough, David,' I'd said, and he'd smirked like a naughty boy.

'You'd rather I said it than anybody else though, Bruce, wouldn't you?'

David was a difficult friend to have. Liberals were his meat and drink. He had two cards: the queer card and the fascist card. He played them hard and fast and watched the wishy-washies squirm. Heike couldn't stand to be in the same room as him. Her flesh crawled whenever he kissed her hello. In the past he'd shown me some vulnerability and asked for a little trust on it. I found it difficult to turn someone down under those circumstances.

I polished off the whisky and gargled with the ice-cold Löwenbrau. David snapped his fingers at a waiter and pointed at the empties.

'You're looking seedier than usual, Bruce,' he said, lighting up some dreadful brand of menthol cigarette he liked to smoke. 'You look like the kind of person I had to beat off me in dark little cinemas in Soho. Ugh! Unbearable people.'

'I had my car crushed by two forty-foot containers on Tin Can Island today. No change of clothes, no shaving gear, no toothbrush.'

'You haven't hauled me out here just to borrow money, have you?'

'I have money. This is rare, I know. All I want is some information.'

'I'm always giving you help and information but . . .'

'You work for the High Commission, that's what you're supposed to do.'

'. . . but what do *I* get in return?'

'What more do you want? You get a salary, a car, a house, a maid, a cook, a gardener . . .'

'A kiss. A chaste little kiss.'

'Oh, for Christ's sake, David.'

'You started it with the "I love you" business.'

'I was *in* the car when they started crushing it. You're lucky you're not supervising having me cut out of a steel ingot. I'm tense, nervous . . .'

'Sorry, 'course you are.'

'You still haven't found your Apapan docker?'

'Er, not exactly,' said David, staring off into the night. The waiter came and unloaded the fresh drinks. I reached for my pocket as if I'd felt a kidney stone on the move. David held up his hand and signed for it.

'Might as well let Her Majesty buy the odd round.'

'She's very generous.'

'Not as generous as she used to be,' he said, and drained the rest of his first beer. 'What do you want?'

'Napier Briggs. You called the other day asking about him.'

'Did I?'

'You said you didn't, but we know you did.'

'Ah, Napier,' said David, with natural cadence, a travesty of pity leaked into his face. 'Another lost soul. Utterly pathetic man. You said he'd died.'

David liked using callousness for effect.

'You were a bit more interested in him than that, weren't you, David?'

'Was I? As I recall, you brought him up.'

'Why did you pass him on to us?'

'He wanted me to do something but he wouldn't tell me anything, wouldn't give me any details. All he could say was, "Two million dollars, I've lost two million dollars and all you can do is tell me to go home." A terrible bore. I told him about an American we'd heard of the week before who'd dropped two and a half mil on a "fees and taxes" scam but, like all of them, he thinks he's a special case.'

'Why didn't you send him to Adjeokuta?'

'We've been asked to screen people beforehand. If they're time-wasters. If they're not prepared to talk. If they've done something illegal themselves. We generally don't send them on to him. He has his hands full enough, as you'd expect.'

'Did he come to you at the High Commission?'

'Briggs? Yes, eventually. But I met him at a party first. An American woman. Strudwick. Her husband's an international lawyer, Graydon Strudwick. She's called Gale. Your type, I'd say. You know, blonde, actressy. I think Graydon's her fourth husband.'

'Since when has that been my type?'

'Just something to say, Bruce. Try to relax, for God's

sake. What do I know about what men want from women. I can't even see the point of breasts.'

I knew a Gale from my London days, who, apart from having a very good nose for sex and money, had also developed an intuition for the right marriage. She'd married her boss, then her boss's boss and finally her boss's boss's banker. She'd been living in some department-store cake of a house in the Ivory Coast capital, Abidjan, the last I'd heard. After that many marriages I couldn't remember the name of the last one.

'Gale,' I said. 'Her maiden name's not Glass, is it?'

'We're boring out here, but not that bloody desperate.'

'Blonde, you said.'

'She's pretty voracious by all accounts. Doesn't stick to her husband, unless that's locker-room talk.'

'I didn't know you played sport.'

'It's never stopped me going into the locker room.'

'This Gale, she's blonde, ice-blue eyes, little bee-stung mouth, medium height, slim, in fact very slim, with very slim long legs that blokes are always on about wanting to die between?'

'You're boring me to death now, but yes, you've got her. That bee-stung mouth. I thought she'd had collagen implants and I asked her what it felt like. No, she didn't like that at all. I shouldn't use me as an intro. Now I remember, she was married before to somebody called Teller, a banker in Abidjan.'

'Grant Teller. That's Gale. Good old reliable Gale, she's pulled it off again. Strudwick. That's good,' I said. 'Sounds like densely packed money being stacked on a table. Very much her kind of thing.' I knocked back the whisky and took a pull of the Löwenbrau straight from the bottle.

'There's no need to behave as if you've come straight off the rigs, Bruce.'

'You got an address and phone number for her?' I asked. He slipped a pocket diary out and read it off to me. 'When did you meet Napier at this party?'

'Sunday the eleventh.'

'And after that?'

'Afternoon of the twelfth.'

'You didn't see him again?'

'No.'

'In those two meetings he didn't mention any names, where he'd been, anything?'

'I don't know. I'll have to look at my day book. I wrote up a report on him in case we had trouble later.'

'So you weren't that surprised?'

'Oh, no. He had it written all over him, Bruce. Victim. They find their killers, those people. They can't resist them. I was *mildly* surprised at how violent his death appeared to be.'

'Anything on the inside track I should know about? Have you got somebody over there apart from the Honorary looking into it?'

David's brain didn't even stop to think. He had synapses in there that could cross-reference and still let him talk.

'Your car problem, was that to do with Napier Briggs?'

'You don't miss much, David.'

'Are you working on something?'

'What're you going to give me, if I tell you?'

'Like?'

'Could you check a couple of truck registrations for me?'

'What!?'

'You heard.'

'No.'

'Come on, David.'

'I can. Of course I can. But I'm not going to.'

'It's two numbers . . .'

'Forget it, Bruce. I *like* my official car. If I poke around in your business I might lose it. Get your numbers checked elsewhere.'

'I haven't asked you to *do* anything about my car, have I?'

'No,' he said, 'you know you're on your own with that kind of thing.'

'As British citizens abroad we're on our own with everything unless it's business and there's a drink in it for the lads.'

'Don't get like that, Bruce. We've always been what I think the Americans like to call "nonparticipatory".'

I poured my Löwenbrau out and sat back in the dark and watched people accustomed to luxury float about in the marbled cool interior of the hotel. David got another menthol going. He wanted to know about Napier Briggs, which meant that he had something on him too.

'Who's the lucky guy?' I asked.

'Oh, nobody,' he said, looking at his nails as if he'd just bagged a Hollywood star. 'Just a waiter. God, it's amazing what you have to go through.'

'He doesn't read Wittgenstein in his spare time?'

'Fortunately there's not much talking.'

'You want to eat something?'

'Very kind of you, Bruce, but I'm rather booked up . . . for a change.'

'You want to be careful out there, David. Where that guy can lead you is a long way from the High Commission, a long way. You might not find your way back.'

'And how would you know, Mr Politically Correct, Kiss My Arse, Liberal?'

'You've already told me the type you go for.'

'Oh, Ali, he's OK. He's just a waiter.'

'I'm sure Ali's OK. He's got a job, some money. Maybe some more money now. It's his friends I'd be worried about. His friends with no money, no jobs and sharp noses for the milky-white *oyinbo**. You don't know what it's like outside the barbed-wire compound, or maybe you're guessing at it and you think it's exciting.'

'I'm not a hothouse flower, Bruce.'

'You don't have to be in this climate.'

'Very clever. All us delicate little lovelies running around in the open, you mean? Unprotected.'

'I wouldn't like you to be a victim like our friend.'

'Napier, yes, you didn't say . . .'

'I don't get my truck numbers. What *do* I get?'

'I can't say.'

'Then let's talk when you can say.'

David took me to a store where I bought some clothes and supplies. He dropped me at the guesthouse where a couple of guys were arguing with a cab driver over

* *oyinbo* – white man

129

their fare. I got out of the car and leaned back in to have a final word with David but he beat me to it.

'You didn't tell me why you're still chasing Napier Briggs?'

'I'm being paid to.'

'Who by?'

'My clients' details are always private and confidential,' I said. 'And who from your lot's so interested in him anyway?'

'You can read what you like into it, Bruce. But I can assure you all we're doing is routine and the sooner we're off it the better.'

'It's the first time I've been aware of a routine.'

'We do our best to be inconspicuous.'

I closed the door and he gave me a stiff backhand wave and put the car into reverse. The two guys rowing with the cab driver had carried their bags inside and the cabbie was getting back into his cockpit. David pulled away, heading back into town. I got in the passenger side of the cab and told the driver to follow David's car.

It was on an impulse. I had nothing better to do and I'd let this ugly side of my personality win for once – I was going to get some leverage on David. There was no telling, in this business, when it might come in useful.

He looked as if he was going to cross the Five Cowrie Creek over the Falomo Bridge but he cut back and went down into embassy land and crossed the creek on to Lagos Island close to the British HC. He drove into a maze of streets in the Brazilian Quarter and parked up at the first opportunity. I paid the cabbie off and followed him on foot. There was no name to the street. It was off Bamgbose right in the middle of the island.

We walked for some time, David easy to follow at some distance in his cream silk shirt. He was moving at quite a pace for the heat and I was disorientated and in a sweat by the time we reached a terrible little bar called the Gaiety at the bottom of a building which wore its structural problems on the outside. He went in through a door frame plastered with Guinness stickers. I crossed the road and stood on the other side of a line of parked VW Beetles. He looked around in the badly lit room and headed for a corner. In a few minutes he was out on the street again with company, an African, shoulder height to him but twice as wide, wearing a black T-shirt yelling NO OPTION. He wore it with the sleeves rolled up over some bonecrusher shoulder muscle and tucked into a pair of tight white jeans. They turned directly right into a black hole of a doorway in what looked like a burnt-out block but which had a single blue light on the top floor. David, appraising the man from the rear, hoiked out the T-shirt and jammed his hand down the back of the tight jeans in a rough proprietorial fashion. His friend yanked it out as if it was a hanky and he was on for a sneezing jag. He held on to David's wrist and hauled him up the stairs, which he mounted two at a time.

No light came on in the building. The blue light remained. I got bored and felt disgusted with myself for following someone who, although he wasn't a close friend was a lot more than an acquaintance. Was I seriously going to use this? Was I going to get myself into a situation where I would go to the ambassador and tell him that one of his senior officers was enjoying some rough trade down at the Gaiety? The guy'd probably look down his nose at me and say, 'We all go down there, my dear boy.'

The African in the white jeans came out of the doorway and turned back into the bar without looking around. I waited, getting a little nervous now. Five minutes passed, ten minutes. Did he kill him?

David's cream shirt appeared in the gloom. He leaned up against the door jamb. His hair was hanging over his forehead and he was holding his silk shirt together at the chest because all the buttons had been ripped off. He ran his hand through his hair and set off down the street with his hand holding his side and a limp. He looked into the bar, his head floating on his shoulders, wanting to catch a glimpse, wanting to go back in there, for God's sake. He thought better of it and headed back to his car. I followed him to make sure he got there. I checked on some landmarks so I'd remember the place and hailed a cab to take me back to Y-Kays.

I sat in the back of the cab, the streetlighting rushing through the car in rhomboid flashes, and thought that Napier Briggs was proving to be a lot more complicated than even Bagado could have imagined. David was interested in him for sure, even a bit nervous about him. This time he'd cobbled together some crap to slip out of the slightly embarrassing fact that he hadn't passed Napier on to the colonel at the 419 squad. So why did he send him to me? To get him out of Nigeria, which is one thing. Or maybe it went further and they wanted to push him into Cotonou where, seeing as he was a 'victim' and on the way out anyway, he could be shut down with a lot less fuss. It was going to be interesting to see how much more trouble I could get into while I was in Lagos.

I called home from the reception of the hotel, hoping that Helen might still be there and could go over to Bagado's house with the truck registrations. Bagado had plenty of friends in the Lagos force who could do a little job like that for him. Heike picked up the phone.

'It's me. I'm in Lagos,' I said.

'Right,' she said, sounding flat, exhausted.

'I wanted to get some truck numbers to Bagado. Is Helen still there?'

'She's gone for the night. Give them to me. I'll drop them round.'

I gave her the numbers.

'Selina went back to London,' she said.

'I know,' I said. 'I'm working for her. Are you all there, Heike?'

Heike's breathing came down the phone in pants with all the stresses uneven.

'I'm all here . . .' she said, now unable to conceal the distress. 'I don't want to tell you this over the phone, but you have to know. Moses's blood-test results came today.' She struggled, the ugly angles of the words catching in her throat. No sound came out. She started crying. I put my elbow up on the desk and dropped my head into my hand. My bone marrow had gone cold.

'He's HIV positive,' she said.

Chapter 12

I crawled on to the hard bed in my cell at Y-Kays and lay there in the dark with an early-model air conditioner giving me the sensory deprivation I needed. I'd taken the precaution of a bottle of whisky in my room and drank fingers of the stuff without concentrating on the measures. A multicar pile-up built in my head. Before the wreckage was complete I put a call through to Gale, who surprised me by picking up the phone when she must have had a regiment of gofers to lift a finger for her.

'Gull Strud –' I said, still on my back, my face and head numb as if I'd had four hours' root-canal work.

'Who is this?' she snapped back.

'Sorry, Gale Strudwick,' I said, sitting up and getting it out straight.

'*I'm* Gale Strudwick, who the . . . who are *you*?'

'I'd like to be able to say I'm all Bruce Medway but I'm only half here.'

'Who's the other half?'

'He's called Johnny Walker.'

'Well, let me speak to him – he's always been the more interesting.'

'Buh!' I said. She laughed. 'Sorry, he's too far gone.'

134

'That really is you,' she said. 'Still getting shit-faced and it's way past your bedtime.'

'I'm over forty now.'

'Oh my God! I can't bear to think what you look like. You were so beautiful. Where are you?'

'Lagos,' I said, 'and thanks for the compliment, they're thin on . . .'

'Where in Lagos?'

'Adeola Hopwell, Vic Island.'

'That's just round the corner. Why don't you . . .'

'Because, Gale . . .'

'Right. You're so shit-faced you don't know the difference between your poontang and your pecker.'

'Those bankers have made you poetic.'

'Yeah, I'm doing creative-writing lessons for assholes.'

'Are you around tomorrow?'

'Am I *around*?'

'At home.'

'You mean rather than nipping down to the Sheraton for the Bruce Oldfield show, before hopping across town to choose the foie gras for luncheon, before zipping out to the beach, then cocktails, bridge at the club and dinner with my aunt. All that shit, you mean?'

'Well . . .'

'Nobody nips, hops or zips in this town. We hide behind walls, hover around panic buttons . . .'

'Linked to the shrink,' I said. She laughed. 'You're free, then?'

'You know, I've missed that sledgehammer irony,' she said. A lighter clicked, a sharp intake of breath. 'I'm at my best at eleven thirty, that's a.m. So come then.

We'll have a few drinks and . . . a few more. Then maybe I'll let you have a sandwich. How's that sound?'

'What do I get in my sandwich?'

'Oh, I've got some fish paste in the back of a cupboard somewhere.'

'Is that what you call caviare now?'

'I'm *that* rich, Bruce,' she said, 'but . . . yeah, anyway, what do you do with yourself these days?'

'I meddle in people's affairs.'

'How nice.'

'I collect debts, recover losses, find people, uncover mysteries, rummage in drawers, lift up carpet corners, take husbands out of freezers before they get served for Sunday lunch . . .'

'You're a PI,' she said.

'Is the first word of that "Piss"?'

'Right, see you tomorrow.'

I refitted the phone, got my head up for some more Scotch, but it leaked everywhere and ran down my neck into the pillow. I drifted into sleep, hollow and miserable, trying not to think too much about Moses.

I was stabbed awake later, terrified, as if I'd found myself in a mortuary fridge. I'd dreamt a dream with no pictures, just darkness and rippling over that an even blacker darkness. The air con was freezing, my trousers stiff. I kicked off my shoes, found a blanket, shivered and tried to think about lighter things, but they wouldn't come. So I tried nothing. Nothing wasn't allowed. Only blood was allowed. The deep dark, black arterial blood that thumps in the core of us and contains more than just cells and platelets.

Sleep came in the gash between night and dawn. I dropped fathoms in seconds and surfaced in minutes without the benefit of decompression. The phone was ringing so loud it was shaking me by the head.

'Duh,' I said.

'Bruce? Bagado.'

'Guh.'

'The trucking companies. I've got the names.'

'Fuh.'

'Pen?'

'Nuh.'

'Get one.'

'Yuh.'

'It's nine thirty Bruce.'

'Not six?'

'Not six. Two names. Get the pen.'

'Right.'

'Seriki Haulage, Awaya Transportation. Both of them are up by the Ojota Motor Park. I'm calling the Land Office now – you'd better get moving.'

He clicked off. I wrote the names on the Scotch bottle. I thought I'd been impaled on a railing. My neck and arm . . . and then it came back. The whole big, beautiful, blue yesterday came back to me. A vision wave set off down the room, hit the wall and slopped back up to me. I called reception and told them to send out a boy to get some over-the-counter analgesics. I made it to the bathroom and lay under the shower like a derelict in the last-resort city shelter.

By 10.30 I'd gone back to the basic principles of trousers and got into them. Minutes later I was behind a cup of coffee and thinking of other uses for the slab of sweet Nigerian bread. I found one. Covering the soft-boiled eggs.

After twelve hours' air con the heat outside was like walking into a warehouse of boiler lagging. I stabilized myself in the back of a cab and breathed back crises and counted palm trees. They were building security barriers at both ends of the Strudwicks' street. When the cab driver saw the state of the gates to the house he dropped me off.

I rang the bell and looked up at the video camera as instructed. Behind it a small sign said 'This fence is electrified' and behind that were five pronged spikes along the wall and four strands of angled wire beyond them. It was not a light decision to shake this place down. A small door opened in the solid steel gates and a uniformed guard beckoned me on to the tarmac drive.

Inside, set back from the perimeter wall about fifteen feet, was another fence, a chainlink job with barbed wire on top.

'Is that mined?' I asked the gateman.

He whistled. My ears rang. He looked down the run made by the fence. A cloud of dust appeared and out of it two black-and-tan monsters. They flung themselves against the chainlink which ballooned and bounced them back on to their size-twelve paws.

He tipped his cap and pointed me up the drive. The house wasn't visible. The tarmac drive snaked through huge mounds of hibiscus and was lined at intervals by fanned voyager palms which looked like unpaid attendants ready to cool the odd person on foot. I broke through a line of shrubs and headed across the lawn rather than put a mile on my hike by following the drive. The house was a large white cube with a flat roof and shuttered windows all encased by steel bars.

The solid mahogany door had a brass seahorse a foot long facing out of it. I was going to give it a swing but the door opened on Teflon hinges and a liveried boy took me through the house, which had the smell of a private collection. The stairs and the gallery above the entrance hall were sealed off tastefully by thick Spanish-style bars and the rooms off the gallery all had steel doors.

The boy and I burst through some French windows and trotted down stone steps to an Olympic-size pool. There were four wooden-framed calico awnings arranged at one corner, under which were some wrought-iron, pewter-coloured Roman campaign chairs with fat yellow cushions. They surrounded a wrought-iron table with a two-inch-thick piece of glass on top the size of a Harrods window. I sat at the table and watched a large, expensive-looking cat make its way around the pool.

The liveried boy left me, returned a moment later and hefted a twenty-pound ashtray on to the table. He placed a packet of Kent, a silver lighter and a little brass bell next to it. The cat approached, gave a disdainful left and right glance and hopped up on to the table. She nosed around a little and sat down. The pool lapped, the heat rapped, the birds stayed in the bushes.

'Get off the table, Carmen!' Gale shouted.

Carmen flung a leg up in the air and set about washing her bottom.

'Frigging cat,' said Gale. Carmen looked up briefly and went back to it.

Gale thumped into a chair and lit a cigarette. She

tinkled the bell and straightened her sunglasses, which were two ovals suspended from a horizontal red wood line. Her long blonde hair crashed around her shoulders and her lipstick added a peach stripe to the white filter of her cigarette.

'She's Graydon's,' she said, easing the lapel of her peach silk robe open and crossing her legs, which were still long and slim.

'Graydon?'

'Graydon Strudwick the third – husband.'

'Fourth, surely?'

'Fourth husband, third Strudwick.'

'That's my first Graydon, I think.'

'Graydon Hepplewhite Strudwick,' she said. 'Not a Christian name in sight. Drink?'

'I'll take a beer off you.'

'Bring Mr Medway a beer, please, Ali.'

The name cut through the skeins of dead brain tissue.

'Löwenbrau, Heineken, Budweiser or Labatts?'

I turned to look at Ali and was thrown to find it wasn't the same boy who'd opened the front door. Ali was an older, bigger, tougher specimen and even in the purple-and-green-trimmed livery I could see that those shoulders belonged to David's little hard man.

'Löwenbrau, please, Ali.'

'A bottle of Veuve Cliquot on ice and two flutes, Ali. Go.'

'Veuve Cliquot,' I said out loud, straight in from the pueblo.

'For the Veuve Strudwick,' she said. 'I feel like a god-damn widow out here. Oh my Gad!' She ripped off her sunglasses. I sat forward expecting a body to float to the

140

surface of the pool. She leaned over and kissed me on the lips firmly with nothing in it. 'I forgot to say hello. Jesus. I see the same assholes day in day out I can't even raise a sneer. I'm sorry, Bruce, forgive me.'

'It'll cost you your first born.'

'You got a lo-o-o-ong wait.'

She gnawed at the arm of her sunglasses and sat down. Her peach robe was open all the way down now. She wasn't wearing underwear and the bikini waxing had been drastic. She smiled at me and slowly folded the robe over herself.

'What does a poor little rich girl do with herself all day?'

'You tell me, my imagination's dry right now.'

She put her sunglasses back on and bit a thumb. Ali brought the drinks. The Löwenbrau sweated while Ali popped the Veuve and filled a flute with a practised trickle. He backed away. We drank. I cried.

'How is it with number four?' I asked.

'OK . . . to begin with. The money's great. The sex *was* good. We came here. The end.'

'The money still looks good.'

'Yeah, but we're here.'

'You were in Abidjan before with Grant.'

'I didn't like that either. Something happens to guys when they get out here. They make dough like you wouldn't believe, they chew fat with ministers, they kiss our ruler's ass, they get to feel all important and then the rest of their lives look like fat-free frigging milk.'

'But do you love the guy?'

'Love? You still reading novels and poetry and shit?'

'You don't love him. Leave him. You've done it before.'

She rubbed her money fingers at me.

'And, hey, I'm not so young any more. I mean you, you're handsome. OK, so you lost your beauty but at least you're kinda rugged, good-looking. Me? I'm getting like a wrinkly old red capsicum.'

'You'll get a settlement.'

'PNA. That's prenuptial agreement to you, and thanks for disagreeing.'

'The PNA's got to be more than a ten spot a week.'

'I get the house on Kiawah Island and two hundred thou . . . a year, Bruce, a goddamn year. I need that a month.'

'The tears are welling, Gale.'

'That's because you're cheap. Anyone in the US'll tell you they need ten mil to quit.'

'And Graydon's got that kind of salad?'

'The guy's got green fingers. What d'you think we're here for?'

'The sunshine and the rain?'

'Oil.'

'I thought he was a lawyer.'

'The kinda law he was doing out here was guys'd call him from the john and ask if they could zip up without getting caught. I mean, Jesus. He doesn't mess with that stuff any more. The guy moves for his own account. He kisses ass where he has to and shovels it away.'

'You ever come across a guy called Napier Briggs in any of his stuff?'

'Sure,' she said, without thinking about it, 'Napier was one of Graydon's brokers.'

She stood up then and moved off as if she'd had an idea that needed walking about. She rearranged her robe and smoothed it over her buttocks that were still as taut as a teenager's – the word 'cellulite' not allowed in the house.

'I'm still all there, Bruce,' she said, used to having men's eyes on her. Insulted if they weren't. 'You had your chance way back and you blew it.'

She was referring to a time back in London when she'd sat next to me in a bar, bought me a whisky sour and asked, straight out, if I wanted to have sex with her. I said I'd like some small talk about poetry and ballet first. She'd said she didn't have the time. She was competing with a friend to see who could bed the most men in twenty-four hours. I passed. She gave me her number in case I changed out of a pumpkin before midnight. I didn't, but I had seen her again. She'd won with twelve.

'You're not looking for Napier, are you, Bruce?'

'No.'

'But you're interested.'

'That's why I brought it up.'

'I'm not going to seduce it out of you now, Bruce. You either bring yourself off or put it away.'

'Such sweet words.'

'It's to do with my sex life with Graydon.'

'What are you after, Gale?'

'You first.'

'Napier's been murdered. I want to know why.'

'Spicy. Hot.'

'You?'

'I want to get some dirt on Graydon so I can bust this PNA.'

'Is there any dirt to be found?'

'If you've got green fingers there's always dirt under the fingernails.'

I finished the Löwenbrau. Gale filled the other flute,

topped up her own. The cat walked over to Gale's end of the table.

'Are we celebrating?' she asked.

'I don't usually do divorce work.'

'This isn't divorce work. It's a criminal investigation into my husband's affairs.'

'Criminal?'

'Now you're gonna tell me you don't do criminal work either. Whaddya do, Bruce? Candy monitor for kiddywinks?'

'If I know it's criminal I try to stay clear. African jails aren't so nice.'

'Well, pal, you're cutting yourself off from ninety-five per cent of the business population in West Africa. You ever give someone a bribe?'

'Sure . . .'

'You're a criminal. Revise your company code of ethics. Christ, you're investigating a frigging murder, if that's not criminal . . . now raise your goddamn glass.'

'Wait on, Gale. What do I get out of this?'

'I am gonna give you access to the Lagos business community at the very highest level. You'll be flying in exactly the same circles as Napier Briggs used to and if you can't find out from those guys what happened to him, you ain't never gonna find out.'

We chinked glasses. The champagne went off in my head like a firework. She turned her back to the table and the cat put its head on one side as if sizing things up.

'You need a front, Bruce. You can't come snooping around my parties as a gumshoe.'

'How about a commodity trader?'

'D'you know anything about it?'

'Back of a stamp's worth.'

'Forget it. These guys'll open you up.'

'But I do know somebody who is a commodity trader and I'm strong enough on shipping to be able to pass myself off as her chartering department.'

'You eating her?'

'No.'

'What's her angle?'

'You don't have to know everything.'

'Gimme a name.'

'Selina Aguia.'

'Italian.'

'-ish.'

'Cool. We got some Italians. She blab the lingo?'

'Yes.'

'She like to go to bed?'

'Christ, Gale. Ask her yourself. You're not shy.'

She moved away from the table. The cat stretched out a paw and a claw caught in the fine silk and opened up a silent rent about a foot long across Gale's behind.

'Hey,' said Gale, so that I thought she'd noticed, but no, she knocked back the Veuve and made an expansive gesture to the sunlight on the pool, 'you know something? I'm enjoying myself for the first time in months.'

Chapter 13

I slept off the champagne in the first three hours of a ride up to the Ojota Motor Park. In the last half hour I held on to my head and thought about what Gale had on offer. She'd invited Selina and I to party on Sunday afternoon. All the big hitters were going to be there to kiss the ass of one of the new presidential candidates, some chief whose name she couldn't remember. After that she'd got into the second bottle of Veuve and invited me down to the pool house to see her new stippling technique. I hadn't fallen for that and had refused everything else, including the fish-paste sandwich.

It was a hot and dusty late afternoon in Ojota. The sun was scarfed with some horrible bruise-coloured chiffon and the breeze was set at the right level for zero cool and maximum crap to pick out of your eyes. The Awaya Transportation yard was empty apart from a flat-bed on blocks and a watchman who looked as if he'd been tyre-ironed.

There were three trucks in Seriki Haulage and two of them had registration numbers I was interested in, both of them big old Leylands with the stuffing knocked out of them. The yard was small, walled in by breeze

146

blocks with broken bottles on top. There was space only for the trucks, a wooden shed of a sales office and a corrugated-iron shack of a service area where the earth was stained black and piled high with engine blocks, axles and old pistons.

A fat guy was doing something fiddly with the valves and jets of a carburettor. Two boys were rewinding copper wire around an alternator. A charcoal brazier shimmered the air where three soldering irons were being heated in the red-hot coals. Another man sat on a tyre worn smooth which he slapped and thumped like a tam-tam.

I went over there. The boys looked up and said, '*Oyinbo*,' and laughed. The big man kept on with his carby. The tam-tam didn't break time.

'One of you a driver?'

The drummer worked up to a frenzied pitch and finished on a loud *tok*!

'How can I help you?' he asked.

'Do you drive one of those Leylands?'

'The sales office be over dere, *oyinbo*,' said the fat man without looking up from his work.

'I don't want to hire the truck. I want to ask some questions. That's all.'

'He not free to answer you questions,' he said, looking up now. 'Sales office over dere. Dey answering you questions.'

A man stood in the doorway of the sales office, his hands on his hips, a neat round pot of a belly stretching his white T-shirt which had some red scribble on it, as if he was doing some light bleeding.

'Do you remember,' I asked the driver, 'around early

to mid-January, taking some containers from Tin Can Island . . . ?'

'Listen,' said the fat man, putting down the carby, and twitching at one of the boys who sprinted across the yard, 'he don' know nothing. He be de driver. He jes' pickin' the load, he don't know wass in it. You wanna aks question this be de man.'

The man from the sales office was on my shoulder now. He wasn't pretty. His face was pitted from small-pox and, along with the tribal scars, he had some that came from unsuccessful social interaction. They talked in Yoruba. The word *oyinbo* occurred frequently. The boy closed the yard gates. The driver picked his nose. The other boy fanned the brazier.

The sun was still hot and the Veuve was giving me a splitter. I moved to the doorway of the shack. There was a work bench in there with a couple of table vices on either side and on the wall a range of tools all out-lined on a board.

'You got some questions,' said the sales office man.

'I wanted to ask about a load he carried back in January.'

'That your business?' he said, his face nastying up, not having far to go.

'Yes, it is.'

'You working for somebody?' he asked, riveting the words into me.

'Myself,' I said, twisting a bit of sneer into it, trying to get tough, making a big mistake. The man's eyes flickered at the mechanic.

'You!' he said, pointing at me so that all I could do was look down his hammerhead finger. Then one, two, hup! The mechanic hit me with a right and left in the gut and lifted me on his shoulder and slammed me down on the work bench. My head flicked back, hitting the wood hard and the green roof closed in on me.

My tongue was out a foot trying to lick some air into my lungs, which had been squashed flat by my diaphragm and was all up around my thyroid. They'd locked my hands into the vices and the mechanic was winding wire flex around my legs and the table.

Then the ugly guy appeared in frame above me. I looked away into the corner of the shed. There were two gas cylinders – oxyacetylene. I went back to Ugly. Anything could happen in here.

'Who you working for?'

'I told you.'

'You looking for drugs? What you looking for?'

'Information.'

Ugly flicked his head and spat some Yoruba over his shoulder. The mechanic appeared with a soldering iron glowing red in the darkness of the shed. It was out of control now. The guy was either psychotic and I was headed for the lagoon with a truck axle around my ankle or they were doing the best job of scaring me I'd seen in five African years.

'What you wan' aks?' he asked.

'Nothing important.'

'Why you wan' aks it then?'

'Pass the time of day.'

Ugly didn't like that. He gave the iron to the mechanic and stripped my trousers and pants down. The boy brought a fresh iron and I did some very convincing whimpering.

'Now you tell me, *oyinbo*.'

'I wanted to ask him where he went with a truck back in January.'

'You wan' know the answer?'

'If he remembers.'

'None of you fucking business, *oyinbo*. Thass the answer.'

There was a sizzle and a crackling and a sharp scorching pain that made me scream and filled the shed with the stink of burnt hair. I thought about digging for a deeper scream but the pain didn't go any further. My hands came out of the vices. I leaned over and puked. They released my legs. I was drenched in sweat.

'Now fuck off,' said Ugly. 'And don' come back. You wan' aks questions, you aks you own people.'

I slid off the bench and did my trousers up and looked around for a piece of something that I could stick in the guy's head. The mechanic took hold of me and ran me out of the workshop so that I landed in the bald tyre the driver had been sitting on. I was surprised to see a look of concern in his face. I was still looking for that piece of piping when Ugly heaved me up and shoved me towards the gates. I ended up in the dust outside the yard, my flies open, minus a shoe and any shred of dignity.

I wasn't seeing so well but I did find the shoe. The sky was darkening. I made my way back to the motor park. A bar appeared with a wooden verandah painted blue and pink. I found myself holding on to its railing, needing some help. Two men dragged me to a table and I doubled over and did some sweating into the floorboards.

'You want a drink?'

'Hold on,' I said and leaned over the railing and vomited again. Somebody gave me a damp rag and I wiped myself down.

'Just get me a taxi,' I said.

A smashed-up Peugeot came by a few minutes later. I crawled in and propped myself up in a corner.

'Where you wan' go?' asked a voice.

'Y-Kays, Vic Island,' I heard myself saying, and heard it repeated by seven voices.

The taxi took me across the lagoon on the Third Axial Road from Ojota to Lagos Island. I saw the water over the lip of the window, dark purple for a minute. I was breathing like a winded dog. Night fell while we were out there on the water. The city looked as friendly as home from the lagoon. If you didn't know about those hard, beaten streets, those stinking, overpopulated, jammed-solid streets and you hadn't been tickled with a poker you might be in danger of thinking that Lagos was a reasonable place.

It was after 8 p.m. by the time I got back into Y-Kays. The girl at reception said there'd been some calls for me, all from the same person, a Nigerian who hadn't left his name. I got myself to the room and under a shower. I inspected the burn which was a streak through my pubic hair, the skin scorched and blistered underneath. I had to get some antiseptic on that in this climate. The phone rang. I did some internal bleeding and made the monumental effort of answering it.

'Yes,' I said, smoothing the hair across my bruised gut. 'Yes,' I repeated.

151

'*Oyinbo?*'

'That's me. Old whitey. Who's that out there in the Lagos sky? You the Prince of Darkness?'

'No, no. I'm the driver.'

'The driver from Seriki's yard?'

'Yes, sir.'

'How'd you get this number?'

'I was there when they put you in the taxi.'

'I hope you're more polite than your friends.'

'That was a bad thing they did.'

'Yes, well. What do you want? Tell me your name first.'

'No names.'

'OK. So tell me what you want.'

'To talk.'

I didn't say anything. The phone hissed. I dried myself off.

'If you want to talk, my friend, you have to fill in the bits where I don't.'

'We should meet.'

'It's easier over the phone . . . and safer.'

'No.'

'I see.'

'We should meet.'

'Ah . . .' I clicked at last. 'You want some money. How much?'

'You have CFA?'

'Better than niara.'

'Fifty thousand.'

'Forget it. Good night, my friend.'

'What do you want to pay?'

We banged on for a few minutes and settled on ten

thousand CFA. He said he wanted to meet tonight. I told him I was in no state to go anywhere. He said he would meet me in a blue Datsun Cherry at the entrance to the Tafawa Balewa Square by the horse statues at 10 a.m. tomorrow. We hung up. I told reception not to give my name to anybody under any circumstances.

I went to switch on the air con and heard a radio playing outside. It was the news read by the sweetest Nigerian voice I'd ever heard. 'The situation tonight,' she said, 'is somewhat dicey, and reinforcements will have to be sent to the region . . .' Now, why can't I meet people who talk like that?

Lagos. Thursday 22nd February.

I ate heavily in the morning and went out and bought a new shirt, electric blue with red slashes – not tailing gear. The girl in reception hauled me over and asked for money for the room. I gave her some for keeping her mouth shut plus my laundry. The phone rang. She said it was for me.

'*Oyinbo?*'

'Who's that?' I asked, hearing a different voice.

'Wilfred can't make it.'

'Who's he?'

'The driver.'

'Who are you?'

'A friend.'

'Why? He change his mind?'

'He got a job. He want meet you tonight.'

'Not at night. No way.'

'OK, you tell me.'

'I'll meet you on the road by Bar Beach where Akin Adesola Street meets the sea.'

'Two o'clock.'

'This afternoon.'

I dumped the phone and wondered why names were suddenly being used and decided to get careful. I spent the morning getting myself downtown and into Companies House. I looked up Seriki Haulage and found it belonged to someone called Ben Agu and that Awaya Transportation was owned by Bof Nwanu. The offices were registered in Ikeja somewhere, but I wasn't going out there for fun.

The traffic was at a standstill on Lagos Island and I had to walk it across Five Cowrie Creek and pick up a taxi outside the Ivorian embassy. It took me to Bar Beach, which wasn't a beach any more since it got swept out to sea in a cyclone.

The palm trees thumped past the window and the sea breeze mingled with the cabbie's air freshener which hung from his rearview in the shape of a plastic tortoise. I wondered what tortoises and fresh air had in common and decided I'd never make it in marketing. Then I saw the Datsun and thought marketing's got to be better than this, even if you do spend a week talking about nozzles on lavatory cleaner.

I told the cabbie to stop and reverse up to the boot of the Datsun. There was nobody in the car unless he was sleeping. A moped puttered past. The cabbie looked at me. I did a 360-degree scan. Nobody. I got out and circled the Datsun. Empty. No keys in the ignition. The car in gear. No floor carpeting. A hole where the radio had been. The keys were in the boot. I had a weak feeling in my stomach.

I opened the boot.

It doesn't take long for the maggots to get started on things in West Africa. Wilfred, if that was his name, was seething. He was in the foetal position with his back to me, his neck twisted over his shoulder so that even I knew it was broken. His back was lined with deep grooves, as was his forehead. There were holes in his cheeks and where his eyeballs should have been was charred a deep matt black. It's terrible what an oxyacetylene torch can do to human flesh.

Chapter 14

Lagos. Thursday 22nd February.

The cabbie didn't say a word, just pulled away, looking at me out of the corner of his face. He was nervous. He knew the colour white people were supposed to be.

'You vomit out the window,' he said after a minute.

'I'm OK,' I said, breathing back the heavy breakfast, trying to filter out the taint of tortoise air freshener.

Snooping wasn't working. The level I was at, you snooped around, you got your car smashed to a Dinky, a chargrilled pubis and a welding course for psychotics. The business was being taken seriously down to the lowest possible level.

I checked out of Y-Kays with a damp shirt and a plastic bag. In the hours it took to get to the Eko Bridge Motor Park for the long-haul taxis to Cotonou I persuaded the cabbie that there was only one future for him and it didn't involve a past which featured our visit to Bar Beach. He was a young man, but wise enough to know where he'd never been.

I waved him off at the motor park but didn't take a taxi. I still had the Hotel Ritalori to check. A strange choice for a white man fresh from London – not near the airport, not downtown either. I walked across the bridge and took a cab from the railway station to the Surulere district.

The cab wrestled its way into another jam. I was keen on getting into a temporary vegetative state but the radio was on and that beautiful voice was giving out the ugly incidents of the day – 'A blue Datsun containing the dead body of thirty-two-year-old lorry driver, Wilfred Aketi, was found on Bar Beach late this afternoon. A police spokesman said that his neck had been broken and his body badly burned using an oxyacetylene torch. They are treating the case as a gangland murder. Now for a summary of the main points – Petrol shortages continue in Lagos . . .' The cabbie jabbed the radio and Highlife filled the car. Who wanted to know about petrol shortages in a half-million-car traffic jam?

The Ritalori was a modern hotel with a swimming pool and an exclusively Nigerian clientele. Why did Napier come here when his big buddy Graydon was out on Vic Island? If he couldn't afford the Eko Meridien he could have slummed it in the faded grandeur of the Federal Palace or bummed it in Y-Kays. Napier wasn't stupid enough to think he could get his money back on his own, not in this city of roaring humanity. He must have had a Nigerian contact. Someone who lived close to the Ritalori. When that line didn't work he went to Graydon, Graydon to David, David to me. Something wasn't right. If Gale had painted Graydon straight he had to be a lot better lifeline than the High Commission or me. And there was something else – Graydon employed Ali, Ali gave David sexual favours, David sent Napier to me. That stank.

I checked in at reception under my own name, which

157

was unavoidable. I gave the guy a couple of thousand CFA and asked him if he'd come across my half brother back in January. It took some time and another thousand before he found Napier. He'd stayed two nights. The night he arrived, when he checked in at 3 a.m., and the following night. He must have had a friend.

I put a call through to Bagado, who was back in his old routine and working late in the office at 8 p.m. I asked him if he'd found Napier's address book in the Hotel du Lac, which he had.

'How many Lagos numbers in there?'

'Five.'

'Graydon Strudwick?'

'Yes. Two for him.'

'David Bartholomew?'

'British High Commission, yes.'

'The other two?'

'Robert Keshi in the storage department of NNPC.'

'That's interesting.'

'He won't talk. I've called him three times.'

'The other one?'

'Emmanuel Quarshie. He won't talk either.'

'Is he in the Surulere area?'

'Yes,' he said, and gave me the number and address. 'You got anything for me?'

'Loose ends,' I said. 'But ones that end painfully. Did the Land Office show?'

'Not yet. No computer.'

'You spoke to Strudwick?'

'He said Briggs came to a party on Sunday eleventh Feb. He said he was surprised to see him, not at the party, they have open house every Sunday, he just didn't know he was in town. I asked him if he thought Briggs was anxious. He said he was always anxious. He said the man was a broker, it was his job to be anxious. You live on lots of little two per cents it makes you worry. That's the kind of thing I heard from Graydon Strudwick. Flannel.'

'The money he's got buys bolts of the stuff,' I said. 'Bondougou on your back?'

'He's letting me get on with it, but he's watching.'

'He knows, Bagado.'

'That's why I'm here,' he said. 'He asks after you. I've told him you were off Briggs. I said there was no money in it.'

'He take that?'

'I wasn't so nice about you.'

'You told him about the high-heeled boots, the miniskirts, my nights on street corners?'

'And more.'

'My heart of gold?'

'If you'd had one you'd have pawned it a long time ago.'

'Sometimes I think you believe this stuff.'

'Your form in ethics wouldn't get the betting up.'

'When I'm up for a sainthood I won't ask you for a reference.'

'Just go and talk to Quarshie,' he said. 'Beatification's a long way off.'

I gave myself a mouthwash of the right stuff and spangled my brain with a Heineken. I dialled Quarshie. He demanded a name in a plummy English accent. I gave him Steven Wright.

'Do I know you?' he asked.

'We have a friend in common.'

'Who's that?'

'Look, before I tell you my business there's something you should know . . .' I cut into that with a mouthwash and let it hang.

'Well?'

'It's not going to go away, Mr Quarshie. *I'm* not going to go away.'

'I don't follow.'

'Napier Briggs.'

'Oh, my God! I can't . . .'

'Listen.'

'I'm not . . .'

'You are, Mr Quarshie, you just don't know it,' I said. 'Have you been threatened?'

'By whom?'

I shut up.

'Why should I be threatened?' he said.

'Let's talk about it. Tonight.'

'Tonight. I can't.'

'You can,' I said. 'It has to be tonight.'

'Why?'

'Because then it's over and you can go back to living.'

'You know where I am?'

'I do,' I said. 'But, Mr Quarshie, don't call anybody else before I come. Are you on your own?'

He said he was and told me how to find his house in the street. The only one with gates and those painted red oxide. I hung up and the phone rang immediately.

'This is Prince,' said a voice.

'Prince who?' I asked, looking for a punchline.

'Prince!' he said, exasperated.

'Prince of Darkness, Prince Charles, Prince Sihanouk. Which?'

'I'm black.'

'If you've been drinking,' I said, 'you haven't done enough.' I slammed down the phone. There are arse-holes everywhere in Lagos trying to get an inch of your tail.

I found a street hawker outside with a spare lad and asked him to take me to Quarshie's. It wasn't far from the hotel. I gave him a few niara and he beat it. There was no streetlighting, just auras from the houses which made the beaten earth road darker. I found the gates, they were embossed with a large 'Q'. There was no watchman, a quiet neighbourhood. A little further on was a mango tree and a box underneath it for people to sit in the shade. I took the box, went into Quarshie's compound and placed it a metre inside.

Quarshie hadn't invested in outside lights – get the 'Q' on the door before you mess around with security. The house was middle-class professional and there was a light on in only half of it. Through the net curtains I saw a short stocky man standing in the middle of his living room. He was hunched with his hands in his pockets, pushing down his trousers, which looked as if they were being inexorably hauled up his arse by the thick braces he was wearing. His tie was off, his white shirt open at the collar and his heavy black-rimmed specs dragged on his face. He stared at a bare section of the wall in front of him.

In the corner of the room was a bar with a little red barrel on the counter with 'Watney's' in gold on it. On the shelves behind were bottles arranged to fill the space

– Vat 69, Bols Avocaat, Blue Curaçao, Bailey's Irish Cream. Cocktail hour looked like hell in this house.

Next to the bar was an open sliding door to a mosquito-screened verandah. I went down the side of the house into the back garden. I checked over the eight-foot-high back wall and found another garden. I walked back and slipped the catch on the screen door of the verandah which whinged but didn't turn Quarshie's head. I went through the sliding door and behind the bar.

Quarshie must have been trying to find his inner child or locate his id because he didn't move, not even when I poured myself a Vat 69. I rested my elbow on the Watney's barrel, which was only for show, and remembered bad nights in empty London rooms with Party Sevens up to the ceiling. I'd just found the mini fridge when Quarshie, as if warned by the ancestors he'd been summoning, slowly turned.

'Good evening.'

'Mr Wright?'

'Don't let me disturb you.'

'Help yourself,' he said, that plum still in his mouth.

'Were you educated in England, Mr Quarshie?'

'Millfield and King's College, London.'

'What did they teach you there?'

'A lot I didn't need to know about engineering.'

'I thought everything was important in engineering.'

'Not if you're going to work in Lagos.'

'Did you meet Napier Briggs in London?'

'Yes,' he said. 'There's Black Label in the fridge, I'll take one.'

I ditched my Vat 69 into an empty ice bucket and

poured us both a Black Label. Quarshie came to the bar and laid a flat hand on it to support himself and socked back the whisky.

'Cheers,' I said. 'Did Napier stay with you, Mr Quarshie?'

'He was in the Ritalori.'

'For a night.'

'He came here. He didn't stay.'

'What did he want to talk about?'

'I don't understand your interest.'

'He lost a lot of money and he's been killed.'

'I know, but who are you? You're not police. You don't look very Scotland Yard.'

'I told you. I'm a friend. I don't like seeing friends ripped off and killed.'

'Then you have no weight, Mr Wright. No weight to throw around like you're doing at the moment.'

This annoyed me. I looked under the bar and came across a long plastic-handled rat's-tail ice pick. The sort they use to have a go at those long oblong bars of ice you see guys selling in sackcloth. I tapped the counter with it.

'You've got a choice, Quarshie,' I said. 'You can speed up our little chat so that we get to the nub a little quicker than we are right now or I'll stick this through your hand, nail you to the bar, get round the other side of it and pummel your kidneys so you piss blood for a week.'

Well, people had been getting a lot tougher with me over the last few days. I'd call that *piano* rather than *fortissimo*. Quarshie didn't. He backed away from the bar. I got out from behind it.

'I'm in a bad mood, Quarshie. Now let's get down to it.'

'Put the ice pick down.'

'Sick it up or sweat it out. I don't care what you have to do but tell me the Napier Briggs story.'

'He was a bloody fool,' he said, and I knew it was going to take time to get Quarshie to tell the truth.

'Or just inexperienced in the African way?'

'Both,' he said. 'How much do you know about the Nigerian situation?'

'Politics?' I asked. 'You've got a military dictatorship that wants to stay in power but it's being forced by the people, by outside pressure, to return the country to civilian, democratic government. There were some elections. Big Chief Billionaire was, how did they put it on the BBC, "widely recognized" to have won them. They were annulled. There was a bit of a crisis, the Big Chief announced himself president, the military came down hard. The man's in jail and not feeling very well.'

'Yes,' said Quarshie. 'It quietened down for a bit. Then the military made a mistake. They executed the environmental activists for the murder of the four tribal chiefs. Now the pressure is on again for democratic elections, not just from the West but other African countries as well. The military is looking for candidates.'

'Very nice, Quarshie. What's it got to do with Napier?'

'An example.'

'Make it a short one.'

'A chief customs officer in this country has a privileged position. You can make a lot of money. It's a much-sought-after job.'

'You're going to tell me about "fronting", how these

164

guys have to pay their superiors to maintain their position and lifestyle.'

'Yes, and of course this goes very high. Right to the top.'

'Where's Napier, Quarshie?'

'You can imagine how expensive it is to become a presidential candidate.'

'Napier was scammed for a campaign contribution?'

'There are three candidates lobbying. Chief Benjamin Oshogbo. Chief Babba Seko and Chief Kaura Namoda.'

'Napier thought he was going to pick up a couple of million dollars in Benin and instead he got killed. Why and which of that lot killed him?'

There was a crash outside. Quarshie's next visitor had just taken a tumble over the box. I hung on to the ice pick.

'People who know something and look as if they're going to start talking have been killed in this business, Quarshie. I hope you're not next.'

'I have no option,' he said, opening his arms. 'It's all out of my hands.'

I went back out through the verandah and hopped over the garden wall, skirted a pool and ran down by the side of a house. I vaulted the front gate and landed in a parallel street to Quarshie's. I ran into the dark. I ran to the Ritalori. I ran up to my room. I locked the door. I slept with my hand under the pillow, the handle of the ice pick in my fist.

Chapter 15

Cotonou. Friday 23rd February.

I'd got back around lunchtime to find that Heike hadn't gone into work and that Moses had gone back to his village. She'd tried to stop him, had tried to convince him that Western medicine was the only way to tackle HIV at this stage, but he had to go and see his man. He'd said that his village doctor had already cured people with AIDS let alone HIV. He'd gone down the Jonquet taxi park at seven in the morning and taken a car to Accra. There was nothing to be done.

Heike and I shared a bottle of wine over lunch and did what we always did with a long afternoon ahead of us and nothing much to do. We made love and slept.

'What is this vile thing?' asked Heike.

'A stiletto,' I said.

'Is it?'

'No, it's an ice pick.'

'Wasn't Trotsky killed with one of those?'

'In Mexico and what the hell was he doing there?'

'It's creepy. I'd rather it lived outside.'

'You don't have to kill people with it, you can just use it to break up ice.'

'Could you?' she asked, getting back into bed with me.

'You mean, am I cold-blooded enough, or is it sharp enough for the job?'

'It looks evil enough . . . but are you?'

I took a handful of breast and kissed her nape. She squirmed away and faced me.

'Tell me.'

'No, I couldn't.'

'I'm not sure I believe you.'

'Then what are you doing in bed with me?'

'I *have* asked myself that question.'

I slid a hand between her thighs. She squeezed me out.

'I wanted to ask you something about Selina.'

'What's happened?'

'Do you think she's a lesbian?'

'No.'

'You sound definite.'

'The cufflinks guy?'

'That only lasted six months.'

'And she made a pass at me,' I said. 'Well, she let me know there was some chemistry.'

'Same here. What did you do?'

'I went to Lagos. You?'

'I spilled whisky down my front.'

'On purpose?'

'No, I missed my mouth.'

'Come on, Heike, that must have happened to you before.'

'Don't be guilty of the most pathetic male fantasy, Bruce.'

'I'm not. Men have made passes at me.'

'When you were younger . . . a lot younger.'

'Thanks for the boost,' I said. 'Is Selina back yet?'

'She got in from Paris at two in the afternoon yesterday, dropped her bags off and I haven't seen her since.'

I liked that about sex in the afternoon. All that time for lazy inconsequential talk. None of that urgency about having to sleep to get up in the morning. There was an added dimension to the intimacy with the noise outside of people having a day while we played truant in bed. It also took four and a half hours out of the afternoon and I could walk straight from the bedroom and into a drink without a hint of guilt, which was what I did. Selina was there lying with her feet over the end of the sofa. She looked up from her magazine.

'What have you been doing?'

'Sleeping.'

'It sounded like afternoon sex to me.'

'I'm a lively dreamer. And you?'

'I never dream.'

'The sign of an atrophied inner life. You should seek spiritual renewal or maybe just a drink.'

'Got one.'

I poured a beer and filled a bowl of pistachios.

'Where've you been all night?'

'Heike noticed.'

'Over thirty your maternal instinct comes on strong.'

'You mean you worry all the time.'

'OK, don't tell me. I don't give a shit.'

'I met a Nigerian guy on the plane. We had a drink at the Sheraton, we sang to each other in the karaoke bar, I went to his room and finished with him at about four o'clock this afternoon. OK?'

'I'm proud of you.'

'He's forty-one years old, married with two wives and eight children.'

'I feel unaccomplished.'

'He wore a condom too. Fifteen, in fact.'

'How *was* England?'

'Bad,' she said. 'My mother didn't turn up to the funeral. Said she would and didn't. There were only four of us at the crematorium.'

'Blair?'

'He was there. Dad's brother too. And an African.'

'What did the African have to say?'

'He stood at the back and left before the end. What happened in Lagos?'

I told her about the car, the beating and the body. I gave her Gale's invite and told her our roles, but I didn't say what I was going to have to do for Gale.

'I suppose I owe you a car,' she said.

'It wasn't much of a car, but there'll have to be something on the expense sheet.'

'How much do you need for a new one?'

'I'll have to talk to Vassili.'

'Who's he?'

'A Russian who deals in second-hand cars across the lagoon.'

Selina went into her room and came back with a small holdall. Inside was one and a half million French francs. She picked up a block of about a hundred thousand francs and gave it to me.

'Enough?'

'For three of the cars I've got in mind. You're planning a long campaign with this kind of money.'

'Things might be about to get complicated.'

'Not more so?'

'More so. You know where this money came from?'

'Selina Aguia Limited?'

'Thanks for the compliment,' she said, 'but no. I was the only beneficiary in my father's will and there was only one thing in it that wasn't repossessable by the bank, the building society and the leasing company. A safe-deposit-box key in the ALPbank in Zurich.'

'And I thought he was a busted flush.'

'So did I.'

'So what was in the lucky box?'

'Just over seven million dollars in four currencies.'

'Lottery money?'

'Let's buy a car,' she said.

Heike came with us to Vassili's, not because Vassili was the best company in Cotonou but for the simple reason that he had the best vodka in Cotonou. He had a collection of twenty-four vodkas in his freezer and all the flavours were home made. He had a piri-piri vodka which he made by soaking red chillis in fifty-two per cent alcohol. He had another which was made with Scotch bonnet chillis and I'd seen big strong men drink that and buckle like thirteen-year-olds at pop concerts. Heike was coming because she knew if she didn't she'd never catch up.

We found a wreck of a Renault 4 taxi which took us past the sprawl of the Dan Tokpa market and crawled us over the slope of the Nouveau Pont into Akpakpa. Vassili lived with his Beninois wife and three children in a house with a large yard full of cars, none of which would get through an MOT in their country of origin. Occasionally he pulled in a Mercedes or a BMW for a

170

special client and we'd see him swanning around Cotonou in air-conditioned bliss for a few days.

He'd started the business by buying stolen cars ripped off from the streets of Paris and driven trans-Sahara to Benin. Then the heat came down in the early nineties and the Algerians started fighting each other and that killed the business. Now his cars came in on huge Ro-Ro ferries and all the paperwork was legit.

Although Vassili hadn't been on a Russian diet for more than a decade there didn't seem to be anything that could stop him from getting fat and blubbery. He had a head like a big, round cabbage and a body like a sack of spuds. He drank huge quantities of beer and vodka and his face was as red as borscht. The only time he wasn't bright red was the 'morning after' when he was grey and on those occasions he disconcerted by looking like Brezhnev in state outside the Kremlin. He spoke fluent French but had only learnt English since being in Benin. I had confused his brain by telling him there were eight ways to pronounce the letters 'ough' and now any word with anything approximating those letters would get scrambled. 'Daughter' came out as 'dafter' and 'laughter' as 'lawter', 'ought' as 'ufft' and 'tough' as 'tow'. Things got even more complicated after the vodka and we usually lapsed into French or I'd get started on the Russian.

We did the business first. He turned the genny on to light the yard and pulled the dogs out. He didn't bother with *gardiens*, who spent their time thinking of ways to roll him over, but had four German shepherds who were unbribable and only fed once a day, in the mornings.

171

'Your end down there, Bruce,' he said, pointing into a corner. 'This all jet set up here.'

'Any five-oh-fours?'

'Two,' he said, holding his gut on either side as if he was about to punt it over the wall. He waddled to the corner, gasping in the heat. He had a shirt/short combo on made out of Dutch wax whose major design feature was car number plates. His heart must have leapt when he saw that stuff in the market but why an African should want to buy it was one of those retailing mysteries.

Vassili kicked a 504 with a brand new Sebago Docksider and said: 'This one for you.'

'You got a special price for an old friend?'

'No, but I tell you this car work good.'

'How much?'

He took an unfiltered Gitane out of his pocket and lit it.

'Everything good inside. Perfect motor. New clutch. Gear change like lawing in the sun.'

'Lawing in the sun?'

'Yes, easy, like that,' he said, and flung an arm back as if he was with his girl on the coast road from Monterey to Big Sur.

'Steering?'

He grunted and set himself solid as a sumo.

'But listen,' he said, and ran his hand through his black greasy hair and put the Gitane in his horse-hoof mouth. He started the engine. 'Like my wife at night.'

'How are the kids?'

'Ach! You know. The eldest still miserable. She don't

172

like being a *métisse*.* I bufft her a bicycle for her birthday. She cry. Hah! She cry as if I smack her. Nevertheless,' he said, another favourite word used for holding attention, 'the boy is good. Lawing all the time. He never complain. The baby? The baby is a baby. Crying all thruff the night. Drive me mad, but lovely. You gonna buy it? Listen.'

We listened. I looked at Selina. She shrugged an eyebrow. We bought it. We went inside and did the business on the freezer. I said I'd pick it up as soon as the papers were ready. Vassili opened the freezer. He put on a pair of gloves and removed two bottles as if he was taking detonators out of a nuclear device. A cuckoo clock struck nine in the next room. Vassili roared into some distant corner of the house and his eldest daughter came in, long-faced, carrying a tray with four shot glasses and some cashew nuts.

We flipped back two lemon vodkas each and then Vassili stopped us with a finger.

'New one,' he said. 'Mango.'

We worked on the mango for a few minutes.

'Furthermore,' he said, getting expansive post-sale, 'the world is going off to shit.'

He roared in Fon again and the daughter came in again with some sausage and gherkins. Vassili put the lemon and mango away and brought out pineapple and papaya.

'Why's the world going off to shit, Vassili?' asked Heike.

'I tell you, Heike, you have no idea. That Gerhard, he no want to buy that jeep?'

* half-caste

'Is that all?' I asked.

'No, no. I just remember. He want a jeep. I got one. No, the world going off to shit because three days ago something happen. A Kazakh man came to me. Here. In my house. A tow-looking Kazakh bastard. We drink something. We speak Russian. He tell me he know I buy and sell car, maybe I want to try something different. Like what? You know what he got?'

'A Lada?' said Selina.

'This not funny business, my friend. That Kazakh bastard offer me plutonium. Weapons grade. He offer me an atomic bomb. I tell you. That's why the world going off to shit.'

'Was he serious?'

'He came to see me. He show me the paperwork, where it come from. I don't know.'

'Were you interested?' asked Selina, pushing.

'What am I going to do with atomic bomb and kids in the house too?'

'He must have approached you for a reason,' said Selina.

Vassili gave her some pure Brezhnev in Red Square overlooking an army parade in −27°C.

'I'm sure he didn't stop off just because you're a brilliant second-hand car salesman,' she said.

'Who is she?' Vassili asked me, the room suddenly colder than Tomsk in January. I took him by the elbow and whispered to him about Napier Briggs's murder and how Selina had just buried him. He defrosted down to −2°C. Selina wouldn't let go.

'I mean, Vassili, somebody wouldn't approach you and expose themselves to you as a nuclear-arms smuggler if for one second they thought you were a legitimate trader who would dump the security forces on them.'

An aircraft passed overhead on its way into Cotonou airport.

'You tow bitch, that's what you are,' he said, and we laughed a little harder than we wanted to. Vassili poured the papaya vodka.

'Maybe it's time for me to try the piri-piri,' said Selina.

Vassili lifted out a bottle of clear red liquid encased in ice. He poured a shot, it was as viscous as syrup.

'This one cold,' said Vassili.

'You going to answer my question, Vassili, or tell me to fuck off?'

'Drink!'

She flipped it back, a shudder passed through her body. She replaced the glass.

'Peppery,' she said, lightly, and Heike roared.

Vassili went back into the freezer and came out with something that he had to beat the frost off. He poured something into the glass that flowed like black-cherry treacle.

'More old,' he said.

Selina was in a sweat now. Her shirt dark between her shoulder blades.

'Some history,' said Vassili, looking at the glass. 'In nineteen seventy-two they made coup in Benin. The president was successful and in nineteen seventy-five he made popular revolution. He made link with China, North Korea and Russia. I come here nineteen eighty-three. I am Russian. I do very well from contact with people. They like me. I am white but no imperialist.

175

I know people in government and slowly the government making things easy for business. I am in good position. *Bon bon. Très fort avec le président.* Nineteen eighties very good for me. Then nineteen ninety the socialists out, and right-wing president come in. I'm still strong but I have to be careful. People look to my car business. I go more straight. Now this year we have another election. The socialist coming back. He an old man but they like him, say he going to win. Like Russian people the Beninois not all happy with the free-market reform. Maybe next month *je suis plus fort avec le président.*'

'The Kazakh made you an offer because of your contacts? I don't . . .'

'Drink!'

Selina snapped it back. Another shudder and this time a cough. She tried to say something but no sound came out. Vassili leaned forward.

'*Pardon? J'ai pas compris.*'

Selina's short *brosse* haircut darkened at the roots with sweat. Trickles appeared and ran down her jaw.

'Spicy,' she said in a hoarse whisper.

Vassili grinned and opened the freezer. He pulled out a bottle so thick with ice that when he beat off the frost there was only a thin black line visible through it.

'More old,' he said and tapped the top with a small hammer. He poured a liquid as thick and dark as Black Strap Molasses.

'Do *not* drink that,' said Heike.

'Men,' I said.

'More history,' said Vassili.

'Tell me,' said Selina.

'In nineteen seventy-nine Russia invaded Afghanistan. I was eighteen years old. Afghanistan on the border there so the army take lot of boys from Kazakhskaja, Uzbekskaja and Turkmenskaja. Very tow young boys in that part Russia, but not as tow the Afghan. They killing and torturing and is very dirty war. I get out. Run away. Desert. There were five of us. Two Kazakhs, two Uzbeks and me. The only way is forward thruff the enemy and into Pakistan. We go back to Russia – you can lose yourself there but you have no life. So we go to Peshawar. The two Uzbeks killed by bandits in the Khyber Pass. Me and the Kazakhs make money smuggling guns. I leave to Karachi. Take ship to Dar, Durban, Luanda. I end here. Cotonou. The first country where I speak the language.'

'The Kazakh bastard deserted with you?'

'Drink!'

Selina tipped back the glass, sucking in the still viscous liquid. There was a two-second delay then she dropped the glass and clutched her throat. The sweat sprang out of her face and all down her arms and legs. She dropped straight to the floor, landing on her backside. Vassili roared in Fon and the daughter came in with a beaker of thin yoghurt which he poured down Selina's throat.

I picked her up and put her on the sofa. Vassili sent for more yoghurt and towels. She was crying now and clear snot ran in channels from her nose.

'A tow bitch,' I said. 'And a stupid one.'

'Fuck you,' she mouthed.

The cuckoo gave us ten.

'How the hell does he live with that thing?' asked Heike.

177

'For the wife,' said Vassili, throwing a towel. 'She like it.'

Selina pulled herself together, drank more yoghurt, towelled herself down, went to the door and spat out into the yard. Vassili returned the mature piri-piri to the freezer and pulled out some apricot.

'Was I right?' asked Selina.

'Yes. The Kazakh was my friend.'

'Was?'

'No. Still my friend. I tell him friendly like. No deal. He offer me old things. Antiquities from Afghanistan too. Lovely. I buy some. It's OK. But plutonium . . .'

We left soon after. Vassili gave us a calabash of yoghurt with some clingfilm over it. He said Selina was going to need it when she went pee-pee in the morning.

We dropped by the Milan and bought a pizza (no chillis) to take away. We drank cold beer and ate. Selina rolled herself a joint the size of a Havana cigar and smoked it with very little help from Heike or me. We'd got used to the African view of dope-smokers, that they were no-shirt losers, shoeless drifters, lower than Special Brew drinkers from back home.

At midnight Selina stood up and asked if we had any Ecstasy in the house. We shook our heads. She ran her hands over her breasts and hips and gave an impatient, exasperated jiggle.

'I've got to go and get laid,' she said, 'unless you two are game?'

Chapter 16

Cotonou. Saturday 24th February.

'Where are you going?' asked Heike.

'See Bagado,' I said.

'You're going to *leave* me with her?'

'She came back?'

'I barricaded the door in case she got in with us.'

'She's . . .'

'. . . an animal.'

'I thought we were Generation "Excess" and they were just "X".'

'You think she's always been like this?'

'Maybe her father dying . . .'

'I *hope* that's it. You should have been in the back seat on the way to the *Milan*. More hands than Shiva on a Saturday night.'

'I didn't know you were . . .'

'Because you were talking a load of shit to the driver.'

'Next time . . .'

'You'll bring a bucket of cold water with you? I should be able to handle this on my own. I'm a middle-aged woman for Christ's sake. But she's so strong. She's got wrists on her like a sculler.'

'*You're* not middle-aged yet.'

Heike slumped back on to the bed.

'I'm not even half way through?'

'You've got to hit forty to be middle-aged.'

'What makes you think you're going to live to eighty?'

'Whisky.'

'Selina's ageing me. My vital organs feel like pensioners.'

'My theory is – too much testosterone.'

'Yes, I've heard girls inject themselves with the stuff – it makes them predatory and as thick as pig shit.'

'Why'd they want to be as thick as pig shit?'

'It's a contraindication the drugs companies don't tell them about.'

'I'm taking Selina to Lagos today. Give you a breather.'

'That well-known city of moral rectitude and Christian virtue?'

'I'll cufflink her to the bed.'

'Wrong, Bruce.'

'I'll be good.'

'Kiss me, you idiot.'

The late morning was hot by way of a change. I took a *taxi moto* to Bagado's house. The courtyard, a large patch of beaten earth, half shaded by the spread of a mango tree, was full of people. His wife sat over an aluminium calabash of boiling oil while his eldest daughter gave the yam some stick. The middle girl, a real beauty called José-Marie, played with the boy, who'd taken to wearing shorts since I last saw him. He staggered up to me and pointed a finger and said: '*Yovo.*'* They learn young. The rest of them I didn't know, and Bagado probably

* white man

180

didn't know some of them either. He did know that they were all his responsibility and that there'd be more now that he'd got his job back. I was shown into the living room where there were two armchairs and a sofa which looked as if they'd been scrapping all night. Bagado was sunk deep into one of the armchairs with his mac on as usual and his hands steepled. I sat on the central ridge of the sofa so that I didn't disappear behind my knees.

There was a wooden table between us with four lace doilies and a china ashtray with the legend 'I cum from Looe' in the middle. The walls were scrubbed clean to an uneven colour between grey and brown. On one was an English clock with barometer attached which read 'Storm' permanently. Opposite Bagado was a reproduction Gaugin which he'd told me was called 'Where do we come from? What are we? Where are we going?'. Questions I fought with daily and came out underneath.

The clock ticked. The family noise outside smothered now that the paterfamilias was in session.

'I suppose you want a beer,' said Bagado.

'Not if you'll starve.'

'No, no. We have beer. Cashew?'

He roared a name. A threadbare curtain parted behind his head and a young man stepped into the room holding a tray with two glasses, an old whisky bottle full of cashew and a bowl.

'We've been expecting you.'

The boy put down the tray, poured La Beninoise into two glasses and left.

'That's André. He wants to go to university.'

181

'A nephew?'

'No. His father died of cancer last year. I've taken him in. He's a good boy. He will go to university. You never went?'

'I didn't like school. Too many people telling you what to do.'

'Followed the money. Thought it would buy you freedom. Mistake.'

'Lectures, classes, tutorials, they didn't appeal.'

'Yes, well, none of us is free.'

'Bad week with Bondougou?'

'There's never been a good week.'

'Your Napier Briggs investigation?'

'I was doing rather well. I know what happened now. I had a car located in all the right places. I had a Lagos registration, even a name, a suspect.'

'You arrest him?'

'He's out of the country. I needed permission to link up with Lagos.'

'Now Bondougou's handling it?'

'And I'm working on the drive-by shooting of a rice importer in the industrial zone.'

'You going to give me that name?'

'Emmanuel Quarshie, BSc. London.'

'Did you know it when I hit you for the number?'

'Of course.'

'I could have used it.'

'I didn't want him to know. I wanted you to work out where Mr Briggs spent his time in Lagos. You'd have scared him.'

'I did anyway. Had a little rush of psychosis at the end of a tough week.'

'Did he talk?'

'If you're interested in Nigerian politics, which is not my kind of muzak, yes, he talked. He implied that one of the presidential candidates lobbying the general tapped Briggs for some campaign funds. We didn't get round to which one.'

'You were interrupted?'

'He'd called some home help before I turned up.'

'Do you think it's true?'

'I had Napier down as a sardine swimming with shark. After Quarshie I started thinking he had some teeth. I thought if that toxic waste is the stuff Napier shipped then maybe he issued a little threat and if the shark was a presidential candidate and he saw a nasty exposé looming he'd have bitten back . . . hard.'

'So he went into the *cocotiers* to pick up blackmail money?'

'That's why he wanted me with him.'

'But you *haven't* linked him to the toxic waste.'

'Apart from the way I was getting trodden on in Lagos when I started sniffing around, no. But our friend Napier wasn't a poor boy scrabbling in the gutter.'

'Ah! There was a will?'

'A safe-deposit-box key with a jackpot of US dollars seven mil.'

'He's not sounding like a four-one-niner any more.'

'All that paperwork smells right. The scam letters and then the sting, but I've always wondered how the gang knew when to hit his account. Broking houses don't often hold that kind of cash, and if they do they don't hold it for long. It goes straight on to the overnight money markets before being passed on to the clients.'

'He cheated his own clients?'

'You don't end up with seven million dollars in a Swiss box unless you've been a bad boy and you know a lot about being one.'

'So he could have been going into the *cocotiers* to pick up his *own* money.'

'There's a lot we don't know about Briggs, but I'm flying to Lagos with Selina tomorrow and we're partying with the people he worked for. Maybe some clams'll start opening. I'll keep an ear open for Bondougou too.'

'Do that. He's nesting over there and I don't know who with.'

I drank beer and popped cashew. Bagado sawed his chin and communed with Gaugin. The clock chimed twelve.

'How did they get Briggs out of the *cocotiers*?' I asked.

'You want to know whether you should be embarrassed?'

'I'm embarrassed, Bagado.'

'I wish I could say you learned from your mistakes.'

'Is this a knuckle rap?'

He shrugged.

'Briggs was chloroformed. You must have left him alone for a few moments. They weren't very subtle about their business.'

'They didn't have to be with the police on their side.'

'I like your spirit, Bruce. Just listen. They bought a one-litre bottle of chloroform from the major supplier in Cotonou. I have a description of the buyer from the manager of the shop. The car they used must have been around some time on the Boulevard de la Marina because several of the girls out there saw it. Two of them went up to it. One of them talked to the driver. The other even remembered the registration number in case she saw it later on. A different girl saw Briggs thrown into the back of the car and watched while it took off and turned right just before the conference centre. They must have been playing gangsters in the car because we had no trouble finding their route to a derelict warehouse in Cadjehoun. One other passer-by even took the registration. You know we had that carjacking and street-shooting incident in Porto Novo last month? Citizens have been very vigilant since then.'

'When did they dump the body?'

'About three a.m. The car crossed the border to Badagri just after four fifteen.

'How was he killed?'

'Broken neck eventually.'

'And they were all African? No whites involved.'

He nodded.

'Nothing from the Land Office still?' I asked.

'I'm hopeful.'

I told him about the car, my beating at Seriki Haulage and the dead body of the driver. That bought him out of the chair and set him pacing around the room, flicking his teeth with his thumbnail. I gave him the haulage companies' directors' names, Ben Agu and Bof Nwanu. I ran him through my conversation with Quarshie.

'He doesn't say anything, does he?' said Bagado.

'Played for time until meals on wheels came.'

'I keep thinking about the army – what they were doing around Akata village, keeping people out, protecting the waste dump . . .'

'Making sure nobody ran away.'

'That too. Those soldiers were nervous. They seemed scared, their guns always ready. Those workers must have been prisoners.'

'Lifers looking for a half chance?'

'If that's true then what Quarshie is saying about presidential candidates feels right. What happened to you, the driver who was going to talk – it all fits.'

Bagado wrote down the names of the three presidential candidates in his notebook and said he'd do some digging on them.

'If the level we're operating at is as high as Quarshie makes out I'm headed for the meat grinder,' I said. 'They know who I am now.'

'At one level. The lowest.'

'Quarshie can't be that low down.'

'True. You'd better stay out of his way.'

'He'll talk. He'll give some kind of description.'

'First, you didn't use your own name, and second, an African's description of a white man is . . . you know . . . you all look the same. Like we do to you. Black curly hair, flat nose, brown eyes, dark skin . . . useless.'

'That's cheered me up, Bagado. The guy went to London University, for Christ's sake, he's used to white people.'

'Doesn't make any difference,' he said, sweeping the room with a levelling hand.

'I'm six foot four inches tall.'

'And Quarshie?'

'Short and stocky.'

'Right, everybody looks tall to him.'

'I will still be going to Lagos, Bagado. I'm not backing

out. I'm being paid. Remember what you said about me to Bondougou.'

'I think,' said Bagado, stopping in the middle of the room, 'I feel a speech coming on.'

'Already?'

'A small one. Your mettle needs strengthening. You're lacking purpose.'

'Did you ever think of going into the holy orders?'

'As a matter of fact . . .'

'Good career move. You'd be a star.'

'Nigeria is a country that should be a showcase for Africa. Oil brought us the biggest financial opportunity of any country on the continent, and that includes the South African gold and diamond mines. There are one hundred million Nigerians and most of us are hard-working, intelligent and love life. And yet our country is a broken-down, polluted, utterly corrupted place with most of our oil wealth either going to numbered Swiss bank accounts or paying interest on the national debt. Are we going to stand silent while this country is taken over by a man who imports toxic waste, who has dealings with organized crime, who has people killed? I say no.

'You maintain this stance, Bruce, that you are only interested in the money, but I don't believe it. You've been in Africa for more than five years, you've never been back to Europe in that time . . .'

'Never had the money.'

'You're African now whether you like it or not. You're one of us.'

'And I know my duty.'

'Right.'

187

'Let's find out who we're up against. If it's a presidential candidate with access to army help and the mafia. Then we'll have to see.'

'Remember your client. Your precious client. Maybe she'll decide something different. Her father was brutally murdered and revenge is a strong-burning fuel.'

'Her appetite's carnivorous too.'

'All I ask, Bruce, is that you don't do anything illegal. Not here in Benin.'

'Thanks for the warning.'

'I'm a policeman now.'

'And I'm a *Private* Investigator.'

'But you'll still tell me things I need to know.'

'If it doesn't breach client confidentiality.'

'I see.'

'You've got to hand it to Bondougou,' I said. 'He knew what he was doing.'

Chapter 17

I was back home at 1 p.m. The flight left at 3 p.m. The door was locked to Selina's room. Heike made a salad. I fried up a cheese omelette. We called Selina. No answer. We ate and made coffee.

'Maybe she's not in there,' said Heike.

'You think she's taken a twelve-foot jump into the neighbour's garden and talked her way through their house just so she doesn't have to face us in the morning?'

Heike gave me a slow shrug, plugged a cigarette into her holder and lit it.

'I would,' she said quietly.

'I don't think she gives a shit about last night. You would, but she doesn't.'

'I wouldn't sexually assault my hostess in the back of the cab.'

'Why are you whispering?'

'Oh, fuck off.'

'Five minutes, Selina,' I shouted. 'If you're not out in five minutes it's all off.'

I slumped on the sofa and sipped coffee. Heike watched her smoke stretch itself out in the languid air. We waited the full five minutes.

Selina's door opened. She stood for a moment in her flat sandals, khaki shorts, a long-sleeved white silk shirt and a pair of very black wraparound sunglasses. She cocked her head at the door and left. We followed her down to the Pathfinder. I noticed a large bruise on the inside of her thigh as she got in the back. We drove in silence to the airport.

Heike stopped outside the airport entrance. Selina got straight out and walked into the terminal. I told Heike not to hang around.

'She doesn't look too happy to me,' she said. 'Talk to her.'

'Do you think she'll talk back?'

'Be charming, Bruce, you used to be good at that.'

Selina handed me a boarding pass. We went into the departure lounge, sat on some plastic seats and sweated while two guys put together some pallets of crates of whisky out of the duty-free store. They wheeled them out to the Nigeria Airways plane which stood on the tarmac a hundred yards from the building. They called our flight and the anarchy started. We ran for the doors and burst out into the thick, hot after-noon air.

There was no question of flight attendants showing us to our seats. You sat where you could. The aisles and rear seats were taken up with whisky. We threw our bags into an overhead and got our backsides down. Three people got sent back to the terminal.

The plane manoeuvred its way out on to the runway with seven of the overheads flapping open and the back of my seat bust, supported only by the crates of whisky on the seat behind. The toilet door banged open and shut when they applied the brakes. There was no crew in sight and no word from the captain.

190

A couple of weeks earlier the military dictator's son had been killed in an aircrash in Nigeria and the minister of transport had come on to the World Service to tell us that most Nigeria Airways internal flights were 'nothing better than flying coffins'. I didn't think I needed to mention this to Selina, and anyway, she wouldn't have twitched. She was cool. Those wraparounds said butt out to chit-chat.

It was a short hop to Lagos, the plane barely bothering to get above wave height over the Gulf of Guinea. Soon we were banking sharply over the sprawl of rusted corrugated-iron roofs with holdalls and hats flying around us. A man in a blue shirt with epaulettes and black trousers was thrown to his knees in front of us. He grinned insanely. He was probably the pilot working his way to the back for a pee. Anything was possible.

We landed at Murtala Mohammed airport, the pilot taking his time to go into reverse thrust so that we had to swing away a little wildly from the perimeter fence. There was no applause. We cruised to the terminal in silent tears.

Our papers were in order but it still cost us 5000 CFA each to get into Nigeria. They're like that there. We fought like Vandals with the cabbies and drove the price down 1000 per cent. Selina sat in the back like a mother accused of murdering her children and said nothing in the four hours it took us to get to Y-Kays.

We took our room keys. I drank beer and danced in the air con and put a call through to Selina, who didn't answer. I went out to the Peninsula restaurant and sat on their terrace and ate brilliant Chinese food and looked at the lights flickering on Five Cowrie Creek.

Back at Y-Kays there was no change. Selina was locked in her room and hadn't been out. I put a call through, she didn't answer again. I packed it in for the night. I'd just opened a slim volume of Philip Larkin I liked to travel with when the phone rang.

'Any drink your side?'

'Not any more.'

'I'll bring some.'

I got dressed, made the bed, turned off the table light and put the overhead on. I sat at the table with the Larkin on show and slapped some unambiguous, sexless charm on my face thicker than pan stick. She knocked and brought a bottle of Red Label in with her. I found some glasses. She fingered the Larkin. Turned on the table light and cut the overhead.

'They fuck you up, don't they?' she said, referring to the Larkin.

'My parents didn't,' I said, pouring the whisky.

'That you know of,' she said.

She sat on the end of one of the beds. She wore a black T-shirt over the same shorts, no shoes. She lit a cigarette.

'I've been out of control,' she said. 'Had to shut myself down for the day. Pull myself together.'

'Did you eat?'

'You sound like my mother.'

'Ninety per cent of emotional trauma is hunger.'

'For what?'

I called reception and asked them to send out for some jolloff rice and a bottle of beer.

'It got out of hand last night. That piri-piri vodka. Then the grass. I went to the New York New York

192

afterwards, met a couple of French guys and went back to their hotel with them. The Aledjo. They had a bungalow. We drank some stuff they had there. Pastis, I think. Then it sort of happened . . . one of the guys liked to get rough. I got this bruise and some burns . . .'

'They raped you?'

'It wasn't rape, Bruce.'

My mouth opened but the words didn't come.

'I liked it.'

'Selina, your father's just died. You were close to him. You've just buried him on your own. Now you're trying to . . .'

'Spare me the bullshit, Bruce. Don't start telling me I'm trying to replace my father's love and using sex to do it because my head's not on straight, I'm emotionally distraught, I'm buggered up inside, because I'm not.'

'I won't then.'

'I've always been like this, ever since I was a kid playing games in the back garden I've been on for it. It's the way I am – I've just had a job admitting it to myself, that's all. Been feeling guilty about my appetite. Thought I should have a loving, monogamous relationship and couldn't understand why I wanted to go off with . . . with anything that moved. I thought there was something wrong with me.'

'Maybe there is.'

'Maybe the time'll come when I have to go and talk to somebody about it, but right now, just so you know, I'm OK. More than OK.'

'Even without Napier?'

'Even without him. It's been a release. I mean, he screwed up his relationship with my mother, tried to fit these other relationships into his life somehow and didn't succeed and now it's all over.'

'Did the money make a difference?'

'I hope that wasn't a nasty thought.'

'Finding out that your old man was a bad boy. Does that give you a bit of licence?'

'To be bad too? Do you think I'm bad?'

'Not so far. Not so long as you realize that Heike and I don't swing.'

'Swing? Now that's a word. A sixties word. Such an innocent word for a decadent practice. You baby boomers had a way with words.'

The boy arrived on cue with the jolloff rice, some irons and a bottle of beer. The jolloff, tinged red from being fried in palm oil, was studded with pieces of chicken. Selina polished it off without raising her head, wiped her mouth and fingers off and nodded, agreeing with whatever she'd just thought.

'Maybe I am bad. At the very least I'm perverted.'

'You didn't answer my question about your father.'

'We don't *know* that he was bad.'

'We know he shipped some toxic waste. We know he's got seven million dollars in a deposit box, not even in an account. A box, Selina. That's because Swiss banks are tougher than before. You can't deposit dough like that into an account without answering questions. And another thing – we know he had a lot of his owners' money stripped out of his account in a so-called four-one-nine scam. What happened to that? Well, I'll tell you – I reckon that's what he was going to pick up in the *cocotiers* the night he got killed. So don't tell me how blameless . . .'

'OK, so he was bad. We just don't know how bad. He didn't leave me a list of names saying these are the saps I fucked over in my life, give them a wide berth. He left me a key *nada mas*.'

'I've got a problem that I didn't have yesterday until you told me about the money.'

'To do with my father being a bad guy?'

'To do with going into the *cocotiers* with your father to recover his stolen money. I thought I was chaperoning him. Making sure he didn't get slapped.'

'And now?'

'Well, it looks like a big risk for him to have taken with seven mil in the treasure chest. Him knowing who he was dealing with. You know he asked me if I had a gun that night?'

'You had a gun?'

'He *asked* me if I had one. He was playing nervous that night and I thought firearms were the last thing he needed.'

She lit a cigarette and ran her hand through her crop.

'That was nearly exciting.'

'Thanks, I've been working on my narratives.'

'But I can't help you.'

'Was he just being greedy?'

'Still can't help you.'

'So that's it. He was a bad guy. He liked to play in the mud. He liked to get dirty. Don't you think he deserved to get slapped?'

'Slapped, maybe. But not whacked, and not like that.'

I told her about the body in the blue Datsun and Quarshie's lesson in politics.

'So? They're powerful and ruthless, we knew that already,' she said.

'This is one of the richest countries in Africa and the people your father mixed with want to control it. There are no rules at that level and white people don't mean a thing.'

'Are you trying to talk me out of this?'

'Maybe some of these people tomorrow will know you.'

'They won't if I know Napier,' she said.

'You know there's probably no going back after tomorrow.'

'Well, I'm still in. Are you?'

'If you can bring yourself to tell me anything about your father that's got a shred of truth in it.'

'I wouldn't know where . . .'

'You must have been through all his stuff back in London. The house, the office. You must have turned those places upside down. There must have been something somewhere to show how seven million dollars got to be in a safe deposit box.'

She crushed the cigarette out, poured herself a gob of whisky and offered me one. She sat and thought and worked out how little truth she could get away with.

'Graydon Strudwick,' she said after a few minutes.

'The money came from Graydon?'

'There's no evidence of that. There's just meetings in Zurich.'

'In a diary?' I asked. 'Anything else in the diary apart from "my meetings with Graydon"?'

'He had a complicated love life.'

'Any names?'

'No. Just X and Y.'

'It couldn't have been that complicated without Z,' I said. 'Did your mother run off around the time when X and Y appeared?'

'She *did* go off with Blair.'

'Not answering the question. Did you do a media course in that MBA Napier paid for?'

'It looked like X was the problem.'

'Not-so-innocent Napier.'

'He always painted himself as the injured party.'

'What happened to his business after your mother and Blair left?'

'It went through a bad time.'

'And then it picked up around the time Napier started coming to Nigeria and meeting Graydon.'

'There was a coincidence.'

'Do you know how they met?'

'No.'

'You're being a little tight with your lips.'

'I'm employing you.'

'Why?'

'I can't do this alone, but in business, I don't trust people. You tell people too much and they start thinking for themselves.'

'You tell people too little and they do the same thing *and* they go down the wrong track.'

'There's an element of risk in everything.'

'I've taken a lot of risks for you so far.'

'And you're going to be well paid for that.'

'But no inside track.'

'To give it to you brutally – the management doesn't share everything with the employees.'

'You know more than I did when I was twenty-five.'

'Maybe you didn't get fucked over until you were older. Maybe you didn't know anything that was useful that you could tell someone so that they could use it and fuck you over. Maybe . . .'

'I had a sheltered childhood.'

'Maybe you did.'

Chapter 18

It was a rare day along this coast when the breeze had been stiff enough during the night to clear the pollution and leave the air fresh and breathable. The sun wasn't shining through some fifty denier tights for a change, but slapped straight down on to the wild-headed coconut palms, the fluttering fanned voyager palms, and even the frowzy, flappy banana palms managed to look chic. There were shadows, clear and sharp, and out on the water, ships that were usually lost in a nylon haze cut shapes on a blue sky that would normally be bleached to ash.

I was wearing a pair of crisp off-white chinos, a petrol-blue viscose short-sleeve shirt and a pair of blue-and-burgundy docksiders (no socks) and, for once, I didn't mind how I was smelling. Selina wore a big, baggy, wide-flared pair of blue-and-white-striped pyjama bottoms with a navy sleeveless top with just one button holding her in. She sat in the rear of the taxi with her arms stretched across the back of the seat and an ankle crossed over a knee while an expensive flip-flop kept pace with what was going on in her head. She smelled of something vigorous like Eau Sauvage or one of Calvin's concotions. She'd discarded the wraparounds and brought out some very dark, gold-rimmed lozenges that did little to protect her eyes but a lot for her style. Her crop stood up spiky and alert without looking moussed and the red lipstick she'd applied looked as if it tasted good.

The watchman wouldn't let the taxi in and we walked it up the drive arm in arm. This time the house was fronted by cars and the cheapest was a BMW 7 series. The front door was open and we legged it through to the pool and an hilarity of voices. Ali approached with a trayful of flutes and we restrained ourselves by taking one each. The champagne was brick cold and fizzed right out to the inner ear.

Gale glided through the crowd, unmissable in an ochre sarong split up to the crotch to the tantalizing point which had the men slitting their eyes. She had a matching bikini top which squeezed her breasts inwards and upwards and a couple of drops of champagne were clinging there with sheer delight.

'Don't worry,' she said, kissing me on the lips, 'this trash won't be staying for long.'

I introduced Selina. Gale drank her in and got instantly blotto. She gave her a kiss on the lips too. Everything looked set for a long, strong afternoon. A man with pink tinted glasses, silver hair on his head but none on his body, approached and tried to impress himself on us.

'Get lost, George,' said Gale. 'Go bore Tilana over there by the bushes.'

George backed away and did as he was told.

'You have to be brutal with that type,' she said, 'or he'll bore your hair limp. Now, let's get you out of the mayhem and into the inner sanctum.'

Gale took Selina's arm and led us around the pool past the hungry eyes of various other types of George who stood with their hands resting on the waists of the willowiest African girls I'd ever seen off a catwalk. We got shot of the mêlée, rounded a corner of shrubbery and headed across a piece of lawn to a walled garden.

'They don't belong to them, Bruce,' said Gale over her shoulder. 'All provided by the house. Know what I mean?'

'One of your inventions?' I asked as we entered the walled garden.

'How many of these you seen in West Africa?'

It was spectacular. The walls were maybe twelve feet high and supported a domed structure of aluminium pentagons overgrown with orange, red and purple bougainvillea and passion flower. The sun still broke through to dapple the terracotta floor tiles and the water in an oblong pool whose fountain had been paid to trickle at a level just below consciousness. Fans whirred silently in the roof but not so strongly that napkins, silk shirts and underwear would get sucked up into the thermals above.

The walls were lined with plants and creepers. Interesting shrubs, which only grew on mid-Atlantic volcanoes, had turned out to impress for the occasion. Tendrils of this and that stretched out to caress attractive women, who leapt and brushed them off quickly, spilling their drinks on to bold men's trouser fronts. The space was big enough for forty people to mill without crushing.

At one end was a raised platform where there

was an arrangement of an open square of swinging sofas. I'd seen swinging sofas before – all fringes and florals – with half-inch tubular frames which behaved like experienced drunks on the verge of collapse but miraculously holding it together. These ones were German engineered, Italian designed with British décor. You could have gone down a rollercoaster in one of them.

Two of the sofas were occupied by a man on each. One of them had to be Graydon. A man who looked as if his tan, his perfect, golden, even tan went right up to the patch behind his scrotal sac. A man who looked as if he had been born between sets at a country-club tennis court in Beverly Hills. A man whose manicure was more expensive than most people's orthodontistry. A man wearing the crispest, whitest shirt, the darkest, richest, naviest-blue shorts, the springiest, most mushroomy-coloured espadrilles of any that's graced the portals of Saks 5th Ave. Gold-diggers' spades were tinnitus to him. He held a highball of Perrier with a twist of lark's song in it and rolled his finger against his thumb as if he had a bogey to flick.

On the other sofa was a different animal altogether. A huge-headed man with wire-wool hair and olive skin which hung a little loose around the neck. His face held up a pair of heavy-framed tortoiseshell sunglasses, the arms at least an inch thick, with lenses so black life must have been like looking into hell. His jaw had the solidity of peasant stock, his mouth the luxuriance of an opera villain. He was wearing a pillar-box-red polo shirt and he bench-pressed at least 200 pounds from the way the material snagged on his shoulders and

202

chest. The gut wasn't so clever, needed a little work. That was heading west over his belt, which held up a pair of black trousers. He wore red socks to match and black loafers with nothing fancy. He smiled, at something Graydon might have said if he'd have moved his lips, and revealed big white teeth, tablet-size. He leaned over to a side table and picked up a cigar he'd been smoking earlier and relit it. He swilled something red around in a glass and sunk it and held up his hand to show Graydon he didn't need refilling.

Gale was introducing Selina to a Nigerian whose name was Robert Keshi who'd been in Napier's book under NNPC storage department. Gale had her arm around Selina's waist and, smaller than her, had to go on tiptoe to whisper something in her ear. Selina put her arm around Gale and whispered something back. They parted and Gale came over to me.

'She's gorgeous,' said Gale. 'Is she all yours?'

'She's no one's.'

'Nice to have another around.'

'Who's the other single white female?'

'Me, of course, and don't say anything bitchy, Bruce. I bitch for the USA. I'm their great medal hope in the Fuck You Olympics.'

'That Graydon over there?'

'Yeah, we'll let him warm up first. He doesn't drink,' she said and closed a nostril with a finger. 'Mum's the word. He won't start on the toot until Franconelli goes.' Gale leaned in. 'The Italian does *not* approve.'

'How did he find out?'

'Maybe Gray offered him a line and he gave him a finger up the ass.'

'What's Franconelli's connection?'

'Business, Bruce. It's all business.'

'Concrete?'

'Toot and smack for all I care.'

'Don't joke about it, Gale.'

'Who's joking?'

'You don't need me for this.'

'I *need* you. Come on. I want to show you something.'

Gale led me back to the house, swatting at the creeps around the pool. We turned a hard right inside the French windows and powered through a forty-five-foot living room which had three cream leather sofas in it drawn up to a smoked-glass table set on an acre of parquet flooring. Gale had her arms out as if she was flying, as if she'd had some toot. She stopped at the door and gave me a pirouette.

'Steel doors,' she said, and pointed to another doorway across a corridor. 'Steel doors to the kitchen.'

We turned left down the corridor. She pointed to a door on the right.

'Graydon's study. Locked.'

She pointed to another door further along on the right.

'Security,' she said, and turned the handle. 'Unlocked.'

It was a closet room with eight monitors set into a huge cabinet on one wall. There was a console and a chair. The screens showed scenes from outside the house. The party around the pool. An empty front door. The driveway outside the front door. Outside the front gate. The perimeter walls.

'You saw the barrier we're putting up in the street,'

said Gale. 'This is kinda normal for Lagos. You know, there's a lot of armed robbery, people smashing into your home and, well, killing you. It's death for murder and armed robbery so you might as well rob 'em and pump 'em. Less chance of a witness.

'OK, so we can afford to have sliding steel doors to seal off this part of the house. We got a staircase that goes up to the roof. We got a reinforced roof so a chopper can land and take us off to the US Navy when it all goes rat shit. But nearly everybody in Lagos has a place they can retreat to. It's serious stuff out here. I might look like a businessman's wife, Bruce . . .'

'But in fact you're a fully-trained anti-assault blah-blah-blah.'

'Right.'

'I promise I won't break in.'

'Other people have got this kind of thing,' she said, pressing a button on the console. The images on the monitors changed to the house interior. 'These are all the ground-floor rooms. Nothing strange about. You want to see where the suckers go once they get in. This . . . is a little more unconventional.'

She clicked another button and this time four of the monitors came up with empty bedrooms, the others remained blank. Gale opened up the cabinet which showed four VCRs.

'Graydon likes to video his guests?' I asked.

'He's a creep,' she said. 'He doesn't even have to do it. Most of these guys are so glad to get a piece of black ass they'll do anything for him. He does it so that he knows he's got that power in reserve.'

I thought about David and Ali and wondered whether

he'd been stupid enough to transgress in the house. At a party like this he probably had the opportunity. Christ, this would make him sweat.

'Great dirt, Gale,' I said. 'But not usable.'

'It's a character reference, Bruce. I don't want you going in to bat against Gray without knowing about his fastball, no, I mean his forkball or slider or whatever they call that shit. What do they say in England?'

'Googly.'

'Jesus. That sounds tricky. Well, that's what he's like. Googlies everywhere. He's got wealth, intelligence and most of all charm. The number of stupid bitches I've seen go in on Gray spitting blood and come out wanting his babies . . . it makes me puke.'

'Does he video your bedroom too?'

'Uh-uh, nor his own.'

She clicked the monitors back to house exterior. The gates were opening up to a Rolls Royce. We watched it draw up to the front of the house. It had a flag on the bonnet.

'Here comes the chief,' said Gale.

'What's with the flag?'

'He's practising,' she said. 'I better go get Gray fired up.'

We went back down to the party, skirting the pool away from the riffraff.

Inside the walled garden Selina was no longer talking to Robert Keshi but had moved up on to the dais and was sitting talking to Franconelli on his swing. Graydon was leaning forward off his and seemed close to having a good time. Gale flitted through the crowd and took Graydon by the hand and led him away.

Franconelli was sitting sideways with his leg cocked up on the sofa and leaning over the back. There was a guy behind who was joining in the conversation. I took a drink and moved closer. They were speaking Italian. I was strictly 'restaurant' in that language so I left Selina to get on with it. I went looking for Robert Keshi.

I never made it to Robert Keshi. I'd become a part of the Selina phenomenon. The whole party was talking about her as if they were her bestest friends.

'You're with Selina, aren't you?' asked a blonde woman in a gold sheath who must have reaped them like corn in her youth and was doing her best now, but with a tired sickle arm.

'That's right. I'm Bruce,' I said, trying to keep the smile contained, didn't want to get shit-eater's cramp early on.

'Marcella Jones-Cassatta,' she said in all seriousness. 'That's my husband over there, Gryf. He runs Graydon's bottled-water company in Austria.'

'You sound Italian,' I said.

'Yes, but with the Welsh bastard thrown in,' she said, and laughed at her little joke which she made frequently. She swung her hair back over her strapless shoulders and produced an Art-Deco cigarette case from her purse. She smoked filterless so she had to pick strands of tobacco off her tongue with a long painted nail.

She probably didn't make that joke in Gryf's hearing, or if she did she cracked it on his cauliflower-ear side. The man was front-row-forward material, international rather than club level.

'Who's he talking to?' I asked.

'Graydon's art-buyer in Europe.'

'Your husband likes art?'

'Look at him,' she said without contempt. Gryf took three inches off a beer he held in a grazed knuckle hand. 'Piss art, maybe. Shall we move over here a little?' she said, and slipped her hand up my shirt arm and cupped the bicep which she squeezed and let go.

'Another one of your compatriots,' I said, nodding at Franconelli.

'He's a southerner,' she said, explaining everything.

'What does he do that allows him up on stage?'

'He'll tap dance for you . . . on your balls.'

'A vaudeville Italian?'

'He'd cut them off if he heard you say that.'

'Can't laugh at himself?'

'I don't think he's ever had to.'

The garden went quiet for a moment. The pressure change of a celebrity's imminent arrival. Gale burst in and flicked her wrist. Everybody put their glasses down. Graydon came in with a huge Nigerian of at least six foot three and weighing a good three hundred and fifty pounds, maybe more with the quantity of Dutch wax he had built into his ceremonial robes. We all clapped.

The crowd parted and the Nigerian waded through us up to the dais, shaking the odd hand. Graydon accompanied a woman who must have been the chief's wife, and not his first. She was tall and slim and achingly elegant. She looked down as she walked as if there were print marks on the floor for her to place her feet in. She wore a single piece of stiff Dutch wax which went from orange, through crimson to deep arterial red. It was cut low at the front so that the gold chain holding a tiny chandelier of diamonds looked no less than a million dollars against her perfect black skin.

'May I present to you,' said Graydon, reaching the dais, 'the next president of the Federal Republic of Nigeria. Chief Babba Seko.'

'Not quite,' said Marcella under her breath.

The chief came to the front of the dais and shook Graydon's hand.

'Thank you,' he said. 'Thank you.

'My friend, Graydon Strudwick, is, as always, thinking way ahead. We are at the beginning of an arduous road, and there are many competitors in the race. But I believe our esteemed military leader is thinking very positively at the moment and I hope it will not be long before this great country of ours is returned to the hands of its great people.

'This, my friends, is not a political occasion. We are here as Graydon's guests. He wishes us to enjoy ourselves, which means I must shut up immediately. My wife and I would like to thank you and the Strudwicks for such a warm welcome. Thank you.'

During the speech the chief's retinue filed in. Not many for a man of his importance, a mere dozen. One of them had found his way to Marcella's side, a mid-thirties guy who looked as if he'd studied Ralph Lauren at school. His face was in a permanent state of amusement, although his expressions were minimalist. His only curiosities were an enjoyment of his own lips and the proprietorial way he had placed a hand on Marcella's behind. This must have happened before, but still Marcella stiffened, checking her radar for Gryf's whereabouts. She introduced the man to me, just to get that hand off her rear end.

'Bruce?' she asked.

'Medway,' I filled in.

'This is Ben Agu.'

The MD of Seriki Haulage and I shook hands.

'How is it . . . ?' I started.

'Oh, fine, fine,' said Ben.

'. . . working for the great man?'

'Ben's going to be the chief's campaign manager once the military dic – leader has given the go-ahead for elections,' said Marcella.

'Bof and I will be heading up the team,' he said.

'Bof?' I asked.

'Bof Nwanu. Bof worked on the Bush administration's campaign.'

'The one he won or the one he lost?'

'The ninety-two campaign,' he said, smiling.

'He's made for it, don't you think?' said Marcella.

'How long do you think it's going to be?'

'There should be an announcement about the candidates by the middle of the year with the elections to follow six to nine months after.'

'You don't think you'll get strung along?'

'The people won't have it,' he said.

'Do they matter? I'd have thought South Africa and the US are more important this time.'

'It doesn't matter where the pressure comes from as long as it's the pressure for change.'

Marcella slumped on to one foot and propped up her smoking elbow with her hand.

'If the campaign hasn't started, what are you doing with yourselves now?'

'Business. We need to raise money. "Our man" doesn't have the same advantages as others. He's not, for instance, a billionaire. We work, and of course we have our benefactors.'

'What sort of work?'

'I was going to ask you the same question,' he said, his face as still and concentrated as a stalking leopard.

'Commodities,' I said.

'Commodities,' he said. 'Interesting.'

'You?'

'Well, apart from road haulage, storage, construction and taxis we do as much import/export as we can.'

'Commodities?'

'Cocoa . . .'

'Palm oil, timber, sheanut, maybe?'

'Sheanut,' he said. 'I haven't met many white men who've even heard of sheanut.'

I slipped into the role of complete arsehole with preternatural ease and Ben came alongside so that we could throw jargon at each other and feel important. My God, I even ended up talking to him about free fatty acid content and mobile labs and loading systems. Marcella had to hold her breath to keep her tits from sagging with boredom. Ben Agu became a close personal friend.

'Are you alone here?' he asked finally.

I pointed out Selina on Franconelli's couch and Ben glued his eyes to her behind. Marcella started an impatient jiggle in her hip and hit Ben on the elbow.

The chief suddenly raised a huge middle finger as if to tell the assembled company where to go and Ben was off and at his side.

'Sod him,' said Marcella, and drained her flute.

It was important for Ben to be at the chief's side. Lunch was about to be served. Gale had been through the menu with him. He had his own personal tin of Beluga, Ben had to check it. The chief was convinced he could get poisoned at any moment. He would only drink champagne opened in front of him and only Krug 71. The melba toast for the caviare had to be just so thin. Ben was in charge of 'our man's' stomach. He was the most important aide on the team.

Marcella grabbed another flute and sighed from down the back of her knees. Ben Agu was pointing out Selina and me to the chief. The chief was doing some sage nodding as if he was bored shitless. Ben realized his mistake and backed off. Timing. Get the man on a full stomach.

Marcella said something about black men which I missed. She'd rattled through the last flute and whipped another off a passing tray. Graydon moved off the dais and looked through the crowd as if he'd lost his yacht in a marina. He stopped in front of me, a hand in his pocket, the other offered. I shook it. He was glowing with health. His skin shone from years of oils and unguents pressed into it by expert fingers. He smelled better than a bed of roses.

'You're Selina Aguia's partner?' he said. 'We should talk.'

'Hi, Gray,' said Marcella. 'How's it going?'

'Hi, Marcella,' he smiled.

'I didn't know they had announced the presidential nominees,' she said.

'They haven't,' said Graydon.

'Oh really,' she said, with ludicrous mock surprise.

Graydon gave Marcella the same hooded look I'd seen on his cat when it was stalking Gale. He didn't like drunks. This was not a problem for me – if I had the mechanism inside me that made me drunk I wouldn't drink so much. Graydon liked control and he liked others to be controlled. Maybe that was why he was a toot man – it gave him the illusion of complete control.

'Catch you later, Bruce,' he said, patting my shoulder.

Marcella giggled. I could tell from the back of Graydon's head that he'd heard.

The party rolled on. People edged towards the table, which was being loaded with food – lobster, crab, salmon, prawns, quivering mounds of mayonnaise on ice, a fantastic quantity of antipasti – but there was a large gap in the middle. Everybody seemed to know what was going in there except me. They all had little spoons and plates at the ready.

There was a rush of excitement and Ali came in with a silver tray two inches thick with crushed ice and a slag heap of caviare on top that must have snipped $5000 off the bottom of Graydon's pocket money. The company fell on it. Extremely polite knock-down-drag-out fights developed. Women appeared with their shoulder straps askew and an earring missing, but with a molehill of Beluga that could have got them two nights in the George V.

The tray was down to water by the time I got in there

so I had the swordfish carpaccio and ciabatta with a half lobster. Selina appeared on my elbow and kissed me on the ear.

'We're in,' she whispered.

Chapter 19

By the late afternoon, when the houseboys had started putting out the smoking mosquito coils, there was only the hard core left. The chief was on his third bottle of Krug, and Ben Agu and Bof Nwanu were getting on down with the willowy 'companions' who'd hijacked the sound system and were giving the Afrobeat a belt. The chief's wife was sitting in the corner of his swing sofa sleeping soundly. Franconelli was inhaling some prewar Armagnac. Gryf was still on the beer, his lack of neck curiously friendly now. The Moët-fuelled Marcella had gone for more cigarettes and Gale had taken Selina off to 'freshen up'.

I, obviously, looked fresh enough. I'd stopped drinking when I saw what the champagne had done to Marcella's mouth, so I didn't have a craggy canyon migraine. I'd even refused whisky and had opted for the Perrier with a hint of lark song. The virtue was pouring off me as I'm sure Graydon could have pulled out some golden elixir, hand-distilled by ancient crofters from water drawn at the highest point of the river Livet.

Selina and I had been offered a job. Well, the chief had given us space in his office on one of the four floors he occupied in Elephant House on Lagos Island. Ben Agu and Franconelli had independently talked things through with the chief and the chief had come to the momentous decision that although they were doing their best to sell commodities there wasn't anybody in his organization with the first idea about them. Ben Agu had told me on the quiet that this, their only foreign-currency earner, was actually losing them money. The other businesses generated niara, which was crashing through the floors and gaining momentum.

Bof and Ben were flowerpot men. They knew how to run a business but they didn't know a lot about international trade, and they were low on top-level European contacts. Napier must have fitted in like a dream. Selina and I had turned up gift-wrapped for the party. Not only did we have the London office and the African know-how, we were new faces, and not ugly ones. There's nothing an expatriate community craves more than fresh blood. They're like an isolated desert tribe who need their blood-lines strengthened with new genes.

Night fell. The wall lights came on in the garden. Franconelli and the chief talked football. The chief was still enraged at the Nigerian team being pulled by the military from the Africa Nations Cup after they got petulant over South African flak on the environmental activists' executions. Graydon stifled yawns. Gryf and I stood out of the great man's aura and talked inland waterways of Great Britain, a special interest of Gryf's.

Abruptly, the chief decided to leave. His wife, who'd been out for three hours, was instantly awake and delighted. We all shook hands and did some mock pleading. Graydon was looking dangerously bored. He eyed Gryf, and I saw some mischief flit behind his glassy pupils. He put an arm round him and they walked the chief back up to the house.

Franconelli and I were alone in the garden apart from his man who, now sitting behind the swing sofa, wore trousers that didn't ride over his lumpy ankle. This was no country for jackets so it was the only way to pack.

Franconelli twitched his eyebrows. I went over but didn't feel chummy enough to join him on the swing. I sat on a stool opposite him. He flung a hand over the back of the sofa and rubbed his stomach with the other and ruminated.

'You don't drink,' he said in a slight American accent. 'It's good. Stay sharp, right?'

I didn't want to ruin my chances of having a drink in his company again so I came clean.

'I'm off it. Malaria and alcohol don't mix.'

'There's a lot of it about this time of year,' he said, giving me a pained look which I didn't understand. 'You known Graydon long?'

Now he'd taken the tortoiseshell sun bins off, his face had lost a lot of its glamour. Around his eyes was charcoal black as if the man hadn't slept all the way through in years. There was some shrewdness there too which he probably liked to keep out of mixed company on a sunny day and there was sadness as if he felt sorry for all those wives whose husbands had gone for short walks and never returned. That was Franconelli's mix, a strange one – power and pity.

'Met him today for the first time,' I said.

'Oh, right,' he said, and gave his fingers a gimme twitch. The help put a baton in his hand and Franconelli unscrewed a Havana cigar. 'Don't smoke?' he asked,

217

and rammed a hand down his pocket for a clipper. He took a divot out of the end.

'I'm not a health freak, Mr Franconelli.'

He grunted and lit up and blew out plumes of smoke that smelled like an expensive saddle shop.

'You're different,' he said. 'You're not like these other assholes. You don't fight for the caviare, you don't do champagne, you don't chase the black tail on offer. You're not a fruit, are you?' I didn't pick up all of the last question. Was he admiring my restraint on the desserts? I thought I'd hold on the smartass reply. He shrugged away the silence. 'No, 'course you're not,' he said. 'You came with Selina. Nice-looking girl. This the first time you met Graydon . . . so how come you're here?'

'I know Gale. We were in London the same time, years ago.'

'You know Marcella too. I saw you . . .'

'Never met her before in my life.'

'She's a whore,' he said brutally. 'Big trouble. She likes black guys. Gryf should keep her in line. So you looked up Gale and she invited you?'

'That's it.'

Female laughter hopped over the wall. Franconelli leaned over to an ashtray and rested his cigar. I needed rescuing. I didn't like playing whelk to Franconelli's winkling.

'Selina's a great girl,' he said, rubbing his hands together. 'How long you and her been together?'

'How do you mean, Mr Franconelli?' I stalled.

'You work with her, right?'

'I didn't know if you were asking a personal question.'

He picked up his cigar again and took a huge drag and I suddenly had a feeling about what he was asking.

'You and Selina . . .'

'We work together,' I teased.

'That don't . . .'

'I've never been big on office love, Mr Franconelli. Bad for the concentration.'

'Right.'

The guy fancied her. Double her age and the guy wanted her. His man over the back of the swing was shaking his head as if he couldn't believe his boss was saying these things. Franconelli's head turned. Selina and Gale stumbled into the garden, arm in arm, giggling.

'Graydon said you guys were out here not dancing,' said Gale.

Franconelli sat back and set his swing going. There was a grunt from his man as he knocked him off his perch. The boss smiled. I smiled back.

'I haven't been able to dance since Louis Prima,' said Franconelli.

'Oh come on, Roberto! Highlife, juju, fuji, Afrobeat, King Sunny Ade,' she said, and gave us a pirouette, slow and full of rhythm with her arms stretched above her head.

'You got it, Gale,' he said. 'Me? I was born with lead in my feet. Can't move like these Africans can.'

'Come on, Bruce,' she said, grabbing my hand. 'Talk to him in his lingo, Selina, get him moving.'

We left the walled garden and rounded the shrubbery to the pool glowing blue in the black of the lawn. All the downstairs lights were on and the windows were shaking with sound.

'Your neighbours must love you.'

'They're inside,' she said, and pushed me in the bushes.

'Come off it, Gale.'

'Trouble,' she said. 'Look.'

Out of the French windows came Gryf holding Marcella by the hair. He threw her down the steps to the pool. She ended up on all fours, a tear in her gold sheath, screaming.

'This is too much, Gale . . .'

'Shut up, Bruce,' she said. 'It's a domestic. You wanna go play knight to the damsel, you'll wake up next Christmas with an ice bag for a brain.'

Gryf skipped down the steps and hauled Marcella up by the back of her dress, which split in two and came off. She was naked underneath. Graydon appeared at the French windows with his hands in his pockets.

'It's time to stop this shit,' I said, and barged past Gale to the pool.

'Asshole,' she whispered after me.

Gryf slapped Marcella across the buttocks. She crashed forward through the tables and chairs which slowed him down so she could get to her feet. He hit her with a back-hander across the face and she fell through more furniture.

'Gryf!' I roared, but he was hurling chairs into the pool. Marcella made it to the grass and ran down the garden. Gryf yelled at the furniture. I spun him round by his shoulder. He was sweating and smiling. There was light foam at the corners of his mouth.

'Come on, Gryf,' I said.

He took a swing at me. I ducked and he ended up

facing the pool. I jammed my hands into his kidneys, ran him forward and sent him sprinting into the water. There was a tremendous crash as the water parted and then caved in over Gryf. Tables and chairs were knocked over by the quantity of water that exited from the pool and Gryf, after some moments, burst on to the surface like a harpooned whale.

Gale was up the steps now and talking to Graydon who was shaking his head in amazement. I picked up Marcella's dress and handed it to Gale and told her she'd need some safety pins. Graydon was humming with blow.

'Christ,' he said, 'Gryf damn near emptied the god-damn pool.'

He turned, walked off down the hall and took a right, going the other way to his study to avoid the dancing in the living room.

'Gryf saw one of Graydon's videos?' I asked Gale.

'Ben and Marcella last weekend,' she said. 'You learn something if you hang around long enough. We're all silk and diamonds on the surface and blood and dirt underneath.'

'Maybe it's time to go home.'

'Sure, but you're back here tomorrow for lunch. It's all arranged with Selina. Just the four of us this time. I can't take any more of this shit. Where'd Marcella go?'

'She's off down the garden hiding from Mr Piggy.'

I went back to the walled garden to pick up Selina. Gryf was out of the pool, staggering around the lawn with several kilos of water soaked into his underpants. He was calling for Marcella, saying he was sorry, telling her it was OK for her to come out now.

Franconelli's bodyguard was standing outside the garden smoking a cigarette. I went to go past him and he put a hand in my chest.

'I like it,' he said, and slapped me on the back.

Franconelli offered us a lift. I turned it down. He insisted, said Carlo would take us. He had some business with Graydon. He called Carlo in and talked to him in a dialect that sounded like Portuguese rather than Italian. We shook hands. Selina kissed him on both cheeks.

We didn't talk on the way back to Y-Kays and went straight up to our rooms. Carlo's car didn't leave immediately so I took a squint in reception. He was dashing the girl some niara bills.

An hour later I was halfway through my second solitary whisky when I got the knock. Selina was dressed for bed – I mean sleeping, not the other. I pointed her over to the whisky and she ignored it.

'That was pretty wild,' she said.

'If you like that kind of thing.'

'How many times have I heard that us Generation Xers just don't know how to have a good time?'

'It takes a lot of experience, Selina. It might look easy, all that stuff, but there's years gone into it.'

'A generation.'

'How'd it go your side?'

'I spent some time with Franconelli, or Roberto as he likes to be called.'

'I noticed.'

'Meaning?'

'He's operating on some ancient code of chivalry . . . he asked me if it was OK to pursue you.'

222

'What the hell have you got . . . ?'

'He thought we were an item. Didn't want to tread on my sensitive parts. I was relieved. I thought he wanted to know how long we'd been working together. We never covered all that stuff. How long is it?'

'Don't ask me.'

'He also sent Carlo with us to check out we were in separate rooms. I've just seen him dashing the girl downstairs.'

'Jesus. These people,' she said. 'That's what it was like with my ex. You don't marry the man, you marry the whole family and everyone's got an opinion. The women twitter in back rooms about underwear and sauces while the guys sit in the front room and talk about whacking people out.'

'Even fashion designers?'

'They're the worst. They don't car-bomb you. They just terminate careers, pull out the plug on companies. Fuck people over. That's why that anti-corruption purge, Operation Clean Hands, was so successful. They were falling over themselves to rat on each other.'

'OK, calm down. Have a drink, for God's sake. Tell me how you worked it with Franconelli.'

'Like all women do, Bruce. I listened to him, I flattered him, I hung on his every word. He might look like a tough guy but he's vulnerable, which is why he plays it close and keeps it clean and likes others to keep it clean. Nothing excessive. He liked you, said you knew how to behave.'

'Did he talk about Graydon and the chief?'

'Only in passing. We were talking more personally.'

'How's he vulnerable?'

'His wife died four years ago, and then only just last year his daughter.'

'Out here?'

'The daughter got malaria which went cerebral and she didn't pull out of it. The wife died in a head-on collision with a truck.'

'Happens all the time. They're crazy bastards on the roads. How old was the daughter?'

'Franconelli did that all the time. Talked about one thing and then asked a question about something totally different.'

'It's catching.'

'She was twenty-five. Same age as his wife when he married her.'

'Same age as . . .'

'We know.'

'You going to see him?'

'I'm invited to dinner tomorrow night.'

'He didn't invite me.'

'He likes you but not that much.'

Chapter 20

Lagos. Monday 26th February.

Over breakfast I told Selina about the connection between the containers shipped out on the *Paphos Star* containing toxic waste and the two haulage companies Seriki Haulage and Awaya Transportation. I linked in the sweet-natured welcome I received at the former with the information from Companies House about the two managing directors Ben Agu and Bof Nwanu. I mentioned their relationship to Chief Babba Seko. I asked her about Quarshie and drew a blank. I gave her Quarshie's lesson in Nigerian politics. She got very excited. I cemented the story in by telling her that Bagado's investigation had shown that Quarshie's car was used to abduct Napier and that Bondougou, who'd masterminded the trashing of Bagado's career, was now effectively blocking any communication between Cotonou and Lagos.

'Chief Babba Seko killed my father.'

'It *looks* like it. There are some links, like the toxic waste, but they aren't direct. Babba Seko doesn't *own* those haulage companies. We don't *know* the owner of the land in Western Nigeria where the waste was dumped. Your father was a pal of Quarshie's, but does Quarshie *know* Babba Seko?'

'Well, I'm there. Agu and Nwanu are close enough to the chief to *be* him.'

'We'll do some work for the chief, we'll get into his business, his office and then we'll find the link.'

'And then we'll sting him.'

'Sting him?'

'The police aren't going to do anything about it so we will,' she said. 'I don't kill people, and I don't think you do either. So we'll do the next best thing. Whack them in the bank balance.'

'Hold on a minute,' I said. 'I don't remember that bit of my contract.'

'There's got to be retribution, Bruce.'

'I don't remember you saying that I was going to be involved in handing it out.'

'I smell milk.'

'Burning?'

'No. You. Skimmed milk. Virtually not milk at all.'

'Come on, Selina. I've got to live here. You get your justice and fly away. I *live* in Cotonou ... and there's Heike to think about too.'

Silence.

'Maybe there's a way of stinging him *and* serving him up,' she said.

'I'm listening.'

'I don't know it yet. I don't know who I'm dealing with. I mean, I've got a good idea but I'd like to get a bit closer ... Could we get a newspaper to take the story? Find a rag supporting another candidate ...'

'Army. The army was out on the toxic-waste site. Bagado reckons the labourers were lifers. Nobody would touch it.'

'Unless they weren't actually army.'

'How long's it going to take you to prove that?'

'OK, we just don't tell them about the army.'

'Do you know how many newspaper editors are in prison? This is the "climate of fear" you've always heard about and never been in. They're not going to print it just because you're white. Go take a look at Kirikiri Prison. From the outside, that's all you need. It's a big stinking rat trap of a deterrent. It's not Ford Open Prison with newspapers, afternoon tea and racing on the telly. They'll check you and your story out.'

'Ideas, Bruce. I'm trying to save your ass, remember.'

'Let's nail him down first, then you can smother him in honey and leave him for the ants.'

I was glad I hadn't shown my real talent at the party. We came out of Y-Kays and it was as if the day had taken both barrels of a shotgun in the chest. The air was dead and heavier than a corpse. We took a taxi which nudged its way forward on bald tyres and made my feet feel sore. We crossed Five Cowrie Creek and Selina saw her first body. Obscene and bloated, it bobbed like a tractor-tyre inner tube in the harbour. People stopped on the bridge to look.

We joined the Lagos Island traffic jam and didn't move for an hour. The pollution doubled. The sluggish heart of the city, this diseased muscle fed by furred and hardened arteries thick with lead-poisoned blood, stopped.

We paid the cabbie and walked to Elephant House. The lifts were working but there was a crowd waiting for them with the desperation of account holders in a banking crash. We went up to the sixth floor in a silence crammed with human desolation, the unspoken mantra singing in their heads 'We are the lucky ones, we are the chosen.'

Ben Agu met us and took us through some brown doors and dark passageways to his office, which was as cold and dank as a leaking mausoleum. A curling Maerskline calendar hung on one wall and another from AMObank behind Ben's head. The window was covered with a piece of orange material which had been used as a field dressing. A fly, suffering from whatever's terminal for flies, buzzed, lost height dramatically and ditched into a cup of pens where it buzzed throatily on and off for a couple of minutes.

The chief had not arrived. Ben offered coffee. We accepted. He tried to show us that his intercom was working. It wasn't. He left.

'A man could die in here,' I said.

'And they wouldn't know for a week.'

'Not by the smell, anyway.'

'Are we sure we want this coffee?'

'If it means we're jet-ambulanced out of here.'

I looked at the *Daily Times* which was open on Ben's desk at the funeral pages. When people die in West Africa the family put a notice in the newspaper with a photograph of the deceased. Staring out from the centre of the page with a forlorn expression on his face was Emmanuel Quarshie. There was no mention of the cause of death. I flicked back through the pages to the local news section and saw the headline – 'Engineer found dead at home'. A quick scan revealed that Emmanuel Quarshie had died of a gunshot wound to the head – suicide, it was thought.

Ben came back to say that the big man had arrived. I thought I'd heard a fanfare from the air-con duct. We went up to the next floor. The chief's office was about eight of Ben's in one. The white carpet was so thick it had had to be snipped to get the door open. The chief, in white robes at his desk, looked like a snowbound polar bear. He had heavy specs on, stretched wide by his fat head. He spoke on the phone, holding the piece between finger and thumb as if he was listening to a good cigar.

We took the two seats available, which were comfortable but low, and I looked at a photo of the Nigerian national football team up on the wall. Ben stood at a respectful distance. The chief finished his call in his own good time.

'My friends,' he said, 'you are welcome.'

The girl came in with the coffee. The chief took the Manchester United mug and crashed back into his chair. Selina had Norwich City while I toyed with Blackburn Rovers.

'Cantona!' roared the chief, sipping his coffee. I looked at Ben, assuming this was a Yoruba exhortation to get on with it. 'Eric Cantona!' said the chief.

'A great player,' I said.

'No, no,' said the chief, wagging a huge finger, 'a visionary.' He looked at Ben. 'Is this Nescafé?'

Ben glanced at the girl, who'd just made it to the door. She nodded.

'Yes, sir.'

'If I find this is Red Mountain, heads will ro-o-oll.' He roared with laughter.

'I think coffee would be a good thing to get into,' said Selina, taking up the torch.

'Coffee?' asked the chief.

'Robusta coffee. It's cheap on the London market at the moment. Too cheap for most people to start buying out here. What do you think you could deliver that for in Lagos?'

'Coffee? Cheap?' asked the chief. 'Have you ever noticed, Miss Aguia, that no matter how cheap the coffee price in Africa, Nescafé never goes down?'

'Well, sir, the beans represent less than ten per cent of the retail price and robusta a fraction of that.'

'Quite so,' said the chief. 'A travesty. The people of my country break their backs planting and nurturing and harvesting for a pittance so that multinationals can make a fortune from advertising, marketing, packaging, labelling, wholesaling and retailing.'

'And there's the speculator's cut too, which is what we're here to discuss.'

'How much would that be?' he asked, pouncing with both paws on to the desk.

'Last year the robusta market gave as much as one thousand eight hundred dollars a ton clear. I don't think it will get that high again, but maybe one thousand three hundred dollars is attainable.'

'But . . .'

'There's transport to . . .'

'We have our *own* haulage companies, our *own* agents,' said the chief.

'Well, if the market moves there could be a gain of around one thousand four hundred dollars a ton.'

'Then we should buy a hundred thousand tons at once,' said the chief.

That was about three times the total world robusta

230

crop so I left Ben to answer that one and drank coffee. Selina's mouth remained open for some time.

We talked like that for about half an hour, throwing figures around, discussing the merits of cocoa versus sheanut, how palm oil was coming along, what would happen to cotton this year. Then I said:

'Have you ever considered rice?'

'Rice?' roared the chief, who had taken to standing at the window looking out over the lagoon with his fists in his kidneys. 'We don't grow enough rice as it is.'

'I mean *importing* rice.'

'But there's a ban on imports, Mr Medway.'

'Of course there is. But not into Benin . . .'

'Tell me about rice going into Benin,' said the chief.

'You open up a Letter of Credit for say fifteen thousand tons of parboiled rice in the Bank of Africa in Cotonou. You don't have to put up too much cash because rice is as good as money. The bank regards its own Letter of Credit as security. As soon as the ship is loaded in, say, Thailand, and has left with an arrival date in Cotonou you send buyers to the bank to deposit money against the lots they want to buy. By the time the ship arrives, about a month later, all the rice is sold. Some buyers turn up at the ship's side with trucks, others you warehouse it for them in the port.'

'How do we access the buyers?' asked Ben.

'Through agents in Cotonou. There are three agents with the whole business sewn up. You have to do a deal with them.'

'What's the money?'

'The difference between the landed cost and the retail price in Cotonou is about four hundred per ton.'

'But here,' said Ben, 'because of the ban, the retail price is much higher.'

'I think perhaps you've seen the potential.'

'But here,' said the chief airily, turning away from the view, 'as you so rightly say, Ben, there is a ban.'

'Which is why there's a premium,' said Ben.

'Which is why the future president of the Federal Republic of Nigeria cannot be seen to be smuggling, cannot be seen to be profiting from putting food into the mouths of the common people.'

'Yes, sir,' said Ben.

The chief turned back to the lagoon and straightened his hat, which didn't need straightening. I could hear his brain working like a barrel calculator. Duty, plus transport, plus bribes, plus Nigerian customs, plus warehousing, equals ... well, I knew what it equalled. I'd done the deal in my head a thousand times before. Even selling on to a wholsesaler there was at least $200 per ton in it. Over 15,000 tons, that was looking very like $3,000,000. From rice? How could that be right?

But it was. The problems were finding a supplier, getting in with the bank and hitting the right deal with the agent. Three things that were impossible for me, but for someone with the chief's connections ... I remembered the AMO-bank calendar in Ben's office.

'You could open a Letter of Credit with AMObank,' I said. 'They're Nigerian, aren't they? And they have an office in Cotonou.'

The chief's ear was tuned to me. He flapped his palms on his backside. As soon as we were out of the room he was going to be on that phone, snapping and snarling down it like a hyena.

'You'll have to excuse us,' I said. 'Selina and I are having lunch with Graydon. Should we call later?'

'No, no. Yes. All right. Very good. Yes, yes. You must go. Mustn't keep Graydon waiting. Send him my regards. Thank you.'

Chapter 21

'Rice,' said Selina, looking at the traffic and annoying the driver by flicking the door lock up and down.

'It just hit me in the meeting.'

'Oh yeah?'

'We were thinking about export not import. It was a lateral hop.'

'You sounded as if you knew what you were on about, sounded as if you'd done some thinking, sounded as if this wasn't the first time . . .'

'Hey, Selina, back off. You're not the only one who's allowed ideas. I happen to have an office opposite a warehouse where once a month about five hundred tons of rice comes in and five hundred tons goes out. I'm curious. I'm not always crowded out with things to do. I go down to a friend of mine at an agent's in Cotonou and ask him about rice. He tells me how I can make three million dollars if I know the right people. He tells me because there's the outside chance that I'll bring him somebody who can help him do the deal. He tells me . . .'

Selina leaned over and shut me up with her lips on mine. She thrust her tongue in between my teeth, held my head and worked me over good.

'Now shut up,' she said. 'You're boring the shit out of me.'

'Why did you have to go and do that?'

'Kiss you, you mean?' she asked, and my eyes connected with the driver's in the rearview.

'If that's what it was?'

'Yeah,' she said. 'A bit of a snog.'

'More like a buccal sap.'

'Romantic.'

'Dental.'

'Why don't we, you know,' she said, putting her hand on my knee, 'just for fun. You don't have to tell Heike. I won't.'

'Just keep taking the pills and you'll calm down.'

'Fuck you.'

The driver's eyebrows went over a speed bump.

'Why doesn't anything ever happen here?' she asked.

'Waiting's the game in Africa.'

'I don't mind waiting if there's something to do.'

'Work on Franconelli,' I said. 'He knows things. He likes you. He wants to fit you in.'

'Between his sheets.'

'Not interested?'

'He's not the type to let a girl go on top.'

'What about Graydon?'

She shot me a look which made the driver duck.

'Graydon doesn't do anything ... not with other people, anyway.'

'Is that what Gale said?'

'He's a spectator. Doesn't like to get his knees dirty.'

'And Gale?'

'Don't be sneaky, Bruce, it doesn't suit you.'

'Nobody tells me anything. I have to find it all out for myself.'

'That's your job.'

'And what are you? My sleeping . . . client?'

'I knew you wouldn't say "partner". You're such a tease.'

The traffic eased up as we got on to Vic Island and the driver stunned himself by getting into second. Selina put her face on, which in the light breeze didn't slip straight off. The cab dropped us off and because Gale knew the day was dead on its feet there was a Nissan Patrol waiting to take us up the drive.

'Did Robert Keshi, that NNPC guy, say anything to you?'

'No,' she said, taking hold of my arm as she got out of the car.

'He's an oil man. Your father knew him.'

'I know.'

'Did your father know a lot about oil?'

She stopped and we faced off.

'Are you a brilliant actor or just very dumb?'

'I like asking obvious questions.'

'My father was a shipbroker specializing in chems, gas, clean and dirty. Less than fifteen per cent of his business was chems and gas. The rest was putting crude into Northern Europe and shipping clean out of the refineries.'

'So it's all about oil?'

'God, Bruce.'

'Well, your father was a bit of an actor too.'

'After Blair my father never let anyone near his business. Not even me.'

'You learnt from him.'

'Let me ask you a question,' she said. 'Why do you think the chief has asked us to work for him?'

'Make him some money. He's got an expensive patch coming up.'

'You don't think Graydon and Franconelli could solve that problem. You don't think that what they've got going together is enough to keep the chief in Krug?'

'I don't know whether the word "enough" is part of Babba Seko's vocab. In the oil-boom years when Bonny Light hit thirty-five dollars a barrel the president instigated a "clean hands" operation. They found people with ten *billion* dollars in their foreign accounts. Do you think they knew how much "enough" was?'

'I think you ought to look at this as a bit of a game, Bruce. A game with three major pieces in it and a couple of little guys. Guess who we are?'

'Let's have some lunch.'

Ali met us at the door and led us down the hall to the living room with the cream leather sofas. The house was closed off to the outside world and the air con was wintery. Sitting on the sofa was like reclining on a dead man. Ali took the drinks order. We sat in silence. The time ached past. The art on the wall did little to fill the mind. A huge white canvas with an off-white square, off centre, off the wall.

Graydon came in with a cashmere cardigan on over his polo shirt. His shoes squeaked on the tiles and annoyed him. He slumped in a sofa, rubbing his fingers and thumbs together and seemed to take aim at something over Selina's shoulder.

'Central air con,' he said. 'There's nothing we can do about it. Gale'll bring you some clothes. How did it go with the chief?'

'He listened to what we had to say,' said Selina.

'Amazing,' he said, hitching a trouser. 'You must have been talking about soccer.'

'Eric Cantona featured,' I said. Graydon glazed.

'Ben there?' he asked.

'Yes.'

'That's O K. He does the detail. Ali!' he roared. 'Perrier and nuts.'

'Do you have any contacts in India or Thailand who could supply . . .'

'Opium?'

We laughed nervously. Graydon didn't.

'You know how it is, Graydon. Powerful people can lay their hands on almost anything in these countries.'

'I've never been in India and I'm out of Thailand now. Try Franconelli, he's strong out there.'

'What about the States?' I asked.

'For what?'

'Rice. Parboiled.'

'Too expensive.'

'Could you get a price for us out of the US Gulf or East Coast?'

Gale came in wearing a baggy white polo-neck. She threw us some jumpers. Lunch was served. We never got our drinks. We sat down to a chef's hat of crab soufflé, a rhombus of salmon in nectar, a cylinder of chateaubriand in mustard with a tower of julienned vegetables, an ingot of chocolate in what has to be called a *jus* or a *coulis* or you're dead. We drank Puligny Montrachet with the fish, Chateau Batailley with the meat and a Setubal with the sweet. Gale ate a corner off each dish and drank most of the Puligny Montrachet.

Graydon didn't even touch the first three courses but ate three plates of chocolate. We talked about the sperm count of the Western male.

'What's the point in outproducing when you can be out-reproduced in a few generations?' said Gale. 'We're the suckers. The Africans are playing the long game.'

'And the Chinese?' asked Graydon.

'No women,' said Selina.

'Takes two to tango, Gray,' tinkled Gale, which iced his Perrier over.

'Plastics,' said Graydon.

'Oestrogen in the plastics,' said Gale. 'We'll be a world of women, hermaphrodites and homosexuals.'

'Well, it'll make great TV,' said Graydon. 'Shall we go to my office?'

Graydon left, Gale waved us out after him. We followed him into his carefully lit study, whose only natural light came from a single skylight high in the roof. A cabinet containing a collection of videos was open and Graydon slid it shut as he walked to his desk. He indicated that we should sit at a circular table away from the desk. Graydon picked up a newspaper off his desk and threw it in the bin. He sat and remained silent for some time. The gallery lighting in the room pointed up a singular cracked terracotta hand, an alabaster sandalled foot snapped off at the ankle, a set of marble genitals, and a hand, forearm and elbow emerging from a block of stone. The broken, the maimed and the incomplete. What did this say about Graydon's psyche?

'Excuse me a moment,' said Graydon, and he got up and left the room.

'Gray's not with it,' said Selina.

'Hasn't had his toot yet. He'll be back,' I said. 'Just listen at the door a minute.'

I opened up the video cabinet. Good old anally retentive Graydon had them in alphabetical order. Each video was initialled. I picked out the only D. B., thinking of David. There was no N. B. for Napier which was interesting. I put the video in Selina's handbag and retrieved the newspaper from the bin. I found it open at the same funeral page as Ben Agu's – sad old Quarshie. Selina clicked her fingers. I flicked through the newspaper. Graydon swept back in. Selina was inspecting the genitalia.

'Whose lunch is this?'

Graydon roared.

'Lunch!? Oh, yeah,' he said. 'That was sold to me as a piece of a destroyed statue of Paris from Troy.'

'No kidding.'

'Well, maybe. It's all stolen and sold on. Shall we?' he asked, looking at me standing by his desk with his newspaper.

'This guy Quarshie,' I said, 'I've heard his name somewhere. Wasn't he at your party on Sunday?'

'He was supposed to be. Goddam tragedy. The guy shot himself Friday morning.'

'Oh, right. He was an engineer, wasn't he?'

'Yeah, he did some plans for me for a floating jetty off the coast at Port Harcourt.'

I dropped the newspaper back into the bin and we all sat down at the circular table. In five minutes Graydon outlined a deal where Selina's company would buy 120,000 tons of Nigerian crude from a company based in the Caymans called Neruda. The interesting difference was that, although her company would take title to the product as soon as it was on board a ship she could charter herself, she wouldn't actually have to pay for it until it was delivered in Europe. She would take a commission on the shipping and she was guaranteed a minimum of fifty cents per ton on the oil. Graydon was giving her the opportunity to become an oil trader without putting up any money.

'There are some obvious questions, Graydon.'

'Well,' he said, 'I don't want to do the work myself. I don't want to pay tax. I don't want the market to know what I'm doing. I want an established London-based business to do it. You're not in the oil business which gives me confidentiality, but you are in commodities which means you're not a schmuck.'

'But why me, us?'

'In business it's possible to be scientific, with people it isn't. I go for a feeling, an instinct. How can I ever know someone well enough to let them into my world? I can't. They can bullshit me with professionalism, they can slap me with their education, they can stun me with their CV. I could run psychological tests and get a murderer. I could pay a consultant and he'd select the square pin for the asshole. I feel good about you. I'm giving you a single opportunity to see if you fit. If you do, we're richer. If you don't, it's only one deal and how many of them are there in a day?'

'You're offering me . . .'

'I know what I'm offering you,' he said. 'But don't snatch. Think about it.'

The phone went. Graydon flopped behind his desk and picked it up.

241

'Hi, José, hold the line a moment,' he said, and looked up. 'That's all, folks. Gale'll see you out.'

Gale was in the living room with some coffee on the go and an ashtray full of butts at her side. She flicked violently through *Hello!* magazine as if she was hoping to come across herself.

'Where'd they get all these assholes?' she asked.

'It depresses me,' said Selina, looking over her shoulder, 'but I can't resist seeing how they look. It's like porn.'

'Yeah,' said Gale. 'Fascinating *and* boring. How'd they come up with a formula like that?'

'Hair salons,' said Selina.

'How'd it go with Gray?' asked Gale.

'He made us an offer. We're thinking about it.'

'Nobody ever lost money on Gray's back,' she said. 'Except me.'

We walked out to the car. The heat fell on us like a rapist, its hot tongue in every crevice.

'You know,' said Gale, 'the first time Napier turned up here Gray offered him a deal.'

'Oh yeah,' I said. 'Who introduced him?'

'That foreign office guy. The one I reckon's a fruit. David. David Bartholomew.'

'Well, maybe he has a weakness for blondes,' I said.

'Then why didn't I get anything?' she asked.

Chapter 22

We watched a clip of the D. B. video in the owner's apartment at Y-Kays. Selina sat with her legs crossed and foot nodding while I talked the owner out of hanging in there with us for the show. I fast-forwarded the tape for a minute. She tapped her cheek with her finger, waiting, impatient. I hit play.

'Ooo, that looks painful,' she said.

David was trussed up on the bed, his left wrist tied to his right ankle and the right wrist to the left ankle. From the tangle of limbs another rope ran up to a choker around his neck so that every time he moved he cut the air flow to his windpipe. David's penis had been stretched tight and taped to a point just below his sternum. Ali was lying on the bed naked, stroking his large erection a few inches from David's face. David attempted to inch forward. Ali judged him too close and gave him a savage little kick in the testicles which sent David off into a paroxysm of strangulated pain. I stopped it. Selina was disappointed. I packed the video away and went to call David about his diplomatic bag.

In the evening a car picked Selina up and took her to Franconelli's for dinner. I took a taxi to the Peninsula restaurant, where I'd arranged to meet David. I'd expected it to be cooler after dark and sitting out seemed better than chilling off in the air con, but if anything it seemed hotter, closer, more airless and the fans weren't cutting it either. David and I drank lots of cold beer and worked our way through table napkins and excellent Chinese food.

'Is this the first time you've taken me out to dinner?'

'It's only because I need to soften you up.'

'I knew it wasn't out of deeply felt friendship.'

'Wrong, David. You've been in the FO too long.'

'I've gone all gooey inside, Bruce.'

'Sweet and sour?' I asked, and passed him the plate.

'Mmmm,' he said, giving me a penetrating stare. 'You're worrying me.'

'How much?'

'Generally . . .'

'Let's talk personally.'

'I've never been one to let things get on top of me. Perhaps that's been my mistake . . . you know, being queer,' he said, grinning.

'I don't need everything spelled out for me, David,' I said. 'Jesus, what happened to all that elegant scholarship?'

'You want some Plautus? I'll give you some.'

'Yeah, well, translate for me, my Latin's shot to hell.'

'But the Latin's so perfect, so sweet and tight, so economic with everything except the truth – *Homo homini lupus* – you see? A man's a wolf to another man . . .'

'Thanks for that.'

'. . . until he finds out what he's like,' he finished flatly, and socked back his beer.

'You're calling *me* a wolf. Since when have I known what you're like?'

'I've told you I'm queer.'

'What's sexuality?'

'Something to make you hide if you're me.'

'I've never used or held that against you. I wouldn't call that lupine, would you?'

'We'll see,' he said. 'So, what are you softening me up for?'

'I'm preparing myself to trust you.'

'Do you think you would have got in this far without my trust?'

'Got in this far to what?'

'Napier, Graydon, Gale, the chief.'

I looked at him for some time. His face didn't move. His eyes remained fixed on mine.

'Do you?' he asked again. 'One word from me and you're gone.'

The sweet and sour congealed in the silence that followed. I drank beer for support, my bombshell looking squibby now amongst the destroyed Chinese food.

'The last time we met, I followed you into the Brazilian Quarter to the Gaiety Bar.'

'You surprise me, Bruce.'

'The next day I met Gale and got a closer look at Ali.'

'He's got something, don't you think?'

'If you like a little brutality.'

'You never went to public school. You don't understand the nature of punishment,' he said. 'So what now? Are you building up to a little blackmail?'

'A little help. I give you some, you return the gesture.'

'Ask me.'

'Why did you pass Napier on to me?'

David picked up a prawn which had been puffy with tempura but had collapsed in the heat. He bit it off at

245

the tail, which he flicked out over Five Cowrie Creek.

'Napier and I were friends.'

'Like we're friends?'

'Ah, well,' said David, laughing. 'Maybe better. We saw more of each other, you know, spoke on the phone and such.'

'Yes, Gale said you introduced him to Graydon. Any reason why you made out you didn't know him?'

'I thought it would be easier for you that way. I thought it would keep you on the outside, which is the safest place to be. You've been more persistent than I expected.'

'Why was it friendly of you to pass Napier on to me?'

'Get him out of here. He was getting "troublesome", as the Nigerians say.'

'Over the toxic waste?'

'An accumulation of guilt, I think. He was being threatening, which is not a good idea in Africa.'

'Threatening the chief and his political ambitions?'

'Yes,' said David, concentrating on his food.

'So how did you get him to come and see me, and why?'

'I negotiated a way out for him. That he would be allowed to leave the country . . . quickly. The waste would be moved to a different site. And a sum of money would be paid to him. I told him to go and see you with some cock-and-bull story and enlist your services. He said you were not very cooperative. Too inquisitive. And the black fellow . . .'

'Who did you negotiate with?'

'You won't know him.'

'Try me.'

246

'Emmanuel Quarshie.'

'And who's he?'

'You see?'

'Just tell me.'

'He was someone acceptable to both parties.'

'The chief and Napier? Graydon and Napier? Maybe even Franconelli?'

David didn't answer. His brain was ticking over faster than mine had ever done. I prompted him again and he gave me a dazed look, the thinking not quite done.

'You're a man of some sartorial elegance, David,' I said, which grabbed his attention. 'Did I tell you the story about that tailor up in Niger? The pinstripe man?'

He shook his head.

'A friend of mine went to him. Got the best suits made for him since Savile Row went up in price. The man was gifted so my friend bought his material in the UK and had him run things up in Niamey. He brought him some pinstripe one time and when the tailor called him to say the suit was ready he said he'd even got a half metre left over. My friend was surprised and went over there and as soon as he walked in the room he knew he was looking at one of the best pieces of couture he'd ever seen. The cut was immaculate, the styling superlative and the workmanship was outstanding but . . . the suit was unwearable.'

'The half metre left over,' said David. 'Too small or what?'

'The pinstripe was horizontal. The tailor had never seen pinstripe before.'

David howled.

'The only thing it was good for was for writing music on.'

David roared.

'That's what your story's like, David. Immaculate cut, horizontal pinstripe.'

David shut up.

'Did you speak to Napier on the night he died, David?'

'In the afternoon he called . . .'

'At night.'

The traffic roared across Five Cowrie Creek. David took one of his white menthols and lit it with a gold lighter. He sat sideways to the table and crossed his legs, a suede brogue twitching at an empty table.

'No,' he said, and I didn't believe him.

'What's Quarshie to the chief?' I asked, wanting him off balance.

'Family. Don't ask me what . . . but that's it.'

'Was that the best intermediary for Napier?'

'He trusted him. It was nothing to do with me.'

'Quarshie's car picked him up the night he died in Cotonou.'

'Maybe that's why Quarshie shot himself,' said David, taking a long blistering drag from his mint fag. 'You're trickier than you look, Bruce. How do you know Quarshie?'

'Maybe it's time for you to ask me what I've got for you.'

'I can't think that you could have anything to help my situation.'

'Because you're in control of the information and I know nothing?' I asked. David smirked. 'What *is* your situation?'

'Your turn to talk,' said David.

'What do you think of Graydon?'

'He's high most of the time.'

'You think that makes him a little weird?'

'His wealth makes him weird.'

'You know he has a security system?'

'Who doesn't?'

'He's even extended the system to the bedrooms, David. The guest bedrooms . . . are monitored.'

David dumped his unfinished cigarette in the ashtray, uncrossed his legs wildly, clipping the table hard with his knee and set off at a run into the restaurant. He fled into the Gents. I ordered whisky for two and looked at the lights dancing on the water.

David flopped back into his chair. The sweat stood out in gobs on his pale face as if he'd had a rush of malaria. He knocked back the whisky and told the waiter to bring the bottle. He mopped himself with gathered napkins. I asked him if he was OK.

'Yes, yes,' he said. 'I don't often get a bowel movement so when one comes along I take it.'

'I have the video,' I said, quietly. He closed his eyes.

'Have you watched it?'

'Just twenty seconds or so to make sure it wasn't one of you playing with a plastic elephant in a foam bath.'

He laughed but it came out as a sob.

'Does that help your situation?'

'It relieves something I didn't know about, so not really.'

'Drop this Ali guy.'

'I can't.'

'It's not like it's heroin, David.'

'But it's bloody exciting, Bruce. I can't tell you . . .'

'Keep it like that,' I said. 'Have you finished with that chicken and cashew?'

'Oh, for God's sake,' he said, and waved the plate at me.

'I don't know about you, David, but I reckon that video's worth more than horizontal pinstripe,' I said. 'So tell me about your friendship with Napier. What did you talk about?'

'He told me that his wife had run off with his partner. Blair somebody. I didn't really listen that much.'

'Does he have any children?'

'He said he didn't.'

'Known him long?'

'Three years.'

'You talk about oil?'

'Oil and shipping.'

'Did you give him information?'

David nodded.

'You're drying up, David. More whisky?'

'I gave him information on contracts for building projects. Floating jetties for oil tankers. Natural gas liquefying and storage plants. Boring stuff like that.'

'You were handling other companies' contracts?'

'I knew everything that was going on.'

'So you became good friends,' I said. 'Did you know of any oil scams that Graydon was pulling with Napier?'

'Should I?'

'You knew about the toxic waste.'

'Only because Napier didn't like it.'

'What trouble did he cause?'

'He said he'd talk.'

'And then there'd be no "Hail to the chief"?'

'Quite.'

'And the money? He said he'd been four-one-nined out of two mil.'

'I don't know everything. I do know that he was obsessed with getting ten million dollars together. That was his idea of a nest egg. I negotiated two-point-seven million dollars for him through Quarshie.'

'Did he rip off his own company?'

'How's that pinstripe looking now?' asked David, getting desperate.

'Not quite wearable yet.'

'Where's the video?'

'In my room,' I said. 'But I have great need of your silence, David. So it stays with me for the moment.'

'Well, I'd call that lupine, Bruce.'

'I'd call it "not stupid", which is a change for me.'

The waiter cleared our plates. We hammered the whisky bottle. David smoked hard.

'What do you know about Franconelli?' I asked.

'I've met him at Graydon's.'

'What's his game? Toot and smack, as Gale says?'

'I don't think so,' he said. 'He likes real business.'

'Oil and construction?'

'The Italians don't do badly in Nigeria.'

'They have an innate understanding of the system.'

'Exactly.'

'Did Franconelli know where Napier was getting his information from?'

'You pretend to be slow . . .'

'Do I?'

'. . . but you're not. Napier didn't tell Franconelli about me.'

David gnawed on a toothpick to give himself more to do.

'What do you do for Graydon?' I asked.

'Nothing.'

'How does he use your weakness for Ali?'

'He hasn't . . . yet.'

'That's right. You said. So why were you giving Napier any information at all?'

'You *are* slow.'

'You just said I wasn't.'

'I thought you'd got there a long time ago and you were playing coy.'

'You and Napier . . .' I said.

'That's right,' nodded David. 'We were lovers.'

'He was staying with you before he came over to Benin?'

David nodded.

'Is that why his wife ran off with Blair?'

'Not because of me. He'd had others before.'

'And what about you and Ali?'

'I don't expect you to understand queers . . . gay relationships. Total fidelity isn't always a requirement. Or rather, we're faithful but we recognize that we have certain needs to be satisfied and give our partners freedom to do so.'

I poured more whisky and asked for the bill.

'Do you think that Franconelli knew about the problem between Napier and the chief?'

'I'd have thought so. But there's a game between those three – Graydon, the chief and Franconelli – that doesn't allow for the free flow of information. You know it's not uncommon in partnerships of three powerful people that one wants to be on top. Personally, I think Napier was important to Franconelli and he wouldn't want to lose him. The chief saw him as a threat and did.'

'And Graydon?'

'Who knows. Graydon's motives are money and mischief.'

The bill arrived. It was so big in niara I paid for it in CFA.

'You won't find out anything looking from the outside,' said David.

'But I'm getting to be on the inside now,' I said. 'You must be very upset about Napier's death.'

'There's not a lot I can do about it, and that's been the story of my life.'

David drove me back to Y-Kays. We didn't talk. He had the radio on. That charming voice was telling us how good things really were underneath it all.

Chapter 23

By midnight I was having a rare shopping dream in which I was getting everything I wanted and had the money to pay for it. I came out of it into the humming, frigid darkness and a knocking that wasn't the ancient air con. I turned a light on, stumbled to the door in a T-shirt and underpants and unlocked it. Selina was leaning on the door jamb, smelling of perfume, liquor and Franconelli's cigars. I held on to the top of the door and closed my eyes. I was suddenly very wide awake as a cool hand slid into my underpants and gripped my penis. I grabbed her wrist, her sculler's wrist and she tightened her grip.

'I'll yank it off,' she said, her face close now, her lips nearly at my chin, her lipstick-and-cigarette breath mingling with mine. She smiled and planted a kiss.

'Let go, Selina.'

She kissed me again and moved her hand up and down firmly so that I hardened. I let go of her wrist. She relaxed slightly. I pinched her hard on the underside of her arm. She squealed and let me go. I reeled backwards.

'You little bugger!' she said, and kicked the door shut with her foot. She threw her handbag down and stepped out of her shoes. We faced off like a couple of wrestlers. She darted in at me. I grabbed her wrists and swung her round so that she landed on her back on the bed.

'So masterful,' she said.

'Just stop it, Selina,' I said. 'Just fucking stop it!'

'Jesus,' she said, propping herself up, 'that's the first time I've heard you say "fuck".'

I pulled on a pair of jeans, sat on the end of the other bed and ran my hand through my hair.

'I guess that means you really don't want to do it,' she said.

'That's what it means.'

'It was only meant to be a bit of fun,' she said, 'and I can tell you, that's been pretty thin on the ground this evening.'

She found her handbag and shoes, lit a cigarette and sat down in front of the whisky bottle and two glasses.

'In the absence of a decent fuck I suppose I'll have to settle for a drink.'

'Didn't Franconelli come through?'

'Not on the first date, Bruce. What do you take me for?'

'I've no idea.'

'Not with Franconelli,' she sneered. 'The guy'd think I was a whore. You've got to tickle these Eyeties like trout in a fast stream. You can't just go in there and grab.'

'Unlike . . .'

'You're not *married*, Bruce. It was only a bit of fun. I had a hard time with Roberto and I was a bit . . . fruss.'

'Pour the drinks.'

She splashed it into the glasses and handed one over.

'I could tell you were enjoying it,' she said.

'I like sex, Selina. You're an attractive woman. But

I've messed around before, so many times before, it's amazing how long it takes to learn the lesson. Sleeping around does my head in. So I don't do it any more.'

'You love Heike?'

'Yes.'

'You should tell her.'

'How do you know I haven't?'

She shrugged and sipped her drink with her little finger raised.

'Well, I thought you were fair game,' she said, wiggling her pinky at me. 'But if you've got a ring on your finger . . .'

'Heike tell you I was fair game?'

Silence, the rasp of a match, smoke folded into the draught from the air con.

'She told me about her "affairs".'

'Was that a plural?'

She nodded, cocky now.

'While she was with me?' I asked.

'There was Wolfgang,' she said, holding up her hand and counting off the fingers. 'The one she worked with in Porto Novo.'

'That's one.'

She laughed dirtily and looked up in the air for inspiration and counted through to her fourth finger, irritating the hell out of me.

'I made a mistake,' she said. 'It was "affair" singular.'

'Pour yourself another drink. You're going to need it.'

I was raw now, livid and I wanted to hurt. She looked anxious.

'Why was it you said your mother left your old man?'

'*Calmez-vous*, Bruce,' she said, getting desperate, 'that's "chill out" in baby boomer.'

'Something about her promiscuity, wasn't it? Your father not giving a damn, being weak.'

'He just let her run around . . .'

'It was because he was queer, Selina.'

'Queer? I think gay is the term you're reaching for, Bruce. We say "gay" in the nineties.'

'Not any more, Ms PC. The preferred term is "queer". More manly, less trite.'

'Whatever.'

'She came back and found him banging a boy on her bed.'

I regretted that. One step too far. Her chin wobbled and tears rolled down her face. I felt about as lovely as four-day-cold lamb.

'And how the fuck do you know that?' she shouted through the wreck of her face, snot and tears pouring down the corners of her mouth.

'I had dinner with his lover tonight.'

'Oh, fuck you! Fuck everybody!' she said.

The bathroom door slammed behind her. The taps ran. I gritted my teeth and tried to force the last few moments out of existence.

She came back in after five minutes and sat at the table.

'They fuck you up, they really do,' she said and lit up. 'My dad and his algebraic fucking love life. Who needs Z when X and Y are blokes? Jesus. And he never told me. My mother punishing him, chasing and screwing all those guys in front of him. What a mess. And . . . and this was supposed to be a celebration.'

'About what?'

'Roberto can get the rice.'

'Where from?'

'Thailand.'

'That's good.'

'They can't talk to each other, these guys, can they?' she said.

'What did you and Roberto have to talk about?'

'Yeah,' she said, 'that was pretty hard going. I mean, he looks sophisticated enough, he's wealthy, he's been around, but the guy hasn't seen a film or read a book in his life and he won't talk about anything interesting like politics because it's man's business.'

'Did you try football?'

'It was close, Bruce,' she said. 'There was something else going on there tonight. His men were around. Carlo and a couple of other guys. I think Roberto is having a respect problem.'

'Anything specific?'

'They didn't like me being there and they showed it. They shouldn't have had the nerve. The capo should be the man of steel and the men should be prepared to die for him. There just wasn't that total devotion. I had the feeling they thought Roberto was losing it. Going soft.'

She went back into the bathroom and came back with her face in the towel.

'That guy in the video. The white guy. He wasn't my father's lover, was he?'

I nodded. She shuddered.

'What a life.'

'He told me why the chief wanted to get rid of your father.'

'So it *was* the chief?'

'I thought it might have been Franconelli but he was getting information out of Napier on construction projects. David, the guy in the video, was feeding him.'

'Why Franconelli?'

'Just the way they killed him. It wasn't very African.'

'How sure are you about the chief?'

'David negotiated a way out for your father with the chief. He used an intermediary called Quarshie. Bagado said Quarshie's car picked up Napier in the *cocotiers*.'

'What was the deal?'

'Two-point-seven million dollars to get out and shut up. David said Napier was after ten mil to retire. It looked as if he was going to get it.'

'Cheaper to kill him.'

'Except Napier had it confirmed to him that he was going to be allowed to pick up. He told me he had had it from the highest authority.'

'Who was that?'

'The chief himself, I don't know,' I said, 'but he still asked me if I had the gun.'

'He was being greedy,' she said, and I saw an idea spark in her head. 'Greedy.'

'There's something you should know about Gale.'

'She's greedy too?'

'She's not for free.'

'How much?'

'She got us in this far and she has to be paid off.'

'Yeah, I know, but how much?'

'Not money. Just dirt on Graydon so she can break her prenup and bust him for ten million dollars.'

'What is it with ten million?'

'The difference between Moët and Krug.'

'So, we do some digging.'

'David talked about the big three, said there wasn't exactly a free flow of information between them, said there's always one who wants to be bigger.'

'Power,' said Selina, landing on it hard. 'It's all about power. The three of them're trying to fuck each other over and we're the go-betweens. They can't talk to each other so they use us. Well, now, maybe we can do something here.'

She threw the towel on the bed, grabbed a cigarette and paced the room without lighting it.

'That chief's a greedy little fucker,' she said, 'and he wants to get one up.'

'You're not thinking about Gale.'

'Don't worry about her. We'll get the dirt on Graydon. What I want to do is nail the chief and I think I know how we can do it.'

'This *does* involve me.'

'What?'

'The retribution bit.'

'Don't go soft, Bruce, because this *is* going to need some spine.'

'I'll try.'

'We're going to sell the chief a nuclear bomb . . .'

'You want to hear me say it for the second time? Fuck.'

'. . . or at least the basic ingredients for one. You remember Vassili's friend? The Kazakh bastard? What did he have? Plutonium, enriched uranium. Whatever. We have a supplier. What we need is a set-up.'

'How is this going to be a hardship for the chief, you know, to be the proud owner of a Little Boy?'

'Little Boy?'

'That's what they dropped on Hiroshima, just so you don't think we're playing with toy guns and caps.'

'Well, that's the point. The chief's ripe for it. Think about it – having his own, personal nuclear device – he'd love it, almost as much as he'd love his own football team.'

'But how does this hurt him, how does it end up stuffing him?'

'The endgame is that the chief loses a lot of money *and* he gets caught holding nuclear material for which I believe the penalty is death.'

'And we at this stage are suddenly and miraculously uninvolved.'

'I didn't say it would be easy but you've got to admit there's potential.'

'For complete disaster. You're not an adrenaline freak, are you, Selina? You don't go paragliding, sheer-face rock climbing, or shoplifting in a bikini?'

'Are you with me or not?'

'You've given me an idea with no plan. How are we going to persuade the chief to buy? How are we going to persuade him that what the Kazakh bastard has got is genuine? How are we going to get money out of the chief for nothing but the promise of delivery? How are we going to set him up without implicating ourselves?'

'Small print, Bruce. Fine tuning.'

Chapter 24

It rained heavily in the night for an hour. The power went off, cutting the air con. The sweat and the roar of the rain on the corrugated-iron roof woke me. I'd slept for three hours and a wedge of hangover had been sledgehammered into my head. I thought about David and Napier in a tumble-dryer sort of way – just rolled them around, hypnotizing myself. Napier had stayed with David. David had negotiated a deal and sent him to Benin. Napier had been certain about the money. We'd gone in to get it. He'd been killed. It didn't hold together. I felt suddenly nauseous.

I drank water and ate aspirin. The rain stopped. I drifted like a shoal of fish and suddenly rushed into sleep to be woken instantly by Selina's knocking.

We walked most of the way to Elephant House, but it was cool from the rain and still overcast. Ben was waiting for us like a cougar for a couple of she-goats. He'd got a fax addressed to Selina on behalf of the chief from a Thai supplier confirming availability of 15,000 tons of parboiled rice at a good price for immediate shipment ex Bangkok subject to Letter of Credit terms.

Within an hour there was still no Babba Seko, but

Selina had agreed a price with the Thais and had found a ship which could meet the supplier's delivery dates. She fixed it subject to charterers' confirmation.

The chief came in at eleven and arranged a meeting with AMObank in Cotonou to discuss the Letter of Credit terms. At eleven thirty the chief, Ben and I left for the airport to pick up the late-afternoon flight to Benin. Selina said she would wait for Bof Nwanu who was due to show her a parcel of coffee in a warehouse in Lagos. She would take the evening hop to Cotonou and join us at the Sheraton.

The traffic was solid. The chief and Ben slept. I frayed my nerves thinking what Selina would do left in the office on her own. We just made the flight and got out of Cotonou airport as night was falling.

Although the chief had slept all day, like a lion who'd had his killing done for him, he was tired out and needed a lie-down before the important business of the day, which was the Italian theme night at the Sheraton. He told us to reconvene at 9 p.m. I took a taxi home.

Heike was listless, depressed and running for the toilet in mid-sentence. She said Vassili had shot her sick day to pieces, phoning every hour to tell me that the car was ready. I asked her if she'd been to the doctor and she sneered and said there was no point for a stomach bug. I looked at the blackberry smudges under her eyes and told her that malaria could start with diarrhoea. She said that mosquitoes didn't bite her, that she'd eaten fish last night which was a mistake and that I should leave her alone and pick up the car so that Vassili didn't bother her any more. I didn't mention Selina.

I took a *taxi moto* out to Akpakpa and found Vassili

with another white man, a heavily bearded guy with no fat on him and blue-white eyes that looked as if they belonged to a husky. They spoke in Russian. I wondered if this was the Kazakh bastard, but Vassili didn't introduce me and I didn't want to get involved. I sipped a couple of lemon vodkas with them and got irritated by the way their conversation stopped when they looked at me and resumed when they looked at each other.

'How's Selina?' asked Vassili, when his friend stood up to go for a leak.

'She's coming over from Lagos tonight.'

Vassili explained something to his friend, who listened by the door and leaned a hairy, sinewy forearm up against the wall. He grunted and played with his balls then went out into the yard.

'He doesn't speak English, your friend?'

'Only French and it's good for me to speak Russian. Makes me ... you know ... emotional for the old country.'

'What's his game?'

'He has no game. He's just visiting. We're talking.'

'What's so interesting?'

'He's been telling me about something called red mercury. You know it?'

'I've heard of it. I've heard it's nothing. Expensive nothing.'

'That's what the Americans say. That's what they hope.'

'The Germans too.'

'Yes,' said Vassili, tossing back a shot, 'but my friend disagrees.'

'How would he know?'

'He used to work at Chelyablinsk-65 up in the Urals and after that at a research reactor in Tashkent.'

'An interesting man.'

'If you're interested in that kind of thing. I prefer vodka.'

'What's he doing here?' I asked. 'Nobody just visits Benin.'

'He looks for work.'

'Selling cars?'

'Why not? It's money.'

'It's not nuclear science, though, is it?'

'There are too many nuclear scientists. How many people want someone who can design a plutonium reprocessing plant? Who needs to reprocess plutonium? A lot more people want to buy cars and nobody wants to kill you if you do that.'

'Why should anybody want to kill him?'

'He has knowledge. He could sell it to unpopular people. Iraqis, for example. That would upset other people. Americans. He's telling me it's big problem. There are two thousand scientists, in Russia, now, who can build a bomb ... but where's the work? How do you earn a living?'

'This guy can build a bomb?'

'No, no, no. He worked in plutonium reprocessing. But now they dismantle the missiles. These missiles will produce a hundred tons of plutonium and four hundred tons of uranium. Where's his job gone? Who needs to reprocess plutonium now?'

'Tons? A hundred *tons* of plutonium?'

'Tons, my friend, and it only takes five little kilos of

plutonium to make a bomb. A hundred thousand kilos of plutonium stretched out over the whole of Russia. Well, that could easily become ninety-nine thousand, nine hundred and ninety-five kilos, no? You see the problem. There are people who understand the technology with no work, and there's the material, too much material.'

'And then there are people like your Kazakh friend . . .'

'Yes. He said he had six and half kilos. So you see . . .'

'Your friend here . . . he really wants to sell cars?'

'No. I try to persuade him. He wants me to speak to the government. Get him government job. You see, he's a Russian, they like to work for the state. I tell him if the government want to start a programme like that, what they need him for? They buy the material, they buy the scientist but what they need more than anything is the engineering. A nuclear bomb isn't just plastic explosive and a detonator. It takes precision. This is something we must thank God for.'

'How do you know all this, Vassili?'

'The Kazakh bastard tell me last week.'

'How long's your friend going to be around?'

'Some time.'

'Have you spoken to Selina?'

'Not since the night she drank the piri-piri vodka. My God, she's some woman. If I wasn't so fat,' he said, slapping his gut.

Vassili introduced me to his friend, Viktor. He gave me the keys to the Peugeot and went through the documents. I drove back across the lagoon and didn't even notice how the car was running, purring like Vassili's wife. I was thinking about Russians. How they all come together in one place. How suddenly they all know something about nuclear bombs. How they're all so well tuned in to the boodle frequency . . . for communists. Or maybe it was the vodka culture that brought them out of themselves.

Heike was asleep when I came in at 9 p.m. I called a lawyer friend of mine. A woman with the unlikely name of Isabelle Lawson, a Togolese with Ghanaian family, bilingual and very strong on Francophone and Nigerian law. I asked her if she was interested in advising on the Letter of Credit and told her to wear something suitable for the Italian evening and wait for my call.

I was late but the chief didn't mind. He had Selina, who had miraculously arrived at 8.30 p.m., to talk to. She had the look of an athlete at the top of her game. She radiated confidence and the chief was basking in it like a sunbathing python with a pig inside.

We talked about the meeting with the Cotonou rice agents, and in covering the AMObank Letter of Credit details, I mentioned Isabelle Lawson. The chief told me to bring her on. Within half an hour we were eating bowls of pasta and talking *scaloppine* like any bunch of business people on a jolly. Ben was sitting with his hands clasped behind the back of his chair. He could see the chief's boiler was close to the red line over Isabelle, and it was the only way to stop his own hands dancing across the table and losing him his job.

We split at midnight, as pumped as a sales crew after a guru session. I dropped Isabelle off at her home in the Cocotiers district and took Selina back to the house. She wanted to hit the New York New York with me but I told her Heike was off games. I asked her what she'd been doing all day.

'Covering ground,' she said.

'Does the chief know how you got the rice?'

'No way.'

'But Franconelli knows who it's for?'

'Sure.'

'Does Franconelli get anything?'

'Maybe.'

'He agrees things on a "maybe"?'

'Maybe.'

'Is this the client talking?'

'Nice car,' she said, and lit a cigarette.

'Thanks,' I said. 'You still want to sell the chief some nuclear material?'

'I don't think there's anything he wouldn't buy off me now.'

'I might have the answer to a problem.'

'Which one?'

'Verifying the product,' I said. She didn't leap. 'Not so interested after all?'

She shrugged. We continued in silence. I eased the car up and down the troughs of the dirt road and pulled up at the gates. I opened them and drove in behind Heike's Pathfinder.

'Did you tell Heike about our little tussle last night?' she asked.

'There didn't seem much . . .'

'So, no. Right?'

'Vassili knows you, Selina,' I said. 'You're a tow bitch.'

'That's not what Franconelli thinks. Roberto to me.'

'Wait 'til he gets to know you better.'

'He's in love with me.'

'That was quick.'

'Older men fall for me.'

'So the rice deal's a gift. A love token.'

'He's not that sentimental.'

'I thought he might be after what he's been through.'

'That's true. It wasn't as expensive as it should have been.'

'What's he want?'

'He wants to know how Graydon's oil deal goes.'

'Why?'

'He's involved.'

'So how come he doesn't know?'

'They don't trust each other, these guys.'

'So what was all the ground you covered?'

'The next bit'll cost you.'

'Forget it, Selina.'

'No sex.'

'Just a chaste little kiss?'

She laughed, ditched her cigarette and crushed it with her foot. She tapped her bottom lip with her finger.

'You have to promise me something.'

'What do I get if I promise?'

'You get to give Gale what she needs.'

'I wouldn't call paying Gale off my responsibility.'

'You also get a bonus.'

'Of what?'

'Whatever's left in the bag by the time we're finished. You've already got the car.'

'I lost one too.'

'That's right, you did. It feels such a long time ago.'

'Is that it?'

'And I'll leave you alone for ever.'

'Don't go and break down crying now.'

She gave me a withering smirk and folded her arms.

'Well?' she asked.

'So what have you got?'

'Promise first.'

'What do you want me to do?'

'I want to pull the plutonium scam on the chief, but you've got to help me right to the end. No chickening out.'

'Babba Seko must not end up with any of that material.'

'He won't. I promise.'

'And you mustn't say a word to Heike.'

'About last night?'

'About selling plutonium to people like Babba Seko.'

She giggled and flicked her lighter on and off.

'OK, it's a deal,' I said. 'Your turn.'

'I've got proof that the chief and Graydon between them have ripped off Roberto for around twelve million dollars on these oil scams.'

'You know, all you got to do is tell Roberto that and those guys'll be concrete moorings for floating jetties out in the Gulf.'

'I know,' she said, 'but where's the fun in that?'

Chapter 25

When Franconelli told Selina he wanted to know about the oil scam she'd read him absolutely right. As soon as we were out of the office she hit the nearest PC. She had one piece of information from Roberto, which was the name of the company through which they worked the Nigerian end of the oil operation – BASOLCO. One snag. She needed a password. Not even Babba Seko was that stupid and, anyway, it was Ben who'd set up the system.

It didn't take female intuition to know that the password was going to have something to do with the boss. She spoke to his secretary. She was the daughter of the chief's wife's brother which gave her the chief's wife's maiden name. Great. It didn't work. Misread the man. Not personal enough. This did get her into the chief's office though, tagged by the secretary and there it was, up on the wall – the photograph of the Nigerian national football team. Who was the chief's favourite player? Rashidi Yekini. She volleyed that at the screen and scored.

The BASOLCO accounts were done by shipment. The sale was made. The money was paid into the Caymans, Neruda account. The expenses were deducted – the freight to the shipowner, the larger bribes directly into safe-haven accounts and the smaller ones in a lump in Nigeria. There was nothing strange about any of this except that fifty-eight of the seventy-two shipments made over the last four years had been done by four ships – the *Limnos III*, the *Ohio Warrior*, the *Red Solent* and the *Mithoni VII*. They were all Panamanian flag vessels. Each ship was owned by an individual Panamanian company and those companies were owned by a holding company called LUNEXCO S.A. of the Cayman Islands. What drew Selina was the name of the managing director of the Panamanian companies – José Marcos. She remembered the phone call Graydon took in his office – 'Hi José.' – and we were dismissed.

She called a friend in London who was an expert on offshore companies and asked if he could do some digging around on LUNEXCO. He came back within the hour to say that LUNEXCO was solely owned by Graydon Strudwick. Then she looked at the freight rates. She spoke to a broker in the oil department at Clarksons in London. The freight rates were consistently between $1 and $2 per ton above the market level and there had always been other ships in the area who would have, in the broker's opinion, been prepared to drop the market rate even further. The only time the cargoes were fixed at market levels were on the fourteen occasions when one of Graydon's ships weren't around.

That seemed typical of Graydon – not in it for the money but the humiliation. He wanted to be able to sit on the swing sofa with Franconelli and think, 'I'm ripping you off, spico.' Just like his videos did, it gave him power.

If Franconelli got hold of this it wouldn't be the money that would get Graydon killed, it would be the lack of respect, and, if Selina was right, respect was something Roberto was having trouble with right now.

Selina came across the second set of BASOLCO accounts as she was closing down. In these accounts everything was the same except that the bribes paid to the important people with offshore accounts (one of whom was Robert Keshi, the guy from the storage department at NNPC) were twenty-five per cent higher than in the original BASOLCO accounts. She flicked through some of the chief's offshore bank accounts and came across one in Madeira which had amounts corresponding to the loading on the bribes. The chief was doing the same thing, gently ripping off Franconelli for around $100,000 a shipment.

One thing that Selina couldn't find was any indication that these cargoes of oil were paid for. There seemed to be no sums of money going from BASOLCO into NNPC, although she matched a lot of names from the NNPC personnel listed in their published Year Accounts with the people receiving bribes into offshore banks from BASOLCO. Another thing that wasn't clear from these accounts was whether Graydon knew what the chief was doing and vice versa.

The reason Selina had been talking to Clarksons was that she wanted to fix a ship from Port Harcourt to a refinery in Rotterdam with the 120,000 tons of oil Graydon had offered her. There were three ships and she worked all of them. One of them was the *Ohio Warrior*, which fell out of the running early on because she wouldn't drop her rate from $2 per ton above the market. The broker was puzzled and Selina fixed the cargo on a vessel at 25 cents per ton below the market rate. It looked as if Graydon was using her to persuade

Franconelli that the BASOLCO shipping operations were straight up.

That was why she'd been looking so athletic at the Sheraton that night. She had a one-megabyte floppy in her briefcase which told the whole story and she'd just made $80,000 on her own crude shipment without raising a sweat.

Now she was lying on the sofa with a splash of Black Label and thinking about Viktor and what his knowledge of plutonium reprocessing could contribute to the end of Chief Babba Seko's political career.

'I've already spoken to the chief,' she said.

'About the nuclear stuff?'

'I just ran it past him. Said it in a conversational way that a Russian friend of mine had been offered some gear.'

'Did he bite?'

'No.'

'Nibble?'

'No.'

'Sniff?'

'No.'

'He had his mind on other things.'

'It was before Isabelle arrived.'

'He wasn't in the right mood. Not thinking about the right thing. Not thinking about his presidency.'

'Why don't you try him? You hooked him on the rice. Maybe he only listens to men. He didn't treat Isabelle like a hotshot lawyer, did he?'

'Maybe you've done enough already. It's planted. Let's see if it grows. Even if it doesn't you can always dob him in to Roberto and walk away.'

'You hope.'

'Yes, I do.'

'No sense of challenge.'

'Just a sixth sense for trouble and – as Bagado says – it always finds me.'

'Am I with the right guy?'

'You're the trouble,' I said.

'You going to lend me your car keys?'

'Goodnight,' I said, and lobbed them over.

Cotonou. Wednesday 28th February.

In the morning, Heike was hot but not sweating. I was losing my nerve about the malaria diagnosis. She said she was feeling OK apart from the diarrhoea. I told her to go to the Polyclinique. We had a fight. She called in sick to her office. I told her to take something for her stomach. We had another fight. I made an appointment at the Polyclinique. She asked me if I was ill. I gave up. She was old enough.

Selina gave me the floppy of the BASOLCO accounts and I put it in the poetry section of the bookcase between Heaney and Hughes. We drove downtown and took our coffee and croissants in La Caravelle before driving out to the port area for our meeting with the agents at 8.30 a.m.

The agents' director was a Nigerian, an Igbo, who spoke fluent French through a permanent wince from a stomach ulcer. He was the only African I'd ever met with one of those. Ben and the chief were on time and we were filing into the director's office when Ben turned and put his hand on my chest.

'This is an African thing,' he said. 'You understand?'

We went back to reception and sat the meeting out amongst the rubber plants and magazines called *Container Week* and *Commodities Hotline* from last year. Selina was puce with fury. She didn't know how lucky she was. A European can't stand the African Way. A European likes to get to the point. The African likes to discuss everything but the point. I've been in meetings where Africans have danced around the point for hours with no noticeable drift towards the nub and then, suddenly, an agreement has been reached, hands shaken, the office vacated, and old whitey's been left still drumming his fingers on the desk with nothing written on his notepad.

At about 11 a.m. there was a cheer from the office, as if they hadn't been discussing business but had hunkered down in front of some old replays of the Africa Nations Cup. They filed out with an agreement written over their faces. Ben steered Selina off to a waiting taxi and the chief put his hand on my shoulder and leaned on me all the way to my car. We drove downtown.

'I had a Peugeot once,' said the chief, as if it had been a favourite toy when he was eight.

'Good cars.'

'Oh yes.'

'Paris/Dakar.'

'Quite. An African car.'

'They make them in Nigeria, don't they?'

'Mmmmmm,' he murmured, as if relieving himself in a swimming pool. 'What do you think of Nigeria, Mr Medway?'

'It's a mess and it shouldn't be.'

'And why do you think it's a mess?'

Careful here, I thought.

'There's nobody *running* the country, they're just *controlling* it.'

'A fine distinction,' he said. 'You should be a politician.'

'I don't have the necessary qualities.'

'Which are?'

'Unshakeable vision and unfathomable optimism,' I said. Well, I didn't want to blow it with 'unshakeable arrogance and unfathomable insincerity'.

'I have a vision,' said the chief, quietly, as if he was admitting that he'd written a short story and would I like to read it.

'That's why you're a presidential candidate,' I said.

'Not yet, but yes.'

'Am I allowed to know your vision?'

'Of course. It's that Nigeria will be strong again. That we will be the number-one country in Africa. That the continent will look to us for leadership in economic affairs and . . . for defence.'

This is the African way – from Peugeots to plutonium without mentioning it. We sat outside A M O bank and discussed Nigerian foreign policy for fifteen minutes while Ben and Selina sat in the taxi behind. By the end still nothing had been said, but I was in no doubt that the chief was in the market for any amount of weapons-grade plutonium we could lay our hands on, and he was in no doubt that I would be able to supply it.

We were included out of the meeting with

AMO bank and Isabelle Lawson. Selina was shaking and I had to grip her upper arm and drag her to the indoor shrubbery before she mauled someone.

'What are we doing here?' she asked.

'We're entourage. The chief's an important man. He's so important he has two white people who sit outside his meetings waiting for him.'

'I'm humiliated.'

'Your time will come,' I said. 'He wants the gear.'

'He does?' she said. 'Oh boy, am I going to enjoy fucking this guy over.'

After the meeting, on the way to lunch, Isabelle told us the terms of the deal. The chief was required to deposit $500,000 with the bank. As soon as the ship was loaded the bills of lading would be sent to AMO-bank, who would hold them until the balance was paid by the buyers sent by the agents. When the value of the cargo was reached the bills of lading would be released to the chief. Nice business if you can get it.

The chief retired after his lobster and Ben made it clear that Selina would be needed in Lagos while I should start moving things in Cotonou. I dropped Isabelle off and headed across the lagoon to Akpakpa.

Vassili was in his yard pacing around and yabbering in French down one of the new mobile telephones which had been available since the Francophonie conference. He nodded me into the house, where I sat alone for two minutes until his eldest daughter came in with two Petite Beninoise beers and a bowl of cashew. She looked as if she'd lost a kitten, and rebuffed my four stabs at conversation with monosyllables.

Vassili collapsed into an armchair and threw his feet

up on the table. He grabbed the beer and slugged half the bottle. His daughter watched him from behind a curtain to the kitchen. He flashed her an irritated look and she bled away into the house.

'You know someone who wants to buy a Mercedes 300 series diesel?'

'Do I look like it?'

'Mmmm,' he said, doubtfully. 'What do you want? The Peugeot OK?'

'The Peugeot's fine,' I said. 'I want to meet your Kazakh friend.'

The beer stopped halfway to his mouth. He looked steadily and directly into my eyes for a minute. One of his dogs barked in the yard. He didn't flinch. The air hissed in the room like a gas fire.

'Does he have a name, your Kazakh friend?' I asked.

'No,' he said. 'We call him Mr K. Why do you want to see him?'

'I'm interested in what he has.'

'Don't joke with me, Bruce.'

'No jokes.'

'You have a buyer?'

'Well, it's not me, Vassili.'

'What's he want? Your buyer.'

'I don't know what Mr K's got.'

Vassili nodded and fed his mouth with cashew from the silo of his fist.

'Mr K,' he said, 'never deals direct.'

'With the principal?'

'That's right. It's a big responsibility for you. The money. The product.'

'Why doesn't he deal direct?'

279

'Experience. He learn to stay clear. Friends have been killed. Set-ups are common. This isn't a set-up?'

'It won't worry him if it is, will it?'

'I mean you. You're not being set up?'

That spanner went clanking into my machinery and lodged itself somewhere, not vital, but where I could feel it.

'She's a very interesting woman,' he said, 'Selina.'

The beer bottle clinked against his teeth. He tipped it, looking at me out of the side of his face.

'Just ask Mr K if he'll see me.'

'He'll talk to you. You won't see him. He's a careful man.'

'Viktor can call me too. If he wants to make some money.'

'My God,' he said. 'And me?'

'You'll find a commission somewhere out of all this.'

He grinned. I stood and drained the beer. Vassili struggled to his feet. He slapped me on the back twice but didn't say anything.

I drove back across the lagoon, the water shivered in the wind coming off the sea, the jungle bristled on the shoreline. Dust swirled around the Dan Tokpa market so that people walked with their arms across their faces. Clouds bunched in the sky due north and my Peugeot's engine missed a couple of beats.

As soon as I walked in the house I knew there was something wrong by the quality of the silence. Helen was sleeping on the kitchen floor. Heike's bedroom door was shut. My ears were ringing as I reached for the door handle. I looked over my shoulder but it was only the tension in the room pushing me forward. I opened the door.

Heike's head and neck were drenched in sweat. Her hair plastered over her face in oily streaks. There was a dark halo on the pillow where her head lay. The blue sheet twisted, and dark too, stuck to her body. Her eyes were shut and she was panting, muttering as if in a religious trance. Malaria.

I tore the wet sheet off her, wrapped a dry one around her and a blanket, picked her up and ran down to the car with her. Twelve minutes later I was carrying her up the steps to the Polyclinique. Three minutes after that she was in a private room with air con and a French woman doctor holding her eyelids open and shining a torch in there but getting nothing back. My insides felt like bagged freezer meat.

'Does she take anything?' asked the doctor.

'No.'

She rolled Heike over and stuck a thermometer in her anus and issued a rattle of instructions to the two Beninois nurses who ran out of the room. Four minutes later she removed the thermometer.

'Forty-point-six,' she said. That was a hundred and five in my language and the fear crept up my neck and banged around in my brain like a madman amongst the dustbins.

The nurses came back in with a bottle of lime-coloured Quinimax solution with glucose. The doctor asked if they'd put the nausea suppressant in and the nurses, wide-eyed and as scared as me, nodded. The doctor plugged the needle into Heike's vein and turned the drip on. The nurses bathed her temperature down with cool water. The doctor shone her torch into Heike's eyes again.

'Has it gone cerebral?' I asked. The doctor didn't answer.

If you hit malaria hard early on there was nothing to fear. The parasites injected by the mosquito when it bit didn't get a chance to multiply in the bloodstream. If, however, the malaria was allowed to get on with it, the parasites multiplied, poured around the body in the bloodstream and entered the vital organs, including the brain.

It then became cerebral malaria and the chances of dying were very high. Pure quinine was the only anti-dote. That and a lot of luck.

The nurses left when Heike's temperature dipped below the 100 mark. I walked around the bed obsess-ively checking the drip. Then I leaned with my forehead against the slatted window and watched the afternoon dying. I had the terrible thought that this is what hap-pened. This was how it ended. On an unremarkable sunny afternoon a long way from home.

Outside people came and went. Nurses changed shift. Cars arrived and moved off. Night fell. The traffic thickened as everybody left work and thinned as the evening meals were taken. Then it was quiet. Heike didn't move. The doctor came in again and removed the drip, checked her temperature and looked into her eyes.

'It's up to her now,' she said. 'Does she like to fight?'

She waited for an answer until she realized that she wasn't going to get one. I was stunned by the black hole I found myself looking into, tipping into, falling into. I was going to lose her.

A cool touch on my forearm made me start. The doctor, a very small woman, no bigger than a twelve-year-old, looked up at me. She had bags under her eyes, puffy skin from working indoors in the tropics and maternal hair. She'd seen the despair, the complete desolation in my face, seen me looking out across some night-time rocky desert. I knew because looking back into her fifty-year-old green eyes I saw something unusual, something I hadn't seen for a while, something I didn't come across in my line of work. It pricked my eyeballs.

'Does she?' she asked again.

'Oh yes,' I said, and I was going to add to it, but this whole life opened out in front of me, not in scenes, not in takes of film that have always flickered and whirred in my head, but just light, a strong, far-reaching light. I swallowed but the conker in my throat stayed. The doctor left.

A nine-inch striplight shone above Heike's head and lit her face in what seemed to be an anagram of her own. Black-and-white shapes which produced an effect which wasn't her. I felt foolish and angry, in fact I felt everything. I found myself on the cutting edge of feeling – a thousand cuts and still living. I turned the light out, sat by the bed, held her hand and, like the drip she'd just had removed, drained my will into her.

I stayed like that all night. I reckoned that I'd feel her if she tried to slip away and hold on, dig my heels in.

Cotonou. Thursday 29th February.

In the morning, dawn took fifteen minutes to paint us into the room. We were still here. Outside the traffic cleared its throat. The cobblers walked along tapping their boxes, looking for work. The night shift left, putting one foot in front of the other.

At 9 a.m. the doctor came back in and took another blood film. The result of the last one had come through at an astronomic 2000 parasites per cubic millilitre. She said they'd put her on another drip after lunch and told me to go home for a while, change my clothes, shower.

I got home at lunchtime and listened to the answering machine. Vassili and Bagado had called and wanted returns. Selina too. She sounded nervous and left a Lagos number I didn't know. My gums tingled.

I called Vassili and told him I was in room six at the Polyclinique. He said Mr K would be in touch. I called Selina, a houseboy answered and said she was unable to come to the phone. I wanted to avoid Bagado for the moment. I packed some clothes for Heike, my stomach turning at her body's imprint on an old dress, a pair of shoes. The phone rang.

'Was that you before?' asked Selina.

'Where are you?'

'The chief's.'

'Why didn't you come to the phone?'

'They're being difficult. They know somebody's been in their computer system. There's a floppy missing from the office. Are you getting anywhere?'

'Heike's unconscious in hospital. Malaria.'

'Christ.'

'Is this whole deal going off?'

'Not yet.'

She hung up. I went back to the hospital. Heike was on another quinine drip. The parasite count was still high. She was shivering now and under blankets.

I watched another afternoon die, holding on to Heike's wrist feeling her pulse – a thin, thready, tinkering beat. Sweat began to bead on her forehead and I tore off the blankets. I put my head on her lap, reassured by the gurglings of her intestines and watched the glass darken in the windows. I closed my eyes and squeezed out that thought that was hammering to come in. If she . . .

I surfaced in the dark, in a desolate sob, and ransacked my brain to find out where I was. There was a hand on my ear. It wasn't mine. I lifted my head. Heike had moved her hand. It was cold, but not that cold. Her eyes were moving under her lids.

Chapter 26

'My ears are ringing,' she said.

'It's the quinine.'

'I'm thirsty.'

I poured her several glasses of water and she drank them down.

'I'm going to vomit,' she said.

She half filled a bucket. I had a bizarre vicarious satisfaction in her release. She slumped back on to the pillow.

'What the hell is going on?' she asked, as if this was something completely unnecessary for her to be going through.

'You've been in a malarial coma.'

She looked at herself in the narrow bed. She felt the plasters on her arm from the intravenous drip. Her fingers were shaking.

'Why am I shaking?'

'You've just had your second pint of quinine solution.'

'You were right.'

'You scared the living shit out of me.'

'Did I?'

'You can slip away, just like that, you know?'

'Come here,' she said, and held my face with trembling hands. 'This is a terrible admission – I should have listened to you.'

'It's not in your nature.'

'You *can* talk an awful lot of shit.'

I told her I loved her and that we didn't have to fight straight after her brush with death, we could leave it a couple of days.

'Why do I always have to nearly die before you say you love me?'

'Is that true?'

'The last time you said you loved me was when you rescued me from that American creep.'

'No, I've said it since then.'

'I'm not counting any time when you've had more than a bottle of wine and four whiskies and that's . . .'

'. . . nearly all the time.'

'But you can kiss me, if you want,' she said. 'If you don't mind me being a bit pukey.'

There was a knock at the door. The nurse poked her head in and said there was a boy in the reception area who wanted to talk to me. Heike gave me one from her stack of long-suffering sighs and I tried to make it better by kissing her hand. She waved me away. I followed the nurse.

It was 9 p.m. The boy saw me and started walking out of the hospital, through the gates and round the back of the parked cars under the trees outside. He took me to an old jeep which I recognized as one of Vassili's. He opened the back door and I got in.

It was dark in the car and apart from the aura coming through the trees and shrubs from the hospital there was no light. I could see that the man in front had very long hair but that was all. The rearview was turned up.

'I'm Mr K,' he said in English. 'Vassili said you want to talk to me.'

'You have something for sale.'

'You have an interested party?'

'What are you selling?'

'Vassili says you work with a policeman.'

'Not any more.'

Some time struggled past. He shifted in the front seat as if he was about to turn round.

'I know you very well,' he said.

My guts dropped. The silence built inside the car. He lit a cigarette that smelled like dried camel dung. He didn't offer me one. He straightened a length of his hair, fanning it out to the shoulder. He had a gold ring on the third finger of his right hand.

'Your girlfriend's sick. Her name is Heike Brooke. She works in Porto Novo for Gerhard –'

'Are we doing business, Mr K?' I cut in. 'Because if we're not I'd like to go back in there and look after her. I'm sure you're very knowledgeable about me. Vassili knows everything there is to know. I respect that. But you're either going to tell me what you've got or not, and we can take ten minutes less time to do it if you start now.'

'I have six and a half kilos of Plutonium 239, ten kilos of red mercury. Half a kilo of Californium 252. The price is ten million dollars. I am already talking to the Libyans. Do you understand the products I have for sale?'

'I'll find out.'

'Leave the car. Contact Vassili if you want to proceed.'

I got out and went back into the hospital, thinking everything's $10 million these days. The car's headlights came on and it pulled away in the direction of the airport.

I left Heike sleeping at 10 p.m. and went home. I called Vassili and asked for Viktor. We arranged to meet in my office downtown in twenty minutes.

Viktor and I sat in the bare essentials of my office, without a light because the fuse had blown downstairs. We drank beer while he gave me a layman's brief on nuclear bombs in the simplest French he could muster.

The red mercury that Mr K was selling would be in the form of a high-density gel. It was made by dissolving mercury antimony oxide, which was red, into mercury. That was irradiated for twenty days in a reactor and any excess mercury evaporated off, leaving the gel. To make a bomb the californium 252 would be added to the gel and that compound would become the explosive chemical detonator that surrounded the plutonium 239 at the core of the bomb.

The red mercury, he told me, had a high density which gave good compression to the plutonium which was necessary to bring it to critical mass. The californium produced neutrons which would initiate the fission reaction early. The ultimate effect was, in fact, a neutron bomb, and even I remembered that the neutron bomb had the desired effect of killing people while leaving property intact.

The advantage of buying the red mercury and californium with the plutonium was that the buyer would get more bangs for his buck. A normal bomb would need either 5 kilogrammes of plutonium 239 or 15 kilogrammes of uranium 235, but by using red mercury a bomb maker could significantly reduce the plutonium/ uranium required. By how much, Viktor did not know.

Viktor could see he was making me nervous with the

cool and detached way he talked about these weapons of mass destruction, which were in raw form perhaps not far from where we were speaking. He tried to reassure me that anybody with these ingredients would still be a long way from making a bomb.

'Unless,' I said, 'he wants to pay one of you guys a million bucks to come over and fix it.'

Viktor gave me an acknowledging jump of his eyebrows. I asked him if he would be able to identify genuine product without opening the boxes and killing us all. He said there would have to be some documentation with the product and he would certainly be able to tell if it had been properly packaged and came from somewhere in Russia.

'If your buyer wants to go ahead,' he asked, 'how much are you going to pay me to help you out?'

'That depends on what he buys it for.'

'How many people are in the deal at your level?'

'Two.'

'So how about we split it three ways . . . whatever the difference is between the seller's price and the buyer's?'

'That's not a decision I can make on my own.'

'Have to talk to the lady?' he asked, wringing the contempt out of his voice as he spoke.

Viktor left. I called the chief and got Ben. I told him I'd opened the discussions. The chief came on the line and asked how much. I told him that it depended. He said he would send Ben across in the morning. I asked to speak to Selina. Ben came back on and said she'd gone to bed. We hung up.

I bought a pizza to take out. I didn't turn the lights on at home but walked around in the polygons of light cast by the streetlamps outside. The fridge held a wrinkled tomato and enough booze for a party. I had to stop living like this. I poured myself a highball of white wine. I closed the fridge and saw him again. The man out on his balcony looking down into the black garden, his arms out stabilizing himself on the rail. What was he looking at? I got up on the kitchen sink and peered down there myself. Nothing. Maybe this was where he came to take a look at himself. Ah, well. We could all use some of that. Not too much. Not so much that the self-doubt crept in and the self-disgust, because all that left was the high dive into blackness.

Cotonou. Friday 1st March.

I woke up at midday with the phone going and my mouth dry and caked, as if I'd taken a bite out of a wax apple. It was the chief's secretary calling from the office saying Ben would not be in Cotonou until five thirty that evening and that he would like a meeting with the seller of the goods tonight. I asked after Selina. She hadn't been in.

Ben and the chief were keeping us apart.

This was how mistakes were made – when you were alone. I wouldn't have minded a talk with Bagado but I was outside the law now and any hint of it to him and I had no doubt that he'd jug me for it. Heike was in no state. She'd kill me too. Víktor, I didn't trust on the meetings we'd had. The way he'd pushed on the money, those eyes, and anyway, he was Vassili's man. Vassili, well, in Vassili there was a conflict of interest now. I called him and asked him to arrange for Mr K to be in the Sheraton car park at 8 p.m.

I drove to the hospital with some food for Heike. She was going through her third and last quinine drip. Her parasite count was down but they wanted her to stay another night and take a course of Fansidar. I sat with her through the afternoon and, while she dozed and ate, developed a range of stress-management exercises. I left at 5.30 p.m. to pick Ben up from the airport. He came in late and brought some chill air down with him from 20,000 feet. Suddenly I'd become lower than dirt.

He was silent on the way to the Sheraton while I gave him the nuclear briefing and told him about Viktor's role. He took a room and kept me waiting in the marbled lobby until two minutes to eight. I decided not to waste my time and gulped down a few pints of draught lager which came in dimpled mugs and gave me a pang for Clapham and a seat in the dark at the back of the Prince of Wales.

Ben smelled the beer on my breath. I was free fall in his estimation. We went out into the night, another hot and humid one but with a stiff breeze whacking off the sea. The tall palms in the massive car park rattled, but not in the nervous way that they did in the *cocotiers*. They were calmer, more self-assured, moneyed. The jeep was off in the corner. I knocked on the rear window and Mr K popped the rear door locks. Ben sat behind Mr K's long-haired head.

'No names,' said Mr K as soon as we were settled. 'Talk.'

'You have some goods,' said Ben. 'We're interested in buying them but before we go anywhere I have to

292

know whether ten million dollars is your final price because if it is we can terminate discussions now.'

'The product is under offer to the Libyans.'

'That doesn't answer my question.'

'This is Africa.'

'Is that an African price?'

'No.'

Some cars streamed past on the road outside the Sheraton's grounds. They turned left at the security gate and drove swiftly up to the entrance. Silence resumed apart from the wind in the palms.

'Tell me how the business will work,' said Ben.

'The English here is the intermediary. When we have agreed terms you will make a deposit of fifty per cent of the value of the goods to him. When he has received the money he will inform me. I will tell him where to find the goods. He will have twenty-four hours to hand over the goods to you and for you to inspect them. At the end of the twenty-four hours he will bring the money to me.'

'And if we're not satisfied with the goods?'

'You complain to the Consumer Protection Society,' I said, letting the beer do some talking. Silence. Unimpressed silence.

'You return them and keep your money,' said Mr K quietly. 'And if that works to your satisfaction we'll proceed with the second drop.'

'The second drop?'

'I'm not giving you all the goods for half the money.'

'Why can't we do it in one exchange?' I asked.

'Because it takes time to get the goods into position and this is how I like to work. It's safer for you too.'

'Yeah, what *about* me?' I said. 'There's a lot of weight on my shoulders.'

'You,' said Mr K, 'had better make sure you're getting well paid.'

'But why me? Why can't there be another intermediary.'

'Because you're here,' said Mr K, and lit one of his camel-dung smokes.

'There are others. Plenty of others.'

'You approached me. You've been vouched for. Any complaints from the buyer?'

'No,' said Ben. 'Let's talk money.'

That was the end of my involvement. Five lines for the one most likely to get killed. I didn't listen to the haggling. Tomatoes, cars, nuclear bombs, it's all the same. The final figure was $6,350,000, $3 million payable as the deposit.

Then came the shock.

Ben said he would need until three p.m. tomorrow to confirm. Only eighteen and a half hours to confirm this deal. This was going too fast. This was going too fast for the people who were supposed to be planning the sting. This was being taken out of our hands. I needed air.

Ben and I walked back to the hotel. There should have been plenty of air out there, fresh and with a sea bite to it, but I couldn't breathe it. I leaned on the back of my car and tried to loosen my throat off.

'Where's Selina?' I asked.

'We think it's better that she stays with us until this is over, in Lagos. It's more comfortable for her there.'

'Are you telling me she's a hostage, Ben?'

'A gilt-edged security, Bruce. This is a dangerous

business. We're insuring ourselves. Three million dollars is a lot of money.'

This is what happens when you try to sting the stingers, I thought, the wasp meets the scorpion. We were going to get creamed.

'I want to meet Viktor tomorrow,' said Ben. 'Arrange it for eight a.m. here. I want to get the ten o'clock back to Lagos.'

'If you confirm, where do we exchange?'

'Nigeria is very sensitive now. The military are too nervous. There's too many people listening in Lagos. We'll do it here. I have a brother with a warehouse in the industrial zone. The keys will be delivered to you once we've confirmed. It's a big place for storing cotton seed, but it's empty now apart from a few hundred tons. I think that will work. Anything else?'

There had to be something else. There had to be something to slow this thing down. Ben turned and started back to the hotel.

'There has to be a payment for this. I mean a fee. Viktor isn't for free, and there's me and Selina.'

Ben turned fifteen yards off.

'It's normally the seller who pays the commission, isn't it?' he said, and disappeared through the glass doors of the hotel.

He was right. What had I been thinking of? I knew what I'd been thinking of. I'd been thinking – 'Where's my sting? I haven't got one. The one with the big idea was in Lagos.'

I went home and called Vassili and asked for Viktor, who wasn't there. I told him to get Viktor to contact me. I sat on the edge of a chair and forced a beer down, which sat in a tight plastic bubble in my chest. I converted to whisky but it wouldn't go down past the bubble, it kept backing up, hot and sour into my mouth.

Viktor called at 10 p.m. I told him to be at the Sheraton in the morning. I wondered if Ben spoke French or Russian. Well, that might slow things down a bit.

I didn't sleep. I wrestled with the pillow, I fought with the sheet and then I went subliminal and woke up shattered and flayed as if I'd been pushed down the Cresta run in my birthday suit.

Cotonou. Saturday 2nd March.

At 9 a.m. I got a call from Ben summoning me to the Sheraton. As I was leaving, the hospital called asking me to pay a bill and pick up my wife. Things were moving so fast and out of control that I'd even got married without knowing it.

Ben was satisfied with Viktor. I didn't ask how they communicated. He said that if he confirmed at 3 p.m. I should go to an address in the Cocotiers district and ask for Mr White. He would be arranging the $3 million. He suggested I take a suitcase. I thanked him for doing my thinking for me. It annoyed him and I felt his radar lock on to me.

'You might have heard,' Ben said, 'of a British businessman who was killed in Cotonou a week or so ago.'

'Killed or murdered?'

'I suggest you find out for yourself. It might concentrate your mind. His name was Napier Briggs.'

I paid the bill at the Polyclinique and took Heike home. She was weak, too weak to notice that I couldn't eat, that I was holding on to my stomach and bringing up acid, that my bowels were liquid. I put her to bed and looked for somewhere to hide $3 million.

I went down into Moses's apartment and fingered his few belongings and found myself missing him badly. But then I tried to think of him, and I couldn't remember him, I couldn't picture his face or imagine what he would say. It was different now and he wouldn't be the same man again.

I went into the bathroom and found a room off that which Moses used to store some cooking things. There was a ledge above it which stretched out over the garage and became its roof. It looked perfect for the money.

Ben called at 2.45 p.m. I hoped it was to cancel, to say that he couldn't get the money together, that the whole thing smelled bad. But no. He confirmed and told me that I was going to have to pick up the keys to his brother's warehouse from his office next to the Hotel Babo. He suggested I check the place over and I told him not to patronize me. There was a thick silence and I knew I'd pissed him off again.

'Did you find out about Napier Briggs?' he asked, and hung up.

I called Vassili and asked him to have Mr K call me at 7 p.m. I drove out to Mr White, whose security man told me to come back at 6 p.m. I picked up the warehouse keys from Ben's brother's office and went downtown to buy the cheap suitcase I should have bought before I went to see Mr White. I could see Ben grinning and thinking, 'What an asshole.'

I went across the Ancien Pont to Akpakpa and turned off the main Porto Novo road into the industrial zone. It was another three kilometres of rough road to the warehouse, which was itself on a deep sandy track.

There were two warehouses, each a hundred metres long with about ten metres of beaten earth in between the two. Behind them was some scrubland and another unfinished warehouse with just the concrete cage of the structure but no floors, walls or roof. The *gardien* pointed me to the warehouse that was more or less empty. I gave him the keys and he opened it up.

There were four doors evenly spaced down each side. Each door was big enough to admit a truck for loading. The warehouse was a concrete cage filled with unrendered brick and had a steel-gabling structure in the roof supporting some corrugated sheeting. The few hundred tons of cotton seed in four stacks were in the middle of the warehouse. There were two doors at that point and about five metres between the stacks. There was light overhead too. I opened the door on the far side. There was a ramp up to the warehouse floor from a dirt track. I locked up and left.

Mr White was ready to see me this time. I walked up some outside stairs and into a large room on the first floor of the house. There were two large men by the door and both were armed. Mr White was an American, a balding guy of fifty with gold-rimmed specs which put me in mind of the advertising hoarding for glasses out on the wasteland in *The Great Gatsby* – all-seeing but no feeling. I sat down on a chair about three metres from his ludicrously small desk and put the suitcase down. An Oriental was feeding notes into an electronic counter behind him and stacking them off into a old cardboard bleach box. A single netted bed stood in the middle of the room. Mr White clasped his hands and made his thumbs talk to each other.

'I had a bit of trouble getting this together at such short notice,' he said.

I nodded and looked at his wrecked feet twitching in his cheap blue flip-flops. The phone went. He snatched it up.

'Yeah, he's here,' he said and held out the phone to me.

'There's no need to count it,' said Ben.

'You're always trying to tell me my business.'

'You can trust Mr White.'

'I don't know how much you told him to put in there.'

'Ask him.'

Mr White held up three fingers. I gave him the phone. He listened for a few seconds and put it down. The Oriental boy brought the box to the desk. Mr White presented it to me. I picked out a block of $100 bills.

'Most of it's hundreds,' he said. 'The last four hundred thou's in twenties.'

I spot-checked the blocks of currency and added them all up. I put it in the suitcase and left.

I drove home fast and put the suitcase in Moses's flat. There were no messages on the machine upstairs. I sat on the edge of the sofa and waited. At 7.10 Mr K called. I told him I had the money.

'I'll call you at . . . four thirty tomorrow morning,' he said.

'Nine hours? You can get it together in nine hours?'

'Why not?'

'It's a Sunday, for God's sake. I mean, don't you need more time?'

'Not at this stage.'

'*I* need more time.'

'You've got twenty-four hours from four thirty tomorrow morning. You haven't got anything else to do, have you?'

'What about my commission?' I asked, not giving a damn about my commission, just trying to haul back on the reins somehow.

'Go on,' he said, and when I didn't answer immediately he added, 'but be reasonable. Percentage men piss me off.'

'I'll think about it.'

'Just say it.'

'Ten per cent.'

'I'll be looking for someone else to do the second deal.'

'What about this one?'

'Two and a half is fair,' he said.

'Fairness doesn't come into it. If we were being . . .'

'Maybe you should think about it some more,' he said, and hung up.

I pulled my scalp back with both hands and gritted my teeth to try and get some thought into my brain. All I saw was myself being charged down a narrow road.

I drove to the office for something to do and picked up some beer from the supermarket on the corner. The *gardien* gave me a DHL slip and said there'd been a delivery this afternoon. It was something else to do. I cracked one of the beers and swigged it as I drove out to the DHL office in the Cocotiers district.

They had a cuboid package for me. It felt like poly-styrene with something weighty inside. The sender was Napier Briggs Associates from the Eko Meridien in Lagos. This felt like one of Ben Agu's games. I drove back to the office and put the package on the desk and looked at it while I finished another beer.

I slit open the DHL plastic envelope. There was a sealed polystyrene box inside. I stripped off the black tape and split the cube. I threw it across the room and, like an idiot, ducked below the desk. The damn thing was smoking. I looked to the door, the window, the balcony, and in those vital seconds it didn't explode.

What was smoking was now lying on the floor. They were two blocks of dry ice. There was also a clear plastic package. I picked it up and put it on the desk and studied it. Then I reeled back, stumbling over the chair and skidding on the polished floor tiles trying to get away from it.

It was Napier Briggs's mouth.

Chapter 27

That was enough for me. I didn't want to spend any more time out in no man's land – the unsupported pawn up for sacrifice. I wanted the backing, the cover of a major piece. I wanted to be one of those decisive pawns that stands out there and occupies a position.

Ben and the chief had found out who I was. They had my office address now. I didn't remember them knowing anything about me, which meant that Selina was talking, bargaining. I didn't blame her. She was in a vulnerable position and an even more vulnerable position if the chief knew, as I now suspected, that Napier Briggs was her father.

It was time to bring in a slogger.

I called Gale. The houseboy took his time. The line crackled and echoed.

'Who is it?' she asked, in that glassy voice of hers when she was a little drunk and getting lippy.

'Bruce. It's time we had a talk. I've got something for you.'

'Yeah? Like what?'

'The dirt you were after.'

Something broke, like that unseen membrane that can hold two lovers apart for what seems like a lifetime. Her voice oozed down the terrible line, rippled like honey from a spoon.

'Then we should meet, Bruce, my darling.'

'We should,' I said, 'and it had better be tonight.'

'You're in Lagos?'

'No, but I'll get there.'

'At one in the morning, Bruce. That's a border and some traffic you've got to deal with.'

'Anything wrong with one in the morning?'

'I'm not allowed out late.'

'You a teenager?'

'I'm married.'

'Go and play bridge with one of your pals and make a diversion on the way home. I'll be in the Eko Meridien at one a.m.'

'What's so goddamn urgent? I mean, Jesus, Gray's money's not going to run away.'

'One o'clock,' I said and hung up.

I phoned Vassili and told him to tell Mr K that 4.30 a.m. was not workable, that I would call later with a time that was. I drove home, checked Heike, who was calm and sleeping, picked up the floppy from between Seamus and Ted and, at 9 p.m., left for Lagos.

Lagos. Sunday 3rd March.

It's only seventy-five miles to Lagos but you should never think of getting there in anything under four hours from Cotonou. It took me four and a half and I was lucky with the traffic downtown. I rolled into the Eko Meridien car park at a little after 1.30 a.m.

I headed for the lobby but a light toot from a Mercedes 190 with its engine running stopped me. Gale was

303

listening to the radio with the air con on and doing some concentrated smoking. I got in next to her. She was wearing a cream cotton strappy minidress with no bra. Her nipples had hardened against the material in the cold of the car.

'I should do this more often,' she said. 'It's been a blast for my confidence. I had guys hitting on me nonstop in that lobby. Three offers for "champagne in my room". I mean, shit, that's not bad for a little old housewife. Jesus, Bruce, you look like something Gray's cat honks up once in a while.'

'When you've put the strychnine in its food?'

'You're full of ideas.'

'Yeah, and this is the best I've been feeling all day.'

'You be careful. You don't wanna end up round somebody's roses.'

'It's the closest I'll get to being in a bed of them.'

'Hard day at the office?'

'A zinger.'

'So what'd you make me drag my ass out here for?'

I tapped the steering wheel with the floppy.

'A three-and-a-half-inch floppy, wow. You haven't gone and pirated your latest computer game for me, have you, Bruce?'

'You show this to Roberto Franconelli and he'll take a couple of rubber truncheons and beat a tattoo on Graydon's testicles until they're the size of pumpkins.'

'That sounds a little strong for my purposes,' she said. 'Graydon's an asshole but I don't want him killed. You got anything fluffier?'

'Graydon's not going to part with ten million dollars for a soufflé.'

'I was thinking more sponge less hardtack.'

'Then you'll have to kiss Roberto's ass and make him see that maybe Graydon's been a little out of line and should get his knuckles rapped. That maybe he should pay a little fine to his wife and give the capo back what he's ripped off plus interest.'

'You're sounding a little pissed.'

'If you had balls and they were in the vice mine are in, you would be too.'

'I'm not sure about this, Bruce. This is sounding kinda . . .'

'I'm going to Franconelli's with this floppy. You can come with me and plead for Graydon's ass or you can let me fly and watch Graydon get weaved through a cattle grid. Let's go and make a phone call.'

'You mean *now*?'

'It's tough being pushed around. Believe me, I know.'

'But *I* didn't push you around.'

'No, but it's my turn now, and I've chosen you.'

We got out of the car and walked to the lobby. Gale put a call through to the Franconelli household. He wasn't up. Carlo didn't want to wake him. Gale held the phone in a limp wrist and gave me the 'too bad' look. I tore the phone out of her hand.

'Carlo, this is Bruce Medway. Gale and I want to talk to Mr Franconelli. It's inconvenient, I know, but tell him there's a life involved. Tell him it's Selina Aguia's life. Right? You understand? *Capice*, or whatever you guys say?'

I held the line for a good seven minutes. Gale smoked

two cigarettes and took the nails of one hand down to the half moons. Carlo came back on and told us to come up straight away.

I followed Gale to Roberto's house. It was in a secure street similar to the Strudwicks'. Carlo had phoned down to the guards to admit our two cars. We drove through the steel gates and up through the usual heavy-security situation to the house.

The house was a square block, a bunker that looked as if it had the strength to take another ten floors on top. The windows were all barred and shuttered. The front door was steel with shipyard rivets and no knocker. Carlo met us and took us upstairs to Franconelli's office.

Roberto was sitting on the corner of his desk clipping the end off a cigar. He was wearing blue silk pyjamas, a yellow silk dressing gown and black velvet slippers with gold crests on the toes.

There were two other guys sitting on a low black leather sofa. They had guns clipped to their belts. They propped their faces up with their fists, stretching their mouths to the size of mental patients'. Carlo shut the door behind us. Franconelli lit his Havana with an extra-long match.

'All of you wait outside for a few minutes. I want to talk to Mr Medway alone,' he said, and blew out the match with smoke from his mouth.

The door closed behind them.

'You drinking tonight?' he asked.

I nodded.

'Grappa? It's all I got up here. The whisky's down.'

'Grappa's fine.'

'Before we talk business,' he said, uncorking the grappa, 'I want to ask you something.'

He poured the drinks in small shot glasses. We saluted each other.

'What did Selina tell you about me?' he asked

'That I should even think of coming to your house at this time of night asking for help?'

'She tell you I was soft on her?'

'She said you were interested.'

'Just interested?'

'She said you might be in love with her. But she's still young, Mr Franconelli. Maybe she was mistaken.'

'No, she wasn't,' he said, and walked behind his desk and sat in the leather scoop chair in front of his PC. 'She tell you about my wife and daughter?'

I nodded. He smoked at the ceiling for a few moments.

'I look at you, Mr Medway, and I can see that there's something going on. You've got a life going on. There's something burning, something pushing you. I've looked at myself these last four years, more the last year, and I see nothing but a dead man. I smoke, I drink, I eat, I do business. Nothing more. Then I meet Selina and I find what's been missing. But you're right. Carlo's right. She's young. She's younger than my daughter. I don't want to make a fool of myself. I want you to tell me if I'm making a fool of myself. You understand what I'm asking?'

'Carlo doesn't like Selina?' I asked, trying to smooth myself out for the lie that was coming.

'He's afraid for me, I think.'

'Well,' I said. 'As far as I know you're not making a fool of yourself.'

'That's good,' he said, looking pleased. 'Now we can talk business.'

He pressed a button under the lip of his desk. The others filed in and took seats. There were just about enough for all of us in the room. Franconelli poured a grappa for Gale. Carlo and the boys sat dead-eyed.

'Where's Selina?' Franconelli asked me.

'Chief Babba Seko's house.'

'You said she's in trouble. Why?'

'Because of this,' I said, and threw the floppy on the desk.

He turned on his computer. Opened a drawer and took out a pair of heavy-rimmed specs. He checked the floppy for details of the programme and copied it on to his hard disk. The BASOLCO accounts came up on to the screen.

'I have these same accounts. You going to tell me what it means?'

I told Franconelli what Graydon and the chief had been doing since his wife had died, since they'd seen him getting distracted, since they'd seen him starting to go down.

There was an extraordinary physical change in the man. Before he'd looked human, the blood slick around his veins, his face heavy but impassive, his eyes shrewd but compassionate. Now it was as if I could see the arteries narrowing, the blood thickening, the pressure rising. His arms and pectorals shook. His carotid popped out in his neck. The pressured blood began to do strange things to his face – purpling it, darkening it. The purity of his anger left him with a white rim to his mouth, a thin white line around his liverish lips. He blinked at the heat coming off his eyeballs.

'Now, Roberto . . .' started Gale. I held up a hand.

The young men on the sofa tensed. A half smile appeared on Carlo's face and he stretched his neck as if his collar was chafing. Franconelli stormed around the room, torrential Italian pouring out of him as if he was an actor rehearsing lines for an opera. Carlo followed him with approving eyes, his body still. Franconelli's fist was opening and closing as if he was pumping his own, thick, enraged blood around his body. He stopped in front of me.

'Why'd she do this?'

'I think you asked her to, Mr Franconelli.'

'I asked her. I tell her to tell me to . . . fucking language. *Non parla Italiano?*'

'No.'

'I told her to look at the oil. That's all.'

'I don't think you did.'

'And you!' he roared, turning on Gale. 'What the fuck are you doing here?'

'She's come here to ask for leniency.'

'You come here to plead for your husband's ass?'

'I've come here to beg you, Roberto,' said Gale, catching hold of the tempo fast.

'Beg me for what? Not to kill that fucking bastard husband of yours?'

'I know . . .'

'Gale is part of the reason Selina broke into the chief's system.'

'Why?'

309

'She's sick of Graydon . . .'

'She's sick? I'm sick. Graydon. Fucking man,' said Franconelli, using his fingers to show us that Graydon liked to stick himself with needles and pump himself up.

'Gale asked us to find information on Graydon so that she could leave him. She can't live with a man like that.'

'No. Nobody can live with a man like that,' he muttered. He spoke in Italian to Carlo who stood up and walked over to Gale.

'Bring him here, now.'

'Roberto,' said Gale, standing up, 'don't kill him. I'm begging you not to kill him.'

'I give you my word,' he said, 'I won't kill him.' They left the room. 'What does she want?'

'She wants enough money to be able to leave him.'

'Like how much?'

'Ten million dollars.'

'You know, that *stronzzo*, he could give five times that and it would be nothing.'

'Selina's situation is more complicated,' I said, wanting to get out of here, away from these people. 'I was sent this package today.'

I threw the polystyrene block on to the desk. Franconelli looked at it. His body stilled. He made a decent show of opening the box but I knew, at that moment, that it was his. He had sent the box. He knew what was inside.

'What is it?' he asked, but I wasn't convinced.

'It's the mouth of a man called Napier Briggs.'

'Who is he?' he asked, and that was enough for me. Franconelli knew Briggs better than his own aunt.

310

I told him how Napier Briggs had been found and waited to see if he would keep the lie going.

'And what does this have to do with Selina?'

'Briggs was making himself dangerous to the chief, so they killed him. Now they're threatening me. They're holding Selina and threatening me to make sure things go smoothly.'

'What things go smoothly?'

Now I knew why Franconelli had sent the package. He was listening to me with every cell of his body. Right down to the dead skin on the back of his heels he was listening to me. He wanted to know what was going on. He knew there was something and that it was important but he didn't know what. He'd thrown Napier's mouth into the works to raise some information. Franconelli straightened himself as if he'd realized he was looking as hunched as a toad.

'She's arranged for him to buy six and a half kilos of Plutonium 239, ten kilos of red mercury and a half kilo of Californium 252.'

'She's selling him a *bomb*?'

'Just the ingredients.'

'Has she gone crazy?'

'She'd planned it so that the chief would lose some money. Something has gone wrong. Now the chief is threatening. I need your help to get her out.'

'Why does she want to cheat him?'

'You should ask her that yourself. I'm the paid help. She doesn't tell me everything.'

'What are you doing with her?'

He knew who I was and what I'd been doing. If I wanted his help I had to keep my mouth shut.

Franconelli leaned over the desk at me, looming dark and turbulent like the coming rainy season.

'I'm helping her.'

'Why?'

'She's paying me.'

'You don't look like the kind of man to sell nuclear bombs to people.'

'I'm poor. She said he wouldn't end up with any product. Now it's out of control and I need your help.'

It had been his mistake to make out that he didn't know Napier Briggs. Now he couldn't ask the question he wanted to ask without looking a fool and Roberto Franconelli was not in the business of looking foolish.

'Chief Babba Seko,' said Franconelli, pushing himself back off the desk, 'is a man who is coming to his moment.'

I told him about the proposed exchange at Ben's brother's warehouse in Cotonou.

'Carlo'll go with you when he comes back. You show him the warehouse,' he said, and wrote down some numbers. 'You call me when you're fixed up.'

'How can I guarantee that the chief will come with Selina?'

'You *make* him come,' he said. 'Where's the money?'

'With me.'

'Recognize your strengths, my friend. You're the principal now. Lay down your conditions for the exchange. Who's supplying?'

'A Russian. But the goods will come via me.'

'Then you're the one in control. Tell him he *has* to be there.'

'He'll be suspicious. He'll know I'm trying to get

Selina out. The exchange is only for the first half of the product.'

'Why?'

'The Russian wants it that way.'

'Let him be suspicious. He'll bring his men to the warehouse. But maybe he's made a mistake doing the business in Cotonou. He's got a private army here. He'll only have maybe six to ten men there.'

'He said Nigeria's too dangerous at the moment.'

'True,' he said, and sat at his desk again. 'So, you tell him what you want. We'll wait for your call. The rest is for us.'

He clasped his hands, fingers tapped knuckles. The white rim around his mouth had gone. A man his age should be careful of a temper like that. I sipped my forgotten grappa. Franconelli picked up his forgotten cigar. He relit it and loosened off his dressing gown. He put a hand up his pyjamas and massaged his heart as if he knew he'd done it wrong. It revealed a thick hairy belly that had a layer of fat that filled the contours of muscle underneath. He put an ankle up on a knee. The fly of his pyjamas gaped and a short, thick, brutal penis emerged. He didn't notice.

I was too tired to move. I should have left but there was Carlo to come. It was after two thirty in the morning now. A car pulled up outside and Franconelli stirred. He tied himself up in his dressing gown again. A few minutes later Carlo brought Graydon and Gale in. They didn't look as if they'd been talking in the car on the way over.

Graydon was dressed in a paisley-design silk dressing gown with some yellow Moroccan *barbouches* on his feet and a pair of fuchsia-coloured pyjamas.

'Carlo said it absolutely can't wait until a civilized hour in the morning,' said Graydon.

'It can't,' said Franconelli, and Graydon's jaw muscles bunched. 'You never seen Graydon in short sleeves, have you?'

I shook my head.

'Show him, Graydon.'

'What is this?' Graydon whined.

Franconelli nodded at Carlo, who was standing behind Graydon's chair in the absence of a seat. He hoisted Graydon by the collar and with one movement pulled the gown and the pyjamas off Graydon's shoulders. He had eczema rashes in the crooks of both elbows.

'You started on your feet yet?' asked Franconelli.

Carlo let him go and Graydon shrugged his clothes back on, looking at Gale as he did so.

'The *Red Solent*, the *Ohio Warrior*, the *Limnos III* and the *Mithoni VII*,' said Franconelli.

Graydon smiled.

'I'll see you straight,' said Graydon.

'You couldn't see me straight if I came at you on rails.'

'A game, Roberto. Just a few million bucks. We understand each other.'

'We don't,' he said. 'You think I'm playing games with you?'

Wall-to-wall silence. Three-dimensional, double-density silence.

'Your wife came here to beg for you,' said Franconelli.

Graydon didn't even look at her.

'What does she want out of it?' he asked.

Franconelli laughed.

'You got to know each other better than that. If any-body deserved each other it was you two. Maybe what they say about opposites is true.'

'I don't remember *your* wife being *that* nice,' said Graydon.

Graydon couldn't resist it. That was his problem. An addictive personality. Looking basket-wise on the guil-lotine he still had to have his say. Franconelli saw that there was no talking to him. He walked over and slapped him hard across the mouth so that Graydon fell to the floor at the feet of the men on the sofa. He got himself up on an elbow. His hair was jogged out of place and blood coated his lip, which was swollen in a corner. With the veneer cracked he should have started looking smaller. Carlo put him back on his chair.

'You're going to make a couple of phone calls,' said Franconelli. 'One to your bank in Zurich to arrange a transfer of ten million dollars to your wife who has saved your ass. The second to your lawyer who is going to arrange for those four ships to be sold to one of my holding companies. I think four bucks should see the deal through.'

That breezeblock silence was back in the room. Six pairs of eyes would have weighed a lot on anybody else, but Graydon was built different and he let the silence go on until it was stacked to the ceiling, then he said:

'I don't think I am, Roberto.'

Chapter 28

Carlo drove me to Cotonou in my car. He started to tell me I should buy myself something with air conditioning then stopped and stuck his elbow out the window. He didn't want to talk about that – bored himself easily.

'You don't like Selina, Carlo?' I asked.

'I like her fine,' he said, slowing for a police roadblock. They waved us through. 'But not for Mr Franconelli. She don't want to be his wife. I seen girls like that.'

'She's doing him some good.'

'No. You the man doin' him some good. This the first time he shaped up in years. We been runnin' around for those guys and they been fuckin' us in the ass for our trouble. Now Mr Franconelli wakin' up. You goin' to see something. I'm tellin' you.'

He might have carried on talking for all I know. My head dropped and I slept until we arrived on the outskirts of Cotonou at 6.30 a.m. I took him past the warehouse and then to my office downtown. I gave the *gardien* some money and told him to buy coffee and croissants and make a copy of the warehouse key for Carlo. I left Carlo in the office and went home.

Heike was still sleeping. Helen arrived, put one of her tooth-cleaning sticks in her mouth, and started sweeping the floor. I called Vassili and told him to get Mr K to call me in my office in half an hour and to tell Viktor to be there as soon as possible. I went back to the office and had breakfast with Carlo. At 7.30 a.m. the *gardien* brought the key, Carlo brushed himself off and left. Five minutes later Mr K called.

'What happened?'

'I had to go to Lagos,' I said.

'Problem?'

'Nothing's easy.'

'It's solved?'

'We're ready.'

'A set of keys will be delivered to your office. They belong to a Renault 18 parked where the jeep was the other night in the Sheraton.' He gave me the registration. 'You should be there no earlier than eight fifteen a.m. The goods and documentation are in the boot. Leave a message with Vassili when you have the car. I hope you still have the money.'

The line cut. Fifteen minutes later Viktor arrived. I sent the *gardien* out again for more breakfast. Viktor, in a loose-fitting short-sleeve shirt which he wore outside his jeans, laid a palm on the desk top and tapped it with his thumb. I asked him to stop. He went out on to the balcony, his Reebok sneakers squeaking on the floor. Time passed in rashers. The boy came back with some croissants *ordinaires* because the *au beurre* were finished. Viktor asked him to go and buy a *pain chocolat*. I opened some windows but the heat was everywhere. The caffeine made me sweaty and breathless.

There was a knock at the door. I shouted for the boy to come in. No answer. I opened the door and found an envelope leaning against the jamb. The car keys. The boy arrived with the *pain chocolat*.

317

We left for the Sheraton, me driving, Viktor with the keys and spitting flakes of pastry from the *pain chocolat* over the front of the car. We pulled up alongside the blue Renault in the Sheraton car park. Viktor got out and slid into the driver's seat. We drove back to the house. I parked the Peugeot outside and got Viktor to reverse up to Moses's apartment. I opened the door. Viktor popped the boot on the Renault. There were four boxes in some kind of heavy-duty plastic with the nuclear insignia on each and a black vinyl briefcase. We lifted them out. They must have weighed around twenty-five kilos each. Viktor took the briefcase into the apartment and sat on the bed with the bedside lamp on. He lifted the documents out which were broken up into four batches, each one in a clear plastic zip-up sachet. All the typing was in Cyrillic script. I read off the codes on the sides of the boxes and Viktor placed a set of corresponding documents on each. He opened up the first sachet.

'This is seven hundred grammes of Plutonium 239. It's originally from Tomsk-7 Western Russia. It's made up from eighteen batches.'

He flicked through all the papers, counting off the batches and checking a signature at the bottom.

'These are all signed by Major-General Dimitri Lentov who runs the Tomsk-7 facility. This plutonium is made up from small consignments sent from Tomsk-7 to a research laboratory in Tblisi. Three hundred grammes here, two hundred and fifty there. Then as the product moves around the Tblisi facility, slowly, slowly it gets lost.'

'So all the documents show is where the material originated?'

'You can't get official documentation for material *stolen* from the Tblisi facility. *Ça, mon ami, c'est impossible.*'

'So the material could be bogus?'

'Of course. If you were selling to a government, like the Pakistanis, say, they have a facility to check the quality of the goods. Here we just have copies of the documents of origin and the boxes to go on. The documents tell me this is genuine weapons-grade plutonium and to my eyes the boxes look genuine. What's actually in them? Ah, well. But let's not open them up.'

I left Viktor to his work and went upstairs to phone Mr K. Heike was up and eating. She was looking sharp, which made me nervous. If she knew what was downstairs it would be the end.

'They said I have to eat,' she said. '*Je dois bouffer fort.*' She put an arm around my neck and kissed me. 'Tense?'

'Still.'

'Don't be about me.'

'I'm coming down from it.'

'We should go away for a weekend. I should get some rest. We could go to Grand Popo, as long as they take all those gouty anchovies out of the *salade Niçoise.*'

'Sure.'

'I'm drowning in your enthusiasm.'

'Just a few things to sort out first.'

'I won't ask,' she said. 'What are you doing in Moses's flat?'

'I thought you said you wouldn't ask.'

She sucked in air as if she'd cut herself with a knife.

'Take a shower,' she said, 'and call Bagado.'

'He's called?'

'Left messages. Two.'

'I can't talk to him now.'

'You don't look that busy.'

'I'm taking a shower.'

'All day?'

'That was a public announcement.'

'We're gratified.'

After the shower, even in new clothes, I still felt dirty. I found the icepick in the kitchen drawer and slipped it into my chinos pocket, which was just long enough to take it. I went back downstairs. Viktor had packed away the documents. I told him we had to move the product out. We packed it in the car again and drove down to my office.

They were killing another sheep outside on the concrete ramp below the balcony. I parked up next to the butcher who was hauling the guts out of the carcass. I trod in the blood as I got out of the car. My foot skidded away from me and I just saved myself from landing on my arse in it. In the office, my sticky shoe kissed the tiles and left perfect prints in the dust. Viktor sat on the client side of the desk while I called Lagos. Ben Agu answered.

'Are you ready?' he asked.

'I'd like to speak to the chief.'

'*I'm* handling the details.'

'Let me speak to the chief, Ben,' I said, cheerfully. He hesitated and put the phone down. I heard the chief lumber across the room and sink into a leather chair which gasped.

He didn't say anything but breathed in a congested way down the mouthpiece.

'I'm ready,' I said. He didn't respond. 'I have some conditions.' He tapped the side of the phone and sighed.

'You'll have to come to the warehouse and bring Selina with you.'

'Not this time,' he said.

'Yes, this time.'

'Only when we complete the transaction.'

'No,' I said. 'It won't work like that. I want to see her every step of the way.'

'You can talk to her now.'

'I don't need to because you're bringing her with you tonight.'

'Tonight?'

'This isn't a business where hanging around is advisable.'

'What time?'

'Eleven o'clock. That should give me enough time.'

'She'll go back with us.'

'Of course.'

'How many people will you bring?'

'Just me and one other. Ben knows him. We don't want the world there.'

'No, no. You are right.'

'And your side?'

'The three of us.'

'And no arms.'

'Arms?'

'Firearms.'

The chief started laughing, slowly at first but he built it into a guffaw, a gut laugh, a tear-jerker, a bowel-loosener. There must be other people who would find that funny – tell a guy not to bring a pistol when you're selling him a nuclear bomb – but not me. I slammed the phone down.

I pulled the *gardien* up again and asked for more coffee. I put my feet up on the desk. The phone rang. I let the answering machine take the call. It was Bagado. I clasped my hands tight across my stomach. He said he knew I was there and shouted at me to pick up the phone. Viktor licked his lips. Bagado said he had important information on Napier Briggs. It was nothing that could help me or him now. I let Bagado use up tape. He clicked off after a minute. Viktor didn't inquire.

I paced the office and grew some sweat patches on my shirt. Distant music came over the traffic – drums, trumpets. The coffee arrived. I went out on to the balcony and breathed in some disgusting air. Viktor joined me. The music was louder. A straggle of people stopped at the roadside to watch. A phalanx of robed dignitaries preceded a coffin held aloft. A group of women followed supporting one of their number who was the distraught widow. The band played out of tune and time as if the man's death had destroyed the natural order of things. They walked to the junction. The traffic stopped. They crossed the road to the cathedral.

I went back into the office, drank coffee and put funerals out of my head. Viktor stayed out on the balcony. I called Franconelli and gave him the time for the product exchange. I told Viktor we had to kill some time.

He asked me if I knew somewhere where we could go and drink some beer and watch women take their clothes off. He said that would use up some time, you know, in a nice way. I told him stripping was not something they did a lot of in Africa. You either went the whole hog or not at all – no halfway house. Viktor smoothed his beard over his face and shook his head. AIDS, he said, it was a problem.

We could always go and play pinball in La Verdure, I said. He wasn't terrorized with excitement until I told him that there were always two or three girls there and he shouldn't find it too difficult to persuade one of them to go upstairs and take her clothes off for him. He shrugged and asked me if I'd ever had sex with a black girl. I said it was none of his business. He asked me if I knew a lyric from a rock song which went something like, 'Black girls, they just wanna get fucked all night, but I ain't got that much jam.' It sounded like the Rolling Stones, I said, but I didn't have Jagger's phone number so he could talk it over with him. I was beginning not to like Viktor very much.

We drove to La Verdure. I parked up against the railings and we went in and ordered two *demi pressions*. There were no girls, just a shrunken French alcoholic in a red shirt four sizes too big for him. I took five games of pool off Viktor and then we had Sunday lunch. We ate a *terrine de lapin*, *côte de porc grillé*, and a *marquise de chocolat* in a thin *crème anglaise*. We drank the quarter *pichet* of red each that came with the set menu. The girls turned up. Viktor went back into the bar. Time was dead on its feet and wouldn't move on even if I looked at the second hand.

Viktor negotiated with one of the Beninois girls to go upstairs and take her clothes off, but even he realized this was not going to push the clock forward too much as the girl was wearing a blouse, a skirt, a pair of knickers and two shoes. Even if she was a master of the art, which I doubted, she was going to have her work cut out to stretch that over five minutes. I told him to go and buy seven veils. He renegotiated to include a *pipe*, a blow job. I felt sick. They went upstairs.

Another girl who looked as if she'd have had to jump from the fourth floor to get into the lycra sheath she was wearing twanged her way over to me. She was grabbed by a sailor whose gut rested on the glass of the pinball machine, a tattoo of a pair of breasts danced on his bicep as he played it. He smelled of ripe cheese and I could tell that the girl had to search for the hero inside herself just to put an arm around him. I needed to get out of here. I was resenting Viktor's stamina for the situation. He'd been up there six hours now, well, eighteen minutes, but you know how it is when you're the gooseberry.

Viktor came down around teatime. I was playing pool against my alter ego. The dark side was winning. Things had progressed. They were holding hands. They walked over as if I was Daddy and could take them home now. I said I had to get some sleep and that we'd take a bungalow in the Aledjo. I didn't want to be anywhere where anybody could find me. I drove like a good cabbie with the two in the back kicking the doors out in a struggle that should have left them wearing each other's clothes.

I went to the reception and booked a two-bedroomed bungalow. I found a critical situation in the back of the car when I came back. I asked them if they couldn't just hang on for a moment. The answer was, apparently, no.

I got them into a bedroom using some sheepdog skills

I'd picked up from afternoon television when I was a lot younger. I fell on to the bed in the other room and folded a pillow over my head. I dropped into a world which was no less complicated and terrifying, but had the dubious benefit of jerking me awake so that at least I knew it wasn't real.

Chapter 29

It was 10 p.m. Sunday night. Two columns of oblongs lit the wall behind the bed. The air con couldn't subdue the concentrated pumping from the next bedroom – Viktor finding something out for himself, not having to listen to a rock singer tell him. I hammered on the door.

'*Allons-y, Viktor!*' I shouted.

'*Je viens,*' he said, and increased the tempo.

'*Oui,*' whinnied the girl.

Right.

I checked the car. It was hot out there and the air coming off the sea a few hundred metres away had halitosis which followed me around like those people in offices who feel the need to get close and breathe on you, see if you faint. The product was still in the boot.

There was the faintest flicker of lightning far away over Nigeria, so far that there was no sound. Viktor shambled out of the bungalow.

'*Quelle heure est-il?*' he asked.

'*Dix heures et quart.*'

He whistled to himself, amazed at his own stamina, letting me know he was impressed. We got in the car. I drove.

'*Elle va rester ici?*' I asked.

'*Je vais revenir après,*' he said, sticking an elbow out of the window, putting a foot up on the dash.

We cruised into the industrial zone a half kilometre from the Aledjo. The traffic was light off the main Cotonou–Porto Novo road but the air was still thick with heat and fumes. We drifted through a residential area. Africans who'd made something in the communist era had bought for nothing out here and now small concrete palaces were going up. We merged back with the industrial zone and turned up the sandy track to the warehouse. A single *gardien* slept on a wooden bench outside. There was nobody else around. The few houses opposite the warehouse were either unfinished and boarded up or just footings in the sand with long grass growing in them. It was 10.30 p.m.

I paid the *gardien* to get lost until dawn. Viktor opened up the gates and drove into the compound. I unlocked the warehouse doors in the middle and Viktor reversed up the ramp. He cut the engine and left the lights on. I closed the doors and found the light switch. Two of the three lights came on, one in the middle and one over the Renault. Viktor killed the headlights. I took a torch from the glove and walked up and down the warehouse. It was still empty apart from the stacks of cotton seed in sacks. I checked the roof. In the centre, on the other side from the Renault, a pulley hung from the lowest girder and a rope dropped from it to the top of the cotton-seed stack which was maybe three metres below the roof.

Viktor stayed in the car, sprawled across the front seats with the door open, one foot hanging out, the other resting on the frame of the open window. I sat on a couple of sacks and listened to cars crescendo and diminuendo. The storm I'd seen earlier came fractionally closer – thunder creaked lengthily. Eleven o'clock came and went. I killed four mosquitoes, one fat with blood from a snort off Viktor who was now snoring.

An old tiredness settled on me, one which had started maybe five years ago and never been slept off. It was the kind of fatigue that probably occurred in eighty-year-olds, that pushed them down into the bed and helped them decide that maybe it would be quieter if they gave up the struggle and fertilized the soil instead. It was a weight but a comfortable one. One that sat easy on the body, didn't chafe . . .

The warehouse door I was facing slid open two inches, then a foot. Ben Agu came in with a flashlight. He didn't acknowledge me, but walked up and down the warehouse. Then he stood under the central light, turned off the torch, and tucked it under his arm. He took a mobile out of his pocket and pressed buttons. He spoke quietly.

'You're late,' I said.

He went back to the sliding doors and looked out. After a few minutes he flashed his torch. A car reversed up outside. Red lights glowed on the wall of the other warehouse. A car door opened. Ben slid the warehouse doors to a four-foot gap. The chief came in, followed by Selina. The car's engine ticked over. Its lights died. Ben shut the doors. The chief entered the cone of light in the centre of the warehouse. Selina remained at the edge. Ben Agu joined her but not with a torch in his hand. He had a .38 with a suppressor attached.

'I said no guns.'

'You did,' said the chief. 'I thought security was more important.'

'You've got a driver with you. That makes four not three.'

'There's two men on the gates as well,' said Ben. 'That's six not three.'

'This is Viktor,' I said. He was sitting up now with his heels on the sills of the door. 'The plutonium-reprocessing expert.'

'Is he satisfied?'

'As far as he can be without opening the boxes. He says the documents show where the product originated and that it's weapons-grade plutonium, and he says the containers are genuine too.'

'Where does it come from?'

'Originally Tomsk-7 but it was stolen from a research reactor in Tblisi.'

'He hasn't looked at it.'

'It's not the sort of thing you can fry up in your kitchen.'

'We know where to find you,' said the chief. 'By the time we take the second lot we'll be equipped to inspect the product properly. I have a Russian working on the project already.'

The chief smoothed his hands down the blue robes he was wearing and repositioned his hat. The car's engine cut suddenly. Ben faced the doors which he'd left open a crack. There was a pop as if a milk carton had been run over on the road. Ben jumped backwards, staggered two steps, dropped the gun, put a hand out to break his fall and fell on his hip. He twisted his body towards the light where the chief was standing and tried to say something. His chin hovered an inch above the floor, his eyes widened and his teeth appeared red in his mouth. His shirt darkened rapidly.

A harsh grating sound of metal on metal shattered the silence of Ben's last struggle. A man came through the sliding doors and walked swiftly towards the chief. He had a gun in his hand. A rope looped into the light from above. The gunman bent and scooped it up without breaking his stride. He fitted the loop over the chief's shoulders and tugged it down to his hips. The rope, which disappeared into the darkness of the roof, tightened. The chief shifted. He still hadn't had time to be astonished. The loop slid to his thighs. The rope tightened again. The chief put his hands out and fell to his knees. He was on all fours when, with a tendon-snapping wrench, his legs shot into the air as Carlo and another guy jumped from the stack of cotton-seed sacks holding the other end of the rope.

The chief ended upside down about a metre off the ground, his robes hanging down over his head, his hat a flat blue circle on the floor. He reached for the ground with his hands and grunted thickly as the blood pounded into his head.

Franconelli came in through the sliding doors followed by Gale and another man pushing a wheelchair in which was strapped a person who looked a lot like Graydon but with a clear plastic horror mask superimposed. In the lap of this spectre was some folded yellow PVC and a pair of boots with large steel toecaps. I'd seen a pair of boots like that before. My father had bought me some on the cheap for my first labouring job. They had special flaps that fitted over the laces and were kept in place by a strap and buckle around the ankle. He'd got them from a friend who worked in an abattoir. The flaps stopped the blood leaking into the boots and ruining your socks.

Two more men came in carrying a brown plastic-backed tarpaulin. They unfolded it and dragged it underneath the chief. Franconelli flapped a hand and Carlo lowered the chief to within a few inches of the floor. One of the tarpaulin men took out a penknife and cut away the chief's robes just leaving him with his trousers. He took some plastic cuffs out of his pocket and went for the chief's hands. The chief grabbed him and attempted to haul himself upright but found he didn't have the condition to do it. The man shrugged him off and cuffed the chief's wrists behind his back. The chief's belly, tits and jowls sagged to the floor. He was finding breathing difficult and was sweating heavily. Franconelli flapped his hand again and Carlo lowered the chief to the floor, where he floundered like an elephant seal.

I took a closer look at the man in the wheelchair and decided it was Graydon, but he'd aged twenty years overnight. That smooth, tanned opulence had gone. He was sucked dry, wrinkled and jaundiced. His left leg and hand trembled. His chest was concave. When he bared his teeth to swallow, they looked horsey and loose.

'Yes,' said Franconelli, 'Graydon likes to take his turkey cold.'

'He didn't come across with it?' I asked. Franconelli ignored me.

'Fifteen years,' said Franconelli. 'Fifteen years on cocaine. How much is he up to a day now, Carlo? We gotta be talking grammes of the stuff. Two heavy shots of heroin a day, a speedball or two at the weekends, freebasing, dragon-chasing. Graydon wasn't Graydon. We don't know where the fuck Graydon is.'

Gale was wearing the same cream dress from last night. She was rubbing at some bites on her bare legs with the sandals she had on her feet. She wouldn't make eye contact. Selina took some spray out of her handbag and threw it to her. It landed at her feet. She didn't pick it up.

Franconelli flicked his fingers at the other tarpaulin man, who took the boots and PVC from Graydon's lap. Roberto slipped off his loafers, took hold of the PVC and shook it out into a pair of trousers. He put them on over his own. He fitted his feet into the boots and the tarpaulin man did them up for him. Franconelli stamped his feet. He checked his watch.

'All of us here like to play games,' he said. 'People who play games like to win. If there's a winner there has to be a loser. These two had me pegged as a loser. They took advantage of a situation. A personal situation. And they're going to pay for that. Now *I'm* the winner,' he looked at Selina, 'and because of that you're going to win.' She didn't know how to respond.

'And what about me?' said Gale.

'I kept my word to you. You didn't win because Graydon didn't want you to win. The guy's nuts. What can I say?'

'Just get on with it, Roberto,' said Gale. 'Don't give us any more of this shit about winning and losing. It's a crock.'

That jerked Franconelli's string. He went over to her, the boots clicking on the concrete floor. He said something to her which nobody heard but it left Gale pale and a lot less brassy. Franconelli walked back on to the tarpaulin.

'The Big Man,' he said. 'The *great* presidential candidate for this "*great* country of ours".'

The chief looked up at him from the floor with a big question mark in his face that he couldn't articulate.

'This country will never be great,' said Franconelli, 'until they cut out all the little people like you. The greedy, the corrupt, the stupid, the inefficient – the nobodies who make themselves into somebodies who rule everybody. You're depraved, you're dishonest, you're vulgar. And you have only one ambition . . . to fuck everybody that comes your way. I despise you. I despise your stinking, dirty, noisy capital. I despise your country.'

The chief broke in with something which nobody, including Franconelli, heard. The Italian jerked his head up and Carlo pulled on the rope until the chief's head was an inch off the tarpaulin. Then he got down on his hands and knees, put his face up to the chief's and asked him what he'd said.

'What about *you*? What about *your* country?' said the chief.

Franconelli sprang up on to the balls of his feet and paced back to the edge of the tarpaulin. He had the white rim to his dark lips again. The carotid was pulsing in his neck.

'The only thing we got in common,' he said, 'we both like football.'

He ran at the chief with surprising speed and kicked him with all his weight in the head. The chief's body swung on the end of the rope. Blood poured from a wound in the chief's face. He roared like a cow in labour. The blood pattered on the plastic tarpaulin.

Franconelli gripped the chief's legs to still him. He bared his teeth. His tongue protruded, bigger than a snake's tail, and with frenzied brutality, he kicked him to death. I didn't watch. The sound of those boots on human tissue was terrible enough. It was over in less than a minute. Viktor watched it all, his eyes unblinking as if perhaps he'd seen this kind of thing before. Maybe even done it.

Carlo lowered the chief into the appalling quantity of thick, gelatinous blood that had emptied from his body. Franconelli stepped back. One of the tarpaulin men came forward and cut him out of his trousers and then out of the boots. He stepped into his loafers again and walked off the tarpaulin. They loosened off the rope around the chief's ankles and rolled him into the middle of the tarp. Viktor appeared and helped them move Ben next to the chief. Then they rolled everything up in the tarpaulin and it took the four of them to carry it out.

Gale was sitting on the floor with her head between her knees. There was a large patch of vomit around her. Selina was shaking and white. Franconelli stood in front of her at a distance of three feet. He didn't look like a man who was in love any more, and he'd just executed a demonstration of ruthlessness that no woman, no human being, could stomach. Graydon was wheeled out of the warehouse. Selina glanced over Franconelli's shoulder at the passing Graydon. Then went back to the impassive heavy features of the Italian.

'You killed my father,' she said.

'I don't kill people,' said Franconelli, reminding us what we hadn't just seen.

'Her father was Napier Briggs,' I shouted across the warehouse.

'You can shut the fuck up too,' he said brutally. 'I found that out for myself this morning. Got a call from Naples telling me who Mrs Aguia used to be. I ask you to fucking do something for me and you lie in my face.' He spat sideways without looking, without taking his eyes off Selina.

'Why did you have to kill him like that?'

'The chief?' asked Franconelli. He looked behind him. Carlo and the other men stood there in a state of respectful awe. 'Family matters,' he said. 'You'll find that.'

'And my father,' asked Selina. 'What terrible thing did he do to you that you had to torture and murder him?'

'You can't ask me that question.'

'Why not?'

'Because if I answer that you'd have to go the same way.'

The chill in his voice stopped Selina's trembling. Franconelli turned his back on her. He looked down at Gale and nodded to one of his men who helped her to her feet. They left the warehouse. Two cars pulled away. A distant clap of thunder strode out into the night.

Chapter 30

Early morning. Monday 4th March.

We crossed the Porto Novo road and the railway tracks at 12.40 a.m. and cut through some dirt tracks to another arterial road which went back across the lagoon to the Dan Tokpa market. We didn't cross the lagoon but turned right and headed towards Vassili's house. Selina held on to my arm as if she was going to fall off a cliff. We drove into Vassili's yard.

'*Qu'est-ce que nous faisons ici?*' I asked Viktor, who didn't answer but got out of the car and went into the house.

Vassili came out with a bottle of vodka in his hand and some shot glasses on the end of his fingers. He set them on the bonnet and poured. We knocked back three apiece. Then Vassili and Viktor, speaking in Russian constantly, unloaded the product and put it into a garage in which a thirty-watt bulb was barely lighting the place. Vassili called me into the garage and put a meaty arm around my shoulders. He gripped my left bicep hard with his other hand.

'Don't run away,' he said.

'Do I need to?'

'Take a look at this.'

Viktor dropped to his haunches and snapped the

catches on one of the plastic nuclear containers. He flicked up two metal handles and eased a metal inner case out of the foam-lined plastic sleeve. Two keys were required to unlock the case. He took them out of the briefcase and fitted them into the locks.

'That's far enough, Viktor,' I said.

'A small lesson,' said Vassili, 'in radioactivity.'

Viktor turned the keys simultaneously. I stiffened. Vassili gripped me harder. Viktor lifted off the lid.

'For Christ's sake,' I said. 'What the hell is he . . .'

Viktor picked up a dark-red slab from the top of the container.

'Your first lesson on radioactivity,' said Viktor, in English.

'Plasticine is not radioactive,' said Vassili, and roared with laughter.

I turned to Selina who was leaning against the door of the garage with her ankles crossed, smoking and sipping another shot of vodka.

'You see,' said Vassili, 'Africans think that they live in the only Africa. But Russia is Africa times two. Russia is white Africa.'

'Was this your idea?' I asked Selina. She nodded. 'And you didn't think it was a good idea to tell me.'

'You wouldn't have agreed.'

'I know.'

'I couldn't force you. You had to *be* forced.'

'And what if Franconelli hadn't turned up tonight? What if he'd decided to leave us in it once he knew who your father was? What would we have done then?'

'You going to Franconelli nearly fucked the whole thing up. This deal was supposed to be the smooth one.

It was the next where things were going to go wrong. Still, three million dollars isn't bad for a night's work. Two nights for six million would have been better but . . .'

'You didn't get your murderer,' I said.

'That's true,' she said, and turned her back on me to look into Vassili's yard of cars, 'but what can you do against the mafia? We were lucky to get out of there. What do you think he meant by "family matters"? "Matters of the family" or "family is important"?'

'You decide,' I said. 'It's not an evening that's going to go down in the Book of Deftness and Witty Repartee.'

'Why do you think he had to kill him in front of us . . . like that, with his own feet, for Christ's sake?'

'You're not feeling blabby, are you?'

'Just to scare us?' she asked.

'What do you think his men thought of him afterwards?'

She nodded, turned the corners of her mouth down and smoked some more.

'Where's the money?' asked a voice behind me. A voice I recognized now as Mr K's. Viktor had a big grin in his beard, a long black wig on his head and a gold ring on the third finger of his right hand.

'Is he the Kazakh bastard?' I asked Vassili.

'No, no,' said Vassili, grinning. 'He work in plutonium reprocessing. It's true.'

'Have you got it?' asked Viktor again.

I looked at Vassili. He looked blank, sweaty.

'Answer him,' he said. 'There's no harm in answering him.'

'Yeah, I've got it, Viktor.'

'Then let's go,' he said, 'and get it.'

'It's a million each, is it?' I asked.

'Between four it's seven-fifty,' said Selina.

Silence apart from a buzz from the thirty-watt bulb.

'So, let's go,' I said.

We drove over a quiet lagoon, past a deserted market, through silent streets to my house. I unlocked Moses's apartment and turned the light on. Selina and Vassili sat on the bed. Viktor stood by the door. I went into the back room and pulled the suitcase off the ledge. I took it into the room and dropped it on the floor in front of them. Selina leaned over and unzipped the case. She smiled and took out a block of money. Then the three of us looked up simultaneously, not because there'd been any noise, but because we all knew there was something bad in the room.

Viktor had a gun in his hand. It looked like the one Ben Agu had when he'd come into the warehouse, the silenced .38. He pointed the gun at me and then at Vassili when some Russian language rushed at him from that quarter. They talked for a minute – fast and ugly words. I fingered the ice pick in my pocket but, apart from not wanting to risk my arse for the money, Viktor wasn't exactly presenting me with his occipital bulge. At the end of it Vassili told Selina to put the money back in the case and kick it over to Viktor. He told me to throw Viktor the keys to the flat and to sit down on the chair. Viktor picked up the case and backed off to the door.

'Don't forget that girl you left in the Aledjo,' I said.

'She's dead,' he said, and locked us in the room.

We looked at each other and listened to the Renault

starting up and pulling away. Selina asked if we were going to do anything about it.

'Like what?' asked Vassili.

'Kick the door down and go after him?'

'Nobody touches that door,' I said. 'I'm not explaining this shit to Heike. We're going to wait 'til Helen comes in the morning.'

Nobody moved. It was 1.30 a.m. It was hot and airless with no window and the door closed.

'Was he the Kazakh bastard?' I asked Vassili.

'I can't believe he did that to me,' he said, and we didn't talk about it further.

Helen let us out at 6.30 in the morning. Vassili went straight home on a *taxi moto*. Selina and I sat out on the verandah in the early-morning cool and waited for Helen to make some coffee and run down to La Caravelle for croissants.

'I didn't want the money,' said Selina.

'Nor me, not after that.'

'You're kidding.'

'Can you see me explaining to Heike how I came by three-quarters of a million dollars in cash? And all that blood on it.'

She nodded.

'I lied,' she said, 'I really did want that money.'

'To go with the other seven in Zurich?'

'Yeah, that would have made the round ten.'

'Ten if you'd had the gun. Eight if you were the sharing type.'

She laughed.

'Yes, of course,' she said. 'Silly me. I must be tired.'

I listened to the messages on the answering machine.

340

Bagado said that if I didn't come down to his office this morning at 7.30 a.m. he'd have me arrested. The coffee and croissants came.

'I'll still keep my side of the bargain,' said Selina. 'You can have whatever's in the bag.'

I shook my head.

'I don't want it.'

'You need it.'

'Just give me the fee we agreed. I don't need any more than that.'

'You're a sucker, Bruce.'

'But not a bloodsucker, Selina.'

I was at Bagado's office for seven thirty. He was standing in his door in the blue mac looking agitated. We left immediately at Bagado's walking sprint. We got into a police car at the back of the Sûreté and took off at speed.

'What about my car?'

'You've got a new one,' he said. 'Been busy?'

'I'm on my own now. Double the work.'

'Anything I should know?'

'Just business.'

'I thought so,' he said, and gave me a sad look.

'You know how it is, Bagado.'

'I'm going to give you a break.'

I didn't respond because on the pavement outside the post office I'd just seen the girl Viktor had been with all yesterday afternoon and evening. She was hanging off the arm of a very tense-looking white guy and seemed very much alive. Viktor had learned something from Franconelli, or maybe he had it in him all the time.

'Thanks,' I said, coming back to Bagado, 'but I don't know if I can return the favour.'

'You will.'

'If it's about Napier Briggs, I finished with him a long time ago.'

'And Selina?'

'She's still here.'

'This might be something for her.'

We pulled up outside the Hotel de la Plage, a renovated place downtown, with a beach which had a view of the port's cranes and warehousing.

'Room twenty-two,' said Bagado. 'His name is Martin Taylor.'

'You're not coming in?'

'There's a Mercedes been found on a dump out towards Porto Novo. The driver's neck's been broken. There's two armed men in the back who've been shot and there's two bodies in the boot. Bondougou's sent a twenty-three-year-old down there to sort it out.'

'He'll need some help.'

'And I know Bondougou doesn't want me there.'

Bagado's wheels spun in the sand, gripped and he moved off. I watched him turn right round the back of the hotel and thought – Bondougou, a Franconelli man. I went up to room twenty-two before the hopelessness diverted me to the bar.

Martin Taylor was a big, good-looking man, in a model way, of around thirty years old. He took care of himself. He was wearing loose, baggy jeans and a viscose short-sleeve shirt with a pattern thought up on LSD. He liked running his hand through his thick black hair and he shaved to a charcoal stubble.

He sat cross-legged on the bed in a practised way as if he did regular yoga. I straddled a chair, rested my arms on the back, laid my chin on them and let gravity do what it wanted with my eyelids.

'You look tired.'

'Yes,' I said. 'Bagado says you want to talk about Napier.'

The name jolted him and a terrible look of loss came over his face. I knew why I was here.

'You're "Y", aren't you?' I asked.

'"Y"?'

'You're Napier's new lover.'

'New?'

'You didn't know about "X"?'

'He said he had a complicated business situation down in Nigeria which he was going to resolve, that's all. No Xs and no Ys.'

'You don't know David Bartholomew?'

'No. Napier just left and I didn't hear from him for some time.'

'Like ten days?'

'Yes. Then he called me, said he was in Benin, that it was nearly finished and he'd be back in a few days. We were going to Barbados. I booked the flights.'

'Did he give you my name in case there was trouble?'

'Yes, you've been difficult to get hold of. The *gardien* told me where to find Bagado.'

'How long had you known Napier?'

'Six months. We'd been close for three.'

'You never called him in Africa?'

'He called me that one time, that's all.'

'You know his body's gone back?'

343

'With his daughter, they told me. I didn't even know he had one. I missed the funeral,' he said. 'Do you know who killed him?'

'I know who *had* him killed.'

'Why?'

'If you wait twenty-four hours I'll find out for you.'

I took a *taxi moto* back to the Sûreté and picked up my car. I drove back home and got the videotape of David and Ali. I was just drinking chilled water from the fridge when I saw that guy again, in daylight this time, standing out on his balcony looking into the garden. I opened the kitchen window and I was about to shout at him when I saw what he was looking at – his dog taking a shit in the garden.

I left for Lagos and had one of my worst trips ever. It took me ten hours to get to David Bartholomew's house, by which time it was 7.30 p.m.

I found a surprising situation there. The front gate was still manned by a watchman but there was nobody else in the compound – no gardener, no cook, no maid. The door to the house had been left open. I walked down a dark corridor towards a room at the back of the house which was lit by wall lights only. The central chandelier of the room had been disconnected and lifted off a hook in the ceiling. It lay on its side on the floor. A chair stood underneath the hook.

David was slumped on the sofa in the living room. He was staring at an ashtray that had four burning menthol cigarettes in it. His lips and chin were wet. He blinked infrequently. He had a bottle of Red Label in one hand – a litre bottle half full – and a glass in the other. He drained the glass and refilled it, spilling a quantity on to his trousers.

'Can you spare a glass of that for me, or is it all yours?' I asked.

'Fuck off,' he said, and his hair flopped down over his forehead.

'You don't look as if you're in any state to be repairing light fittings, David.'

'Fuck off.'

I found a glass in a cabinet across the room and a forgotten bottle of Chivas in the back. I poured myself a slug from it rather than wrestle with David on the sofa for the Red Label. I sat in the armchair opposite him.

'You're not going to kill yourself, David.'

'What makes you think I want to?'

'What's the chandelier doing on the floor?'

'Haven't you heard what we buggers get up to?'

'I've brought you your video.'

'Send it to my boss. Sir George Kingsmill, British High Commission, 11 Eleke Crescent, Vic Island, Lagos. He'd be charmed. There's a distinct lack of decent entertainment out here, you know.'

The air con was on full blast but the sweat was pouring off David. His chair was wet from it. He squeezed the bottle between the cushions of the sofa and brushed it back. He found a hanky and wiped his face off. He looked at his trousers, which must have felt wet and said, 'Fucking hell.'

'Still care about your clothes, David.'

'That's all I have to care about.'

'I found out about Napier.'

'Oh yes?'

'Franconelli killed him.'

'The bastard.'

'You probably knew that.'

He snorted, and two jets of snot shot out of his nose. He found the hanky again.

'What a fucking state . . .' he said to himself.

'Do you know why he killed him?'

'I know everything,' he said extravagantly.

'Tell me.'

'Ah, yes. The big confession.'

'I don't think so.'

'No?'

'You're not going to kill yourself.'

'Course I'm not.'

'I'll make sure you don't.'

'Course you will.'

'Now tell me.'

He pushed himself up off the sofa and took an inch off the whisky in his glass and swallowed it as if it was nitric acid. He put the glass down on the table.

'Don't breathe a word,' he said, bug-eyed suddenly and comical.

'David, I've just seen Franconelli kick Chief Babba Seko to death. I'm not feeling talkative. Now get on with it.'

'You see,' he said, looking up to where his next length of bullshit was coming from and fumbling for one of the smoking cigarettes in the ashtray, 'the toxic waste wasn't an isolated problem for Franconelli. It was something he got into for his brother. He should never have done it. He didn't need the money but the chief kept pushing him to do it, to use this land he had up there. The chief wasn't in it for the money either. He just wanted something he could pin on Franconelli if the situation required it. Franconelli had a lot more to lose. He has building projects in the delta region and offshore. Natural-gas storage, floating jetties.'

'The stuff you were giving him help on.'

'Through Napier.'

'Sure,' I said, not really having to listen to all this stuff.

'Franconelli had already put a lot of money in there . . .'

'David!' I shouted at him, tiring now. He stiffened. 'I don't want to hear about Franconelli's financial problems. I want to know why he killed Napier and, if you like, I'll help you. Get you on the right track. The chief and Graydon were close, weren't they?'

'They were working together.'

'On the same projects as Franconelli,' I said. 'Information supplied by N. Briggs. They didn't want Napier dead until they got their information so they agreed to move the toxic waste and give him the money he'd stripped out of his own company on the four-one-nine scam.'

'That was my idea,' shouted David, gleeful as a kid and nearly on his feet until the knees buckled and he crumpled back into the sofa.

'Which one?'

'I told him,' he said, 'I told Napier there was a way out. He'd brokered the toxic-waste deal so he was implicated and it sickened him. He wanted it cleaned up. I told him to offer the building project information I was giving him to the chief and Graydon in exchange for moving the toxic waste.'

'It was in the chief's interests to move it too. He could have ended up in . . .'

'Of course it was. So there was another element to the deal. They would have to pay him money. There was some owing to Napier from Graydon and the rest . . .'

'Up to the magic ten million dollars.'

'. . . came from Napier's company through the four-one-nine scam.'

'You're clever, David, aren't you? No losers. Not bad,' I said. 'What happened to the money?'

'The money?'

'Why didn't anybody show with the money in the *cocotiers*? Napier was going in there to pick it up which means he must have known that Graydon and the chief had the information.'

'But Franconelli,' said David, ignoring me, 'Franconelli's different. Nobody gets away from him. He wasn't going to have Napier out there with a case full of Franconelli skeletons.'

'The vertical hold on that pinstripe's gone again, David.'

'Eh?' he grunted, refocusing on me several times.

'First, the money – why wasn't it there? Second, the chief and Graydon had their information so Napier was free to go and Franconelli, well, maybe he was cool about it too until he found something out . . . How did he find it out, David?'

'Nobody gets away from Franconelli,' he repeated to himself, and belched over his whisky. 'There *was* nothing for Franconelli to find out. I don't know what you're talking about. You're losing me on this, Bruce.'

'I'm losing the man who knows everything,' I said. 'Well, let's come at it from a different angle. I met somebody today.'

'Nice?' asked David, slipping into social ease.

'A friend of Napier's.'

'I was Napier's only friend.'

'What about Martin?'

'Who?'

'Martin Taylor, I met him today. Tall, good-looking, thirtyish. Says he was going to Barbados with Napier. Start a new life.'

David changed colour. He mottled to a yellowing bruise like a sky getting sick before an electric storm.

'The mysterious fucking Martin,' he said, with more venom than a puff adder. 'The *young* mysterious fucking Martin.' David stoked himself up, the booze heating his brain to boiling point in seconds. 'You know, Napier without me, without my understanding, without my comprehension of what the fuck was going on here in Nigeria. Without me, Napier would have been lost. I *made* him, Bruce. I made him all that fucking money. I gave him the contacts. I did all his thinking for him. I did fucking everything. And now he's going to leave me in this fucking shit hole, with these stinking worthless people and run off with his great love. His great *love*. That's what he called him. Shit. *I* was his great love. *I* did everything. Napier couldn't have done anything without my brain.'

'Why did you send him to me, David?'

'You'd help him,' he said, suddenly uncertain.

'You mean *I'd* help *you*. I'd keep Napier away from Lagos, away from you where he could be an ugly problem, where he could turn up like shit on your own doorstep. I'd keep him in Cotonou where he could be killed without any messy inquiry.'

'How could I know . . . ?'

'You knew about Martin,' I said, cutting through him. 'And you're the man who knows everything . . . but only when you want to.'

David sat forward and dumped the cigarette, which was burning his finger.

'I imagine you and Franconelli have got to know each other pretty well by now, David?' I said. 'Or maybe it's Roberto. Now that you've cut out the middleman. Gone direct. I hope he paid you enough.'

David breathed heavily through his nose, the alcohol thumping around his system.

'For what?' he asked.

'For calling Napier in the Hotel du Lac on his last night,' I said. He didn't answer. 'When you told him he could go into the *cocotiers* to pick up the money and you knew he was going to get killed.'

'He shouldn't have been so greedy,' he said, desperately. 'If he hadn't been so greedy he'd have been all right.'

I threw the videotape at him. It hit him in the chest and silenced him.

'Ali couldn't punish you enough for what you've done, could he, David?'

He looked at the tape which had fallen into his lifeless hands. He let it fall to the floor.

'You don't really need that now,' I said. 'Graydon's

as good as dead too. You've made Franconelli king, David. How did you kick it off? Did you tell Franconelli that the information he was getting from Napier wasn't exclusive and that it could be with one little phone call? Jesus Christ, David, you gave Napier the idea and then you killed him with it.'

David yanked the whisky bottle out of the sofa cushions and plugged it between his lips. His Adam's apple jumped as he pulled on the alcohol, trying to get all that horrible stuff out of his brain. I tore it from his hands.

'Don't you be greedy now, David,' I said, pouring myself a splash. 'We've still got to talk about the money, and there's Quarshie too. What was Quarshie doing over there? The engineer, for Christ's sake. What was he doing driving killers around Cotonou?'

'*He* shot himself,' roared David, as if that had not been an option for him.

'The plans he did for Graydon were the same plans he'd done for Franconelli, weren't they?'

David nodded.

'Nobody two-times Franconelli, so Napier, who "came up with the idea", had to die and Quarshie's punishment was to take him to his death. His old university pal. I tell you, David, Napier didn't need his friends around him, did he?'

'If Napier hadn't been greedy . . .' he tried again, and looked up at me as if I'd confirm this to him. I gave him nothing back.

'And talking about greedy, David, what happened to the money? The four-one-nine money. Graydon had the plans, he mentioned them to me when I commented on Quarshie's funeral notice, so . . . You didn't do that as well, David? You didn't take the money as well?'

David's head dropped, the hair hanging from his head in rats' tails.

'It was my idea . . .' he said, and let the words drift away.

'How did it work, David?'

'Quarshie gave him the plans,' he said quietly, to the floor.

'As the first part of the deal?' I asked, and he nodded. 'Then Napier told you about Martin and you sent him to me in Cotonou.'

'And I gave Graydon the contract information.'

'And?'

'I told him he didn't have to deal with Napier, that I was the original source.'

'And he paid you the four-one-nine money while you sent Napier to his death in the *cocotiers*.'

He threw his head back and looked up to some greater power who was never going to be there for him.

'No wonder Graydon took that videotape of you and Ali,' I said. 'You were going to be a very important man to him.'

He picked the tape up off the floor and turned it over in his hands.

'What's the house doing in this state, David? Why are you pissing your brains away? Had one too many visits from your conscience?'

'No. Just Carlo.'

'Franconelli's man, Carlo?'

'I don't know any other Carlo.'

'What did he want?'

David fell sideways on the sofa and sobbed, a jolting retch of a sob.

'Did he explain some house rules to you, David?'

Tears rolled down his cheeks and nose as he nodded against the leather cushions.

'I'm in it now,' he said, to the sofa. 'I'm in it.'

'And just like Napier, David, there's no getting out.'

He folded his arms around his chest, brought his knees up and pulled a face as if he'd just been skewered. Then his features went slack, saliva escaped from the corner of his mouth. He was unconscious.

I drank a good two fingers of whisky and arranged him so he wouldn't drown in his own vomit. I put the chandelier back up on its hook and reconnected the light. I put the chair back in the dining room. I polished off another two fingers and washed the glass out in the kitchen. I drove to the gate, said good night to the watchman and headed back home.

Benin. Tuesday 5th March.

I slept for a few hours on the Benin side of the border, too exhausted to go on. An African woke me at first light, worried that I was oversleeping and might miss the best part of the day. He asked me for a lift to Cotonou. I told him to get in.

There was a lot of traffic pouring into Cotonou at that time and a truck had shed its load, which slowed things down. I got home at 7.30 a.m. and only the thought of slipping into bed next to Heike got me to the top of the stairs.

Heike was sitting at the table with a cup of coffee. She was wearing a light cotton robe and had her heels up on the front strut of the chair. The sun, which had just got up, was slanting through the windows and her dishevelled hair, lit from behind, looked golden. In my broken-down and shattered state I had a flash of certainty. It was something I wanted and dreaded at the same time. I leaned on the table with both hands. She was concerned. I must have looked fresh from a train wreck.

'I think we should . . .'

She started and looked over my shoulder at someone who'd come through the open door behind me. I turned to see Moses standing there looking thin but grinning.

'You're back,' I said.

'Yes, please, Mr Bruce.'

'How was the village medicine?' I asked.

He didn't reply.

'He needs some help,' said Heike.

I crawled to the phone and dialled Heike's office number. I asked to be put through to Gerhard Lehrner.

'Gerhard,' I said. 'Bruce Medway. You remember that favour you owe me?'

'Ah . . .' he said.

The Company of Strangers

Robert Wilson

Lisbon 1944. In the torrid summer heat, as the streets of the capital seethe with spies and informers, the endgame of the Intelligence war is being silently fought.

Andrea Aspinall, mathematician and spy, enters this sophisticated world through a wealthy household in Estoril. Karl Voss, military attaché to the German Legation, has arrived embittered by his implication in the murder of a Reichsminister and traumatized by Stalingrad, on a mission to rescue Germany from annihilation. In the lethal tranquillity of this corrupted paradise they meet and attempt to find love in a world where no-one can be believed.

After a night of extreme violence, Andrea is left with a life-long addiction to the clandestine world that leads her from the brutal Portuguese fascist régime to the paranoia of Cold War Germany, where she is forced to make the final and the hardest choice.

'Displaying once again Wilson's gifts for atmospheric depiction of place, this ambitious experiment is streets ahead of most other thrillers'

JOHN DUGDALE, *Sunday Times*

'A big, meaty novel of love and deceit . . . with this novel Wilson vaults to the front-rank of thriller writers'

PETER GUTTRIDGE, *Observer*

ISBN: 0 00 651203 8

A Small Death in Lisbon

Robert Wilson

A Portuguese bank is founded on the back of Nazi wartime deals. Over half a century later a young girl is murdered in Lisbon.

1941. Klaus Felsen, SS officer, arrives in Lisbon and the strangest party in history, where Nazis and Allies, refugees and entrepreneurs, dance to the strains of opportunism and despair. Felsen's war takes him to the mountains of the north where a brutal battle is being fought for an element vital to Hitler's blitzkrieg. There he meets the man who makes the first turn of the wheel of greed and revenge which rolls through to the century's end.

Late 1990s, Lisbon. Inspector Zé Coelho is investigating the murder of a young girl. As he digs deeper, Zé overturns the dark soil of history and unearths old bones. The 1974 revolution has left injustices of the old fascist regime unresolved. But there's an older, greater injustice, for which this small death in Lisbon is horrific compensation, and in his final push for the truth, Zé must face the most chilling opposition.

'Compulsively readable, with the cop's quest burning its way through a narrative rich in history and intrigue, love and death'   *Literary Review*

ISBN: 0 00 651202 X

The Big Killing
Robert Wilson

Bruce Medway, go-between and fixer for traders in West Africa, smells trouble when a porn merchant asks him to deliver a video at a secret location. Things look up, though, when he's hired to act as minder to Ron Collins, a spoilt playboy looking for diamonds. Medway thinks this could be the answer to his cashflow crisis, but when the video delivery leads to a shootout and the discovery of a mutilated body, the prospect of retreating to his bolthole in Benin becomes increasingly attractive – especially as the manner of the victim's death is too similar to a current notorious political murder for comfort.

His obligations, though, keep him fixed in the Ivory Coast and he is soon caught up in a terrifying cycle of violence. But does it stem from the political upheavals in nearby Liberia, or from the cutthroat business of diamonds? Unless Medway can get to the bottom of the mystery, he knows that for the savage killer out there in the African night, he is the next target . . .

'A narrative distilled from pure protein: potent, fiercely imagined and not a little frightening'   *Literary Review*

ISBN 0 00 647986 3

A Darkening Stain

Robert Wilson

Bruce Medway, fixer for the great unfixed, does not see the disappearance of schoolgirls off the streets of Cotonou, Benin, as any of his business. That is the domain of his ex-partner, police detective Bagado, and his corrupt boss. Bruce has the more pressing matter of a visit from two sweet-natured mafiosi who want him to find Jean-Luc Marnier, a French businessman in for something nastier than a wrist-slapping.

Then an important schoolgirl goes missing and Bruce gets involved, descending into a deeper darkness of police corruption, mafia revenge, sexual depravity and illegally mined gold. To save himself he conceives a scam, one that will excite the natural greed that prevails along this coast and, when executed out on the black waters of the huge lagoon system, inevitably result in death. But then innocence has always been the burden of dark experience.

'Unmissable . . . Unflinchingly imagined and executed. No hint of competition'   *Literary Review*

ISBN: 0 00 713042 2